3-8-14
To Uncle Val & Aunt Flor
With Love,
Elaine

Also by Elaine Doll
Whispers from the Soul

Measures of Passion

Elaine Doll

abbott press®
A DIVISION OF WRITER'S DIGEST

Copyright © 2014 Elaine Doll.

All rights reserved. No part of this book may be used or reproduced by any means, graphic, electronic, or mechanical, including photocopying, recording, taping or by any information storage retrieval system without the written permission of the publisher except in the case of brief quotations embodied in critical articles and reviews.

Abbott Press books may be ordered through booksellers or by contacting:

Abbott Press
1663 Liberty Drive
Bloomington, IN 47403
www.abbottpress.com
Phone: 1-866-697-5310

Because of the dynamic nature of the Internet, any web addresses or links contained in this book may have changed since publication and may no longer be valid. The views expressed in this work are solely those of the author and do not necessarily reflect the views of the publisher, and the publisher hereby disclaims any responsibility for them.

Any people depicted in stock imagery provided by Thinkstock are models, and such images are being used for illustrative purposes only.
Certain stock imagery © Thinkstock.

ISBN: 978-1-4582-1373-0 (sc)
ISBN: 978-1-4582-1372-3 (hc)
ISBN: 978-1-4582-1371-6 (e)

Library of Congress Control Number: 2014900934

Printed in the United States of America.

Abbott Press rev. date: 01/30/2014

Dedication Page

For my mother, Mary Martha Boatman, who filled our home with music.

> *"My heart leaps for joy, and I will*
> *give thanks to Him in song."*
> *Psalm 28:7b*

Acknowledgements

To Sandra Anderson, thank you for your diligent work of proof reading and for holding me accountable to my writing schedule. Many, many thanks for the long hours you stood at my bedside during my hospital recovery, for your prayers, and encouragement. I appreciate you and love you.

To all who lifted me up in prayer during difficult times and expressed your love and encouragement, my sincere thanks and appreciation. It is only by the grace of our Lord and answered prayers, that I am able to finish this book for you, my readers.

About the author

Elaine Doll discovered her passion for writing at a young age, and won her first writing contest at age ten. She attended Madison Area Technical College in Madison, Wisconsin, and has completed five 2-year writing courses as well as other writing workshops. Her articles and inspirational poems have been published in magazines, and this is her second historical romance novel. She is a member of Christian Writers Guild.

Her pastimes and hobbies include: reading, listening to classical and big-band music, and collecting angels, books, and antique glassware. An active member of Hemet Valley Baptist Church in Hemet, California, she is the leader of the Hospital Visitation Ministry.

Elaine was born and raised in California and lives in Hemet, California. She and Charles, her husband, have a blended family of six children, eight grandchildren, and two great- grandchildren.

Chapter 1

Oklahoma City, 1905

"Honestly, Kristina, didn't you see that man watching you?"

Kristina Soderlund was so deep in thought about her plans she'd nearly forgotten her best friend was riding beside her until Doris shouted at her.

"What? No." Why would anyone be watching her? Kristina shrugged it off and kept pedaling. Eyes on the asphalt road, her mind wandered ahead to when she'd leave home and go to college in Boston. After a moment, however, curiosity nagged her. "What man?"

Not that it mattered. She wasn't the least bit interested.

"That man on the library steps was looking you over like a tiger on the prowl, ready to pounce on his prey." All grins, Doris jerked a thumb back over her left shoulder.

Kristina didn't look back.

"That's a stupid thing to say." Doris Langley could be so dramatic at times. No wonder she was always writing mushy poetry and daydreaming about men. She and Doris were closest friends but as different as a pollywog and a rattlesnake.

"He was positively handsome!" Doris swooned so dreamily that she nearly fell off her bicycle.

"You're so funny." Kristina laughed at her friend and shook her head. She didn't care how handsome the fellow was, there was no place or time in her life for a beau. Unlike Doris, whose only dream for her future was marriage and babies, Kristina had more important things to do. Nothing—especially a man—would get in the way of her education and her dream of opening a music studio. "How do you know he wasn't looking at you?"

"Oh no. He was *not* looking at me." Doris's tone was serious. "I saw him perfectly well. His gaze was locked on you, my friend. The way he gobbled you up with his eyes, you'd think he'd never seen a woman in his life."

Suddenly alarmed, Kristina shuddered. An old, recurring nightmare flashed through her mind. The idea of being prey to anyone, especially a stranger, and being stalked like an animal, frightened her.

Hands shaking, she tightened her grip on the handlebars. Hunched forward, she pedaled faster, her nose pointed straight ahead, as if she were to look back and see the devil chasing her. Never mind that the bumps in the road made her teeth chatter, or that her hair flew in every direction. She couldn't get away from the stranger's view fast enough.

"Hey. Wait!" Her friend's words came out in breathless shouts.

Kristina stopped pedaling and, without looking back, she coasted until Doris caught up to her.

Breathing hard, Doris scowled. "Holy pig feathers! What got into you, anyway?"

"He could be dangerous." Kristina's voice quivered and she fought to control her emotions.

"Oh, good grief." Doris laughed and rolled her eyes. "Why would you think that fellow is dangerous? He looked perfectly normal—and absolutely sublime."

There she went with the dramatics again; Doris thought every handsome man was *sublime*. Kristina didn't answer.

She realized her sudden fear was irrational, but she didn't want to explain the reason for her alarm, even though she and Doris been best friends for twelve years. It was too personal to talk about.

She resumed pedaling at a steady speed, glad Doris didn't carry on about the stranger.

A few minutes later, when they reached Doris's house at the edge of town, she slowed and waved as usual. "See you tomorrow."

Thunder rumbled in the distance. Kristina pedaled faster, hoping to get home quickly in case a bad storm developed. The man on the library steps all but forgotten, nostalgia set in as her thoughts reverted to college and moving away from home. Oklahoma City was the only place she knew. She was comfortable here, secure on her father's cotton farm, in the church she'd grown up in, and with her friends. All she knew about Boston were historical things she'd learned in school and the stories Mama Leoma and her grandparents had told her.

Kristina's emotions were a mixture of excitement and apprehension, but attending Boston University School of Music was an important part of her well-laid plan. Passionate about her future, she had no doubts about her success. What was it Mama always said when they discussed her goals? *"All things are possible for those who believe upon the Lord."* Mama was well educated and wise and she knew her Bible well. If Mama said it, Kristina believed it.

She looked forward to her time at the university when she would live with her grandparents. Grandfather Fisk had promised to pay her tuition for two years if she kept up her grades both in high school and college. She was going to do better than that. She'd graduated from high school at the top of her class and she expected to do the same in college.

The asphalt road gave way to dirt and she came to the rough area Papa called the "washboard." Handlebars gripped tightly she pumped hard to keep up her speed. She clamped her jaws together to keep from biting her tongue. Glad when the road smoothed out she breathed a sigh of relief and relaxed her grip. Now that her high school year was finished, she wouldn't miss this ride one bit.

As she neared the lane that led to her house, pounding horse hooves approached from behind. Wondering who it was, she stopped pedaling and glanced over her shoulder to see who was coming in such a hurry. Toby Gallager reined in his old, swaybacked horse so close that he almost knocked her over.

Toby grinned, his yellow, crooked teeth exposed in the afternoon sunshine. "Howdy, Krissy," he said in his long, slow drawl.

"Toby! You nearly knocked me off my bicycle."

"Well, you shouldn't ride that contraption. It ain't safe like my sturdy horse here. Least I got four strong legs under me. I don't know why anyone would ride something with two skinny wheels."

"Humph." She really didn't have anything else to say to the obnoxious coot. He was probably too stupid to learn how to ride a bicycle.

Several times recently, her father had hinted that Toby would make a mighty good husband, but she didn't agree. She'd always had an uncomfortable feeling around him. It wasn't that he was a bad person, or anything she could put her finger on, he simply gave her the jitters. Except for his ugly teeth, he wasn't all that unattractive with his rust-colored hair and interesting green eyes, but he acted strange and talked as though uneducated. Maybe he wouldn't be so bad if he'd keep his mouth shut. She brushed him off like a pesky fly, but he wasn't easily deterred.

If her parents thought they were going to convince her to marry Toby, they were dead wrong. She couldn't imagine why Papa would think such a thing. Maybe it was because Toby was big and strong and a good worker when he helped around the farm. But Papa didn't know what a nuisance he was.

"You just getting home from school, prissy Krissy?"

"Yes." She kept moving, hoping Toby would ride on ahead and leave her alone. He was so annoying. After all, they were both grown up now but he acted like a twelve-year-old.

"You sure do look pretty, Krissy." Toby grinned and wiggled his brows up and down, looking like a clown. "I'd sure as the dickens like to kiss those nice lips of yours."

Oh how dreadful! As far as she was concerned, she'd die of old age before she'd let Toby kiss her. She shuddered and tried to ignore him. It wasn't that she didn't like to be kissed; she had let Orval Bergman kiss her once last year after a school dance, and it was rather nice. But she couldn't imagine letting a varmint like Toby Gallager kiss her.

"I'll let you kiss me when horny toads grow wings and fly!"

Still clopping along beside her, Toby laughed so loud he scared a flock of blackbirds out of a nearby tree. She jumped so hard she almost lost control of the bicycle. What a repulsive half-wit he was.

Thankfully, when she turned onto her lane, Toby rode ahead, probably going to see the new boys up the road. "See ya soon, Krissy," he called.

Never would be too soon.

Riding up the lane toward home, she brushed Toby out of her thoughts, but the sudden fear she'd experienced moments earlier in town returned. Memories of that day in the barn when she was in third grade flashed through her mind. The blindfold, boys, darkness, and pain all rushed back as if it had happened only days ago. Over the years since then she had determined not to allow the childhood experience to ruin her future. But clearly, it still affected her more than she realized.

For a long time, she'd believed the incident was simply a game children played; that's what the boys had told her. "A secret game," they'd said. As she grew to understand what had really happened, it took on a whole new, ugly meaning. The assault in the barn was one thing she'd never discussed with anyone—except God. After a while, she rarely thought about it.

A hole in the lane grabbed Kristina's front tire, jerking her to attention, and she barely dodged a big mud puddle. Sweat trickled down her spine, and she couldn't wait to get home so she could pin her hair up off her neck. It was warmer than usual and humid. The clouds had increased. Glad this was the last day she had to make this long ride, she pushed on, grateful at least, for the bicycle. Mama Leoma had talked Papa into buying it when Kristina began high school, and now it would get handed down to Dyer.

Of course, it wouldn't surprise her if Mama talked Papa into buying Dyer a new bicycle before the next school year. Mama Leoma was really good at talking Papa into almost anything, and Papa seemed to enjoy pleasing her. Like the year he added an extra room onto the house so Mama could have a library and music room for the new piano he'd bought her. Papa worked hard to please his family, and he never complained.

Kristina was six when Papa married Leoma. The stories about how Papa changed his evil, drunken ways when he started to court Mama Leoma were interesting, amusing. Mostly, it was wonderful to hear how he'd changed from a brandy-drinking tyrant to the God-fearing man he was today. She was proud of him, and quite sure there couldn't be a better father in the world. She'd miss her parents something awful when she went to Boston.

The new song she'd learned in music class recently, burst into her mind. She began to sing. Up ahead, seven-year-old Edward Lee pranced around the yard on his stick horse, as if he were astride a great white stallion, and close behind him, nine-year-old Frankie pretended to shoot arrows at his younger brother. Cowboys and Indians seemed to be the only game those two ever played. Roberta Fay, who would be five in the fall, was swinging on the new swing Papa had hung from the big oak tree, her bare feet flying in the air. Dyer was nowhere in sight, but that wasn't unusual. He was probably off with his group of friends, most likely playing church, with him acting as the preacher.

She smiled, her heart filled with love for Dyer. She had no doubt that's exactly what he'd become someday. He'd make a fine reverend. At thirteen, he already had the charisma and speaking ability to carry it off. It wouldn't surprise Kristina if he had half of the boys in town saved and baptized before he graduated from high school. All he needed was some proper training at one of those Bible seminaries her parents talked about.

Kristina drew close to the yard. Brownie trotted down the lane to meet her. His trot was a little slower than it used to be, but the old mutt still had a lot of playfulness and love in him.

"Come on, Brownie," she called. He ran beside her up to the house.

Clean clothes billowed and swayed from the clothesline at the sunny side of the house. On the wide, shady front porch Mama, her belly growing big, and Glenda, Mama's best friend, sat sipping tall, icy drinks, lemonade from the looks of it. They both waved.

She liked Glenda more than all of her mama's friends, even more than Doris's mother, Anna Jo Langley. She remembered the day Glenda came to take part in her father and Leoma's wedding, and Kristina thought she was the most beautiful woman she'd ever seen—after mama. Clearly, Jason Alder had been smitten by Glenda's beauty and sophistication. Mama had said it didn't take him a week to win Glenda's heart and convince her to marry him.

Kristina had fond memories of her parents' wedding day. Papa had been dashing in his dark suit, and Leoma had looked like a queen in her cream-colored, lace and satin dress with pearl trim and her lacy hat with ribbons and flowers.

As Kristina steered the bicycle up to the porch, both women greeted her with broad smiles. Mama asked her usual question. "How was your day at school, dear?"

"Fine." Her routine answer. She stepped off the bicycle, careful not to snag the hem of her long skirt, then she leaned the bicycle against the porch railing and smoothed her skirt into place. Tail wagging, Brownie wiggled and whined until Kristina scratched him behind the ears and patted his back. It was another daily ritual.

"That was a lovely tune you were singing," Glenda said. "It sounded familiar. What's the title?"

"*Sweetheart Be Mine.*"

"Aha. I thought it was something like that." Glenda hummed a measure in her mellow, alto voice.

Mama beamed, pride glowing in her eyes, and smiled. "Kristina will be very successful when she owns her music studio. Isn't that right sweetheart?"

"I expect so. Of course, I have to get through college first."

"You'll do that without a problem," Glenda said. Like Mama, Glenda was always encouraging, and quick to reassure her.

"I hope you're right. It's a little frightening going from our small-town high school to a big uni—"

"Umm. Oh." Mama groaned and bent forward, gasping for breath as she reached behind her, messaging her lower back with both hands. Kristina stopped petting Brownie, and rushed to her mother's side.

"Are you all right, Mama?" The pain on her mother's face frightened her.

"It's just a little warning that the time is getting near. This baby better not come early. It's not due for another three weeks."

Glenda jumped up, taking Mama by one elbow, helping her off the seat. "I think you better lie down. Kristina and I will bring in the laundry and watch the children. You need to go inside and stretch out on the bed for a while."

Kristina took her mother's other elbow, and helped coax her bulging body up off the bench. "Glenda's right. You better rest a while. And don't worry about the children. I'll keep an eye on them."

The clouds had darkened and accumulated overhead, completely hiding the sun. Thunder rumbled again, closer this time.

"Thank you dear. I appreciate that. Keep a close eye on those clouds, too. Don't wait until it rains to bring the children inside. Bring them in right away if you see lightning."

"I will, Mama. They'll be fine."

With her mother settled on her bed, Kristina returned to the clothesline. Glenda followed her out to help take down the laundry. The wind whipped the clothes, nearly snatching them out of her hands.

"Is Mama going to be all right?" Kristina had noticed that her mother seemed to be in pain more often lately, and she worried that something was wrong. She couldn't imagine what would happen if the baby came early and died, like Mama's first baby girl had done.

Glenda dropped the laundry into the basket and wrapped an arm around Kristina's shoulders. "She'll be fine. I think she's been on her feet too much."

"I hope you're right." Kristina wasn't completely reassured. She didn't think she would ever be ready to go through so much discomfort and pain to bear children. It would be just awful having a huge, bulging stomach, and swollen feet so big she could hardly wear shoes. One thing was certain; she wouldn't give up her dreams the way Mama had.

Oh, she loved Mama Leoma, and never thought of her as anything other than mother. She adored and respected her. But she couldn't understand Leoma putting aside her dream of opening a bookshop to marry Papa and have a bunch of babies.

"Maybe after the children grow up I can open my bookshop," Mama had said on several occasions. But babies kept coming, and Mama looked too tired to do much more than change nasty diapers, cook, and clean. The thought almost sickened Kristina. It definitely wasn't what she wanted—at least not for a long, long time. Thinking about childbirth made her cringe. She unpinned the last pair of dungarees from the line.

Lightning flashed and thunder followed within seconds. "Take the laundry inside. I'll bring in the children," Glenda said.

Glenda called the children, and they ran for the back door along with Kristina.

"Wait!" Frankie stopped on the step and looked around. "Where's Birdie?"

Kristina dropped the laundry basket inside the back door, her heart racing. She ran back outside to search the yard. "Birdie! Roberta Fay, where are you?"

Frankie insisted on looking for Birdie too. "I'll go around the house."

"Thank you, sweetheart. Hurry. I'll check the other buildings."

Kristina ran to the outhouse and looked inside. Birdie wasn't there. She ran to the barn, calling and checking every part of the huge structure. Still no Birdie. The only place left to look was the chicken coop. As the first raindrops fell, she ran to the coop and yanked open the door, frantic to find her little sister. She exhaled a sigh of relief. There was Birdie, scrunched up on one of the lower nesting shelves, with chickens clucking all around her.

"There you are." Kristina snatched Birdie into her arms, ignoring the straw and feathers that clung to the child's clothing and hair. "A storm is coming. We have to get in the house."

"All right." Birdie's voice was small, innocent.

Clinging to the child, Kristina latched the henhouse door, and dashed across the yard as fast as she could. Heavy drops of rain pelted her, stinging her skin. Lightning flashed. Birdie whimpered. Heart pounding, Kristina ran faster. All she could think of was getting her little sister to safety. A loud crack of thunder made her jump, and she almost stumbled. A few more steps and she reached the house.

A bath towel in hand, Glenda held the back door open. Kristina rushed through and put Birdie down to be dried. Suddenly, she remembered her books and started back out the door.

"Stop right there," Glenda yelled. "You're not going back outside."

"My books are still in the basket of my bicycle. I have to go get them."

"No you don't." Glenda grabbed her arm before she could get out the door. "You stay in this house; it's too dangerous out there."

"But—"

"No buts. You're all done with school. You don't need those books." Glenda talked to her with the same authority as Mama, but Kristina was pretty sure her mother would go after the books.

"It's a shame to ruin them." Kristina cherished every book she had, no matter if it was last year's text book, or a tattered old story book from her youth. They were sacred treasures.

Chapter 2

AFTERNOON SUNSHINE STREAMED THROUGH the library windows, spotlighting row after row of books. Pilan' Rousseau meandered between two towering shelves, squinting and scanning the selection of topics. Other than exploring a new country or climbing a new mountain, there were few places he'd rather be than among volumes of books. Here there was knowledge, wisdom, adventure, and entertainment. He inhaled. To him, the smell of paper and leather was like the finest, French perfume. His father's vast, personal library, contained over five-thousand books, and Pilan' hoped to rival that number in his own collection someday.

He searched for something more about the early history of the United States, and interesting places in America to explore. Even though he'd been born in Philadelphia, when he was five his parents had taken him to his father's home in France. It was there he had been raised and educated in the best boys' schools. Now that he'd returned to America on his own, he wanted to know everything about this vast territory.

He'd explored the East, finding the history there rich and interesting, but he wanted to travel the breadth and width of the United States. He had two years to explore this country, and he wanted to see it, feel it, and smell it. He wanted to learn about the different people who had come here from all over the world, especially the Native Americans from whom his mother had descended.

Like his father, he was adventurous and curious. Settling in one place for very long wasn't for him—at least not yet. There was a lot of country to see, and he intended to see it all before he returned to Paris to settle down. When he did return home, he planned to open a dance studio where he would teach traditional ballroom dancing.

For now, he had a long list of new places to see, including San Francisco and Los Angeles. But long before he reached the Pacific Ocean, he was going to climb Pike's Peak in Colorado. It was a challenge he couldn't pass up, not because it was the highest mountain—it wasn't—but because his father had done it, and he wouldn't rest until he'd climbed it too.

Running his fingers along a row of titles, he came upon a book about California. He pulled it from the shelf, adding it to the growing stack he already carried in the crook of one arm. Satisfied that he had enough books to keep him occupied for a few days, he found a reading table near the back of the room and set the books down. Settled into a wooden chair, he flipped through the pages of each book, deciding which ones to check out and take back to his room at the hotel.

He'd been in Oklahoma City only five days, and he couldn't help wondering why people settled in such a remote, dusty, place. None of the grandeur of Paris existed here, none of the excitement or excellent entertainment. How could anyone live without a grand opera house, no très bon cafés, or concert halls? Still, he must admit, there seemed to be contentment and happiness on the faces of the people, and everyone was friendly and kind. The town offered all the necessities of basic living, and judging from the construction going on in every direction, and the hustle and bustle from morning until night, the city was still growing. None-the-less, he was convinced it would never compare to Paris. Thus far in his short travels, he'd seen far nicer places than this, as well as worse places. Certain he hadn't seen the most rustic town, he was also certain he'd find none as fine as Paris.

He opened the cover of another book on the stack in front of him. Movement at the opposite end of the table caught his eye. He glanced up just as an attractive woman took the chair on the other side of the table. He didn't have to look twice to recognize her from the day before. It was the beautiful woman on the bicycle. Unable to take his eyes off her, he smiled, waiting, hoping she would look his way. Definitely young, perhaps eighteen or nineteen, she possessed maturity and sophistication beyond her youth. She was one fine lady, *précieuse*. It wasn't difficult to imagine her in the grand ballroom of his grandparents' Paris estate. What would it be like to sweep her across the dance floor in a waltz? Eyes closed for a moment, he imagined such a scene. Yes, he could see it.

The young lady still hadn't looked his way, and Pilan' chided himself for allowing his thoughts to stray so far off track. It would be foolish to think such a fine woman would be interested in him, and besides, the timing was all wrong. Such a distraction, no matter how charming, was not what he needed right now.

A YOUNG MAN KRISTINA had never seen in town sat at the end of the table, a pile of books in front of him. He was a handsome fellow, and she wondered where he'd come from. He didn't look like the typical male citizen in Oklahoma City, although, she supposed she shouldn't judge by his expensive looking attire, or extreme good-looks. But he definitely didn't look like anyone she'd grown up with, or gone to school with.

She pulled her chair up to the reading table and sat down. Not wanting to draw attention to herself, or openly acknowledge his presence, she opened a book and began to read, but she couldn't concentrate. She had a strong urge to say hello, but she wasn't in the habit of speaking to strangers. Staring blindly at the words on the page, she sensed she was being watched. It was impossible to focus on anything the book said when she was so intent on ignoring the man. Maybe he wasn't looking at her at all. Perhaps she was simply being self-conscious. Either way, it was silly of her to act so immature, and it wasn't very friendly of her to ignore his presence.

If he was new in town, she didn't want him to think the folks in Oklahoma City were aloof and unfriendly. That wasn't the case at all. A cheerful smile never hurt anyone, and one was hankering to escape her lips. Unable to help herself, she finally lifted her head and met the man's gaze. His warm smile spread, brightening his face. He nodded. She smiled then lowered her eyes, trying once again, quite unsuccessfully, to focus on her book.

Suddenly, she realized Doris's description of the man she'd seen on the library steps yesterday as they rode home from school, matched this young man perfectly: about six feet of dark, bronzed skin, thick, black hair to his shoulders, finely chiseled brow, nose, and cheeks, and out-of-this-world handsome. Those were Doris's words, and Kristina couldn't dispute them. Could this be the same man that had watched her?

He didn't look at all dangerous. His pale, blue eyes sparkled with kindness, and his smile was polite and genuine. Something about him was very different, almost exotic. She wondered if he was a mix of American Indian and a culture, perhaps from a European country. Although she didn't know much about other cultures, she'd seen people in pictures from places like Italy and France with similar characteristics and aristocratic features.

Kristina gave herself an imaginary kick under the table. *Enough of this.* Reprimanding herself, she attempted to detour her thoughts, but it didn't work. She'd never seen such a mesmerizing person—man or woman. Unable to resist, she glanced up again.

Their eyes met and held.

"Hello." The man's clear, tenor voice was melodious, beautiful.

"Hello." Kristina smiled, her heart threatening to explode.

She sighed much too loudly, hoping the man didn't hear her. Unaccustomed to speaking with strangers, she shifted uncomfortably in her chair. She shoved her hair back over her shoulders and lowered her eyes, determined to read the novel in front of her. For a moment she considered checking out the book and taking it home, but sometimes she enjoyed reading in the quiet library, away from the chaos and noise of home, where her younger brothers and sister were constantly playing noisy games, screaming, and crying. She loved the tranquility of her surroundings here. She could read to her heart's content without interruption—well, usually.

Kristina's love for books had come mostly from Mama Leoma, but she had vague memories of her birth mother reading to her before she had died. As she recalled, Dyer was only a day or two old when their mother had passed away. Even before Papa had married Leoma, when she was wet-nursing Dyer, Kristina had snuggled up next to her in a big, cushioned armchair, and she'd listened to Leoma's soothing, sing-song voice as she read fairytales and nursery rhymes.

Later, when the new babies started coming along, Kristina had lost her place beside Mama, but never her love for reading. What a wonderful thing it would have been, to spend endless hours amidst a sea of books, if Leoma had opened the bookshop she'd dreamed of.

Kristina turned the page and began to read again, this time determined to focus. But, alas, it was impossible to keep her mind and eyes off of the man at the other end of the table. In spite of the constant ruckus at home, she closed the book and stacked it atop the others, then picked them up. Eyes straight ahead, she rushed passed the man, her skirt rustling with each step, and marched directly to the librarian's desk.

The twenty-minute ride home seemed slower than normal today, her mind repeatedly wandering back to the library. She tried singing to divert her thoughts, but nothing kept her mind from straying back to the dark-skinned, fascinating, young man. Most of the boys she'd known in high school wouldn't set foot through the library door, yet this young man had a stack of books. He appeared well-educated, and confident that frequenting the library would in no way threaten his masculinity.

THE GOLDEN DUSK OUTSIDE Kristina's window had turned to darkness, but the night was still warm. She pulled a thin, cotton night gown over her head and slipped between the cool sheets, snuggling her head deep into the soft, feather pillow. It had been a busy Saturday, and she was ready for a good night's sleep. Curled up at the foot of her bed on an oval braided rug, where he'd slept every night for the past eleven-and-a-half years, Brownie snored. She smiled, remembering the day he appeared in the front yard just a puppy, lost and skinny, and she'd claimed him as her own. He'd been her faithful pet since then, and she was glad for his company.

The star-lit night was quiet, a half-moon rising in the east, and at last, the air cooled a little. Kristina welcomed the refreshing breeze that ruffled the curtains on the open window and drifted across her bed.

It reminded her why she liked this time of year, just before the worst summer heat and humidity set in. As she lay back on the pillow, thankful that God had blessed her with another wonderful day, she prayed. *Bless my parents and my family, Lord, and keep us all safe. Please help Mama deliver a healthy baby when her time comes.* She closed her eyes, secure and happy for the comfort and safety of her home and her soft bed.

Somewhere in the distance an owl hooted. Brownie growled.

"Shush, you silly dog. It's just a barn owl." Kristina giggled. Brownie never was much of a watch dog—always growling or barking at all the wrong things. "Go back to sleep."

She'd almost dozed off, when the click-clack of Brownie's toenails moving across the floor aroused her. Kristina threw back the sheet and pushed herself halfway up. Braced on one elbow, she watched as the dog put his paws on the windowsill and nosed the lace curtains aside. He growled again, louder this time, then barked. What on Earth had gotten into him? She'd never heard such ferocious, snarling barking. Concerned now that something more than a hoot-owl had her dog upset, Kristina got out of bed. She started at the sound of rapid movements beyond the window. Footsteps rustled in the brush and leaves, as if someone or something were running away. Her first instinct was to cower back beneath the sheets, but she brushed the thought away, sure it was just a large animal roaming through the yard.

Cautiously joining Brownie at the window, she looked out. Frightened, she sucked in a breath. It was no animal. The dark form of a tall man disappeared into the black shadows across the yard. She jumped away from the window. Her heart raced, and she began to shake.

What if the man she'd seen in the library had followed her home and he'd waited until dark to look through her window? Was he watching her again? He didn't seem the type to lurk in the darkness, and she didn't want to believe her suspicions, yet it was impossible to tell who was out there. Who else could it be? She'd heard rumors of a Peeping Tom in the area recently, but she couldn't imagine anyone she knew doing such a thing. Maybe it was the stranger in the library. She slammed the window shut then wrapped her arms around her shoulders, trembling as she backed away.

Her bedroom door flew open. Startled, she turned and jumped back against the wall, ready to scream. Her parents burst into the room. She breathed a huge sigh of relief and ran into her mother's arms.

Papa ordered Brownie to lie down and be quiet then he turned to Kristina. "What's going on in here?"

"Why is your window closed?" Mama Leoma let Kristina go and crossed the room. She started to open the window. "You need some fresh air in here, sweetheart."

"No!" Kristina rushed to the window, nearly pushing her mother aside, and held the window down. "Someone was out there."

"What do you mean? Why would anyone be out there this time of night?" Her mother's eyes grew wide, disbelieving.

In three giant steps her father stalked over to the window and raised it, sticking his head out the un-screened opening. "I don't see a thing out there. It was probably just a neighbor's dog prowling around."

"No it wasn't. When I looked out after Brownie barked, I saw a man duck into the bushes down by the lane. All I could see was a dark silhouette, but it was definitely a tall man."

"Oh, my." Her mother rushed to wrap her arms back around Kristina's shoulders, holding her more tightly than before, her voice shaky. "I think we'll keep the window closed. Did you see him try to climb inside?"

"No. I don't think he did." The thought brought back old fears and she began to shake. "Brownie must have scared him away before he had a chance."

"It's all right now, sweetheart." Mama brushed Kristina's hair back from her face and patted her back. "Whoever it was, he's gone now. You get back into bed and try to sleep."

"But what if he comes back?" She didn't want to be left alone. For a moment, she felt like a young child again, instead of someone about to celebrate her eighteenth birthday.

Her father kissed her cheek. "I'll make sure he doesn't come back. I'm going to get my rifle and walk around the property. Leoma, you turn the window latch and pull down that shade. Then come lock the door behind me, and don't open it until I come back."

Mama stepped over to the window and did as she was told, lowering the roller shade all the way to the base of the window frame. "Oh, Welby, we never lock the doors. The man was probably just walking across the yard. I'm sure he's long gone by now. Besides, those flimsy latches wouldn't keep a fly out of the house."

"Just the same, you do as I said. And you go back to bed, Kristina. Everything will be all right now, and we'll talk more about this in the morning."

"Yes sir." As she crawled into bed, she wondered if she should tell her parents about the young man at the library, then she decided against it. It seemed unfair to assume he was dangerous when she knew absolutely nothing about him. He didn't appear to be the type of man who would be walking around a stranger's property, or peeking through windows.

It had been years since her mother had tucked her into bed, but Kristina let Mama Leoma pull the sheet up over her shoulders and tend to her as if she were five again. It felt good to know she had the protection and love of both parents, and she tried to relax.

"I remember a Bible verse from the Psalms my mother often read to me when I was afraid," Mama said as she sat down on the edge of the bed. *"I will lie down and sleep in peace, for you alone, O Lord, make me dwell in safety."*

Kristina thought about the words, comforted by them. "Thank you."

Her mother said a short prayer and kissed her cheek. "Good night. I hope you'll sleep now."

"I will. Good night."

Kristina snuggled deeper between the sheets, and chided herself for acting like a foolish child. She knew she was safe in her parents' house, surrounded by their love, and protected by God and a host of guardian angels.

Sleep didn't come, however. The clock in the living room chimed and Kristina counted. Nine. . . ten. . . eleven. Brownie snored, but she was wide awake. It wasn't fear now that kept her gazing into the dark room or tossing from side-to-side, but thoughts that kept rambling back to the young man she'd encountered in the library. Her conscience was in a tight game of tug-of-war. Tell her parents about him, or not? It would be terrible to cause him trouble without knowing who'd been outside her window. She'd thought about the man off and on all evening, and something about him caused a stir in her heart that she'd never experienced before. It was a pleasant feeling, but she knew not to trust her heart entirely. He did seem awfully nice, though. Confusion brought more doubt and sleeplessness. Finally, with a heavy sigh, she made a decision. Right or wrong, she would tell her parents about the man.

At breakfast in the morning, before going to church with the family, she would explain how she'd met the man at the library. And she'd pray it wasn't him who had been at her window.

Chapter 3

STANDING IN FRONT OF a large, oval mirror that hung above a chest of drawers, Pilan' pulled a fresh, white shirt over his head, and grimaced at his reflection as he tucked it neatly into his black trousers. The shirt should have been sent out to the hotel laundry to be pressed before wearing it. Resigned to having somewhat disheveled clothing while traveling, he smoothed his hands over his garments and straightened his shoulders. There was no time to fuss over his appearance this morning. Now that he had a job, he'd have to be more careful about the condition of his clothing. His damp hair had sprung into unruly waves. He ran a comb through it again, attempting to keep his hair off his face.

He glanced at his gold pocket-watch before tucking it into his trousers pocket. Time to head down to the restaurant to work. They'd begin serving breakfast in fifteen minutes, and Potts was strict about having his waiters there on time. Potts had said Monday mornings weren't very busy, but there would be a few regulars who stopped in for coffee and breakfast on their way to work.

Though he could afford to travel around the world many times on the inheritance his grandfather had left him, working in the hotel restaurant helped pay for his adventures. He'd been taught that honest work brings respect and reward. Working with one's hands was honorable in God's sight, he believed, whether it was pulling weeds or washing dishes. His grandfather had taught him, that hard work also makes a man appreciate his life and all he has accomplished. Not that waiting tables was a great accomplishment, but it gave him the feeling of honoring not only God, but also his father and grandfather. It was also a good way to meet new people, and learn more about the places he visited.

Pilan' walked across the room to leave, and stopped short when someone banged on the door. It wasn't the usual knock of the cleaning lady, and he didn't know anyone who would pound on the door so rudely, especially at this early hour. The knock grew louder, impatient. When he opened the door, a deputy sheriff greeted him with a stern glare, and then strode into the room without invitation.

"Good morning sir," Pilan' said stepping aside. Puzzled, he followed the gangling deputy to the small desk where he had an open map, his compass, and his travel journal. He wasn't accustomed to such impolite intrusions. "Excuse me, sir, these are my personal possessions. May I ask what it is you're looking for?"

"Young man, don't be smart with me." The deputy snarled, and lifted his bony, pointed chin. His words came out in a slow, whiny drawl. "Where were you Saturday night around ten o'clock?"

Pilan' thought for a moment, pressing a forefinger to his lips. "I was right here. Well, not here in my room, but downstairs in the hotel restaurant finishing my job. May I ask what this is a—?"

"Your job? The restaurant isn't open that late at night." The deputy shook his head, a smirk on his face, as if he'd caught his suspect in a lie. He picked up Pilan''s snapshot camera from the upholstered chair near the desk and examined it. "Is this thing one of those pictures boxes?"

"It's a camera. Yes, it takes pictures." He took the camera from the deputy. Let me show you how it—."

"Never mind that!" The deputy snatched the camera from Pilan''s hand and examined it. "We have good reason to believe you might have been looking through one of our resident's windows. You been using this thing to take indecent pictures of ladies in their rooms?"

"Absolutely not! Why would anyone accuse me of such a detestable act?" Not only was Pilan' insulted, but for the first time, he knew the indignity of being falsely accused of something bad he'd never think of doing. He'd never been easily provoked, but he had to step back and take a deep breath, or he'd also find out for the first time how it felt to punch another man in the face. After a few calming breaths, he spoke with quiet resolve. "Sir, I am an honorable gentleman. I use the camera to photograph scenery, friends, and things of that nature."

"What about this here map? Looks to me like you're all set to run off."

"I'm on a journey around the country. I use the map to plan my route."

The bone-skinny, flat-nosed deputy cleared his throat and seemed to calm down. He set the camera on the chair. "You're not exactly being accused, young man. You fit the description of a man the young lady saw in the library. She had a scare late Saturday night when someone snooped around her bedroom window, and we're checking all possible suspects. Do you recall meeting a young woman Saturday afternoon in the library?"

"Indeed, I did. I saw a beautiful, young lady, although we didn't converse with one another."

"You're telling me you don't know who she was?"

"I'd never seen her before that. I don't know her name, nor do I know where she lives. She seemed rather shy, and only glanced at me once or twice. We exchanged a polite smile and said hello. After a few moments she departed in a hurry. I've not seen her since."

He didn't dare mention that he'd seriously considered following the girl out of the building to talk with her. Fortunately, he'd thought better of it, and minded his manners. He'd stayed seated and remained in the library for an hour, looking through the books before checking some of them out. After that, he'd returned directly to the hotel for his evening shift at the restaurant.

The deputy squinted, his lips tight, as if he didn't believe Pilan', then he braced his hands on his skinny, hipless waist. He rocked back and forth on his feet, his gaze on the map.

Pilan' looked at his watch again. "I must hurry down to my job, or the restaurant will have unhappy customers waiting for service. I don't wish to be impertinent, sir, but perhaps you might come down with me and speak with my boss. Mr. Potts will tell you I was right there Saturday night, cleaning up after closing. It was eleven o'clock before I left and came up to my room."

From what Pilan' had seen during his short time in Oklahoma City, nearly everyone in town was friendly with Potts, and his boss ran a reputable and popular restaurant. It seemed the customers devoured his biscuits and gravy at breakfast time faster than he could make them, and for dinner, a favorite was his pan-fried steak, fried potatoes, and collard greens with bacon. The hotel guests raved about the cheesecake as well. Pilan' had no doubt that this matter would be resolved as soon as the deputy spoke with Potts.

The deputy followed Pilan' down the two flights of stairs, the only noise an occasional squeaky, wooden step. Pilan' thought about the young lady he'd seen in the library—the one accusing him of this vile act. Why? She didn't seem to be the type to cause trouble for anyone, and he was quite sure she didn't know his name. What would cause her to think he'd been outside her bedroom window looking in? Perhaps she didn't know anyone else to accuse, and since he was new in town it was easy to cast suspicion on him. Though he was disappointed, he wasn't bitter or angry at her, and he supposed he should give her the benefit of the doubt.

Admittedly, after seeing her ride past the library on her bicycle, then seeing her again Saturday afternoon, he found himself thinking about her far more than he should. But his thoughts were pure, simple curiosity, genuine interest. If he were to court a lady, she seemed the type of young woman he'd like to meet and get acquainted with. She was very attractive, obviously smart, and enjoyed reading, and she had a beautiful smile that was hard to forget. He hoped he'd see her again after the real culprit was found and this incident was solved. For now, however, he supposed he'd better lay low.

Pilan' pushed through the kitchen door. His boss was at the stove stirring a huge kettle of grits, steam billowing up from the boiling pot. He introduced the deputy to Potts.

"I know deputy Hank," Potts said without interest or a hand shake, his eyes fixed on the bubbling grits.

It didn't take Potts thirty seconds to convince the deputy that Pilan' was innocent of any crime. If it wasn't the owner's six foot, three-hundred-pound, muscular frame that put the skinny deputy in his place, it was his firm, baritone voice and no-nonsense answers to the deputy's questions. Potts finished answering the questions with a spatula pointed directly in Deputy Hank's face. The scrawny lawman backed away as if he feared his nose might get flattened more with the hot utensil. The lawman had no more questions, or if he did, he kept them to himself.

The kitchen door flew open, and Jake, the other morning waiter, rushed in. "What's going on? We have hungry customers waiting out there." Jake came to Pilan''s side.

"Nothing that needs further discussion," Potts said, glaring directly at deputy Hank.

The deputy sniffed, straightened his badge, and threw back his shoulders.

Jake had quickly become one of Pilan''s confidants and good friends, and Pilan' appreciated his concern. He rested a hand on Jake's shoulder. "It's okay. Everything is straightened out."

Jake frowned long and hard at the deputy. "Well, if you have any questions about the integrity or character of my friend here, I'll tell you. You won't find a finer man in this town, so you better look elsewhere for your suspect."

Jake wasn't shy about speaking his mind, and Pilan' appreciated his friendship and his corroboration. Between the three well-built, tall men staring down at the deputy, it appeared they got the point across quite well. The man was definitely looking in the wrong place for his suspected criminal. Without further words, Deputy Hank lifted his chin, apparently in an effort to look important, and stormed out of the restaurant.

"Thanks men." Pilan' picked up a fresh pot of coffee and went to work.

Potts was a good, honest man and a good boss. Beneath his tough-looking, massive exterior was a kind and gentle Dutchman who cared about the people he hired and about his customers. Clearly, he didn't take kindly to having his employees harassed or accused of foolish shenanigans, and he prided himself in running an upstanding, first-class establishment. Sometimes forgetting his English and slipping into a strong Dutch accent, he boasted about having the best employees and the best food in town. Too bad Pilan' didn't plan to stay more than a few weeks. Even though he knew little about Potts, including his real name, he'd miss both Potts and Jake when he left.

"Just because old Potts vouched for that half-breed, that doesn't mean the man ain't dangerous. You can't be too sure about a stranger with a foreign name like *Pill-ann* Rousseau." The deputy stood as tall as he could. His words rushed out in loud spurts, his hands waving through the air faster than he could speak. "Why, the man had maps all laid out like a thief on the run, and he had one of those picture cameras. A snapshot camera he called it. I don't know what he's up to, but it looks like it ain't no good. I'm sure as the devil going to keep my eye on him."

"You do that, Hank."

Kristina's ears perked up. So his name was Pilan'. What a strange name that was. She wondered if the deputy had pronounced it correctly, but that wasn't important. At least now the man had a name. She tried to remain calm, as if nothing the deputy said had registered or mattered, but she was relieved and happy to hear that the gentleman in the library wasn't the person they were looking for. She hoped he wasn't angry about being suspected.

For reasons she couldn't explain, the fellow had been on her mind a lot. His honest eyes, his broad sincere smile, and the fact that he was looking through a pile of books, all beckoned to her emotions. After all, a man who spent time in the library with his nose in books had to be good. Right? Somehow, he didn't seem to fit the image of a man who would peek through windows or hurt anyone.

It worried her, however, that the sheriff still didn't know who had been prowling around outside her bedroom window. But if she encountered the dark-skinned man in the future, she wouldn't be afraid of him.

Her father nudged the deputy toward the door, giving him a friendly slap on the back. The flimsy man almost stumbled like a newborn calf. "Don't stop looking for other suspects, Hank," Papa said.

Kristina almost giggled but bit her lips together.

The deputy righted his small frame. "You can count on me, Welby. Don't you worry yourself none. Sooner or later we'll catch the culprit."

She wanted to tell the deputy he was watching the wrong man, but she kept quiet. She'd never seen her father so riled up over anything, and she didn't want to make matters worse. It seemed he was just raring to shoot someone. Of course, she knew he wouldn't shoot another person. Would he? Either way, she didn't like seeing him in such a tizzy.

"I'm counting on that," her father said. "You better not waste time finding out who's snooping around the neighborhood and threatening harm to my daughter."

"Well now, let's not go that far, Welby. No one threatened your girl."

"He might have if the dog hadn't scared him off."

What Papa said was probably true, and Kristina shuddered at the thought of what might have happened if the prowler had come through the window, if indeed that was his intent. Suddenly feeling a chill, she wrapped her arms around her body and shivered.

"Maybe so." The deputy nodded with each word.

"Meantime, I'm going to be on the lookout around here, and I'll be carrying my gun. Nobody's going to prowl around my property like that again, or they'll be sorry."

Mama put a hand on Papa's shoulder, trying to calm him. "Now, Welby, you know that's not the Christian thing to say. You're not going to shoot anyone, and you know it."

"Don't be so sure about that, Leoma. When it comes to protecting my family, I'll do what I have to."

The deputy held up a hand to stop the conversation. "Now folks, let's not get too carried away. We've been out after dark watching for anyone who's acting suspicious. Sooner or later we'll catch him, don't you worry." He pointed a bony finger at Kristina. "And you, young lady, just be careful who you talk to. A pretty girl like you can't be too cautious."

Kristina nodded and answered out of respect. "Yes sir."

That didn't mean she wouldn't speak to the man from the library if she saw him again. And she hoped she would see him.

Chapter 4

Kristina watched Mama Leoma drop a big dollop of chocolate icing on the two-layered birthday cake, and spread it into deep swirls.

"It's hard to believe you're already eighteen," Mama said. "It seems it was only last week when your father showed up at my door on that cold, winter morning. He was holding tiny, starving Dyer, and you were clinging to your daddy's leg, half scared to death. Things sure have changed since that dreadful day." Mama smiled, her eyes sparkling with joy. Seconds later, a veil of darkness masked her mother's face. Why the sudden change?

"Leoma?" Welby came up beside Mama and put a hand on her shoulder. "Are you all right, dear? You look upset."

Welby swiped a forefinger through the leftover frosting inside the bowl, and held it up to Mama's mouth. She licked the rich chocolate from his finger and smiled. Eager to have a taste of the frosting, Kristina's mouth watered. Chocolate was her favorite flavor.

"Nothing's wrong," Mama said. "I was just thinking about Kristina leaving for Boston soon. I can't believe she's already eighteen and going off to college."

Papa wrapped his big arms around Mama and held her. Kristina loved the affection her parents showed one another. Papa was so close, she breathed in the smell of his clean shirt and fragrant cologne. She was glad God had put her parents together in unique circumstances, and that their love was solid, rich, enduring. Maybe someday, long after her music business was well established, she would have the kind of marriage they had.

Papa looked at Kristina then turned back to Mama. "It's not everyday a poor cotton farmer's daughter gets to attend a good university. You've been a wonderful mother to Kristina and Dyer, and you've taught them well. Our girl will be fine. After all, she'll be with your parents while she goes to school, and you know they'll take good care of her."

"I know. And she'll do well in school. I'll just miss her, and I'm sure her brothers and sister will miss her."

"I won't miss her," said Edward Lee as he darted into the kitchen licking his lips, his eyes begging for a taste of frosting. "She's scared of snakes, and won't climb trees, and she's a fraidy-cat."

"Now, Eddie," Mama said. "You know better than to talk like that. Your sister is all grown up. Young ladies don't climb trees. As for your snakes, I don't like them myself."

Papa ruffed Eddie's already-wild hair with his big hand. "You'll miss your sister, young man. You just wait and see."

"Won't neither."

With a small spoon, Leoma scraped a dab of frosting from the edge of the bowl, and gave it to her grinning son. "Don't be a stinker. Now run back outside and play with the other children. It won't be long before company comes and dinner will be ready."

Moments later the Langleys arrived, both parents carrying a dish of food. They set the serving bowls on the long plank table, along with the growing array of entrees and desserts. Mama was always happy for Anna Jo's help in the kitchen. She'd admitted many times, if it hadn't been for her kind neighbor and friend, she probably would never have learned to cook a decent meal. They still shared recipes now and then, and Anna Jo was always teaching Leoma some new cooking trick. Kristina often watched and listened, and though cooking wasn't her favorite thing to do, she could do a pretty good job in the kitchen.

"I guess it's time for us men to get out of the kitchen before our wives put us to work." Papa grabbed George's shoulder and nudged him toward the back door. George went along willingly.

"You men get those food tables set up on the shady side of the house," Mama called after them before they got out the door.

"Yes ma'am," Papa called back over his shoulder before the screen door slammed shut.

"Kristina, why don't you and Doris go into your room and visit until we call you for dinner? This is your special day. We can manage without your help." Clearly, by the tone of her mother's voice, the mothers wanted to talk privately.

"All right." Kristina was more than happy to have time alone with her friend. She left the kitchen towing Doris along by the hand.

Before they were out of hearing range, Kristina stopped just beyond the door. She held a finger to her lips to keep Doris silent.

"Have you heard any more about that prowler?" Mrs. Langley spoke in a hushed voice.

"I haven't heard anything lately."

"There have been more complaints, and since Doris heard noises outside her window a few days ago she's hardly slept at night."

Kristina looked at Doris, eyes questioning. Doris nodded.

"I sure worry about the young women around here," Mama said, concern in her voice. "What's this world coming to anyway?"

From where Kristina stood she could see Anna Jo peek at the cornbread in the oven. "Do you think the prowler could be that half-breed everyone's talking about?"

"I don't know. It seems he has a solid alibi according to Deputy Hank. Have you seen the man?"

"Oh, yes." Anna Jo found a hot pad to take the pan of cornbread out of the oven. "He's a handsome creature. Don't you say a word to your husband or mine, but I've never seen a more handsome man. One thing's for sure, he could be a woman chaser. And with his looks he'd reel them in faster than our boys catch catfish."

"Well, we best keep our eyes on our girls." Leoma made room for the cornbread on the warm surface of the stove. "I think everything is ready. Let's have the boys wash up, and call the girls in to help set out the food."

Mama didn't have to call them. Kristina stepped back into the kitchen to offer her help, Doris right behind her. Doris picked up a bowl of potato salad and carried it out.

"I'll take the platter of roast pork." Kristina carried the heavy dish of food out the door.

Just as she set the large platter on the oilcloth-covered serving table, three of the Gallager boys arrived. Toby headed straight toward her. He plucked a piece of meat right off the platter before she had a chance to remove her hands.

Kristina groaned. "Tobias Gallager! Keep your fingers out of the food." She nudged him away with an elbow to his ribs and gave him her meanest frown, not that it stopped him.

Toby just grinned and shrugged one shoulder. "A growing man's gotta eat."

"Well you can wait for everyone to gather, and for Papa to say the blessing before you act like a starved hog." What was it about some men? Kristina huffed and planted her fists on her hips, standing guard between Toby and the food.

"Don't get upset, birthday girl." Toby reached for a strand of Kristina's hair and gave it a little tug. He winked and grinned. "You know I'm just kidding around. Ain't no harm in me getting the first taste of your mama's fine cooking."

"It just isn't polite." Kristina stood her ground, wondering how she had put up with so many years of Toby's relentless teasing. She'd never known a more insufferable, yet almost likeable fellow. They'd been neighbors and friends since before she'd started school. He was eight then, two years older than she, and even then he'd been a prankster. She'd seen him bully other boys but never the girls. He'd only teased them. A few times over the years, until he'd dropped out of eleventh grade, she'd accepted a ride to school with him in his old buckboard. He liked to flirt with her, but she'd never encouraged his actions, and she had no desire to be anything more than a friend.

More company had arrived, and all the food was displayed on the long table. Papa walked over to Kristina's side. With one loud whistle between his teeth and a hand raised to the sky, he quieted the noisy crowd. When the last head was bowed, he said a short but gracious blessing over the food. Papa's faith was strong, and since Mama Leoma had taught him how to read, he read his Bible every day. But he was a man of few words when it came to speaking or praying in front of others.

"Amen. Food's on," Papa said in closing. "You go first, birthday girl."

With a light touch on her shoulder, her father coaxed her to the end of the table to pick up a plate. Right behind her, Toby leaned in to her shoulder, his mouth so close to her ear she felt his hot breath. She jerked her head away. He spoke in a low voice. "You mind if I eat with you? We could sit over yonder together under that tree?"

Kristina took a deep breath. She didn't want to eat alone with Toby, and when she spotted Doris nearby she called out to her. "Come sit with us under the tree." Then she turned to Toby. "Sure, we can sit under the tree."

It wasn't long until a whole group of people spread blankets beneath the shade of the tree and sat down to eat. Kristina was relieved and happy, but Toby looked disgruntled and grew very quiet. The moment he cleared the last morsel of food from his plate he got up and left.

Poor, poor Toby.

Several conversations were going on at one time among the group around her, and Kristina couldn't help but hear someone mention the new man they'd seen in town. Several of the men referred to him as the half-breed.

"He seems awfully suspicious to me, even if he is rather good-looking," said Miss Minnie from the dress shop, her crow-like voice accusatory.

"He does indeed," Anna Jo put in. "But we mustn't judge him when we know nothing about him. He might be a fine, upstanding gentleman for all we know."

Kristina smiled inwardly glad Anna Jo Langley wasn't ready to lynch the man.

"He works in the hotel restaurant, so he's no vagrant." George's affirmation was good to hear, and Kristina secretly appreciated that, especially coming from a church deacon. But anyone could tell by the man's clothing he wasn't a bum.

"Well, I still don't like the looks of him. There's just something about the way he watches people that makes me nervous." Hearsay from the old crow again.

Kristina bit her tongue. She really did like Minnie, and she loved buying clothing in her dress shop. She wouldn't dare say anything to upset her.

Doris spoke up. "Yeah, like the way he stared at Kristina on our way home from school last week. He was standing on the library steps, and you'd have thought he was ready to pounce on her. Couldn't take his eyes off her." The tone of her friend's comment surprised Kristina.

"Oh, Doris. I think you're exaggerating." Kristina couldn't believe what her best friend had said. She'd heard enough from everyone. She raised her voice loud enough for everyone to hear. "Saturday afternoon I saw him in the library looking through a stack of books. A man who spends time reading and learning can't be all that bad."

"Did he speak to you?" Doris was clearly surprised and curious, her eyes wide.

"He said hello."

Doris gasped and spoke in a whisper. "Tell me you didn't speak to him."

"I said hello in return. It's the polite thing to do, don't you think? My goodness. I can't believe what you're saying after the way you swooned over him. You said yourself he was *sublime*. You're the one who carried on about how handsome he was, and you said he looked perfectly normal. Why are you acting as if my saying hello to him was so terrible?"

Doris's cheeks turned as red as her hair. "Well that was before—"

"Before the rumors? I saw nothing suspicious about him." Kristina didn't know why she sounded so defensive. She didn't know any more about the man than anyone else in the group, but it was wrong the way everyone censured him without cause. "Doesn't the Bible tell us God is the judge of all, and for us to judge our neighbors fairly? We aren't supposed to spread slander among our people." Kristina had heard those very words coming from the preacher's mouth and she believed them.

"Kristina! My, my how you go on, dear." Anna Jo's words burned with disapproval. Her friend's mother shook her head several times. "He is *not* one of our people. You must be careful."

Kristina couldn't believe her ears.

Just as Anna Jo finished her warning, Toby rejoined the group. In one hand he carried a plate piled high with desserts, and a half-eaten cookie in the other hand. With his mouth full of cookie, he put in his two bits. "Yeah, Kristina. Mrs. Langley is right. For all we know that half-breed is the prowler that's snooping around at night."

Several others, including Doris, nodded in agreement. Kristina nudged Doris with her elbow. "I can't believe you think that." To the others she spoke boldly. "I'm disappointed in all of you. If Reverend Gilroy were here, he'd tell you not to judge the man's character when you don't even know him."

Silence fell over the group. Some proceeded to eat while others simply stared at Kristina with disbelieving eyes. She'd made her point loud and clear. These were her friends. They'd always been a kind, friendly bunch of people, and to hear them accusing a newcomer of wrong doing when they had absolutely no evidence or cause didn't set well with her. Where had their spirit of brotherly love gone?

She rose from the blanket and excused herself. She didn't mean to sound self-righteous or defensive, yet she couldn't sit by and listen to the accusations and ridicule. Suddenly, she had a powerful desire to get acquainted with the stranger. More than anything, she wanted to know his full name, where he was from, and what he was doing in Oklahoma City. Her heart fluttered wildly as she thought about seeking him out and introducing herself to him. As she thought about the few days left before she would leave Oklahoma City to attend college, a sense of urgency came over her. She had to know more about the man everyone was calling the half-breed.

Though her appetite was ruined, she headed for the desserts. After looking over the selection of mouthwatering cakes, pies, cobblers, and cookies, she decided on a wedge of the chocolate birthday cake her mother had baked. She carefully placed it on a clean plate. Gazing around the yard, she debated whether or not to rejoin the group beneath the tree. The afternoon was sultry and hot, and the tree provided the only available shade in the yard. She'd almost rather roast in the blazing sun than listen to more ridiculous hogwash. Most of what the friends and neighbors had to say was little more than gossip. It was her eighteenth birthday, yet anything special about the day had disappeared. She should be excited and happy, but the day was overshadowed by everyone's concern about the half-breed. That, and feeling betrayed by her best friend, almost brought tears to her eyes.

She took a bite of cake as she meandered across the yard, savoring the moist, delicious dessert. The chocolate frosting was thick and rich, sweetening her mood.

Pilan' spread the map across the small desk in his room, going over the route he planned to take when he left Oklahoma in two weeks. He'd earned more than enough cash to make it to California, but he wanted to make sure he had ample supplies and adequate money for good food and decent lodging along the way. He wasn't as rugged as his father had been during his adventures. In fact, he was probably spoiled. The tales his father told about fighting off wild animals, and enduring treacherous weather while sleeping under the stars with a rock for a pillow, didn't appeal to Pilan'. He'd rough it when absolutely necessary, but to him, roughing it meant sleeping in a small tent with a few comforts, such as a warm quilt and a feather pillow, should he have to stop for the night where there were no hotels or boarding houses.

He ran the tip of a forefinger along the line north from Oklahoma City through Kansas, then west to Colorado. It was a route his father hadn't traveled, and he had little information about what he'd encounter along the way. That, of course, was part of the challenge, the excitement of exploring. He'd heard the land was relatively flat through Kansas and heading into Colorado. After that, he'd have to decide which way to cross the Rocky Mountains. Should he head south again, or attempt the rugged terrain going straight west? He tapped the pencil on the map. Would he attempt the entire journey on horse back, or would he ride part of the distance on a train? It was a lot to consider, and he had to think about the weather, too. It would play a serious role in his decisions. Something else that might alter his plan was the young woman he'd seen in the library. He wanted to meet her, to find out more about her before setting out on his journey again.

Scratching his head he groaned. What was he thinking? After pondering the idea briefly, he decided it was best to forget about her. But the way she stuck in his mind it wouldn't be that easy. Since that day in the library, thoughts of her had plagued him day and night. Until now, no woman had diverted his mind from his travels. Maybe if he could meet her and talk to her, he'd realize she was just another female of no extraordinary importance. If that were the case, he could move on not look back.

A tap on the door jolted him out of his rattlebrained thinking. He dropped the pencil, letting a gush of air escape from his lips as he strode across the room. It better not be that irritating deputy again. He'd had about all he could take of that man. Why the skinny runt of a lawman was determined to hound him, Pilan' couldn't understand. He pulled open the door.

"Howdy, buddy."

"Jake, come in." Pilan' stood back and motioned with a jerk of his head for his friend to enter the room. He'd met Jake when he began working in the restaurant downstairs. Jake had been working there for a year when Pilan' began. He glanced at his watch. Their shift didn't start for another hour. "What's on your mind?"

"I've been thinking about that girl you saw in the library, and I think I know where she lives. I was out riding this afternoon, and a group of folks at one of the farms north of town was having a big shindig or something. I rode up the lane part way before I turned back, but I think I might have seen her there."

For a moment Pilan' considered what his friend said. "If there was a gang of people there she might have been a guest."

"True. I didn't consider that."

Pilan' gave Jake a playful nudge on one shoulder. "I appreciate you trying to find out where she lives, my friend, but I'm not going to go searching for her. I'm going to forget I ever saw her. Besides, it would be my luck I'd get tossed into jail for snooping around where I don't belong. That deputy still thinks I'm some kind of prowler or Peeping Tom."

"He's harassing you even after talking to Potts?"

"Yes, even after Potts vouched for me." Pilan' returned his attention to his map and traced a forefinger along a bold black line toward Colorado. "Here's where I'm headed next, and I'll be glad to leave this town."

KRISTINA HAD JUST TAKEN the last bite of cake when her mother grabbed her belly and bent forward. Mama's loud moan stilled the crowd. Kristina ran to her side, and several of the women dropped their plates of food and rushed from their various places to see if they could help.

"Is it time, Mama?"

Leoma looked up and smiled her nod a definite yes. "It's the real thing this time. I've been hoping the pains would let up, but they're getting stronger. Have your father send for the doctor, and let our guests know the party's over. I'm sorry to ruin your birthday, sweetheart, but I don't think this baby is going to wait for tomorrow. Hurry now."

Kristina thought for a moment then kissed her mother's cheek. "This won't spoil my birthday, Mama. It will be my best present ever."

Glenda and Anna Jo helped Leoma inside while Kristina found her father. As usual, he was talking with a group of men out by the barn. From what little talk she caught as she approached, it sounded like the typical subjects for men: farm equipment, crops, fishing and hunting. Without hesitation, she jumped into the middle of the conversation and grabbed her father's hand.

"Mama needs the doctor right away; the baby's coming. We need to send someone to fetch him."

George Langley broke loose from the circle of men. "I'll go. Welby you stay here with Leoma." George didn't wait for an answer. He ran to his horse and buggy and was gone lickety-split.

Kristina figured if he hurried it was only a twenty-minute ride to the doctor's office, and at the rate Mr. Langley rode away, he'd probably make it in ten. Her father rushed into the house.

The women cleared the food and tidied up the yard while the men took down the makeshift tables. The way everyone pitched in to help, it was no time at all until everything was done. Kristina took charge of the children, and to her delight, Doris joined her.

"I'm sorry for the way I sounded about that man," Doris said. "I shouldn't have gotten caught up in the gossip. You're right. None of us should judge him. Instead we should welcome him and befriend him."

Kristina hugged Doris. "Thank you. I don't know why everyone gets so riled up about him to begin with."

"I think it's because that stupid Toby put the idea in their minds about him being the prowler."

"I think you're right." Kristina looked around and didn't see Toby or his brothers. Good. They were gone. They probably left as soon as they got their fill of food.

Kristina and Doris rounded up the last two children who were down at the creek wading in the water. They helped the parents load children and leftover food into their wagons and buggies. By the time the last buggy pulled out of the yard, the doctor rode up to the house with Mr. Langley right behind him.

"Mama's inside," Kristina informed the doctor. She started to give him directions when she realized Doctor Rhodes had been there enough times to know his way in.

Kristina sat with Doris on the front porch, keeping their younger siblings and Glenda's children outdoors, watching them play tag and other games. Now and then she refereed a dispute, but most of the time there were no problems. An hour had passed. She hadn't heard any sounds coming from inside the house. No groaning or crying out. Since Glenda was assisting the doctor, Jason Alder stayed to be with Papa. Being a doting father, Jason poked his head out the door periodically to check on his two. It wasn't uncommon to see him get down on the ground to play marbles with his son, Thomas, or sit on a blanket to have a tea party with Emma, and her rag doll.

Most of the children were old enough to understand Mama was giving birth to a new baby. Every now and then, one of the older ones would stop playing and sit on the porch with Kristina, mostly sitting quietly and waiting. Glenda's children played nicely with Kristina's brothers and sister. She watched amused by the way Emma entertained and mothered

Roberta Fay. Dyer, of course, now the wise age of thirteen, was not affected by the event, except he didn't like being told to stay outdoors. Much too mature and enlightened for his age, Dyer would rather be at his desk with his nose in the Bible than helping entertain his younger siblings. Other than a short huff and momentary down trodden look, he didn't complain. He was the most patient and cooperative thirteen-year-old boy Kristina had ever known, and he had a special way with children that lured them to him.

Edward Lee galloped across the yard, dropped his stick horse, and plopped down on the step, his eyes inquisitive. "Is the new baby going to be a girl or a boy?"

"We won't know if we have a brother or sister until the baby is born." Kristina hoped that would satisfy the child's curiosity.

"Oh." Eddie jerked up both bony, little shoulders so hard they nearly hit his ears. "I hope it's a boy." With that, he jumped up and hopped down each step like a bullfrog hopping from rock to rock, and went back to riding his stick horse, whooping and hollering like a cowboy rounding up a herd of cattle.

Kristina smiled at the child and shook her head. She didn't mind having to tend her younger siblings, but today, her birthday all but forgotten, her mind was in a far away place, imagining a rendezvous with the man everybody was talking about. What would it be like to feel her hand in his, or have his arms around her? Having never been in a serious relationship with a man, her thoughts and ideas were uncomplicated, yet imagining how it would feel to kiss the handsome young man excited her in ways she'd never experienced.

Oh my. What am I thinking? She had no intention of putting herself in such a position. She simply wanted to know his name and get to know him. She was happy for the diversion when Dyer joined her on the porch again. She loved Dyer with her whole heart, and it never ceased to amaze her how healthy and robust he looked after nearly starving to death as a newborn. They both credited Mama Leoma for saving his life. When he silently put his head down and rested it in cupped hands on his knees, Kristina was alarmed. Dyer never complained about anything and was rarely ill. He'd breezed right through the chickenpox and measles when some children died from the diseases. He was thought of throughout the community as the miracle child, and indeed, he truly was.

"What's the matter?" Kristina placed one hand on Dyer's shoulder. She'd never seen him like this. "Are you feeling ill?"

Dyer's head movement indicated he wasn't sick, but he groaned. "Head hurts."

"Maybe it's the heat." Kristina fanned her younger brother with a square of cloth one of the little girls had been using for a doll blanket. "You've been in the sun all afternoon. After you rest here in the shade awhile you should feel better. Stay here while I get you a glass of cold water."

When Kristina returned with the water it appeared Dyer hadn't moved. Head bent, his eyes were covered with his cupped hands. When he straightened to drink the water he groaned and closed his eyes against the light. After a few minutes, he opened his eyes and swiveled his head in a circular motion. "I think the pain is going away."

"You better sit right here until it's all gone." Kristina had always mothered Dyer more than the younger children, and the bond they shared seemed to be deeper than any of the others. Perhaps it was because of their full-blood relationship. She loved all her brothers and her adorable little sister, just as she would love the new baby, but she still had deeper feelings for Dyer.

The sun hung low in the west, a mild breeze cooling the evening, making it almost bearable. Dusky shadows stretched across the yard. As the sun faded and the temperature cooled, Dyer perked up and said he felt better, but Kristina still worried about him.

With Doris and Dyer's help, Kristina settled the children on a blanket, and gave them each a plate of leftovers from the party. When they were done with their supper she set them free to play again. It was best they stay outdoors as long as possible. She didn't want them to hear Mama's groans and cries as her labor advanced. Even Kristina didn't want to hear the terrible sounds.

Hearing the agony of Mama birthing another baby, certainly took the romantic fantasies and excitement out of Kristina's imaginary rendezvous with Mr. *Sublime*. And helping clean the dirty faces and hands of all the younger children in her charge, before gathering them around her on the porch to tell them some bedtime stories, bolstered her aversion to marriage and having children of her own. She couldn't understand how Mama Leoma endured the pain of birthing five babies. It seemed after all that pain and having one baby die, her mother would never want to have another child, yet she seemed to forget the pain almost as soon as the baby took its first breath. "It's part of God's design," Mama had told her.

All settled on the porch in a small circle, the children listened, caught up in Kristina's rendition of the Bible story of David and Goliath. She added as much drama as she could. Even Dyer sat quietly and listened, even though she knew he could tell it equally well, or perhaps better.

It was getting late and Birdie yawned, letting out a loud sigh. Kristina hoped Mama would have the baby soon and the children could go inside to bed.

At last, before full darkness fell upon the farm, a tiny, shrill cry announced the arrival of the newest Soderlund child. Kristina still had the children gathered around her on the porch, some with sleepy eyes. She breathed a huge sigh of relief and stood, proclaiming cheerfully. "The new baby has arrived."

As she poked her head through the front door Frankie came up beside her. "Is it a boy or a girl?"

"I don't know yet." More important, she wanted to know if Mama Leoma was all right.

Jason came to the door, a mug of coffee in one hand. Before she could ask anything, the answer came from deep within the house.

"It's a girl!" Papa's full-volume shout from his bedroom door was a joyful announcement for all to hear. "Gracie May and Leoma are both fine."

Secretly happy for another little sister, Kristina swept Roberta Fay into her arms and hugged her. "You have a baby sister!"

Edward Lee jumped up and crossed to the other side of the porch, hands firmly placed on his skinny little-boy hips. He stomped one foot. "Ah, pig slobber! I wanted another brother."

Kristina laughed and went to him, running her fingers through his unruly straw-colored hair. "Sorry, buddy. God thought we needed another girl, so he gave us a sister. You're going to love her, just wait and see."

"Won't neither."

Kristina hugged her youngest brother. "Well, I bet she'll love you as much as I do."

Eddie jerked up a shoulder, clearly expressing his doubt, but Kristina knew better.

After saying goodnight to the Langleys and Alders as they departed with their children, Kristina ushered Frankie and Edward Lee to their room then tucked Roberta Fay snugly into her bed. Anxious to see the new baby, she tiptoed into her parents' bedroom. Dyer was already there.

Gracie May was a little, pink bundle with a cap of thick, dark hair. She looked like Mama. Already, Kristina loved her.

When at last Kristina went to bed, she smiled into the dark room. What a day it had been. She was eighteen now, and she had a new sister with whom to share her birthday. All was well with her and her best friend, Doris. And if all went as she hoped, she would soon formally meet the man who had stirred up so much gossip in town.

Chapter 5

Monday from daybreak until noon, Kristina worried and fretted, wondering if her parents could read her mind, or detect that her thoughts were on a man. It wasn't as if she were planning anything unseemly or against the rules. Not at all. Chance meetings happened all the time, and there was no way to know if the *so called* half-breed would even be at the library this afternoon. All she could do was hope.

As soon as she finished the dinner dishes and swept the kitchen floor, Kristina washed her face and hurried to her bedroom, shutting herself in, hoping Birdie wouldn't barge in full of bothersome questions or begging her to read a story. It seemed since Gracie May was born, Birdie turned to Kristina more often for attention.

She slipped into her most becoming summer skirt and blouse. Peering into to the large mirror above her chiffonier, she worried that her mother might question her. Papa had returned to the field or the barn, so he wouldn't see her. She didn't usually fuss so much over her appearance, but today was different. If by some lucky chance she did meet the handsome stranger, she wanted to look her best. She'd taken great care fixing her hair, brushing it an extra fifty strokes, and allowing her natural waves to fall unbound over her shoulders. She lifted the lid on a small box of face powder, patting a tiny amount on her nose and cheeks to smooth her skin. Trying to steady her hand, she hooked a small silver necklace around her neck. She smiled at her reflection, pleased with the results—until sudden niggling doubts taunted her.

Was she being too bold, too secretive?

She would never deliberately disobey her parents, or go against the guidelines and rules they'd insisted upon over the years. Number one rule: never lie. She paused, considering her actions. It wasn't a lie to say she was returning her library books and checking out more. She was an avid reader, and it wasn't uncommon for her to breeze through three or four books a week, sometimes more. If she happened upon a certain gentleman and they talked, she wouldn't keep it a secret. She'd always been an honest, devoted follower of Jesus, and though she hadn't prayed about this situation, she did consider whether hoping to meet the man was right or wrong. But certainly, she wasn't one of those ladies of the night searching for men who were willing to pay cash in exchange for physical pleasures. Heat singed her face thinking of such unholy things.

Mercy me.

Determined to put those thoughts out of her mind, she sucked in a deep breath, and shook her head as she released the air between pursed lips. She had to stop this silliness.

A stack of books in the crook of one arm, she left her room, and called out to Mama who was nursing Gracie May in another room down the hallway. "I'll be home in time to help prepare supper, Mama. I'm going to the library."

No answer.

Kristina tiptoed to her parents' bedroom and peeked in the door. Roberta Fay was napping in the center of the bed. Mama and Gracie May were asleep in the rocking chair, Mama holding the baby close to her breast, a slight smile on her lips. It was a perfect picture of contentment, love. She stepped closer, bending to place a light kiss upon her mother's cheek. Mama opened her eyes and whispered, "I heard you, sweetheart. Put a hat on to shade your face, and be safe."

"I will, Mama," Kristina whispered.

Dyer had been kind enough to hitch Clyde to the buggy and bring them up to the house. He waited near the front door, holding the reins and stroking Clyde's neck and head. "You'll be safer in the buggy than riding the bicycle. The road into town is getting dangerous these days, with wagons coming and going loaded with lumber and building materials."

"Thank you."

Now that she was eighteen, she had been given more privileges and responsibilities, but Dyer worried over her as much as their parents did. She smiled, knowing she was loved and well cared for. All attempts to ignore her fluttering stomach failed as she placed her books on the seat, climbed into the buggy, and took the reins from Dyer.

Pilan' watched the puffy, white clouds against the blue sky, and wondered why they didn't have more days like this in Paris. It seemed the sky went on forever. If only he could capture the picture in color with his camera. He slowed his stride to enjoy the fine day. Upon reaching the library steps, he bound up them two at a time. Beneath large overhang at the top, he paused for a moment, looking for any sign of the young woman's bicycle. He'd hoped she would be there returning her books. Today was the due date stamped on each of his books, so he assumed those she'd checked out when he'd seen her here would be the same. But of course, he had no way of knowing whether she'd returned them earlier in the week. Craning his neck, he looked as far up the street as he could see, but the street was bustling with horses, buggies and buckboards. No sign of a lady on a bicycle.

Disappointed, he pushed open the heavy glass door and stepped inside. The librarian, an antiquated woman with ample girth and a pleasant, round face, greeted him with a smile. He deposited his books on the return desk, and meandered toward the back of the room, glancing every now and then toward the entrance. Lack of air circulation in the room intensified the heat and humidity, reminding him of August in the Louisiana swamp. The only things missing were moss and alligators.

The only other person he saw in the library was a middle-aged woman with braids wrapped around her head, and spectacles perched on her nose. He'd noticed her pat a white handkerchief over her face several times, and he dug into his own pocket for a handkerchief to do the same. Afterward, he checked his pocket-watch to calculate how much time he had before going to work for the evening shift. Swell. He had more than two hours.

Perhaps if he browsed and read for a while, the pretty, young woman who had filled his thoughts and dreams for nearly a month would show up. Then what? Should he approach her and introduce himself to her? It seemed simple enough, and certainly there wasn't any reason he could think of that would go against the proper manners he'd been taught. But he wasn't accustomed to meeting women outside the realm of his family and circle of friends in France.

Until now, no woman had captured his attention so completely that he could think of little else, and he hoped meeting her would get her off his mind. He was a bit timorous because of the visit from the deputy, so he'd have to be cautious, using his best behavior. If the woman became frightened it could cause more trouble for him, and he didn't want that to happen, for it might ruin his travel plans.

He wiped his forehead again with the limp handkerchief, and stuffed it back into his pocket. Attempting to focus on one towering shelf of books, he searched for something new and informative that would take his mind off the woman.

Who am I kidding?

Fifteen minutes passed and he'd selected only two volumes, one about Colorado, and a thick book about Oregon, which included numerous pictures. He flipped through the pages of the latter one, the photographs not holding his attention. His eyes were on the door more than on the book. Giving up his search, he carried the two volumes to a table. He selected a chair where he had a good view, of not only the entrance, but almost the entire room. The heavy books made a loud thump when he dropped them on the table. He pulled out the chair and quietly eased into it, his mind in a quandary, his heart set on seeing a certain brunette with a captivating smile and alluring eyes. He waited. Another ten minutes passed. Inside his pocket, he fingered his watch between his forefinger and thumb. The lady wearing a crown of thick braids checked out several small books and left, leaving the cavernous silence to him, but not for long.

The quiet inside was pierced with a loud commotion outside the building. Men shouted, horses whinnied, a female screamed.

At the sound of the woman's cries Pilan' jumped up from his chair and darted toward the exit, his books forgotten. He rushed through the glass doors to see what had happened, hoping he could be of help. What was customarily a busy but quiet street was now chaos. Men grabbed the reins of agitated horses, trying to settle the animals. People gathered around a small buggy that sat askew, one of its wheels missing.

Then he spotted her. The young woman he'd been waiting for lay sprawled on the street, her long, thick hair fanned out on the dusty asphalt like rippling streams, her hat a few feet away, trampled by horse's hooves and nearly beyond recognition. The silky, white blouse she wore was smudged with dirt and her long, rumpled, blue skirt barely covered her knees.

It took only a moment for Pilan' to bound down the steps to where the young woman lay. When he knelt beside her, he was surprised but happy to see she was conscience. Though she looked directly into his eyes, what he saw first was a blank stare, then confusion. Suddenly, embarrassment flashed in her eyes. Her hands flew to her face, and her head rolled to one side away from him. Pilan' wanted to comfort her, but he was at a loss for words, and he wasn't sure what to do. He patted her forearm gently, not wanting to hurt her.

A small cut on her chin was the only injury he could see, but after such a fall, he feared she must have other injuries, possibly broken bones. He surveyed the growing crowd. "Has anyone gone for a doctor?"

Shoulders jerked up, heads moved from side to side, and not a soul answered his question. A young boy of about thirteen jumped forward on long, gangling legs, arms flying. "I'll go! I'll go!" Before anyone could answer or thank the boy, he was off in a mad dash.

The young woman tried to push up on one elbow. She groaned. Gently, Pilan' pressed one hand on her shoulder, encouraging her to remain still. "Don't move Miss. A doctor will be here soon. Can you tell me your name?"

Her answer was slow in coming, hesitant. "Kristina."

"Hello, Kristina. My name is Pilan'." He wanted to tell her he'd been waiting and watching for her, but that didn't seem quite proper. And this wasn't the way he wanted to meet her. She needed medical attention, not a tongue tied, infatuated stranger attempting to learn all about her.

Blinking and focusing on his eyes, Kristina smiled then flinched. She whispered, warmth returning to her eyes. "I remember you. You have an interesting name. Our deputy pronounced your name pill-ann." She grinned.

Pilan' chuckled. "It sounds like pay-lawn, and it is spelled P-I-L-A-N'. I remember you as well, and I've been hoping to see you again. But this isn't the way I wanted to meet you. Are you in much pain?"

A half-smile beamed up at him. "No. I don't know what happened."

A man wearing a business suit and a black, felt hat stepped forward. Probably a banker, Pilan' thought. "That wheel flew off your buggy and slammed into my horse. Nearly sent me flying off in the street, too. That's what happened, young lady!"

As if Kristina had deliberately caused the accident. It was all Pilan' could do to keep his mouth closed.

"Then the side of my wagon hit her buggy," shouted a scruffy, older man, his face as dirty as his denim overalls. "I tried not to run into her, but her buggy done jerked sideways, and there just wasn't nothing I could do to miss crashing right smack-dab into her."

Pilan' cringed at the man's poor grammar. Here he was a foreigner, yet very particular about talking properly, whether he was speaking English or French. In disbelief, he jerked his head up and glared at the men. "None of that matters right now. Can't you see this woman is hurt?"

Still on bended knee, he turned his attention back to Kristina, smoothing a few strands of her hair back from her face. He couldn't help himself; he had to touch her. He leaned closer, his face within a few inches of hers, to speak without the entire town hearing his words. "I know this is ill-timed, but I must tell you, I was hoping to meet you today—inside the library of course. This isn't the way I'd hoped to introduce myself to you."

"Nor I." Kristina managed a full smile but she winced. "I, too, hoped to meet you today, but in a more graceful manner. Here I am, covered with dirt, and sprawled in the street like a drunk after a barroom brawl. She started to get up, a grimacing frown on her face as she moved.

Pilan' touched her shoulder again. "I think you should lie still, and let the doctor check you over before you try to get up."

Several shouts came from the crowd and feet shuffled. People stepped aside, making a break in the circle of on-lookers. "Here comes the doctor!"

One hand still rested lightly on Kristina's shoulder. Pilan' looked up just as the doctor reached them and brought his buggy to a stop a few feet away. He was easily recognized in his black suit and black hat as he jumped down from his buggy, a large black medical satchel in hand. Before getting down from the doctor's buggy, the young boy who had gone to fetch the doctor sat tall, looking proud and important. Pilan' smiled. He dug into his pocket and found a penny for the boy. "Thank you, young man."

He turned his attention back to Kristina. "You do what the doctor says, and I'll look forward to talking with you at a more appropriate time."

Kristina frowned. "Please, wait. Don't go away."

Happy that she wanted him to stay he smiled and gave her delicate shoulder a light squeeze. "All right. Do you want to send someone to fetch your parents?"

Kristina's head rolled from side to side, her eyes serious. "Only if the doctor thinks it's necessary."

"What about your buggy?"

"I'll repair it." The male voice was husky, possessive. The man stepped out from the crowd. "I'll have it fixed in a jiffy."

Pilan' looked up to see a tall, robust, young man he'd never met. He appeared to be about his own age, but much larger and stronger. Big hands, muscled arms, and denim overalls indicated hard work and strength. He wasn't someone Pilan' would want to tangle with.

Pilan' looked to Kristina for approval. He didn't have any idea who the fellow was, but he supposed a person who would volunteer to repair her buggy must be an acquaintance.

Kristina looked up at the man, immediate recognition in her eyes. "Toby, what are you doing in town?"

Toby shrugged. "Just running an errand for Paw."

"Pilan', this is our neighbor, Toby Gallager. Toby, this is Pilan'."

He reached out and shook Toby's hand, experiencing the neighbor's steel grip. "Nice to meet you."

Kristina smiled at Pilan'. "Thank you for rushing to my—"

"My, my, Miss Soderlund, what has happened here?" The doctor knelt to the ground, examining Kristina's head, arms, and legs.

Pilan' rose. He stepped aside while the doctor asked Kristina scores of questions, poked, and prodded. Kristina, though demure and looking embarrassed again, answered the doctor's questions. The physician took extra time and care examining the laceration on her chin, and wiping away dirt and blood with a clean white cloth. His attentive manner was a clear indication that Kristina was special to him. Or perhaps the doctor treated everyone with such tender care.

When the doctor had completed his ministrations he stood. "Well now young lady, I don't think anything is broken, and you don't need sutures on you chin. Just keep it clean and it will heal in no time. You're quite lucid, so let's see if you can stand up without too much pain."

With the doctor on Kristina's right side and Pilan' on her left, they assisted Kristina to her feet. Her hand was soft in his, and perhaps he held it a little too long, but he wanted to make sure she was stable. At least that's what he told himself.

Kristina immediately brushed off her clothing and tried to smooth her hair, searching the ground, most likely for her hat. Pilan' snapped up the battered chapeau from the street, and held it up for Kristina to see. He brushed off the dust, pushed the top this way and pulled the brim that way, making every attempt to reshape the frilly thing, but it was pointless. The hat was a total loss. "I think it's ruined."

Kristina's hands flew to the sides of her head and she cried out. "Oh, no, Mama is going to be terribly upset when she sees what I've done to her hat."

"Your mother will be so happy you weren't seriously injured, I doubt she'll care about the hat. If it's a problem I'd be happy to replace it with a new one, if you'll allow me." Pilan' would do anything for the woman, as long as she wasn't hurt.

"Thank you, but that won't be necessary. I'm sure Papa will gladly purchase a new one for her."

Much of the crowd had dispersed, heading in every direction, going about their afternoon business.

The doctor gave Kristina a fatherly hug and patted her shoulder. "I'm going to let you go on about your day, young lady, but you mind yourself. If you feel dizzy or get a bad headache, be sure to send for me." The doctor paused, rubbing his chin between a thumb and forefinger. He appeared to rethink his statement. "On second thought, before you run off, Kristina, I think perhaps you should come to my office and let me clean up that scrape on your chin. If you'd like, while you're there, you can wash up a bit and comb your hair."

Kristina kissed the old gentleman's cheek. "Yes, I'd like that. Oh!" Suddenly frowning, Kristina gazed around the area. "Where are my books? I must return them right away."

Again, Toby appeared from behind Kristina's buggy carrying the dust covered books. "I'm afraid they got a little dirty but they seem to be in fair shape, no torn pages that I can see. He looked over the books for some time, his lips tight and moving back and forth before he spoke. "Did you read all them books, Krissy?"

"*Those* books." Kristina took them, blowing and brushing dust from the covers and lovingly smoothing the pages. "Yes, I read every single word in each one. And I intend to check out a few more to read. It would do you good to read a few books, yourself."

Well she put that fellow in his place didn't she? Pilan' held his laughter in check, wondering why Kristina was so sarcastic with her neighbor. Did Toby have special feelings for Kristina that she refused to acknowledge? Whatever the case, it was none of his business.

Kristina turned to Toby. "Will you have my buggy repaired when I'm done here in town?"

Toby puffed up his chest, boastful, almost arrogant. "Sure will. I'll have it done in a jiffy."

"Thank you. Please leave it hitched right here in front of the library."

"You can count on it, Krissy."

"Come with me young lady," the doctor said in his fatherly tone. "You needn't walk all that way in this heat."

She looked at Pilan'. "What about my books? I don't want to carry them to Doctor Rhodes office and back."

He held out his hands, inviting Kristina to place her books in his care. "May I return them for you?"

"Yes, thank you." As poised and pretty as if the accident hadn't happened, Kristina gave the books to him. "I'm sure it won't take but a few minutes at Doctor Rhode's office. I'll be back right away."

Kristina didn't say it outright, but he didn't miss the underlying message in her tone that told him loud and clear, she hoped he would still be in the library when she returned. He watched as the doctor assisted her into his buggy and drove away. From the corner of his eye, Pilan' caught a glimpse of Toby, the glare in his eyes fierce, angry. A chill ran down Pilan''s spine, warning him to be careful around that man. Until he knew the relationship between Toby and Kristina he would be very cautious, only because he didn't want Kristina to get hurt. It was strange that he felt protective of her. He would have done the same to help anyone who might have had an accident, but he felt something different with her, something he couldn't quite identify.

Anxious to return to the library as quickly as possible, Kristina sat very still while Doctor Rhodes cleansed her chin and administered medication. Afterward, she washed her hands and face and did the best she could to put her clothing aright. Mrs. Rhodes came to her rescue with a clean hairbrush and helped Kristina brush the dust out of her hair and smoothed it into place. The reflection in Mrs. Rhode's mirror didn't look too bad, other than the smudge of dirt on her white blouse and a few scrapes. The most noticeable was the one on her chin.

"Would you like a drink of water?" The doctor offered her a tall glass filled with water.

"Yes. Thank you." She emptied the glass and thanked him and his wife.

"May I take you back to the library?" The old family doctor was like a second father and the concern on his face was clear.

It was a short three blocks back to the library, and Kristina insisted she was fine to walk that far on her own. "You've both done so much already." She hugged them both, her fondness for them as deep as any family member. "Please let Papa know if we owe you a fee for doctoring me."

"There will be no fee, my dear," said Doctor Rhodes, fondly patting her back. "You just be safe. And have your father check those buggy wheels more often."

"I'll do that." Churning with excitement inside Kristina waved goodbye and, in spite of some aches and pains, she walked as fast as she could without breaking into a run toward the library. How long had it been? She had no way of knowing the time, but it seemed she'd been gone for hours. Would Pilan' still be there waiting for her? Her heart raced, not just from the brisk walk, but in anticipation of seeing him.

She whispered his name several times, enjoying the way it rolled off her tongue like a measure of music, getting used to the unique pronunciation, wondering what interesting last name would accompany such a unique name.

Pretty sure he had the same feelings and questions about her she hoped she'd have a chance to get acquainted with him. There was so much she wanted to ask him. He'd said he came there hoping to see her. She smiled, a warm, comfortable feeling washing over her, as if he'd been a friend forever.

Then she remembered Toby. She'd never had that same warm feeling around him. The feeling was anything but warm. She wondered if he'd repaired the buggy wheel, if he'd gone home, or if he was hanging around waiting for her. She hoped he'd completed the job and left. The way he'd been acting lately she didn't want to encounter him again today. Why he acted as if he had some claim on her, she wasn't sure, and she didn't like it. He didn't seem to understand that she was not interested in him. When she'd introduced Toby and Pilan' after the accident, she hadn't missed the fiery look in Toby's eyes. Was it jealousy? Possessiveness?

He's just plain stupid, that's what it is.

Half a block away from the library building, with its huge white columns flanking each side of the door, she slowed a bit to cool down. The afternoon heat and humidity soared, causing perspiration to trickle down her spine. Her horse and buggy were right where Toby had promised to leave them. She was relieved and glad when she didn't see him anywhere.

Anticipation high, and anxious to talk with Pilan', Kristina managed to tuck her embarrassment away. Trying to ignore the flutters in her stomach, she rushed up the brick steps. She took a deep breath and pushed open the glass door, unable to hold back a giddy smile—until she stepped inside. She froze.

"Hello, prissy Krissy. Looking for the half-breed?" Toby was loud. Clearly, he knew nothing about the rule of silence in the library, or had any manners. Slouched in a nearby chair he wore a smirk that distorted his face.

"The reason I'm here is none of your business." She kept her voice low, repulsed by his attitude and the vengeance she saw in his eyes. "What are you doing here? You never come in the library, let alone open the pages of a book."

Toby rose from the chair. He sauntered closer to her, until he could reach out and touch her if he chose to do so. Detecting alcohol on his breath, she cringed and stepped back.

"Thought I best come in here and set that half-breed straight about you and me, let him know whose woman you are."

Unfamiliar heat boiled in her stomach and rose to her face. She'd never been so exasperated. The foreign feeling was something she hoped she'd never experience again. She wanted to scream, but out of respect for others in the library, her words came out in a low growl. "That's downright mean, Toby Gallager. I'm nobody's woman but my own, and you know that."

"You been my gal for years, you just didn't know it."

What did he mean? She'd never been anything more to him than a neighbor, and that's all she'd ever be. He stepped closer. She held her ground. His eyes turned dark, almost sinister. Something deep inside warned her to beware. *Don't let him know you're afraid.* After a long pause to calm her nerves and control her voice, a quiet calm that could have come only from God overcame her. She looked into those devilish eyes and forced a smile. "We've been friends forever, but never sweethearts. I won't ever be your girl, Toby. You need to understand that. In a few weeks I'm going away to college, and I bet you'll find a special girl who will want to be your sweetheart."

Kristina glanced around the room, making sure the librarian was in view, and she spotted two other women watching while they browsed nearby. Good. She wasn't alone with Toby. It didn't look as if he agreed with her or planned to leave anytime soon, and she had the feeling he wouldn't give up his idea that she was his girl, no matter what she said.

"You don't need to go off to no fancy college. You're already smart enough. Being a housewife and having babies don't take no special education."

She wanted to correct his grammar and suggest he could use more education himself, but she reconsidered saying anything that might anger him. "That's not what I want for my life, at least not right away. You've heard me talk about teaching music and having my own studio. I haven't changed my plans. By the time I finish school I bet you'll have a wife and baby."

Hands on hips that were lost in his overalls, defiance on his face, Toby leaned in. This time Kristina moved back, hoping he couldn't hear her heart pounding and her rapid breathing. She wanted this confrontation to end so she could be rid of him. *Lord, please make him understand.*

"Don't count on that." Toby's voice was low, menacing. "We ain't done with this conversation, Krissy."

Toby stalked out of the building, determination in his stride. She was shaken, her thoughts scattered. For a moment she stood in the same place, catching her breath, worried about Toby's parting words. So far as she was concerned, she was finished with their conversation, but clearly he wasn't.

Miss Hanna, the librarian, removed her glasses, a frown on her pale face, and came from behind her desk. Old enough to be Kristina's grandmother, she'd been the librarian since the doors had opened. Everyone who knew her loved her for her compassion, and the kindness she showed to people in the community. And she loved to read story books to young children who came in. Sometimes she'd read to a circle of six or eight boys and girls. There were times when Kristina would see a plate of homemade cookies on the checkout desk, baked by Miss Hanna herself, even though there was a policy of no food or drinks in the library.

Miss Hanna touched Kristina's shoulder. "Are you all right, dear girl?"

"Yes. I'm fine." At least she pretended to be, but it would take some time to stop shaking and recover, not only from the accident, but from Toby's insolence.

"You've sure had your share of upsets today, haven't you?"

On the verge of tears, Kristina nodded.

"You be careful around that Toby fellow. I don't like the looks of that young man, or the way he talked to you. I was about ready to send someone for the sheriff, so I was glad when he left on his own."

"Thank you for your concern. I doubt he'll be back."

"Well if he does, he better mind his manners, or I'll have the coot thrown out on his ear." Miss Hanna returned to her desk, defined authority riding on her squared shoulders and purpose in each step. Her wire-rimmed glasses perched back on her nose, she proceeded to straighten and dust the desk.

In spite of her shaky emotions, Kristina chuckled at the image of Miss Hanna, half Toby's size, literally dragging Toby out by his ear and tossing him down the steps. The woman would do it. Kristina sucked in a long breath of air and relaxed. It would do her heart good to see such a spectacle.

It was getting near time to go home and help with supper, but she hadn't had an opportunity to browse through the books. Suddenly feeling tired, she decided she'd forego checking out books today. More upsetting, though, was not being able to speak with Pilan'. Apparently Toby had convinced him that she was his girl. Now she'd never get to know the nice fellow, and the anger she'd felt toward Toby earlier returned. A hard knot formed in her throat. Tears threatened to surface. Not just because her plans for the day were shattered, but she was exhausted from the accident, the walk from Doctor Rhode's office in the heat, and the confrontation with Toby. Now she had a long ride home, and she would have to explain everything to her parents.

She stepped over to the librarian's desk and spoke softly. "I'll return another day to check out some books."

Miss Hanna smiled and nodded. "Be safe going home."

Chapter 6

IF HE'D HAD MORE time, Pilan' would have stayed at the library, no matter what Toby Gallager had told him about Kristina. Somehow, Toby's actions and words didn't ring true with him, and it would have been interesting to stand back and watch the scene unfold when Kristina returned to the library. He couldn't get it off his mind. If the girl really was betrothed to Toby, which he doubted, he figured he may as well pack up and leave tomorrow. He wouldn't mind getting a head start on his trek to Colorado.

The hotel restaurant was busier than usual this evening, and it should have kept his mind off the scene at the library, but it didn't take much concentration to serve hungry customers and help clean up at the end of the night. His mind went over the route he'd take when leaving Oklahoma City, already mapped out and gone over a dozen times. His supplies were bought and ready, except for last minute food and water. But one thing stopped him from leaving early—his promise to Potts. He'd promised to give Potts time to find a new waiter before leaving. He liked his boss, and he enjoyed working for the Dutchman. He wanted to keep his word. And there was Jake, a friend he'd like to have in his life forever. Saying goodbye to Jake and their boss would be difficult. And if he were honest with himself, he'd regret leaving without getting to know Kristina. But what choice did he have?

Entering the dining room to serve a middle-aged man and his lovely wife, Pilan' put on his best smile for the customers, setting aside his ruminations. While crossing the large room, he overheard a conversation between three ladies at a nearby table. He recognized the black-haired woman who, in his eye, resembled an old bulldog with her round, wrinkled face, flat nose, and flabby jowls. The other two, well-dressed, but rather plain women, must have been the bulldog's guests, perhaps from out of town. It wasn't his habit to eaves drop, but most likely he wasn't the only one in the room who heard every word they said. The anxiety in their boisterous voices turned heads and caused curious stares from several guests.

"Belva Taylor told me she heard first hand from the sheriff that the prowler was almost caught outside her daughter's bedroom window last night, but he got away. Just disappeared."

"Oh, my!"

"I heard the same thing from Jeanette Pritchett this morning. What is this town coming to?"

Glad the women were Jake's customers, and making every effort to ignore the gossiping women, Pilan' delivered his patrons' dinners, taking care to satisfy their every need. They, too, were caught up in listening to the trio of ladies and their prattle, but they graciously thanked him for his service.

"Well, if you ask me," the bulldog bellowed with a grunt and snort, "too many of those undesirables are moving into town."

Undesirables?

Just as Pilan' turned toward the kitchen, the woman looked right at him, and immediately lowered her voice to a near whisper. One word, however, failed to escape his hearing.

Half-breed.

It wasn't the first time he'd heard the term, and he didn't like the connotation it held when spoken with such hostility. Were they referring to him? They knew nothing about his background, where he was from, his rich heritage. Perhaps their reference to undesirables was about the Negro folks working in the area of Bricktown, but he couldn't be sure. Growing hot under the collar, he was glad they weren't at one of his tables. What made people judge others by the color of their skin?

Brushing it off as best he could without telling those old gossipmongers what he thought of their biased opinions, he stood tall and proudly strode into the kitchen—right into Deputy Hank.

Pilan' took a step back. "Good evening sir."

Not answering, the deputy puffed up what little chest he almost had.

Pilan' almost choked on his constrained laughter.

Potts stopped peeling potatoes and wiped his hands. Judging by his red face and fierce dark eyes, he was fuming mad. Pilan' could almost see steam coming out of his ears. "I told you, Hank, don't come in here harassing my men. You know doggone well you're after the wrong man."

"Not this time, Potts." He poked a finger hard into Pilan''s chest. "I have two witnesses who said they saw your man here running from their property last night."

"Then your so-called witnesses are either blind or they're liars." Potts moved in so close to the deputy the force of his words could have knocked the scrawny man off his feet. Potts pointed a thick finger in the deputy's face. "You can leave right now. Use the back door the way you slithered in."

Pilan' was amused and surprised by the way Potts spoke to the deputy. After all, the deputy was the law. Pilan' had been taught to respect all authority, and he wouldn't dare talk that way to Deputy Hank. People in the United States, or at least in this part of the country, were more bold and aggressive it seemed, unlike the refined people he'd grown up around in Paris. He wouldn't say it was bad or good, just different. He appreciated that Potts wasn't afraid to stand up for him, especially since he was innocent.

Deputy Hank didn't budge. "You seem to forget who you're talking to, Potts. If you keep disrespecting me and the law, I'll arrest you and haul you off to jail."

Potts laughed. "I respect the law, but I don't have to respect the likes of you. Just because you think you have an old bone to pick with me, don't try to scare me with your idle threats. You know Pilan' is not the man you're looking for. Your phony witnesses are wrong."

With a straight face and all the honesty he could muster, Pilan' put one hand up and interrupted the conversation. He directed his eyes and comments at the lawman, careful not to breathe too hard and blow the twig-of-a-person over. "I respect you and the law, Deputy, and I can honestly say I didn't leave this building last night. I worked until we finished cleaning up. Not only were Jake and Potts here with me, but so was the new dishwasher. When we were finished I went straight upstairs to my room and went to bed. I didn't stir or hear so much as a rat in the wall until I woke up this morning. That was about eight o'clock." Pilan' stopped, rubbing the back of his neck with one hand. "Oh, no, wait. I didn't go right to bed like I said. I took out my violin and played a couple of songs. Then I went to bed and slept soundly until morning."

The deputy looked doubtful, his words sounding sarcastic. "And I suppose you have witnesses to vouch for you—again."

"Yes sir. I said good night to the night clerk at the desk, and I'm sure he saw me go upstairs. He most likely heard the music, too. You can talk to him."

"I know who I can talk to!" Anger in his eyes, the deputy pounded the air with one fist. "And I certainly will. Meantime, young man, you better watch every step you take in this town." Deputy Hank turned toward the back door and stormed out without another word.

SUNDAYS HAD BEEN KRISTINA's favorite day of the week, but attending church today with her family, had done little to remove her frustration and the anger she felt toward Toby for nosing into her business. She had replayed the scene from last Monday over and over in her mind. The sting and embarrassment of the fall, and the disappointment of finding Toby in the library instead of Pilan' still bothered her. She couldn't help but wonder if she would ever see Pilan' again. Sitting down on the edge of her bed, hands folded in her lap, she tried to sort out the confusion in her mind, and to think logically. Meeting Pilan' shouldn't have a place in her thoughts at all. After all, her plans for college and her future were bundled up in one flawless package. So why this obsession?

She wished she hadn't allowed Toby to fix her buggy wheel. That gave him one more reason to treat her as if she were indebted to him. It also bothered her the way he claimed her as his, like a horse or shotgun. If she could avoid him long enough, maybe he'd leave her alone. His being a neighbor, and sometimes a worker on her father's farm would make it difficult. But if she could sidestep the louse until she left for Boston, she'd no longer have to put up with him. She'd also no longer worry about seeing Pilan'. Her feelings about the latter were all mixed up.

Kristina had never been so perplexed—it wasn't like her at all—and she didn't know how to handle such confusion. Being holed up in her bedroom all afternoon, and mulling her thoughts over and over only made it worse. Bewildered and tired of the inner conflict, she stood, took a deep breath, and decided she would walk down to her special place beside the creek. It was at least two hours before her mother would need help with supper, and she had no other chores to do. She'd already practiced her piano lesson for an hour after dinner dishes were done. Looking into the mirror, she ran the brush through her hair several times and examined the abrasion on her chin, glad it hadn't been any worse, and amazed at how much it had healed in six days.

The house was quiet. Mama, Gracie Mae, and Roberta Fay were napping, all three sound asleep. Frankie and Edward were outdoors playing in the barn, or someplace on the property, and old enough to take care of themselves. On silent tiptoes, Kristina left the house, closing the back screen door without a sound.

The sun blazed. The afternoon was already sultry. It would be cooler in the shade of the trees beside the creek. She could hardly wait to take off her shoes and stockings and dip her feet into the cool water. Instead of allowing her mind to return to the embarrassment she'd wallowed in all week, she began to sing, softly at first, then louder as she walked farther from the house. It always amazed her how much joy music brought to her soul, how easily it changed her mood. Nothing else quite compared to it, at least not for her. It was so easy to get lost in a song, to feel freedom from—what? Confusion and chaos? Yes, but even more so, it was freedom to express her passion for life, and freedom to lift her voice to God and sing to him.

One of her favorite things to do was to meander down to the trickling stream at the back of her father's sixty acres where she'd sing, sometimes for hours, pretending the birds and frogs were her students. In a way it was her private music studio. Though it seemed a bit childish, the thought brought a smile to her lips. Alone beneath the trees she sang, dreamed, planned, and imagined the day she'd have a real studio. Sometimes she'd make up songs as she went along, wondering if perhaps she should try writing music. Other times she prayed.

Just as she reached her favorite spot beneath the big tree, a simple song with frolicking rhythm burst out of her, and she danced a little jig as she sang.

The creek rippled and gurgled over rocks and sand, inviting her to refresh herself in its coolness. Off came her shoes. She stuffed her stockings inside before placing them carefully on the ground. She lifted her skirt to mid-calf and waded into the water. It was barely more than ankle deep this time of year, but the cold water was delicious on her feet and cooled her entire body. For a few minutes she waded quietly, soaking in the surroundings, listening to the hushed musical sounds of nature. Hearing a familiar noise she moved down stream a few feet. She scanned the sky just in time to catch sight of a male Scissor-tailed Flycatcher doing his "sky dance," diving in erratic zigzags, and somersaulting as he chortled and cackled. The strange aerial ballet always amused her.

When the bird quieted and flew out of sight, something else caught her ear. She heard what sounded like music in the distance. Standing still, she listened. It wasn't an animal, not a bird. The aria moved closer and became more distinct.

A violin?

The music was pure, the tune a little melancholy, or perhaps reverent. The composer's name didn't come to her. Drawn to the heavenly tune, she listened, not only with her ears but her soul, allowing the elegant solo to soak into her whole being. When the music stopped, she stepped upon the bank of the creek and waited for more. None came. Had it been her imagination? Oh, surely not. Convinced the musician had put away the instrument, she sat down on a rock in the shade and began to sing one of her favorite songs. She sang softly at first, then lifted her voice to the heavens, and sang as if she were performing on a stage. The words flowed freely. *"Love divine all love excelling, joy of heaven to earth come down."*

CERTAIN HE WAS HEARING things, Pilan' craned his neck, turning his ear in the direction of the voice, trying to discern where the song came from. The words were indistinct, but the clarity of the magnificent, soprano voice floated to him as gently as if it rode on the wings of the air. Soon, recognizing the song he'd often sung in church with his parents, he listened for several measures then hummed along. At the beginning of the second stanza, he lifted his violin and began to play along. Eager to hear the singer more clearly, he played as he strolled along the stream toward the voice.

The song ended but he kept walking. Seeing no one after several yards he stopped, and once again lifted his violin to his chin. Strains of *Amazing Grace* drifted from the strings and filled the air around him. He played it slowly, with great feeling as the song of praise deserved. From a distance, the magnificent voice joined in and floated to him on the breeze. Violin and voice united. The purity and beauty of the duet sent a chill up his spine. Never had he felt more reverent or more joy from a song. Driven now by unquestionable need to find the singer, he forged ahead, stopping now and then to listen.

The singer began to sing a new song. He didn't recognize the melody, but it was a beautiful tune, the quality of her voice exquisite, transcending all others. *Praise God in Heaven!* All the troubles and worries of the previous days melted away as he absorbed himself in the music. He felt rejuvenated, spiritually and physically. As he moved forward, he picked up the tune and hummed along. He walked cautiously, not wanting to startle the woman who possessed the angelic voice. But see her, he must.

KRISTINA HAD HOPED TO hear the violin again. Perhaps the musician didn't recognize *Sweetheart Be Mine*, or maybe he or she had gone away.

The last measure trailed off, and she stood in silence wondering if her counterpart was still there.

"Please, don't go away," she whispered. Was the violinist a male, a female? Music must have played a major role in his or her life, for the virtuosity she'd heard could not have come without great devotion and years of practice. She knew nothing about violins, but she did have good pitch and timing, and she knew what she heard was—what was the word? Perfection? Excellence? Crème de la crème. That was it. Crème de la crème. Aside from practice, practice, and more practice, nothing less than great passion and devotion could produce such exquisite music. It had to come from the heart, a gift from God to her ears.

Suddenly the notes of a playful, jaunty, violin tune danced through the air, ousting a flock of blackbirds from the trees, their squawking and flapping wings momentarily drowning out the music. She watched them dart in different directions, then gather again as one choreographed dance in the blue sky. Her smile was instant. She couldn't stand still another second. The music beckoned her to follow it west toward the cotton gin, drawing her step-by-step nearer to the mysterious musician. The moist, cool grass along the edge of the creek soothed her bare feet. Now and then, she paused beneath an oak tree's outstretched umbrella of shade, standing quietly to listen.

Eager to know who played the violin with such reverence and skill, she pushed forward toward a small clearing, where the grass was knee deep and wild flowers were scattered across the field. Lifting her face to the sun as she stepped into the open space, she soaked in the warmth. When she lowered her gaze, just a few feet away was a man with the violin. He lowered the instrument and smiled, surprise on his face. Kristina's feet froze in place. Hands dropped to her sides, her heart danced in lively measures. Never before had she been more spellbound. It was as if a single breath would break the magical spell.

Pilan'.

"We meet again." His voice was as musical and as beautiful as the notes from his violin. He bowed. "Hello, Kristina. Do you have a last name?"

Feeling like a dolt, she nodded, momentarily forgetting her own name. "Yes. It's Soderlund. And you're Pilan'." She struggled with the pronunciation hoping she remembered to say the unusual name correctly. He didn't correct her. "I don't remember; did you tell me your last name?"

"My last name is Rousseau." He stepped closer, stretching out his hand, curiosity in his smile. "I think God must have heard our music and brought us together."

She closed the large gap between them, and offered her hand. He lifted it to his lips and kissed the back of it, leaving her breathless. At last they were properly introduced to one another.

She'd seen Pilan' briefly twice, and each time she'd been enchanted by him. Looking at him now, she realized he wasn't as handsome as she'd first believed. Bathed in afternoon sunshine, his bronzed skin and his glossy, black hair were glorious. His blue eyes radiated kindness. Her heart stuttered. The earlier enchantment had been nothing compared to the ecstasy that coursed through her now. *You're staring at him you silly goose. Now you're acting like Doris.* It was hard not to stare, and if Doris were here, she'd swoon like a witless fifteen-year-old. Pilan' was the most magnificent man Kristina had ever seen—a complete, healthy, beautiful creation by God's own hands. She wondered with half a smile if Adam had been as gorgeous when God created him. Impossible.

With a feather-light touch Pilan' lifted her chin with one finger and looked closely. "I'm glad the doctor didn't have to put stitches in your chin. It would be ashamed to mar such a lovely face."

Speechless, Kristina smiled, but she hated being reminded of her accident. It would take a long time to overcome her bitterness over the lies Toby had told Pilan'. It was a day she'd rather not think about, especially now.

Pilan''s eyes darkened to deep turquoise. He stepped back, a frown slowly replacing his smile. "You shouldn't be here alone with me."

She didn't understand. "You said yourself God must have brought us together with our music. If that is so, is there a reason we can't speak to each other?"

"I want to talk with you, but you are Toby's woman. I fear he is a very jealous and possessive man, and he wouldn't take kindly to seeing us together."

Heat flared up from the pit of Kristina's stomach, and she thought all her inner parts would erupt. "No. I am no man's woman. He lied to you."

"Why would he lie?" Pilan' searched her eyes.

"I don't know why." She shook her head, still angry at Toby. "Lately he's been acting strange. We've been neighbors most of our lives—since I was five. Perhaps he feels protective of me, I honestly don't know. Believe me, I am *not* his woman in any manner, and he definitely is not my beau. He had no right telling you such a fib."

After a moment, Pilan''s smile returned. He seemed to relax, but he hesitated as if trying to find the right words. "I see truth in your eyes. I'm happy to know you have no commitment to him."

"You are?" She loved the way he spoke with such eloquence and a hint of a different accent. Was it French? His last name sounded French so that would make sense.

"Indeed. Tell me, Kristina, when we spoke at the library after your accident, you said you had hoped to see me again. Why was that?"

Being put on the spot, Kristina was slow in answering. The memory of being sprawled out in the street in front of the entire town brought the embarrassment back again.

Putting that behind her as best she could, she answered. "After I saw you in the library I couldn't stop thinking about you. I thought you were the type of person I would like to be acquainted with."

She didn't have the boldness to tell him it was a strong, unexplainable desire to see him again that had kept him on her mind. Was it wrong to desire the acquaintance of a young gentleman? She felt at ease with Pilan' for reasons she didn't understand. He exuded goodness, respectability, gentleness. Suddenly she realized she had no fear of being alone with him, like she might have had in the past. And the uneasiness she felt around Toby didn't exist with Pilan'.

Pilan''s smile broadened; his eyes sparkled. "I felt the same. This is wonderful. Only God could have orchestrated a rendezvous such as this."

"That's true." Kristina was thrilled by Pilan''s revelation.

"When I heard your voice I was driven by some miraculous force to find the singer."

Unable to put two intelligible words together, Kristina slowly moved her head up and down. It was the heavenly violin music that had pulled her toward him. What a huge surprise it was discovering Pilan' in the clearing, his violin tucked lovingly beneath his chin. Hot blood throbbed in her veins, and something akin to wild drums pounded in her heart. What was happening to her?

This didn't fit into her plan.

An afternoon breeze ruffled Kristina's flowered skirt, exposing small, bare feet, giving Pilan' a glimpse of perfectly sculpted ankles. He knew her legs were long and shapely by the mere peek he'd had the day she'd been thrown from her buggy onto the street. As he recalled, they were delightful to look at. Her windblown hair and scrubbed-clean face revealed her true beauty. She had the flawless skin of a porcelain doll, like the one his sister treasured. Kristina's cheeks were kissed by the sunshine, and flowing over her shoulders in silky waves, was the thickest, shiniest brunette hair he'd ever seen. Rather than waste time staring at her, he should be learning all about her, finding out the details of her past, her family, her dreams, but he couldn't take his eyes off her. He did want to know, however, if she'd had professional voice lessons.

"Your voice is beautiful, Kristina."

"Thank you." Displaying a demure smile, she dipped her head slightly.

"Are all your family members musical?"

"Goodness. I don't know. I don't recall ever hearing my birth mother sing, but she died when I was five years old. None of my brothers or sisters has shown an interest in music, but they're all younger than I."

"Your father remarried then?"

"Yes. Mama Leoma has a pretty voice and she loves to sing. I think it was her encouragement when I was young that made me love music."

"But your voice is magnificent. Did you have professional voice lessons?"

"Oh, goodness no. I suppose my voice is a gift from God." Kristina paused for a moment. "You play that violin like a professional. You must have taken lessons for many years."

"Yes. I hated it in the beginning, but my mother and grandmother kept after me until I began to love the sound and quality of the music I played."

"You should thank them for that. May I ask a personal question?"

He had no secrets. "Yes, of course."

"I think it's terribly crude and unkind of people to judge others, and I've wondered why they call you a half-breed."

The question didn't insult him; he was proud of his heritage. "My father is French. He came to America to explore the country, and when he met my mother, a Cherokee, they fell in love and were married. So it is true; I am a half-breed—a very fortunate one."

"And a very handsome one." As she spoke, Kristina's cheeks turned a soft, appealing pink.

"I'm flattered. Thank you. My mother is extremely beautiful, and my father is quite good-looking. When he took Mother home to Paris, she caused quite a stir among all the single women who thought they might trap Father into marriage. His beautiful bride from America made many of the ladies very jealous."

"Your parents live in Paris?"

"Yes. It's my father's homeland. My mother learned the ways of our society quickly, and she fit right in. Although, I'm told all those women who had their hopeful eyes on Father never became my mother's close friends."

"Their great loss, I'm sure."

"Yes."

The afternoon was moving much too fast. Pilan' looked at the sky, checking the sun's position. Worried he'd overstayed his time he pulled his watch from his trousers pocket and flipped it open with his thumb. He took a quick glance then quickly slipped it back into his pocket. "I'm sorry, Kristina, but I must go. I have to go to work soon, and I don't want to be tardy."

He could see that Kristina was disappointed, and indeed, he was as well. There was so much more he'd like to find out about her and he didn't want to say goodbye, but he had no choice.

Now what? Kristina wanted to spend more time talking with Pilan'. It wasn't proper for her to suggest they meet again, and she wouldn't do such a thing. Perhaps she would see him again in the library, but she'd leave for Boston in a few weeks, and there was so little time. There were so many things she wanted to know about him. Something akin to losing one's best friend flooded over her. Maybe getting further acquainted with him wasn't meant to be. The thought saddened her.

"Do you come here often?" Pilan' looking hopeful.

"As often as I can. I like to sing and read over there in the shade." She turned and pointed to the large clump of trees up the stream. Swinging her arm to the right, she pointed across the fields. "That farm over there is my home. There's never any peace and quiet in the house with all the younger brothers and sisters. I guess you could say the shady spot down by the creek is my private get-away."

Pilan''s eyes lingered on her for several seconds, causing another stir in her stomach. He moved to leave. "Well, perhaps we shall meet again."

"Yes, I hope so. I would love to hear you play the violin again."

"I would love to hear you sing again."

Still in breathless wonder, she watched as he took several slow steps backward then turned and walked away.

What a wonderful creator you are, Lord.

Pilan' turned back and waved. "Goodbye, until we meet again."

"Goodbye for now." Not willing to rush away, Kristina stood motionless for several moments and watched Pilan' walk toward town, his long slender legs moving him away from her. Time had slipped by much too rapidly. At last, realizing it was probably time to go home to help prepare supper, she meandered toward her special place beneath the trees to retrieve her shoes and stockings. After several steps she looked back, hoping for one more glance of Pilan', but he had disappeared around a curve. Her heart was full, the violin tunes coursing through her soul over and over until she couldn't help herself. How many years had it been since she skipped through the grass? She was so joyous she skipped and danced all the way home.

Chapter 7

THE MOMENT SHE STEPPED into the house Kristina's joyful mood halted. She'd never seen Mama ringing her hands or pacing the floor as she was doing now. Her mother rushed to her and grabbed both her shoulders.

"Where have you been? I needed you here."

"I went—"

"Dyer is having another bad headache, and I wanted to send you for the doctor. I don't know where your father is. I suppose he's busy repairing fences, or building a new pen or some such thing, but he didn't answer when I called. I didn't know you left, and when I woke up Dyer was in terrible pain. I needed someone to go for Doctor Rhodes."

"I'll go right away. Is Dyer on his bed?"

"Yes." Kristina followed Mama into the room Dyer shared with the younger boys.

A wet cloth was draped across his forehead. Eyes tightly closed, her brother moaned. Kristina bent over and ran her fingers lightly through his hair, smoothing his unruly curls back from his face. She said a quick, silent prayer and kissed his cheek.

"I'll get Doctor Rhodes here as quickly as possible," she whispered to her mother. "Pray he isn't out of the office and busy with other patients."

"Please tell him it's serious."

"I will. And don't worry about supper. I'll fix it as soon as I get back." She kissed her mother's cheek and ran out the door.

The buggy wasn't hitched up, so Kristina saddled their fastest horse. She'd just finished and started to walk the stallion out of the barn, when Frankie and Edward Lee popped out in front of her.

"Where you riding to on Midnight?" Frankie pulled hay from his hair as he talked.

"I'm going for the doctor. Dyer's real sick, and Mama needs Papa up at the house. Can you boys find him and tell him to go in right away?"

"Sure!" Both boys answered in unison and scampered away.

An excellent rider, Kristina didn't waste time. She rode hard, praying as she went. *I know Dyer is your child, Lord, and I believe you have anointed him for special work. He'll make a good preacher someday. Please take away his pain, Father, and make him well.*

She prayed the words over and over, believing God would heal her brother. If only she could take his pain upon herself, she would gladly do so. Until this summer when the first headache struck, Dyer had been a vibrant, energetic young man. He appeared to be a normal, healthy boy, average in height and weight, and he was doing well in school. To him, nothing mattered more than his desire to become a preacher. He was a happy, adventurous young man, full of life, with so much promise. Since the headaches had begun he was often quiet, pensive, and sedate.

She worried about her mother, too. It was no secret that Dyer was Mama's favorite child, even though he wasn't her real son by birth. Mama had nursed him back to good health when he was almost dead, and she'd grown to love him as if he were her own. Anyone could see Mama Leoma had a special relationship with Dyer. That didn't take away from the love she slathered on every child in the family, however. She was the best mother anyone could have.

Doctor Rhodes's office in view, Kristina prayed he would be available to come right away. Since the town continued to grow, all the doctors were kept busy. Back when Doctor Rhodes was the only doctor in town, many times he would come running to the house day or night, or you could walk into his office and be seen right away. He was like part of the family. Lately, however, there were times when they had to wait as much as half-an-hour to see him. What if he couldn't come now? How much longer could Dyer bear the pain? She said another prayer, out loud this time, and reined in at the doctor's door.

Business in the restaurant was slow this afternoon. It was the lull between dinner and supper, and Jake wouldn't be in until just before the evening rush. Potts was busy peeling more potatoes. "Take a break young man. Go out and get some fresh air while you can."

"Yes sir. Maybe I'll take a short walk up the street. I'll stay within view in case a mob comes in."

"No need to worry about that, son." Potts's laughed and slapped a hand on Pilan's back. One of the things he loved about working for Potts was the man's good-natured personality. Sometimes Pilan' thought he himself was too serious. It was probably because in Paris his grandmother, aunts, and uncles were so serious. He couldn't remember hearing much laughter from them.

His grandmother, however, had been a strong influence on him, which he appreciated. He loved her. But he did enjoy the more casual deportment of the people in the United States, and specifically in the middle of the country. With a few exceptions, there wasn't the stuffiness here, or the decorous behavior that he'd grown up with. That didn't mean life in Oklahoma was worse or better. It was simply different, and admittedly, less refined. His grandmother would most likely consider this society uncultured, crude, but he had to disagree.

"I'll return shortly," Pilan' said, walking out the front door onto the busy sidewalk.

He glanced up the street then down, deciding which direction he would stroll, not that it made a difference. The air was hot, the heavy clouds turbulent. It wasn't the kind of weather to linger in very long. Kristina crossed his mind. He hadn't seen her in two days. If he walked toward the library what were the chances he might catch a glimpse of her? Realizing how silly that was, he began walking at a leisurely pace in the opposite direction, no destination in mind. An attractive brick church came into view. He'd considered going there to a Sunday morning service, but he hadn't made it a priority. Perhaps he should go this Sunday. Before he had come to the United States he'd attended church every Sunday with his family. For the most part, it was a ritual. He'd often wondered if there shouldn't be more to church than that. Everything else in this area of America was extremely different, so maybe church services were different too. After thinking more about it, he made up his mind. Sunday morning he would visit the church, and see for himself if there was more to the service than ritual.

He turned and began his walk back to the restaurant. Glad he'd taken the short walk, he felt refreshed. For no logical reason, it seemed as if he felt lighter, happier. Looking up at the sky made him wish the clouds appeared lighter and happier. Instead they looked angry. A sudden gust of wind tore at his clothing. When something struck his back, he thought it might have been a small branch off a tree. He turned and found Toby glaring at him, a long stick in his hand, hatred shooting from his eyes. Clearly, the hard whack had come from Toby.

Reminded of pictures he'd seen of the devil, Pilan' was not only startled, he was momentarily frightened. Not that he was terrified of facing the man, he'd simply never been in a scuffle with anyone, and Toby, a good two inches taller, and forty or fifty pounds heavier than he, was not a man he'd want to fight.

"Hello, Toby." Pilan' attempted a smile, an attitude of indifference, hoping it would fend off the angry looking scoundrel.

Again, as he turned, Toby's stick lashed across his back, nothing between the stick and his skin but a thin cotton shirt. It seemed to Pilan' he had an unfair disadvantage if he was going to defend himself. Not looking back, he walked faster. The restaurant was just a few doors away. Nothing would be gained by turning around and fighting with Toby, but he also wasn't going to run.

"Stay away from my girl, half-breed. You hear me?" Toby poked the stick in Pilan''s back causing sharp pain. Pilan' grunted but didn't stop or turn. Was he being a coward? Or was he turning the other cheek as he'd been taught?

Still walking forward at a steady pace and ignoring Toby's tormenting, Pilan' lifted his hands nonchalantly in an act of resignation. Suddenly, he heard a thud and groaning behind him. He spun around. Curled into a tight ball on the ground, Toby was swearing and crying. Grinning big as ever, Jake stood over the crumpled Tobias Gallager, one foot casually resting on the side of the bully's head.

"I saw that no good cur poking you," Jake said. He reached down and jerked the stick from Toby's hand and used it to poke him in the side. "How does that feel, you dog? You like being poked with a stick?" Jake jabbed him again, harder this time.

Toby swore again and looked up at Pilan'. "You got no guts, half-breed? You not man enough to fight your own battle?"

Pilan' snatched the stick from Jake, and rammed it against the side of Toby's neck. "I'm more of a man than you will ever be. And I'm a gentleman, something you wouldn't know about. There's more than one way to win a battle." He gave the stick an extra nudge and watched Toby flinch. Pilan' started to tell Toby to leave Kristina alone, but he decided to leave her name out of it for now.

"Shall we let the dog up and send him on his way?" Jake still had his foot on Toby's head.

"I don't know." Feeling a little devilish Pilan' smiled at Jake and winked. "Maybe we should poke him a few more times for good measure. He needs to remember how it feels."

"No! No!" Toby squirmed under Jake's foot.

"Well, well." Jake lifted his boot. "The bully doesn't want to take any more of his own medicine."

Several people had gathered. Some slowed for a quick glance, and when they saw what was going on they smirked and continued on their way. One woman stopped and spoke in a deep, hefty voice. "It's about time someone put that ruffian in his place."

"It seems to me this is overdue, Toby." Pilan' broke the stick in half and tossed it away. "Are you ready to get up and act like a real man?"

Toby spit on the sidewalk.

Pilan' looked at Jake and shook his head. "I guess he needs a little more convincing. I don't think he knows how to act like a man."

Before Toby could get up, Jake shoved his foot back down on Toby's head again. Pilan' knelt on one knee, bent down, and looked into Toby's eyes. "We're going to let you up, and I'd advise you to hightail it home. You better think about your actions, and learn how to behave like a gentleman. If that's too difficult for you, you can at least stop bullying and tormenting other people. Nobody likes a hateful, foul-mouthed troublemaker like you, and it certainly isn't the way to win a woman's heart."

Pilan' stood and motioned Jake with a jerk of his head. "Let's send him on his way, and get to work before Potts wonders where we are." Pilan' grabbed Toby's left arm and Jake took the right. They jerked him up off the ground. Before he could get his balance Pilan' shoved him forward. "Start walking," Pilan' ordered. "Don't stop until you get home. And *you* stay away from Kristina. She's too good for you."

Toby turned and opened his mouth, then as he looked from Pilan' to Jake, his mouth closed. Face red, he turned and tromped away, looking madder than a castrated rooster.

Pilan' watched Toby until he was beyond the hotel. Every now and then, Toby would run his hand over the side of his face and his neck. Good. He has a little reminder of what had just happened. Maybe he'd learned his lesson—and maybe not. Young men of Toby's caliber weren't easily changed. The best Pilan' could hope for, was that Toby would leave him alone from now on, but he also worried about what Toby might do to Kristina. Unfortunately, it was none of Pilan''s business. He'd be leaving Oklahoma City before long.

"I'm glad you came along, Jake." Pilan' wasn't sure he could have handled Toby alone.

"Hey friend, when I saw him jabbing your back with that stick I couldn't believe you didn't take him down. Why did you let him do that without fighting back?" The disbelief on Jake's face brought a smile to Pilan'.

"I was exercising my patience."

"Why? Does that have something to do with your religion?" The look on Jake's face went from disbelief to curious. "Like turning the other cheek?"

"I guess you could say that. I don't like to fight. I'd rather win the disagreement with kindness whenever possible." Pilan' had never beat up anyone, but he'd had plenty of anger in him in the past. "When I committed my life to Jesus he transformed me. Trying to win a fight with my fist isn't the best way to do it."

"What is the best way?" Jake stopped walking. He looked baffled.

Pilan' shrugged, not exactly sure how to answer Jake. "Speak with soft words. Walk away."

"It didn't look like that method was working for you, my friend. You mean to tell me you were just going to let him keep poking you?"

Pilan' laughed and slapped Jake on the shoulder. "I didn't have to. You took care of the problem before I had a chance to do anything else. Thanks."

Jake shook his head and started walking again. Pilan' fell into step with his friend, and returned to work without saying any more about the scuffle.

Still dismayed about the encounter with Toby, and thankful for Jake's intervention, Pilan' tried to focus on his job. It wasn't Toby's actions that had him in a quandary. It was his concern for Kristina. He knew so little about her, except that she was a beautiful and talented young woman. Would Toby try to force himself on her?

It wasn't long before a few customers wandered in to the restaurant. He served several couples giving them friendly, impeccable table service, but his mind was going in circles about Kristina, and he couldn't seem to stop it. He'd just set a plate of fried chicken dinner before a customer, when deputy Hank stormed through the front lobby and into the restaurant, his face red and he looked angry. Now what?

The deputy didn't have the manners to save his business for the back room or the kitchen. No sir. He marched right up to Pilan' and shook his index finger in his face. Pilan' took a step back to avoid the temptation to bite the deputy's bony, crooked finger. He'd had about all he could stand of that man; he was a bigger nuisance than flies at a picnic. Pilan' took a few deep breaths, and swallowed the anger he'd just been telling Jake about. To avoid a big scene in the dining room, Pilan' strode into the kitchen without looking back, sure the deputy had to run to keep up with him. When Pilan' was away from the kitchen door he turned around, causing the deputy to crash into him. A head taller and fifty pounds heavier than the scrawny deputy, Pilan' didn't budge. Wondering what the man wanted now, he simply stared into his eyes.

Potts moved in, pointing a large two-pronged fork in Deputy Hank's face. "What the blazing dickens do you want now, Hank?"

"I just had a complaint that Pilan' here attacked one of the Gallager boys. Don't tell me he was working, because I have witnesses who saw both your boys here walking up the street." The deputy stretched upward and stuck his nose in Pilan"s face. He grinned as if he'd won a big poker game. "So what do you have to say for yourself, young man?"

Composed, Pilan' stepped back so he could see the deputy without looking cross-eyed. "You have the facts all wrong. I was walking along minding my own business, just taking a short break and getting some fresh air, when something struck me in the back. I didn't know what hit me, until I turned around and saw Toby Gallager behind me carrying a big stick. I ignored him and kept walking, and he kept jabbing that stick in my back. That's when Jake jumped in and stopped him."

The deputy looked at Jake. Jake had grown up in Oklahoma City, and Pilan' was sure deputy Hank knew Jake and his family well enough to know they were good, honest folks.

"That's the truth." Jake raised a hand as if swearing on the Bible. "I came out of the pharmacy, and when I looked ahead I saw Toby tormenting Pilan' with a stick. Pilan' didn't even turn around to defend himself. He was trying to walk away. After a couple of pokes in Pilan"s back from Toby I decided that was enough, so I took him down."

Pilan' spoke up. He didn't want to look completely helpless. "I did look back once, and I told Toby I wasn't going to fight. I kept walking hoping he'd stop. It's true; there were several witnesses. They saw exactly what went on. I don't know their names, but I'm sure if you ask around, you'll find that Toby is lying."

"From the looks on most of those people's faces, it appeared they approved of how we handled Toby," Jake said. "He only got a small taste of what he deserved. The man is plain mean, and everybody knows it. You should be talking to him, not us."

Deputy Hank grunted, looking first at Pilan' then at Jake. He appeared to search for something to say. When he finally spoke, it was with great effort. "I suppose I can ask around. Maybe I'll go see the Gallagers and have another talk with Toby."

Pilan' nodded.

Potts said, "You do that, and don't waste time getting to the bottom of things."

Potts was red in the face and it wasn't from cooking. He pointed Deputy Hank toward the back door. "Get on out of my kitchen and stay out. You're wasting our time."

Shoulders slumped and head hung low, the deputy slinked out without looking back.

Potts banged the fork twice against the grill. "Let's get back to work. Pilan', this plate is ready for Doctor Rhodes. Get it out there before it gets cold."

"Yes sir." The plate was filled to the brim with an oversized serving of roast beef, mashed potatoes, and rich brown gravy. He picked it up and he hurried into the dining room.

As Pilan' approached the doctor's table with the order, he had to look twice. *Lucky me!* Kristina walked up to Doctor Rhodes. Her knit brow and anxious eyes weren't lost on him. He set down the plate of food. She sounded rushed and upset, saying her brother had another terrible headache.

Doctor Rhodes rose instantly from his chair and put on his hat as he turned to Pilan' "I have to leave. Please apologize to Potts for me, and let him know I'll pay for the food when I return."

"Yes sir. I'll do that."

This wasn't the proper time to talk with Kristina, and he could see she struggled with the same disappointment as she glanced at him. He had to at least acknowledge her. "It's a pleasure to see you again, Kristina."

She smiled and spoke rapidly. "I'm glad to see you, too, Pilan'."

He watched as she hurried out the door on the heels of the physician. Without knowing the circumstances, he whispered a short prayer for Kristina's brother and carried the full plate back to the kitchen.

Kristina stood at the foot of the bed watching and listening to Doctor Rhodes. The doctor pressed his fingers all over Dyer's head, neck, and throat. He looked in his ears, in his mouth and eyes, saying little as he continued to probe. The doctor asked questions of Dyer and Mama and Papa, and he wrote notes on a small tablet, occasionally nodding or shaking his head, which didn't give her a clue about what was going on in her brother's body, or what the doctor thought.

This was a new experience for Kristina. Her nerves were jumpy and her stomach churned. She had unconsciously twisted a wad of fabric from her skirt into a knot, apparently to keep her hands busy. She hadn't seen Dyer look this pale and limp since he'd almost died as an infant. It was heartbreaking to see him like this. A scratch or small cut could be cleaned and bandaged. The doctor could put a splint on a broken arm or leg and hope it healed straight. Most injuries that occurred around the farm could be easily fixed, but a problem inside the head was different. Dyer's problem seemed to be getting worse, and it appeared there wasn't much the doctor could do about it.

Roberta Fay ran on bare feet into the bedroom, chattering and clapping her hands. Mama put a finger to her lips and spoke softly. "Shush be quiet, Birdie. Dyer is very, very sick and we must be quiet."

The toddler copied Leoma, putting a forefinger finger to her lips before speaking clearly in her sweet voice. "Be quiet."

Kristina stooped and lifted her younger sister, settling her on one hip, hoping to pacify the toddler.

Her father touched Dyer's shoulder saying nothing. He looked at Mama and asked in a whisper. "Is it worse this time?"

Mama's eyes were glassy. "It is, and it's lasting longer."

Dyer opened his eyes, squinting. "Hurts."

"I know, my darling boy," Leoma cooed. "I wish I could take away the pain."

Doctor Rhodes seemed to mull an idea over in his head. He looked at Papa. "Welby, I know how you feel about the new hospital, but it wouldn't hurt to let them look at your son. They could take some x-rays, and perhaps they could see what's causing his pain."

"No." Papa's one word was all the answer necessary to stop the doctor from talking any more about the new hospital.

A few minutes later, Dyer opened his eyes and looked around the room. "The pain is easing. I'd like to get up."

"Don't be in such a hurry," Doctor Rhodes said. "I want you to take it easy for a while longer, no running around, and no extreme noise." The doctor turned to Papa and Mama. "He may just be having bad headaches, but it's possible he might have a tumor on the brain. I can't be sure of that, and I don't want to jump to conclusions. That's why an x-ray would be good."

"No." Papa was even more adamant this time. "I don't think those are safe."

The doctor shook his head and sighed, his shoulders suddenly slumped. "Well, if it happens again write down anything that might be helpful, such as foods he ate, whether he fell, or had a blow to his head, that type of things."

"Can you give him medicine for the pain?" Mama touched Dyer's head, her suffering and worry for her son clear in her eyes.

With Birdie still perched on one hip, Kristina stepped from the end of the bed, and moved to her mother's side. Resting a hand on her brother's shoulder, Kristina prayed silently, asking God to take away Dyer's pain.

Doctor Rhodes stood quietly his head lowered, as if seeking an answer. Kristina wondered if he was praying, too. The silence was almost frightening, as if death were taking her brother away. Unable to endure the thought, she straightened and spoke gently. "God hears our prayers. We have to continue asking him to heal you, Dyer."

"Yes, indeed," Doctor Rhodes said. "Until I know what's wrong, I don't want to give him medicine. I'd suggest, Dyer, that you limit your activities outdoors when it's sunny and hot, and get plenty of rest."

"Yes sir." Dyer looked from the doctor to Kristina, love and adoration in his eyes for her. His smile grew until the small dimples in his cheeks appeared. "I'm glad you pray for me, Kristina. Thank you."

Kristina had always thought of Dyer as her little brother, but as he spoke he sounded far more grown up than a thirteen-year-old. He had the wisdom of a full-grown man and the faith of Job in the Bible. She'd never been more proud of him. Her heart overflowed with love.

He had a mission to fulfill, souls to save; he had to get better.

Chapter 8

Kristina found Dyer in his room. Normally he'd be working outdoors and doing chores, but father agreed to follow the doctor's orders, and he'd insisted he could get along without Dyer for a day or two. The younger boys could help with most chores and milking. If he needed more help than Frankie and Eddie could manage, he said he'd send for one of the Gallager boys.

Kristina tapped lightly on the open door and stepped inside. Three boys sleeping in one room sure did make a mess. Something smelled awful. Dirty socks and stinky work shoes most likely. She tried to ignore the foul odor and sat down on the edge of Dyer's narrow bed.

"I'm sorry to interrupt while you're reading. You must feel better."

Dyer lay the book on his lap careful to leave it open to the page he was on. "I'm all right, I guess. Nothing hurts today."

"It's no fun having to stay in the house, though, is it?"

"I don't mind. I'd rather be in here reading than doing farm chores."

Kristina smiled. She didn't want to get all mushy and say things that would make him uncomfortable, but she needed to ask him some questions. Boys Dyer's age didn't understand anything about emotions and love, but he wasn't like most boys his age. Even if he didn't understand, perhaps talking to him would ease her mind. She loved all of her brothers and sisters but she had a special bond with Dyer, and it was easy to communicate with him, maybe because he was older than the others. Or perhaps it was because he was her full-blood brother, though she supposed that shouldn't matter. Yet, for some reason planted deep in her heart, it did. She could talk to Doris, but right now she was concerned about Dyer and wanted to draw closer to him. There was something special about a brother-sister relationship that she didn't quite understand. It was just a feeling. More than that, though, she wanted to spend as much time as possible with him before she went away to college.

"I don't want to go to Boston if you're sick. I'd be worried so much I don't think I could study."

"I'll be all right. There's nothing to worry about. They're just headaches."

"Severe headaches." Her brother didn't convince her that he was fine. It wasn't normal for a young, carefree boy to have debilitating headaches. "How does it feel when the headache starts?"

Dyer shrugged as if it didn't matter. "I don't know. It's just sudden pain that gets worse and worse. It's like getting hit in the head with a sledge hammer. All I can do is close my eyes until it goes away, and they always stop sooner or later."

Kristina flinched. She hurt for him. If only she had some assurance that the headaches weren't a sign of something worse, like the tumor Doctor Rhodes mentioned. Dyer was not only her brother for whom she cared deeply, he was a very important part of her life. She'd loved him from the first day he was born, and she wanted to see him grow up and realize his dream of being a preacher. He would love his congregation, or, as Reverend Gilroy often referred to his congregation, his flock of lambs. She smiled at the mental picture, and she could imagine Dyer's compassionate care and spiritual guidance for each one.

"I hope you're right," she said. "May I talk to you about something else?"

"Sure." Pride shone from Dyer's eyes, probably because his big sister came to him for his advice.

"It's not a big secret or anything." She hesitated, curling her tongue against the roof of her mouth, her lips tightly sealed while she tried to find the best way to ask her question. She picked at a bit of fuzz on his comforter, one that that Mama Leoma had made several years earlier. She took a deep breath. "If a person is from two different nationalities, like half negro and half white, isn't it wrong to condemn or shun them and slander them?"

"You mean like the man everyone in town is talking about, the one they call the half-breed? Some say he's half white and half Indian, or some such thing."

Kristina nodded, wondering how much she should tell her brother. After all, she hadn't told anyone about her chance meetings with Pilan'.

"No one has the right to call him names or shun him." Dyer perked up and went on, seeming more interested. His eyes grew large and filled with curiosity. "Have you seen him?"

"Yes, a few times. He's extremely handsome and nice. He's half French and half Cherokee Indian, and he went to school in France. But he speaks perfect English." Her enthusiasm grew. "And he plays the violin with extraordinary skill."

Dyer slapped his book closed and sat forward. "How do you know all that?"

She couldn't lie. And she couldn't hide her excitement. "I first saw him in the library, so I assumed he was educated. We said hello. The day the wheel fell off our buggy he came to my rescue, and he sent for the doctor. He was so gentle and kind. Then one day when I was down at the creek singing, I heard violin music in the distance. I had no idea who it was, but I followed the creek in the direction of the music, and there he was with his violin. We properly introduced ourselves and talked for several minutes."

Dyer lowered his voice barely above a whisper. "Does Mama or Papa know about that?"

"No, and don't you dare tell anyone. We just talked a few minutes then he had to leave. When I went to town to fetch Doctor Rhodes yesterday afternoon, I had to go to the hotel restaurant where the doctor was having dinner, and Pilan' was serving his food. He works for Potts. There was no time to talk of course, but we said hello again. The poor doctor didn't even get to eat his food. He told Pilan' to return the meal to the kitchen."

"So, you know his name'?"

"Yes. But I heard it first from the deputy, though he pronounced it all wrong. His last name is Rousseau which is French. Don't you think he has a wonderful, interesting name?"

Dyer whispered, watching the door. "Obviously you think he's very interesting. Is he your beau now?"

"No, silly. I hardly know him, but I do like him. It upsets me the way some people talk about him, and Deputy Hank acts like he's just waiting for Pilan' to do something wrong so he can arrest him."

Dyer grinned and shook his head. "Deputy Hank is a dimwitted nincompoop."

Kristina threw her hands to her mouth and giggled. "I can't believe you said that."

"Well it's true. I don't think God was generous with brains when he created Hank. Either that or the man refused to learn anything. His biggest weapon sure isn't his brain, it's his gun, and that's a scary thought."

Kristina laughed and agreed. She wanted to turn the conversation back to Pilan'. "So, do you think it would be wrong if I were to go out with Pilan'? That is, if he were to ask me." She rushed to explain her question. "I mean, it's not like he's asked me to be his girl or anything. We've hardly seen each other enough to become acquainted. But I think he's amazing. I want to get better acquainted with him, and I think he feels the same way."

Almost able to see the wheels turning in Dyer's head, she waited for him to answer. "People around here know what the Bible says about how God created us all equal, but they seem to forget it when someone different like Pilan' comes to town. They tend to ignore the fact that we're taught to love one another and be kind to one another."

She was getting impatient now. "So answer my question. Would it be wrong for me to see him again?"

"I don't think it would be wrong for you to be his friend."

"But what if our friendship develops into a romantic relationship? Do you think that would be wrong? Would it be a sin to marry someone like him?"

"No. Not as long as you save yourself, umm . . . you know what I mean, until after marriage."

Heat crawled up Kristina's neck and face. Hearing such adult advice coming from her young brother embarrassed her. However, she knew he was correct, and she was glad he thought the same as she.

"How did you get so smart?" Kristina reached over and squeezed her brother's hand. "I agree with you on every count. I just wonder, though, what it'll take to make everyone else in town understand."

"I don't know." Dyer paused, frowned, and went on, his words coming cautiously. "Do you know if he's a believer?"

"No. But he talked about God. Why?"

"The Bible says you shouldn't be unequally yoked. That means—"

"I know what it means." She cleared her throat, uneasy with discussing these intimate subjects with a thirteen-year-old boy, even if she did come to him for his opinion. "I'm sorry if I snapped at you. It's all just so personal."

"Yeah, I guess so. But you do have to consider things we're taught from God's word. Sometimes, though, I forget that you are five years older than I, and that much more educated. I guess I don't have to tell you these things."

Kristina smiled. How many younger brothers would acknowledge an older sister's intelligence to her face? "You are so wise, little brother. I respect your opinion."

"Thanks."

She leaned in to hug her brother. "You're welcome. And thank you."

"Will you let me know what happens with Pilan'—especially if he's going to become my brother-in-law?"

Kristina swatted Dyer's arm and giggled. "You silly kid. Yes, I'll keep you posted, if you'll keep it between you and me until I have reason to say something about it to our parents."

"You have my word." Dyer's word was better than gold.

She had no doubt her secret was safe with him. She jumped up and kissed Dyer's forehead. "I know you'll keep it. I better get in the kitchen to help Mama. You rest until you're called for supper. I want you to get well."

Dyer's look of gratitude needed no words. His smile was enough.

PILAN' CARRIED SUPPER TO his room, hoping to have some peace and quiet. It was late and he was hungry, but he was anxious to look through the new books he'd checked out from the library. He'd gone over his travel plan several times and had reconsidered his departure date. He liked the people here, except for that bully, Toby, and his sidekick, Deputy Hank. But they were little more than a couple of pesky flies in a town of good folks. And then there was Kristina. He couldn't get through an hour without thinking about her. He liked her. A lot. He wouldn't mind hanging around town another two or three weeks to see what might develop between them, if anything.

His plate of food was getting cool and the room was stuffy and warm. Opening the window didn't improve it much, but he liked the sound of singing crickets and whatever other critters were outside. He recognized the howl of coyotes in the distance, and thought their cry to be lonely. He put a sizeable bite of roast beef into his mouth and chewed, at the same time mulling over his thoughts.

Music from the bar a block away drifted up through his window, and he preferred the sounds of nature over the rowdy, poorly-played music from an old piano. If he wanted to sleep when he was ready to turn in he'd have to close the window, and hope it would quiet down before too late. One thing was certain. There was little difference between pubs or saloons in Paris, and here in the United States. He'd been in a few exclusive nightclubs in Paris that catered to the wealthy and hired good musicians. There surely were many such establishments in larger American cities, but he no longer inhabited those places.

From what he'd observed, many men and woman were basically the same where ever he journeyed—filled with liquor, the men sought female pleasures for the night and women sought a generous remuneration for their services. That was a lifestyle he'd never explored and didn't quite understand. Being from a wealthy and very proper family, he looked upon such folly as indecent and certainly ungodly. If, or when, he decided to pursue sexual pleasure, he would do so within the bounds of marriage.

Marriage?

That thought hadn't crossed his mind until now. Why now? His thoughts turned immediately to Kristina Soderlund. Not that he'd thought of marrying her; he hardly knew her. However, she seemed to be the type of young lady he'd consider for a partner in life. She was polite, talented, well mannered, and very beautiful. He already knew they had two things in common: books and music. He definitely wanted to learn more about her. No other woman had caused his thoughts to stray from his plans for adventure and travel, and he had no idea if Kristina would be willing to travel from place to place, not having a permanent home for a few years. Didn't most women want a fine house to live in, a passel of children beneath her feet, and a husband to provide all that?

He mulled those thoughts over in his mind while he finished his dinner and drained his coffee cup. His conclusion? With a woman like Kristina, marriage and a family wouldn't be an unpleasant situation.

The sight of his maps, travel journal, and camera on the desk jolted him back to reality. What was he thinking? He had a lot of country to explore before settling into marriage. Kristina probably had plans of her own. She was young. He tried to remember if in their short exchanges she'd said how old she was, or if she still attended school. If he saw her again, and he hoped he would, he'd be sure to find out.

It was late and the day had been long and tiring. The incident with Toby had unnerved him and made the evening long. He wondered what the half-witted numskull would pull next. Toby's persistence in trying to make trouble for him was bewildering. In his twenty-two years of life he'd never encountered anyone like Toby. The man was like a gnat. He couldn't ignore him and he couldn't get rid of him.

His work shirt removed and tossed aside, Pilan' was about to strip off his trousers when someone banged on his door. *What now?* It was after midnight and he didn't want to talk to anyone. Not thinking about who might be on the other side of the door, Pilan' sauntered across the room bare-chested and sleepy-eyed. Half expecting that annoying deputy, he opened the door.

"Whoa there—"

PAIN THROBBED IN HIS head and his stomach hurt. Pilan' heard voices and it took great effort to focus. Where was he? A face hovered over him and came into focus. Doctor Rhodes. Then he remembered a huge fist greeting him in the face last night when he opened the door. So much for hospitality.

"Doctor Rhodes?" Speaking was painful. He groaned and even that hurt.

He lifted both hands in the air and flexed his fingers to see if they were damaged. They were fine. Good, he could still work and play his violin. His head and gut hurt something fierce, though, as if he'd been hit repeatedly with a brick. Oh, yes, Toby's fist. How much damage had Toby done to his face? One hand discovered bandages around his head, the other hand landed on tender, painful skin.

Doctor Rhodes looked stern. "That blasted Tobias Gallager beat you up pretty badly, but you'll be all right in a day or two."

"He belongs in jail. I don't understand why he has it in for me. And how does he get by with his malicious deeds?" Pilan' remembered Toby's warning to stay away from Kristina. Had he seen them down by the creek? Was that what brought on this attack?

"He's a sneaky one. No one saw him do this, but when you didn't go down to the kitchen this morning, Potts sent Jake up to check on you. It appeared you'd been unconscious all night. Jake carried you to my office all by himself."

"How did you know it was Toby if no one saw him?" It was probably a stupid question since he'd been Toby's main target all along, and everybody knew that.

"After we got you to the hospital I gave you some medication to help you sleep, but not before you told us what happened. You probably don't remember answering my questions. You didn't say much and your words were slurred, but you were clear that it was Toby who hit you."

"It was. He didn't give me a chance to invite him in before he slammed his fist into my face." He tried to sit up, but moving his body made the pain in his head and gut worse.

"You might as well take it easy. Potts knows you won't be working today. He had a talk with the sheriff, too, and if you want to press charges against Toby, you just say the word."

"Seems to me there's no use pressing charges if there are no witnesses?" Pilan' had heard about the law in America. In these small cities people like Toby knew how to get around the law. Deputy Hank was a good example of the poor legal system. There had to be a better way than going to the sheriff to stop the scoundrel. Thinking it over, a good idea came to mind, but it might take some time.

Yes indeed, a very good idea. First he had to get out of this bed.

Chapter 9

Hot wind whipped the sheets and towels on the clothesline so hard, Kristina could hardly get the dry laundry unpinned and taken in. Her hair lashed at her face, and she wished she'd tied it back with a ribbon. Struggling between the sagging lines, her long skirt wrapped around her ankles, making it difficult to walk. She'd rather be down at the creek, but on a windy day like this with gusts of dirt blowing in the air, it was too miserable to walk anywhere. She was quite sure, too, that Pilan' wouldn't be out in this windstorm with his violin.

It had been three days since she'd last seen him, and she longed for just a few minutes with him. She loved the way he said her name, with each syllable pausing on his tongue. Just thinking about him made her heart flutter. She scolded herself for her thoughts, and for letting her feelings spiral out of control.

Her arms were full, and the last bath towel was doing its best not to be captured. But she was quick. With the last of the laundry tucked into the large, wicker basket, she hoisted the load to one hip, keeping an arm across the top of the basket so nothing could be snatched away by the wind. Headed for the back door she heard a strange noise. She paused, listened. Something mechanical approached the house.

In spite of the wind, she walked to the corner of the house and looked up the lane. What ever on earth was she seeing? Instead of waiting to see if the contraption would come all the way up to the house, she ran inside and dropped the laundry basket on the end of the kitchen table.

"Mama! Come out front and see what's coming."

Mama Leoma followed Kristina out the front door, and they stood on the porch. Mama shaded her eyes and squinted. Frankie, Eddie, and Birdie came running from various corners of the yard.

"What is it? Who is that lady sitting on it?" Kristina couldn't believe her eyes. "It looks like Auntie Myrtle."

"Well Lordy me. That is Aunt Myrtle driving that motorcar. Wait until your father sees that," Mama said. "Welby! Welby!"

Papa and Dyer came out of the barn. Papa looked dumbstruck. Dyer grinned as the two men ran across the yard and joined them on the porch. Papa rested a dirty hand on Mama's shoulder but she didn't seem to notice. Everyone had their eyes on the visitor. Kristina held her breath, hoping her great-aunt Myrtle would stop the vehicle before she smashed into the house.

The family gathered in a tight bunch. Mama Leoma laughed, her hands crossed over her chest. "Oh my goodness, I can't believe my eyes."

Kristina loved her great-aunt, and she didn't get to see her often enough. She'd heard numerous stories about Aunt Myrtle, usually accompanied by a lot of laughter about the rambunctious and adventurous woman. For one so small she looked mighty brave riding atop that amazing contraption with four big wheels.

"Well for crying out loud." Papa talked above the strange choking and coughing noises coming from the motorcar. "Can you imagine that?"

Aunt Myrtle's vehicle came to a stop several feet from the porch and the noise ceased. It took a moment for the dust to settle, but Mama didn't wait before she ran to greet her aunt. As Auntie stepped down from the fine looking motorcar Mama flew into her arms.

Next, Auntie hugged Kristina and looked her over. "I see my favorite niece has become quite a young woman. Remind me later to give you a little present I brought for you."

"Thank you, Auntie." Great-aunt Myrtle always came bearing gifts for everyone.

"Well, I'll be jiggered. What do you have here, Myrtle?" Papa scrutinized the motorcar, walking around it twice, running his hands over the body, looking beneath it, and admiring the fancy leather seats.

Aunt Myrtle smoothed her long skirt and straightened her windblown hair and wide-brimmed hat, adjusting the ribbon beneath her chin. It was a miracle the tiny woman hadn't been blown off the leather seat.

Auntie's high-pitched voice was jubilant, and just a wee bit haughty. "This fine automobile is a nineteen-o-three Cadillac. Isn't she a pretty thing?"

"Where'd you get her?" Papa and Auntie talked about the automobile as if *she* were an important, living, breathing person and deserved great reverence.

All smiles, Mama watched.

Dyer, who was extremely interested, followed on Papa's heels admiring the motorcar. The other children had obviously seen enough after one inspection of the vehicle and ran off to play.

Not Kristina. She wanted to drive the thing.

Aunt Myrtle answered Papa's questions, her tiny chest *almost* puffed up, her hands flying in every direction as she talked. "I placed an order for it when I attended the New York Auto Show. Oh, my, you should have seen all the new automobiles. I was fortunate to get this one. They took orders for over two- thousand of those beauties, nearer to three-thousand."

Long after Kristina followed Mama and Auntie inside, it took some doing to get Papa and Dyer into the house for supper. So taken with the Cadillac, they were late doing the evening milking. Kristina was all aflutter herself, and she had a bunch of questions to ask her great-aunt. First off, how could she learn to drive such a marvelous vehicle? It didn't seem like a thing most men would favor.

"Well, Kristina," Aunt Myrtle started, her tone resolute, "We women must stand our ground. We must be strong and independent. Of course, I suppose it was in my favor that my husband died young and left me—well I hesitate to say wealthy—but let's just say my needs are well met. I'll never have to struggle or wonder where the next ten-dollar bill will come from, that's for sure, and I don't have to answer to a man. Heaven knows, I wouldn't want any other woman to be widowed at such a young age." She paused a moment and turned to Mama. "You, of all people, understand what I mean don't you Leoma?

But you, with your fine looks, were fortunate to hook a man to take you in right away."

Kristina could see right off Aunt Myrtle's remarks didn't set too well with Mama. Apparently Aunt Myrtle realized it too. She gasped and slapped both bony, ring-laden hands over her mouth. "I'm so sorry, Leoma, honey. I didn't mean any harm by that. You know me and my big mouth."

Mama smiled and half shrugged one shoulder. "Actually, Aunt Myrtle, I am very fortunate to have a wonderful husband such as Welby who wanted me and loves me. When Jeremy died I never dreamed I could be happy again. And look at all the blessings and love that fill my home."

"Oh, yes, indeed." Aunt Myrtle changed her tone and spoke in a low voice. "But do you ever miss the grand house Jeremy built for you? You were so well off with *him*."

This time Mama was steaming. Kristina saw it in her eyes and she understood why. She couldn't believe her ears.

Mama said her piece loud and clear. "That house burned to the ground. When the men of this town rebuilt it for me, Welby did more than his share of work on it. He even went to great lengths to add special touches especially for me, such as a bigger and more beautiful library with elegant bookcases. He spent hours polishing the woodwork until it gleamed. I didn't know until later that he was falling in love with me then."

Mama paused, and her smile turned to something Kristina didn't understand, something that appeared so private and precious it had to be the moment Mama fell in love with Papa.

With barely a breath, Mama went on. "You can't believe my surprise the night of the housewarming. It was Christmas Eve and Welby was determined to win my heart. He was all spiffed up and every bit a fine gentleman. And the gift he gave me was very precious, a sacrifice for sure." Mama took a deep breath and hit her Aunt Myrtle square between the eyes with her firm words. "So you see I didn't have to hook a man who would take care of me. A wonderful man hooked me and won my heart. He gave me his unconditional love, and I fell in love with him. I've been abundantly blessed ever since."

"My, my, my," Aunt Myrtle said through choked sobs. "You not only put me in my place—and I'm glad you did—but you've also touched my heart." She pulled a lace-trimmed handkerchief from her sleeve, waved it through the air, and dabbed the tears off her cheeks. "I do believe I'm leaking."

Everyone laughed.

Mama hugged Aunt Myrtle long and hard. After that everything was fine.

A moment later, Auntie ran a hand over Kristina's hair and kissed her cheek. "I'm surprised a nice fellow hasn't snatched you up by the heart strings and married you. You've grown up to be a beautiful young woman. I thought you'd be married and popping out little chicks by now. Are there no prospects beating down the doors to court you?"

Kristina laughed at the funny way Aunt Myrtle said things; she was so blunt with her words. "Oh, Auntie. I just finished high school, and I've had my eye on something other than men. I'm going to college in Boston. In fact, I'll be going back on the train with Grandmother and Grandfather Fisk. Didn't Mama tell you they're coming?"

"No. I suppose I haven't given her a chance to tell me all the news. That's just fine and dandy, sweetheart. I'm sure you'll find a husband at the college."

"Auntie! You just don't give up do you?" Kristina chuckled. "Many women go to universities and have wonderful careers. Some are even becoming doctors. Do you think it's wrong for me to break some silly tradition our culture has forced on women? We are quite capable of doing more than having babies."

"But don't you want a husband and family?"

"Someday, yes. But first I want a better education and a music studio." She smiled at Aunt Myrtle in her fine silk dress and diamond studded jewels at her ears, neck, wrists, and most of her fingers. "It's not a husband I'll be looking for at college, Auntie. I'm going to study music."

"I see. And how will that help you catch a proper husband?"

Kristina shook her head, and closed her eyes until she could come up with a good answer. Is finding a husband all the woman could talk about? She apparently didn't need one for herself with all her money, so apparently she wanted to make sure all the other females in the family were married to a man who would provide everything for them. That's the way it was done, right? Well that's not the way she was going to do it.

"Aunt Myrtle, I don't need to catch a proper husband. I believe when the time is right, I'll meet the man God has in store for me. Until then, I'm going to enjoy school and live life to the fullest. Who knows, I might even buy myself one of those fancy motorcars, and trek about the countryside on my own—like you, Auntie."

"My, my. You're a woman I can surely admire. And you're right, although God hasn't seen fit to bring another gentleman into my life, and I can't imagine why. I've been widowed nearly twenty years and not a single man has asked for my hand."

Kristina didn't dare say what she thought. It could be that her great-aunt frightened eligible men away with her brashness and independence. And the way she flaunted her wealth on every body part, they probably figured she didn't need a husband, just as she'd implied earlier. Tucking away her opinion, she spoke gently. "Well, Auntie, I think when the time is right God will send a man your way."

Nothing more was said on that subject. Still chattering and giving advice, Aunt Myrtle made herself at home in the kitchen helping with supper. In no time a meal of fried chicken, mashed potatoes and gravy, black-eyed peas, and biscuits was on the table. Kristina took her usual seat at the table, her mind not on eating. Her great-aunt had stirred some unexpected doubts and questions in her mind.

Was it selfish to go off to college to follow her dreams, to think about her own future? She wanted more than marriage and babies. Was that wrong? Should she stay home to help Mama? What if something happened to Dyer? All this tension had her stomach in knots.

Then there was Pilan'. Fabulously delicious Pilan'. *Oh, my. I can't believe I thought that. I'm sounding more like Doris every day.* Glad the words hadn't come out of her mouth, Kristina tried to put him out of her mind, but it didn't work. He was on her mind way too much lately. Since their fortuitous meeting by the creek, she often wondered if he might be the man God had in mind for her. Was it possible? Perplexed, the question played over and over in her head. She liked him but—. No, no, no.

She was positive it was God's will for her to go to college, and later teach voice and piano. She couldn't stay home *and* go to Boston. She couldn't get married and have babies *and* own and operate the studio she dreamed of. And what if she decided against college in order to spend time with Pilan', and it turned out he wasn't the right man? The more she considered the dilemma, the less appetite she had, and the more confused she became.

"Kristina." Papa broke into her thoughts. "Are you with us? We're going to say grace."

She joined hands with Auntie on her left and Birdie on her right and bowed her head. Papa's prayer was short; he liked the blessing brief and the food hot. Amidst the chatter and laughter Kristina dipped small portions of food.

Almost everyone was finished with dinner when someone knocked on the front door. The knock seemed urgent. Everyone at the table stopped and watched Papa rise from his chair, wiping his fingers on his napkin as he left the room. From where she sat Kristina couldn't see the visitor, but one short sentence was spoken when her spine stiffened.

"Y'all, better be on the lookout tonight. That half-breed is on the prowl again." Clearly, Toby was trying to sound important, but he failed miserably. She knew he was lying. "I heard in town that he was snooping around Doris Langley's window again."

How did he know what was going on in town, and why would he be out warning neighbors? That was the sheriff's job. Who was Toby trying to deceive?

She'd heard enough. It was barely sunset, and she was going straight to Doris's house to find out for herself what Toby was all fired up about. "Aunt Myrtle, can you drive that motorcar at night?"

"I sure can. Where do you want to go?"

"To Doris Langley's house in town. She's my best friend, and I want to find out firsthand if Toby is telling the truth." Kristina was already out of her chair putting her half-eaten supper on the kitchen counter. She wanted to leave the minute Toby was out of sight.

"I'm not so sure you should be out this late. It'll be dark soon." Papa sopped up some gravy on his plate with a biscuit. "You could get hurt in that automobile. I understand those things go fifteen or twenty-miles-an-hour." Papa was probably jealous because he wasn't riding along. Actually it wasn't a bad idea if he wanted to go, but before she could suggest it Aunt Myrtle spoke up.

"She'll be just fine, Welby. That Cadillac goes twenty-five-miles-an-hour, and I haven't had an accident or broken down yet."

Mama looked flustered and worried. "Now, Kristina, I don't think you should run off this time of evening. I was hoping you'd play a few songs on the piano for Aunt Myrtle."

"We won't be long, Mama. I bet that motorcar will get us there and back in no time. I'll play some songs when we return."

Mama gave in without an argument, but she didn't look happy. "Just be careful." Then her face softened and she smiled. "And I want a ride in that contraption of yours tomorrow, Aunt Myrtle."

"I promise, Leoma. We'll go into town and show you off in style. We'll even take along the youngsters if you like."

Hardly allowing Auntie enough time enough to gobble down the last of her dinner, Kristina wasted no time getting out the door.

Riding in the leather front seat was much more comfortable than riding a horse or in a buggy, and it seemed to Kristina she sat higher up. When they began to move backward, Kristina gripped the edge of the seat. Startled she jerked her head to look back over her shoulder. "Why are we going backwards?"

"It's in reverse, my dear." Auntie glanced over her shoulder and pushed a pedal on the floor until the motorcar came to a stop."

Kristina sighed, relieved. She'd wondered if they were going to ride into town going backwards. Suddenly, the car lurched forward, and Kristina's grip on the edge of the seat tightened again.

Aunt Myrtle handled the motorcar with skill. As the car chugged and sputtered, turning in a big circle in the yard, Aunt Myrtle squeezed the funny rubber bulb. The loud, honking sound made Kristina jump. Gathered on the porch, the rest of the family waved and laughed. Four-year-old Birdie jumped up and down, clapping her hands.

As her great-aunt turned the automobile onto the main road, the lanterns on the front of the motorcar didn't put out much light, but the evening already promised a bright, moonlit night. And after all, no one had lights on their horses or buggies.

Excited, she smiled, chin lifted, shoulders back. *I'd like to see that ornery Toby try to knock me off of this with his old sway-backed nag.* The motorcar clipped along making much better time than she would on her bicycle or horse and buggy. This was really something. And to think, here she was riding in an automobile before anyone in town had such a fine vehicle. At least she hadn't seen any. Too bad it was getting dark. Hardly a soul would see her riding like a lady of means in Auntie's fancy Cadillac. *Silly me, where is my humility?*

It seemed they'd been on the road only a few minutes when they reached the edge of town. The Langleys' house came into view. She pointed. "Right up there on the left is where we're going. It's that little cedar house."

Auntie pushed pedals and levers and slowed down. She steered the motorcar right up to the front steps and stopped. Kristina wasted no time jumping to the ground. Quick to reach the other side, she offered her great-aunt a hand, but Auntie brushed it away. The woman was as agile as any young person as she gracefully stepped to the ground.

Kristina's knock on the door was quickly answered by George Langley. He looked befuddled, peering over her shoulder. "What have we here?"

"Mr. Langley, this is Great-aunt Myrtle. She's visiting us for a few days. Toby came by and told us what happened this evening—about the prowler. I wanted to come see Doris right away. Auntie was kind enough to drive me here in her motorcar. I hope we aren't calling to late."

"No, no, come in." Doris rushed to greet them, and George Langley stepped outside to peruse the automobile. "It's a dandy," she heard him tell Auntie Myrtle.

Kristina didn't want to talk about the motorcar. She was concerned about Doris, and she wanted to know what happened earlier this evening. She took hold of her friend's hand. "Did the prowler try to come through your window?"

"I don't think so. All I saw was the back of a man running into the trees behind our house. It was still light enough to see, but it happened so fast I hardly got a glimpse of his back."

"Do you think it was the new man in town, the man they call a half-breed?"

"Maybe. I'm not sure. I was changing into my nightgown early because I don't feel very well, so I was going to crawl into bed and read awhile. I heard noises outside my window, and when I walked over there to look, someone in black ran away. By the time I called my father into the room and he looked out, the prowler was gone."

"But you're sure it was a man at your window?"

"Yes. And I think his head was covered with something black, like his clothes. Whoever it was, he's awfully risky, or very stupid, doing something like that before dark, especially so near town. My father went out with his gun to look around, but there was no sign of anyone."

Kristina had seen Toby wear black many times, but a lot of other men wore black as well. It was hardly a significant thing to mention to the sheriff.

She glanced around. Aunt Myrtle and Mr. Langley were deep in conversation about the motorcar, and Mrs. Langley was in the kitchen. Kristina pulled Doris into her bedroom and closed the door. "I have to tell you something. Can you keep it quiet for now?"

Doris sat down on the edge of her bed. "Sure. What is it?"

Kristina felt guilty for not confiding in her friend sooner. They just hadn't been together much the past three weeks, but Doris was still her dearest friend. "I don't believe the prowler is that new man you saw on the library steps a while back. I've talked to him a couple of times since we said hello in the library."

"You have? You didn't tell me you've talked to him." Doris's eyes grew wide.

Kristina told her friend all about the buggy accident at the library, and how Pilan' had helped her. "If he hadn't sent someone for the doctor, I think the whole lot of onlookers would have stood around and gawked. Anyway, I met him again a few days ago, down by the creek and totally by chance. We introduced ourselves and talked for a few minutes before he had to leave and go to work."

"Honest? What did you talk about?" All big-eyed and curious, Doris grabbed Kristina's hands and squeezed tight. "Tell me everything."

It was difficult for Kristina to curb her excitement. She didn't come there to talk about her meeting with Pilan', but it was important to make Doris understand he couldn't possibly be the prowler. She was sure of that. "I was down at the creek—you know where we've gone many times—cooling my feet in the water when I heard violin music. When he played *Amazing* Grace I sang along, only I didn't know it was him. I stepped out of the water and walked barefoot along beside the creek, and suddenly, there he was in the clearing coming toward me. Doris, he's wonderful, and talented, and intelligent. He doesn't even mind being called a half-breed, can you believe that? He told me his father is a handsome, French explorer, and his mother is a beautiful Cherokee. I suppose that's why he's so handsome."

All grins, Doris pulled up her feet under her and propped her elbows on her legs. "So it definitely was you he stared at from the library steps when we passed by. I knew it. Tell me more."

"Goodness. I don't know what else to say; our meeting was brief. I do admire him, though. I believe he's a good person, and it makes me angry that someone is blaming him for prowling around town and peeking in windows. I just don't believe that's true."

Doris unwound her feet and stood. "If it's not him, who do you think it is?"

"I don't know, but I'm beginning to suspect Toby. It seems to me he's the one trying to damage Pilan''s reputation, and how would he know what happened here, unless he was outside your window himself? That's why I'm here now. He came to our house to warn us, and tell us the prowler had been looking in your window."

"Really? I'll tell my father what you said and see what he wants to do about it. Of course, with no evidence we can't accuse Toby. There's no way to prove it."

"Well, I for one am going to keep a watchful eye on him. I'd suggest you do the same."

Doris nodded, seeming lost in thought. "Back to Pilan' and your little encounter, are you going to see him again?"

"I hope so. He's quite fascinating. I want to learn more about him and hear him play the violin again." Almost giddy, Kristina wanted to jump up and dance. Instead, she came to her senses and threw up her hands. "You know my plans, though. I can't allow myself to become involved with him, nor with any man."

"That's too bad." Face beaming, Doris burst into smiles. "Remember Harland Gunther?"

"The nice-looking, blond fellow a grade ahead of us?"

"Yes."

"Didn't he drop out of school before he graduated?" As Kristina recalled his father was sick and Harland had to run the farm.

"Yes. Anyway, he stopped by a few weeks ago, and he asked me if I'd go out to dinner with him. He asked my parents for permission to court me. He was so nervous I thought he'd faint right on our living room floor."

"Did you say yes? Did your mother and father give their permission?"

"Yes and yes." Doris giggled like a sixth grade girl.

Unlike so many of their classmates who were married and already expecting babies, Kristina was in no hurry, but Doris was ready.

"And you didn't tell me?"

"Like you said, we haven't seen much of each other since we graduated."

"True." Kristina didn't like the distance between them in recent weeks. She was curious and happy for her friend. "Did you go out with him?"

"Of course, several times. Tomorrow we're going to have a picnic. I'm making fried chicken and potato salad, and snicker-doodle cookies for dessert."

"Well, that should win his heart." She gave Doris a quick hug. "I'm happy for you; he's a nice fellow."

All smiles, Doris nodded. "He's very nice."

There was a tap on the bedroom door and Doris opened it. Aunt Myrtle stuck her head in. "We should run along, Kristina, before your parents get worried."

"Yes, I suppose." She wished she could stay longer. She hadn't had much time to sit and talk privately with Doris. They had a lot to catch up on and so little time. She'd make a point to visit Doris soon so they could have a long talk before she departed for Boston.

"I'm glad you came to see if I'm all right. Thank you." Doris hugged Kristina goodbye. "I can't believe you get to ride in your aunt's new motorcar." Then Doris turned to Aunt Myrtle. "It was nice to meet you."

Auntie climbed into the driver's seat, adjusted her hat, and fussed with her dress collar for no apparent reason. "Perhaps we can return tomorrow, and I can give you a ride."

"I would like that, but my new beau is taking me on a picnic in the park tomorrow." The freckles on Doris's cheeks blended into a sea of crimson.

"Well you mustn't miss that for a ride with an old, widow lady. Another time perhaps." Auntie tapped a forefinger on her chin and looked at Kristina. "I have a splendid idea. Let's plan a day when I can take you both out to lunch."

"Really, Auntie? That sounds wonderful. We'll have to do it soon, before I leave for Boston."

Her great-aunt beamed. "We shall do that. How about the day after tomorrow?"

"That's fine for me. Doris?"

"Yes, I'd love that."

"Now that that's settled, we should start home before it gets any later. I don't want your parents fretting and fussing with worry."

Kristina hugged Doris goodbye, and bid Mr. and Mrs. Langley farewell as she climbed into the motorcar. "Remember, Doris, be careful and stay alert."

"I will." Doris nodded and smiled.

"We shall see you at noon the day after tomorrow, Doris." Auntie settled into the driver's seat and started the engine.

The Langley family stood on the front porch and watched Auntie turn the car around in a wide u-turn that took up the entire street. Kristina held her breath. Few people were out, and she was relieved that no one was delayed or run over.

Two men on the stoop of a small shop opposite the Langley's house stood and watched. It was too dark to see their expressions, but Kristina imagined they were quite startled. Other than delivery trucks, she hadn't seen another motor vehicle in Oklahoma City, but folks were talking about them. It would probably be no time at all before every man in town had one. Maybe even her father would purchase one, if she and Mama could talk him in to it. As Auntie drove away, she gave the bulbous horn two hard squeezes and waved.

Chapter 10

Kristina's best yellow dress was perfect for church on this sunny morning. She brushed her hair until it gleamed and let it fall back over her shoulders. After examining her reflection in the mirror, she decided to put on some pink lipstick. It made her feel more mature. Looking at herself as she smoothed the rosy pink over her lips, she realized the color made her face appear more radiant. She'd been asked to sing a special solo today so she wanted to look her best. She ran the song through her mind one last time.

"We're waiting on you, Kristina." Her father sounded impatient.

Putting her extra grooming aside, she grabbed her Bible and rushed out of her room. "I'm on my way."

Bumping along in the crowded carriage with her family was unpleasant after riding in Auntie's fancy motorcar. But Aunt Myrtle had gone home yesterday, promising to return before Kristina left for Boston. Kristina looked forward to Auntie's return visit with great anticipation.

Her mind wandered as she rode to church with her family. So much was happening in her life. It was all exciting, but most of all, it bothered her that time to get better acquainted with Pilan' was drawing short. Yearning to see him again, her feelings were all in a jumble.

As her family did every Sunday, they arrived at church several minutes before the service began. The organ pumped out the prelude, played by the ancient, prune-faced, spinster Gilberta. Papa ushered Mama with Gracie May in her arms, Frankie, Eddie, and Birdie down the aisle to their regular pew near the front. Like little ducklings, the three young ones marched in without a peep. Dyer and Kristina entered last, and filled the remaining spots on the pew.

Adjusting to the hard seat, Kristina mentally ran through her solo one more time. She turned to smile at Doris when the Langley's took the pew right behind her. Doris greeted Kristina with a smile and a quick finger wave. Of course, no talking was allowed, and if Kristina dared to say a word to her friend, Papa's magic hand would manage to span the distance between them and tap a reminder on her shoulder. It had been a long time since she'd required her father's gentle discipline. She was old enough to know this wasn't the time to chat with friends.

Just the same, she felt a light touch to her other shoulder, the one farthest away from Papa, and Doris whispered in Kristina's ear. "Good luck on your solo."

Instead of risking a reprimand from her father, Kristina answered with a quick nod.

The church service began with the doxology and prayer. When it was time for her solo the pastor introduced her and called her to the front. This wasn't her first solo. When she was five, she'd been right at home on the platform as a singing angel in the Christmas program. She took her place center stage, and gave the organist a quick smile, her key that she was ready.

Gilberta played a short introduction. Kristina filled her lungs with air, and began the first verse of *In the Garden*.

As she sang the chorus, she was reminded of all the times she'd spent in her favorite place beside the creek—her private garden. She'd often sensed God there with her. The words of the chorus were true; she was never alone. "And He walks with me and He talks with me . . ."

Between verses she glanced at her parents, seeing pride in their smiles, and even on the faces of her younger brothers and sister. She thanked God for this talent and love for music that he'd blessed her with. Scanning the congregation as she sang, her glance suddenly stopped. Her heart caught in her throat for the briefest moment. Three rows from the back was Pilan', a huge smile on his face.

Oh my, take a breath, sing! She almost missed the first word of the last verse, but somehow she managed to refocus on the music and finish the song. Her knees shook as she stepped off the platform and returned to her seat. Oh how she wanted to run to the back of the church and say hello to him.

She hardly heard a word of Reverend Gilroy's sermon, and she almost cheered when he finished the benediction and dismissal prayer. Glad she was on the end of her pew, she exited without waiting for her parents. Pilan' was waiting when she reached the rear of the church. She was so excited to see him she could hardly speak.

When she saw him up close she gasped, wanting to reach up and touch his bruised face. "What happened?"

"Your friend's fist paid me an unexpected visit."

"None of my friends would do that to you."

"It was Toby."

She wanted to cry and scream angry words all at the same time. "He's no friend of mine. He had no right to hit you."

"I'll be all right. Let's not talk about that any more. Your solo was beautiful." Pilan''s smile was her undoing, not because he was blessed with a mouthful of straight, white teeth, but because his smile caused his eyes to shimmer, and it seemed he looked into her heart. Even with his bruised face he was extraordinarily handsome.

Finally, she managed to open her mouth. "Thank you. I'm happy to see you here."

She was full of questions, but her parents were suddenly beside her, curiosity written on their faces.

"Papa, Mama, I'd like you to meet Pilan' Rousseau. Pilan', these are my parents, Welby and Leoma Soderlund."

Hands were shaken, polite greetings were dispensed. Curious smiles and slightly raised brows came back to Kristina. "Pilan' and I met at the library."

Dare she tell them about the recent meeting down by the creek? Was it wrong to keep that coincidental meeting to herself? She didn't think so, at least not here and now. It was a relief that her parents didn't appear to connect Pilan' to the man people in town called the half-breed. They didn't seem at all suspicious, but instead were polite and friendly. And

Pilan' seemed pleased to meet them. Kristina relaxed, suddenly stumped for what to say next.

The Langleys filed past, each saying hello. Doris winked and hugged Kristina before moving on.

"It was very nice to meet you, Pilan'. I hope we'll see you here at church again." Mama's tone was sincere, and for a moment, Kristina wondered if Mama was secretly smitten by Pilan''s ravishing good-looks and his well-tailored clothing. Certain he had that affect on most women, it would be no surprise.

"I'm sure you will," Pilan' said looking at Mama then Papa. "I enjoyed the service. Especially your daughter's solo. Her voice is definitely a gift from God."

"Indeed." With that agreement from Papa, he said farewell to Pilan' then ushered all his ducklings out the door.

Kristina hung back for the briefest moment, not wanting Papa to wait too long for her. She spoke softly. "I'm so happy you came today. I almost forgot the words to the song when I saw you."

"You did a beautiful job. When might I see you again? Pilan''s eyes were warm, his smile warmer.

"I'll be at the creek today after dinner, about three." Her heart grew excited, her cheeks warm. "If you come, will you bring your violin?"

"I'd be happy to."

Everyone had exited the church, and Kristina moved toward the door. "Have you met Reverend Gilroy?"

"No. I'll introduce myself to him. You better run along before your father becomes impatient."

"You're right. Good-bye." Then she whispered. "Until this afternoon."

"Good-bye for now." Pilan' smiled, and nodded adding a quick wink. How a simple gesture could be so personal and romantic was beyond her.

She had to force herself to leave, and she nearly stumbled down the steps. Climbing into the family's carriage, she was thrilled, nervous, and breathless. Pilan' stood outside the church talking to the reverend as Papa pulled away. Kristina couldn't take her eyes off him. She wished she could speed up time; three o'clock couldn't come soon enough.

"Well, my dear, you seem quite captivated by that young man." Mama must have been reading her mind, or watching her closely. Did it show that easily? It was true, but how should she answer such a comment from her mother?

Kristina fidgeted in her seat. Mama sat in the middle of the front seat with Gracie May in her arms, and holding Birdie on her lap, Kristina sat next to Mama. It was impossible to pretend she couldn't hear her mother's prying statement. Nor could she lie; she wouldn't think of doing such a thing.

"He is very nice." She didn't want to share more than that with her parents right now. Her feelings for Pilan' were new and confusing. Her thoughts and feelings were sacred to her, and she didn't want a lot of questions and comments intruding into the inner most parts of her heart.

Papa seemed awfully quiet. Of course, he never said much anyway, but clearly he was thinking hard on something. Had he realized who Pilan' was? She hoped not—not yet. If her friendship with Pilan' developed further, she would like to invite him home for dinner. Then the family would see what a wonderful person he was. Once they became acquainted with him they'd like him. They'd realize the accusations floating around town about him weren't true. And if they heard him play his violin they'd love him.

Nothing more was said about Pilan' until the family was seated for Sunday dinner and the blessing had been said. It was then Papa's questions came out.

"What do you know about that young man, Kristina?" The tone of Papa's voice was courteous but stern.

Where should she begin? This was not the time to hold back information. That would be no different than lying. Kristina thought for a moment and emptied her mouth, supposing she should start at the very beginning.

"I first saw him in the library, as I told you. He had a big pile of books, so I assume he's well educated. Then the day the wheel came off our buggy in front of the library, he was the first person to help me. He sent a boy to fetch Doctor Rhodes, and he stayed to comfort me. He was very gentle and helpful. I suppose that makes him a Good Samaritan, right? She tried to paint the best picture possible of Pilan'."

Neither parent answered.

"Another day when I was walking, I saw him near the creek. He was playing a beautiful song on a violin. He'd heard me singing, and we met in the clearing. We talked briefly. He's very talented."

She paused and put a bite of mashed potatoes into her mouth, hoping she'd satisfied her father's curiosity, and this time for sure, there would be no more questions.

Wrong.

"You know nothing about his background?" Papa patiently waited for her to swallow before she answered.

Is this how a criminal felt when being questioned in court under oath? "He told me his father is a French explorer and his mother is a Cherokee Indian. I think he was born in Philadelphia, but when he was still young, his parents moved to France, and that's where he was raised."

Mama had her questions, too. "He seems awfully young to be traveling on his own. Is he here with his family?"

"No. He said he is exploring America so he could learn more about his birthplace."

"So, I take it he has no regular job; he's just roaming around the country by himself?" Papa's brows lifted, his lips twisted.

"You make it sound like he's a freeloader or a hobo. He works for Potts in the restaurant. I guess that's how he earns enough money to travel, but I'm not sure." Kristina hadn't really thought much about Pilan''s income, or how he could afford to travel for such a long time. It wasn't important to her, nor was it her business.

"I see." Papa's words were clipped. He took a bite of meatloaf and chewed, and chewed, and chewed.

Certain there were no more questions, Kristina sighed a breath of relief and began to eat again, her mind on her rendezvous today with Pilan'. She didn't want anything to ruin it. After all, there wasn't much time left to see him. A feeling of desperation grew within her, bringing with it fresh confusion.

Dyer, who had been silent, put in his words of wisdom. "It seems to me if Kristina is going off to college soon, and this Pilan' person is headed off on some adventure, there's no reason to be concerned." It was a good point. She appreciated Dyer's comment. Maybe it would dispel some of her father's consternation.

"I'm concerned for your sister's safety here and now." He aimed a forefinger at Dyer. "I'm sure you've heard the rumors and accusations about that man, and if they're true he could be very dangerous. I don't want Kristina around him."

Her heart dropped. "But Papa—"

"No buts, young lady. You heard me."

All right. There would be no buts, no argument, and no agreement. Kristina finished her dinner without another word, helped clear the table, and washed the dishes.

Papa went into the living room and sat down in his favorite chair with a farm magazine of some sort, and at once he was snoring. Like every Sunday afternoon, he'd nap for at least an hour or two. Mama was rocking Gracie May in the bedroom, trying to lull the baby to sleep for an afternoon nap. The house rule on Sunday afternoons was to observe at least one hour of quiet. Everyone below the age of ten was required to lie down for a nap, whether they could sleep or not. Edward Lee would be ten in four months, and he tried his hardest to get out of napping, but with no luck, so he read, and invariably he fell asleep with the book haphazardly on his face. When Kristina walked past the boys' room she peeked in. Eddie was still wide awake. She received a glare from him, then a silly face, his eyes crossed, his tongue stuck out. He poked his thumbs in his ears and wiggled his fingers. She slapped a hand over her mouth to muffle her giggles, and moved on as fast as she could to avoid encouraging his silly behavior.

Once in her bedroom, she changed into an everyday cotton skirt— the nicest one made of a pretty floral print—and a crisp white blouse. After brushing her hair, she tied it loosely at the back of her neck with a scarf that matched her skirt, and slipped into a pair of comfortable walking shoes. She rolled up the small blanket she often used outdoors to sit on, and tucked it beneath one arm. A smile on her lips, the blanket under her arm, and a book by Irving in hand, Kristina set out on her Sunday afternoon walk. Without a peep or a squeak, she left the house by the back door.

As she tiptoed down the back steps she whispered. "Sorry for disobeying you, Papa, but I just have to go. Then she offered up a short silent prayer. *Forgive me Lord if what I'm about to do is a sin.* Truthfully she didn't think it was a sin. And besides, not only was she eighteen, she frequently went for Sunday afternoon walks down to the creek. If by chance Pilan' showed up, well then, she wouldn't mention it.

She shifted the blanket and the book to her other arm. Knowing she'd probably not read a word in the book, she'd almost left it behind, but she decided in the end to carry it along. Anything was possible; Pilan' could arrive later than she. There was a chance he wouldn't show up at all. Her heart dropped at the thought, and she knew if that were to happen she'd be too disappointed to read a single word. None-the-less, she was on her way, and the book made little difference. She smiled and lengthened her stride.

EVEN WITH THE WINDOW wide open the hotel room was hotter than Potts' Kitchen. Pilan' was not only in a hurry to get outdoors where the heat of summer would at least be stirred by a breeze, but he was also anxious to see Kristina again. He hoped nothing would keep her from meeting him by the creek. If he hurried, he could surprise her by getting to her spot beneath the trees before she arrived. He slipped on a clean white linen shirt and tucked in it to his trousers. Glancing in the mirror above the small dresser, he ran a comb through his hair. He needed a haircut. He didn't usually allow the thick, black mass of waves to grow long and unruly. Tomorrow morning perhaps, he'd go to the barber.

Not knowing how much longer he'd have the pleasure of Kristina's company before he set off on the next leg of his adventure, Pilan' picked up his snapshot camera and hung it around his neck by the narrow strap, leaving his hands free to carry his violin and some wildflowers, if he found some to pick along the way. He hoped Kristina would allow him to take a few photographs of her. She'd make a stunning picture.

A quick glance at his pocket-watch assured him he had more than enough time to walk to the creek and spend an hour with Kristina. Then he remembered the restaurant was closed on Sundays. His afternoon was free to do as he wished.

What a great afternoon it was going to be. Pilan"s stride was long as he set out. He scooped in a few breaths of fresh air. Even though it was hot, the heat wasn't unbearable yet, and he was glad for the light breeze. The blue, afternoon sky reminded him of his mother's beloved collection of Delft dinnerware and pottery. Were all women mad about collecting glassware and trinkets? He'd have to ask Kristina.

Instead of cutting across private farm land, he walked along the road until it came to the creek, then he followed the trickling stream toward the shaded area Kristina called her private get-away. Making his way along a trail that divided two fields, he wondered if he were walking on Soderlund property at that point. In the distance Kristina's home came in to view, but he didn't see her anywhere. Being Sunday and not yet cotton picking time, it wasn't likely Mr. Soderlund would be in the fields. In fact, no one was in sight.

On both sides of the path where Pilan' walked, the cotton plants looked good, from what little he knew, but the boles weren't fully developed. He tried to imagine Kristina dragging a cotton bag through the rows her back hunched and tired, her fingers sore and bleeding from long hours of picking cotton. A fine young woman with such marvelous talent shouldn't have to toil in the fields. He hoped that would never happen to her. Surely Mr. Soderlund would never expect his grown daughter to pick cotton. There must be plenty of farm workers willing to work for a small wage.

The sun grew hotter and beat down on Pilan"s head, and he wished he'd worn a hat. Suddenly thirsty, he stopped for a moment and set aside his violin case. Kneeling beneath a small tree at the creek's edge, he scooped up a handful of water. It was so refreshing he cupped both hands together and slurped up a second drink. When he'd drunk his fill, he lightly patted his face and neck with his wet hands and stood, ready to walk the last several yards.

Before disappearing beneath the umbrella of the ancient oak, Pilan' glanced once more across the cotton field toward Kristina's home. Ah, what a pretty sight he saw coming his way. There was no mistaking the tall slender body, the graceful gait. He laid his violin case on a grassy spot and waved. Happy to see Kristina waving boldly, tremors of excitement overcame him. Even though the bright skirt that fluttered around her legs was attractive, and the white blouse emphasized her womanly curves, he imagined her in a lovely evening gown of silk and satin, her hair piled high in a romantic hairstyle—what ever the ladies called the styles of the day. Oh yes. She'd fit right in, he was sure. She'd be the most elegant and beautiful woman to ever grace his grandmother's estate, or his parents' château.

Something his father had told him before he left for this adventure in America came to mind—something he didn't want to remember. "You will see many beautiful women, son. Don't bring home a simple, uneducated farm girl expecting to transform her."

Indeed, Father, I won't forget. Kristina may be a farm girl, but she was anything but simple, and certainly not uneducated. She had grace, beauty, manners, and elegance. Even in her plain country attire, she would dazzle the members of his family. His mother had had far less in her favor when his father married her, but her beauty and gracefulness had won his father's heart. Uneducated, she'd been eager to learn about her new husband's culture. She had soaked up lessons in French and etiquette as fast as she could, and she'd emulated the women around her. In a short time she had become the pride and joy of the family, a magnificent wife and mother. No socialite in Paris could rival his mother. He smiled, wondering why he imagined Kristina as the lady of his estate. Such foolishness.

He barely knew this girl. He knew nothing about her plans for the future. Would she be interested in him once she knew he wanted to travel around the country? *Calm yourself my boy. She's only steps away.*

"Hello," Pilan' called, waiting for her to reach him. He didn't want to appear too anxious. He greeted her again, this time in French. *"Bon jour."*

Kristina's smile grew with each step toward him. "Hello."

His outstretched hand grew warm when Kristina placed her hand in his. "I'm happy to see you. I could hardly wait until you arrived."

Pilan''s visions and worries about Kristina working in the fields with common hired hands vanished. Her hand was feathery soft and white, the nails at the end of long, straight fingers, were clean and neatly trimmed. His instinct was to pull her into his arms and ravish her with kisses, but of course being an honorable man, he would do no such thing. To do so would be crude, unbecoming, and downright sinful. He liked her too much to take advantage of the situation, and he was too well taught to be anything other than a gentleman. That, however, did little to diminish his desires.

Ever so slowly, he lifted Kristina's hand to his lips and kissed the back of it. He was tempted to march his lips all the way up her arm, and continue kissing the soft, delicate skin on her neck, but he released her hand after one proper kiss.

CHILLS SKITTERED UP KRISTINA'S spine the moment she saw Pilan' waiting beneath the tree. His kiss on her hand was soft, lingering, and she barely kept her sigh silent. The only bad thing about being kissed on the hand was, well, how could she return the gesture? She was quite sure she shouldn't take one of his hands and kiss it. That seemed plain stupid. The last thing she wanted, was to have Pilan' think she was ignorant.

So she smiled, and smiled some more. When she began to worry her ignorance might be showing, she stepped back and broke the silence with a question. That usually worked in an awkward situation, and she really was curious. "What's that black box hanging around your neck?"

Pilan' touched the box that rested against his stomach. "This is a Kodak snapshot camera."

"How does it work?" She was honestly baffled and interested. It was the first one she'd seen, although she had heard such a thing existed, and she'd seen many photographs, but she had no idea how they came to be.

"Well, I can't explain the technical works, but I can show you how I take pictures, if you will allow me to photograph you."

"Oh, yes." It was most exciting.

Pilan' walked a few feet away, out into the sun. "Come out of the shade and look at me." He motioned with one hand, holding the camera in the other."

Looking at Pilan' was a pleasure she could enjoy all day, although from this vantage point the sun glared in her face and she had to squint. "Now what? I can hardly see you for the sunshine."

Pilan' raised the camera to his eyes and appeared to look through some hole, half of his face hidden behind the picture box. He held the camera with both hands, moving a little this way, then that way, stepping forward then back.

Goodness. It seems like a lot of work, and I won't even get to see the photograph.

"Turn your face a little to the left." Pilan' motioned with one hand.

Kristina did so, and held her breath until she had to breathe or pass out. He didn't say she had to hold her breath, did he? No, she didn't think so. She tried to relax, and at the same time follow his instructions, but she was terribly excited, and it was hard to stand still.

"Perfect. Stand very still now and smile." How was she supposed to smile with the sun blazing into her eyes? Now she knew why people in pictures always looked unhappy. She was a little unhappy with the sun herself, but this was too much fun to complain.

Pilan' walked forward to where she stood. "Would you mind if I try one more?"

"Not at all." In spite of the sun, she enjoyed watching Pilan' with his slender hands and long fingers, his smooth movements. And as much as she hated to admit, she liked his attention. Was that bad? She hoped not.

"That patch of wild flowers would make a lovely setting." Pilan' touched her elbow and led her to the bright-yellow flowers. "Would you mind kneeling here, or would that be too uncomfortable?"

"I brought along a blanket. I'd be happy to kneel on that." At this point she'd stand on her head for him. Well, perhaps not anything quite that extreme. She ran beneath the tree and retrieved the old blanket.

Rather than spread it out, she unrolled it just enough to create a cushion. She knelt on both knees, ignoring the prickly stems that reached over and poked her ankles. At least her long skirt protected her legs. She shifted, adjusted, and settled in what she thought would be a good pose, sitting with her bent legs to one side.

Pilan' leaned a little to the left and a little to the right. When he appeared satisfied, he lifted the camera to his eyes. "Beautiful. Magnificent. Perfect." Pilan''s words of approval rolled off his tongue in waves of passion, his musical voice charged with zeal.

She sat still, her curiosity about him growing. Her body was motionless, but her heart was strumming a new tune, her blood running wild.

She smiled.

The camera box clicked.

Pilan' offered his hand to help her up. She took it, glad for his chivalry. He grabbed up the blanket and handed it to her. "Shall we get out of the sun and sit beneath the shade to visit?"

She led the way, to a spot that was flat and comfortable, spreading the blanket, making space for them both. "I was hoping you would play another song on your violin."

Pilan' waited for her to sit down, then he sat across from her, his long legs stretched out in front of him, one ankle over the other. His legs were comfortably close beside her but not touching. He leaned on one arm, his torso upright. "I'll play a song for you if you'll sing for me. But first, let's enjoy the coolness of the shade and talk a bit."

"All right." Kristina liked his suggestion, liked that he took the lead. She had so many questions about him she didn't know where to begin. Shifting to get more comfortable, she bent both legs to one side, making sure her skirt covered her ankles.

Before she could ask Pilan' a question he spoke. "When I left my home in France to travel around America, I had no intention of meeting a woman, or beginning a relationship. My trip was to be all adventure, no ladies, certainly no romance."

"And . . . that's changed?" She had no intention of interfering with his plans, whatever they were.

Pilan' looked into her eyes, saying nothing for a few seconds. He seemed to be thinking hard, perhaps looking for the right words. "It has changed, but I'm not sure how just yet."

What was he trying to tell her? She remained silent, playing with a twig of grass at the edge of the blanket, waiting for him to speak again.

"Until I met you, I had no desire to get acquainted with a woman. But I find myself thinking about you day and night, wondering about you and your plans for the future. As I told you earlier, you're the type of woman I'd like to know. I'm not sure how our meeting will change my plans, but I can't go away from here without at least letting you know I think very highly of you. I want to know you better."

"I feel the same way, but I don't know what to say." How could it be so hard to find the right words when Pilan' was so easy to be around? She was glad he didn't hesitate before asking a question.

"Tell me about your schooling. Are you finished?"

It was an easy enough question until she remembered her plans for college. "I've graduated from high school, and my grandparents have arranged for me to go to the Boston University School of Music. I'll leave in two weeks.

"Wonderful. That will be quite a change for you, won't it, going from here to Boston?"

"Yes." For a second, disquiet flashed through her mind. "What are some of the places you plan to explore?" Kristina couldn't imagine having the freedom and ability to venture anywhere alone, finding new cities and interesting new places.

Pilan' sat forward and wiped a sleeve across his forehead. "Nothing is absolute, of course, but I hope to climb Pike's Peak in Colorado then go farther west. I'd like to see Los Angeles and the Pacific Ocean, San Francisco, and Portland."

"This country is so big, and there's so much to see." Kristina knew so little about the western part of the country, and she wasn't sure she could converse intelligently about it.

"Yes, it is. Before I go back to France I will spend some more time in New York City. Have you visited any states outside of Oklahoma?"

"Only in geography books."

"Do you ever think about going to other places, wonder what they're like, how the people live in different areas?"

"Not until recently. I thought most towns were like Oklahoma City until I learned about Boston. Mama says it's beautiful, with lots of trees and parks, and big fancy stores. I'm looking forward to seeing it."

"You'll like it, I'm sure." Pilan' asked more questions, made her laugh, made her smile, piqued her curiosity about the rest of the world. Eventually he changed the subject to family.

She was relieved when they stopped talking about the very things that would send them far apart: her departure for college, his adventure west. Yet, she had no right to expect Pilan' to stay, and she couldn't tell her grandparents she wasn't going to Boston with them. She and Pilan' hardly knew each other, and with only two weeks left before leaving, there was little time to become fully acquainted. Still, the tug at her heart, and the thumping in her chest drew her to Pilan'. It was something she couldn't explain or understand.

She was thankful he kept the conversation going, no matter how frequently she was lost for words. He spoke with so much passion about life and family, and he asked important questions. He gave wonderful answers to her questions.

Unlike her large family, Pilan' had only one younger sister. Kristina's family wasn't poor, but they weren't wealthy. Apparently there was no end to the wealth in his family. She lived in a modest farmhouse, where Pilan' described his family's home as a mansion on a huge property with flower gardens and trees; a château he called it. But he spoke about it with fondness and love, not boastful pride. It sounded magnificent. Her home was surrounded with barns, pigs, horses, chickens, and cotton fields—sixty acres of it. Oh, and the outhouse. Papa's pride. Where cotton wasn't growing there was dirt.

Pilan' stood and stretched his arms, reaching down to give Kristina a hand. She rose and thanked him.

"I shouldn't stay much longer. Shall we make some music together?" Pilan' opened his violin case and removed the beautiful instrument and the bow. He handled the violin mindfully, like a treasure he cared for with reverence. He touched the bow to the strings, and adjusted the tuning before he began to play.

Well-played measures of *Amazing Grace* turned the shady get-away into a sanctuary, and entreated her to sing along. So heavenly was the music, it took a moment to catch her breath. When she began to sing her heart swelled. Until recently, she'd never sung with the accompaniment of a violin, and it seemed as if a host of angels came down to join in. By the wonder on Pilan"s face she was sure he felt it too. She closed her eyes and lifted her voice to the sky, immersing her soul in each note.

When the last measure was finished, their combined notes lingered in the air. She looked at Pilan', sharing in the wonder she saw in his eyes. Standing in silence, reveling in what surely had to be God's divine approval, she wiped a tear from her face. Never in church, school, or here in her private haven, had Kristina experienced the presence of God like now.

When, at last, she was able to speak, all that came out was a big sigh.

"Amen." Pilan"s quiet response was equally reverent.

Chapter 11

GRANDMOTHER AND GRANDFATHER FISK arrived, both in jovial spirits, sharing the events of travel on the train. Each described interesting passengers, and painted verbal images of the landscape from a different perspective.

Her grandmother complained that in spite of the sights and adventure, the trip was too long and exhausting. "So much of the country is vast wasteland, nothing of interest to see. And the passengers," she threw up a hand and slapped the air, "were boring and drab."

Grandfather, on the other hand, found it educational and interesting. "I walked the aisle and went from car to car talking to other passengers. It was most interesting to learn where they were going and where they'd been. And you should have seen the wildlife. There were deer, antelope, and all sorts of little critters."

His tales and laughter sounded as if traveling back to Boston with them would be an exciting adventure, in spite of the great distance.

Grandmother flitted around the house, frequently looking out the windows for some sign of Great-aunt Myrtle's arrival. "I'm anxious to see that fancy motorcar of hers. I can't believe my younger sister owns such a thing. Why, she must have paid hundreds of dollars for it."

"Can you imagine?" Mama said.

As she put the good silverware on the table for supper, Kristina listened to her mother and grandmother talking. She made sure everything was set the way her mother had taught her, forks on the left side of the plates, knives and spoons on the right. *Don't forget to turn the knife so the blade faces the plate.* She adjusted each piece perfectly straight.

Bubbling with excitement, Kristina gathered the glasses from the cupboard and put them on the table. Auntie Myrtle had promised she could drive her motorcar when she came back, and she could hardly wait.

"Last time she came," Kristina chimed in, "she took me for a ride in it, and she promised she'd teach me how to drive it."

Grandmother's eyes grew wide. "Is that right? I don't know if I'd trust driving such a wild contraption as that. With all that speed, someone could get killed."

"Oh, Granny, no one's going to get killed." Old folks had such silly ideas.

The table completely set, Kristina's thoughts traveled back to Pilan'. She wanted to see him this evening. However, he had to work until eleven o'clock in the restaurant. Knowing he couldn't come to the creek, she didn't bother going today. The glorious time she'd spent with Pilan' yesterday felt like a month ago, and all she could think about was seeing him again. The longing to be with him and to share their music was new and wonderful. While she didn't fully understand all the conflicting feelings, she continuously mulled over everything about the times she'd spent with him. She planned repeatedly what she'd wear, and what she wanted to say when she saw him tomorrow. Her mind constantly drifting back to Pilan', she had to make an extra effort to enjoy her grandparents.

It seemed Grandma Lillian was a different person than Kristina remembered. She seemed happier and less bossy than the other times she'd come alone to visit. This was only the second time her grandfather had made the trip, and Kristina wished he'd come more often. Her earliest memories of her grandmother Fisk were when she'd been at Mama Leoma's big fancy house before Papa and Mama's marriage. She vaguely recalled times when Grandmother was angry about having Papa in the house, even though he'd been hurt in an accident and couldn't get out of bed. Grandmother had been nice enough, though, to her and Dyer. She'd even sewn a pretty dress for Kristina. She remembered it well.

It was clear where Mama Leoma got her extreme beauty, too. Grandmother was pretty in a classic sort of way, but Grandfather was extremely handsome. His full head of silver hair swooped back over his ears in thick waves. Over six feet tall, he was sophisticated even in his casual trousers and shirt. She'd seen a photograph of him in a suit and necktie, and she thought he was the best looking man alive—well, until she laid eyes on Pilan'.

Unlike any man she'd seen, Pilan''s unique handsomeness was hard to describe. It was difficult to take her eyes off him. One evening soon, she'd invite him to her house for dinner so he could meet her grandparents. She enjoyed being with him, and she wanted him to know all of her family. Kristina had a feeling Grandfather and Pilan' would hit it off quite well, and no doubt, Grandmother would approve of his good-looks and talent.

Supper was served at the big kitchen table, with Papa at one end and Grandfather at the other end. Her father had just said the blessing, when suddenly Dyer pressed both hands to the sides of his head and groaned.

No! Not again. Kristina jumped up from her chair and ran to Dyer's side. His face had turned ashen, his eyes glazed, and he leaned forward, his face dropping toward his plate. Kristina grabbed his shoulders and cried out his name. "Dyer. Are you having another headache?"

It was a stupid question; of course he had another headache. At once, both parents were on either side supporting his body and lifting him out of his chair, as if he were still an infant.

"Hurts bad." Dyer's cry could hardly be heard through his clenched jaw. "I feel sick."

Papa carried Dyer to his room and lowered him onto the bed. "Kristina, take your grandfather along and go for the doctor. Don't waste time."

Without a thought she rushed out the back door, and headed for the barn to hitch up the buggy. Her grandfather was right behind her, finishing the job in no time. "Get in, Kristina. I'll take the reins!"

She'd barely settled in the seat before Grandfather had Lightning trotting out of the yard. The horse was getting old, but he still had a lot of spunk and speed. Papa said Lightning was the best horse he'd ever had. What was it now? Twelve years since he'd bought the stallion. He was still beautiful and strong.

"When are they going to build a hospital in this town?" Having always lived in a big city, her grandparents were accustomed to having everything available to them.

"There's a new one here, but Papa said Doctor Rhodes has been our doctor since I was a baby, and he doesn't trust the hospital. Doctor Rhodes is the best."

"That may well be, but I think Dyer needs more care than Doctor Rhodes is able to give him. I understand his headaches are becoming worse."

"Yes, they are. And more frequent."

Dark clouds were developing west of the city. Kristina watched for signs of lightning but saw none. There were more storms than usual this year, coming one right after another. They tore across Oklahoma faster than wildfire, and she didn't want to be stuck in a downpour halfway between town and home. *Oh, please, Lord. Hold the storm far away until we get home with the doctor. We need your protection.* More importantly, Doctor Rhodes needed to get to Dyer.

Grandfather snapped the reins and urged Lightning into a run. "I wonder if we should have brought Dyer to the doctor's office."

Kristina understood her grandfather's reasoning, but she'd seen how much pain the headaches caused. She didn't think he could stand the bumpy ride. "With all the bumps and dips I don't think he could handle the pain."

"Of course. I didn't think of that." For a city man, Grandfather was good with the horse, and he didn't waste time poking along. A frown turned his handsome features into rugged peaks and valleys of worry.

Thunder rumbled again, a little closer this time, but they were almost to the doctor's office. The moment the buggy came to a stop, Kristina jumped down without waiting for her grandfather. Thank goodness the doctor never locked his front door. She rushed through without a knock or hesitation. He was at his desk, his face buried in a huge book, probably some new medical journal. When she saw there were no patients in the office, she said a silent thank you to God. Before the door slammed behind her the doctor's head jerked up, immediate concern on his face.

"Dyer again?"

She nodded and talked at the same time. "It's real bad this time. Can you come right away?"

Without answering, Doctor Rhodes put on his hat, grabbed his black medical bag. He yelled up the stairs to Mrs. Rhodes. "I'm on my way out to the Soderlunds, dear. I won't be long."

Mrs. Rhodes appeared at the top of the stairs, a pleasant smile on her jolly face. "I'll hold your dinner, dear," she said to her husband and waved.

Kristina barely kept up with the doctor's long strides out the door and to their waiting buggies. Grandfather had the reins in hand ready to go the moment she was settled in her seat.

Black clouds already cloaked the city, turning what little daylight was left to gray. The wind swirled and howled. Kristina tucked her skirt around her legs, holding it against the seat. Even though her grandfather was a strong, healthy man, it was clear he had to fight to keep the horse and buggy under control. She worried they might blow over. A blinding flash of lightning followed by a horrendous boom startled Kristina and spooked the horse. Grandfather's face grew rigid, his hands tight on the reins as he settled Lightning to a slow walk. Kristina sighed, relieved that she hadn't come alone. Grandfather appeared shaken, but continued forward, his lips in a tight line. Rather than push Lightning into a fast gallop, he kept a slow, steady pace. She said a silent prayer for their protection, and if she knew her grandfather, he was sending up prayers, too.

Kristina knew Doctor Rhodes was close behind them, but the roaring wind was so loud it drowned out the sound of his horse and buggy. A loud crack pierced the air. Kristina looked over her shoulder to check on the doctor just as a large tree branch dropped in front of the doctor's horse. The horse reared up, his panicked whinnies echoing in the falling darkness.

Kristina screamed. "Stop, Grandfather!"

Grandfather jerked back on the reins, bringing Lightning to a stop, and Kristina jumped down from the buggy, her grandfather instantly beside her. The fallen branch with its twisted, torn limbs covered the entire road between them and Doctor Rhodes, but she could see the doctor climbing down from his buggy. Grandfather called out in his strong baritone voice. "Are you all right, Doctor?"

"I'm fine." Doctor Rhodes was out of his buggy assessing the situation. "Lucky for us it missed my horse. We'll have to clear this off the road before the rain hits."

Kristina worked along side her grandfather and the doctor, tugging and dragging, huffing and grunting, pulling with all her might to help clear the road. Sharp twigs and limbs reached out snagging her skirt and scratching her arms and legs, but she didn't stop working. Every second was precious. Worried about Dyer, she worked extra hard.

A big raindrop hit her face, immediately followed by a steady downpour. Within seconds the rain soaked them all. Another hard tug by all three of them, and the road was clear enough for the doctor to pass. Without a word they ran to their buggies, and they were off in a cautious trot.

Still catching her breath, Kristina sat back against the padded seat and tried to calm her jittery nerves. She was soaked to the bones and cold, and she hated being caught in this storm. It reminded her of the time her father was out in a storm like this, when he crashed his buckboard and nearly died along with his horse. The images of Doctor Rhodes carrying Papa's broken bloodied body into Leoma's guestroom had faded little with time.

She remembered a lot from that time in her life. It seemed to be a year of tragedy. Her mother had died, her baby brother was starving to death, and their home had been destroyed by a tornado. Leoma had taken in Dyer to wet nurse him, and after the tornado they had stayed at Leoma's until their house had been rebuilt. Before his accident, Papa had slept in Leoma's carriage house, and she and Dyer had slept in a big bedroom upstairs in Leoma's beautiful two-story house. Later, Kristina had learned that Leoma's husband and baby daughter had also died about the same time as her birth mother.

When the tornado that destroyed Papa's house had come through town before hopping and skipping out into the country, it had sent them all rushing down into Leoma's storm cellar. Kristina could still conjure up the damp, earthy smell. A lantern had shed pale, yellow light in the dark hole, but it was still frightening. Up high on the back wall was a tiny window, and she was sure the bolts of lightning were going to jump through that window and get her. The crashing sounds on the cellar door, and the loud thunder, had made her think a monster was beating on the door to get in, but Papa had held her tight and promised her they were safe.

That was before Papa and Mama Leoma had fallen in love. In fact, she'd heard the story more than once about the experience in the storm cellar, and the memory brought a smile to her lips. Both Papa and Leoma had declared they couldn't stand each other. Papa thought Mama was too snooty and highfalutin, and Mama said Papa was an ornery, smelly, booze-drinking, contentious farmer. Mama loved God, church, and reading her bible. Papa loved his brandy, and he didn't much care to read anything. And he sure didn't want to go to church. Being down in that storm cellar had been torture to them both, especially when debris was on the cellar door and they thought they were trapped.

Kristina smiled again, in spite of being caught out in the raging storm. God had sure done a work on both her parents. One would think they'd always been deeply in love and were the sweetest, holiest, God-fearing Christians in town. And, my-oh-my, they truly loved each other now. God sure did some strange but miraculous things. Maybe he would do another miracle for Dyer and heal him.

She said another silent prayer for her brother as they bumped and sloshed along through puddles, and over small tree limbs that littered the road. By God's grace, the rain let up, and they were almost home. When they turned up the lane Brownie barked, and bound down the path to escort them the rest of the way to the house. Her father ran out the front door to meet them before they came to a stop.

Papa dashed to Kristina's side of the buggy and assisted her down. "Thank you, Papa. How's Dyer?"

Without waiting for his answer, she ran toward the house while he helped Grandfather and Doctor Rhodes with the horses. Still dripping wet, she dashed down the hallway and knelt beside Dyer's bed, expecting him to smile up at her and say he was fine.

Mama Leoma took Kristina's elbow and urged her to stand up. She spoke in a whisper. "He's sleeping right now. He was awake for a few minutes, but he said it hurt to open his eyes. We thought it best to let him sleep until the doctor arrived. You go change out of those wet clothes. I don't want you to catch a cold before your trip to Boston."

"Yes ma'am." Kristina raced to her room and closed the door. She kicked off her shoes, dropped the soggy skirt to the floor and stepped out of it. With swift, nimble fingers she unbuttoned her blouse, and peeled the soaked fabric off her skin as fast as she could. She grabbed the first dress she could find to slip into. The moment she was in dry clothing, ignoring her tangled wet hair and bare feet, she hurried back to Dyer's bedroom. She wanted to hear what the doctor said, and if Dyer woke up she wanted to be there.

The house was quiet. Grandmother was reading and entertaining the younger children in the library, far from Dyer's room. Her grandmother had taught children's Sunday school for years, so Kristina was sure she had a bag full of handy tricks in her repertoire to keep the younger children quiet and happy.

When Kristina entered Dyer's bedroom the doctor was beside her brother's bed. Dyer was still sleeping, or so it appeared. Doctor Rhodes was talking to Mama and Papa in a low voice. Still wearing his wet clothing, Grandfather was there as well one hand on Mama's shoulder, the way a concerned father would acknowledge and support his child. Kristina tiptoed in taking a place beside her father.

The doctor asked the routine questions, much the same as previous times. The answers were the same, except this time Mama said he cried from the pain. It broke her heart to think of Dyer being in that much agony. He'd always been strong and active.

Doctor Rhodes listened to Dyer's heart with his stethoscope. "Heartbeat sounds strong and steady. How long has he been asleep?"

"About an hour," Mama said.

The doctor rested his chin on a thumb, a frown working his tired face. "I don't want to jump to conclusions, but as I mentioned before there's a possibility he has a tumor."

Mama gasped. "No."

"I know, dear. I hesitate to believe that's the problem, but this in no ordinary headache."

"But a tumor could kill him," Mama whispered, her words coming in choked sobs.

Doctor Rhodes didn't answer right away. "Let's not worry about that right now. Without x-rays it's impossible to know. It's also possible he's suffering from migraine headaches."

"How can I not worry? What can we do?" Mama raised her voice, clearly out of desperation.

Kristina burst into tears. She couldn't lose her brother. Going to Boston now was out of the question. She'd never forgive herself if Dyer passed away while she was gone.

"There are some things we can try." Doctor Rhodes reached into his satchel and brought out a small bottle of dark greenish liquid. This is a tincture made of cannabis. It's been used for many decades, and it's reported to dull the pain and stop the nausea of migraine headaches. I haven't treated anyone with it, but I've been reading about it. I think it's worth a try."

"If it will help our son then we're willing to try," Papa said.

The doctor woke Dyer and gave him a small dose. He gave Mama specific instructions. "I'll come out and check on him in two or three days."

Chapter 12

HER HEART WAS SO heavy with concern for Dyer if Kristina didn't know better she would have thought an elephant was on her chest, crushing the air from her lungs. She'd cried so much last night she'd slept very little, and she was drained of energy.

Up and behaving normal, Dyer assured the family the pain in his head had gone away during the night and he was fine. But how could he be? The doctor's words lay heavy on her mind. What if the medication only masked the problem? If Dyer had a tumor on his brain, there was no way to know how long he would live. She prayed that Doctor Rhodes was right about the migraine headaches, and that the medication he'd left for Dyer would cure him. *Please, God, let this work.*

Each step along the path beside the cotton field was labored. Though troubled and exhausted, she had to see Pilan' today. As she approached their meeting place, she hoped he would remember to come as they'd planned. He hadn't arrived yet, and as soon as she took refuge beneath the shade, she considered returning home. But she couldn't do that. In spite of her dark mood, she wanted to talk with him. He was a compassionate man, a good listener. Perhaps if she shared her concerns for Dyer with him, he would be a source of comfort and assurance that her brother would be all right.

The shade beneath the tree and trickling water nearby did little to stave off the July heat or the unusual gloominess that hung over her. Clammy from the humidity, her blouse clung to her skin. Sitting beneath the tree, her back against the trunk, she propped her chin on her bent knees and waited. He should arrive any moment, and though she couldn't chase away the worry, fresh excitement about seeing Pilan' welled up in her chest.

A little, green frog, no bigger that silver dollar, hopped nearby, close enough to reach out and touch. A faint smile formed on her lips, and faded when it hopped toward the creek into taller grass and disappeared. There were times when she delighted in seeing the small creatures here, times when she actually sang to them. But now, tired from crying, she closed her eyes, hoping they weren't red and swollen.

Whistling in the distance caught her attention. She lifted her head and watched, listening carefully. She didn't recognize the tune. Focused on the narrow foot path along the creek, she expected to see Pilan' at any moment, but when the person behind the whistling appeared it wasn't Pilan' at all.

Toby. Why was he there? Where was Pilan'?

She jumped to her feet, her energy renewed, but it wasn't happiness that surged through her veins. The way Toby had been acting lately, and the devilish look in his eyes as he came closer, alarmed her. As if the giant oak would protect her, she backed up against the rough trunk, her breathing unsteady. Her fingernails dug into the crusty bark.

"Hello, pretty Krissy!" Toby stopped a breath away, a sly grin on his face, a menacing spark in his eyes. Long muscular arms braced against the tree trunk caging her in.

"What are you doing here?" To say hello would make Toby think she welcomed him. Of course, knowing him it didn't matter whether he was welcome or not. He was the type who did what he wanted.

"Don't you know? I came to see you."

"How did you know I was here?"

"I know more than you think." He snorted "I've watched you down here with that pretty half-breed and his sissy-boy fiddle."

"It's a violin, and you should leave because he's coming any time; I don't want you here."

Alarmed by the vile way Toby looked at her, she tried to step aside and away from the tree, but he kept her trapped between his arms of granite muscle. His face came closer, his nose against hers. His breath smelled of alcohol, his body odor reeking, but she didn't take her eyes off of him. She wanted to duck and run, but he'd grab her for sure. Until now, she'd never been frightened around him, but that edgy feeling she'd experienced lately turned to fear. His boasting that he'd been watching her troubled her, frightened her even more. How often had he watched her? From where?

She wondered if it had been Toby who'd prowled around her bedroom window. Had he looked in while she changed into her night clothes? She shuddered; her stomach churned.

"Oh, I'm sorry, Krissy, your pretty boyfriend isn't coming today. I told him you sent me to tell him how sorry you were that you didn't feel well today and couldn't meet him. He fell for it." Toby's evil laughter sent a chill down her spine.

"How dare you do such a thing?" Kristina glanced around her, looking for a way to escape. Her heart raced. "You're on my father's property. Get off!"

"Naw. You know your paw likes me. He don't care if I come courting you. I'm still thinking how nice it would be to kiss those sweet lips of yours."

"Never!" Kristina shoved her body full-force against one of his arms knocking him off balance, but before she got away she stumbled. Toby caught her with one hand and jerked her up against him. She struggled to get loose, but he was too big and too strong. His hands dug in to her shoulders and her back as he tightened his grasp. His body was hot and sweaty, solid like rock.

"Let me go!" The fear in her voice seemed to spur Toby on.

His vice-like fingers shot pain through her shoulders. "Not until I get my kiss."

"No! I don't want you to kiss me." She spit on his face and stomped her foot down as hard as she could on the top of his foot. It didn't loosen his hold on her. She started to scream, but he thrust his mouth over hers, crushing her lips. He removed his mouth and replaced it with a huge, dirty hand.

"Well, pretty Krissy, maybe if I blindfold you, you won't mind my kisses."

"No!" Her shout was muffled.

The blindfold?

Tears burned her eyes and anger surfaced. She saw the incident in the barn as clearly as if it had happened yesterday—the blindfold, the boys in the dark barn, and pain. So much pain. She'd been grabbed from behind, so she hadn't seen who lured her into their game, convincing her she would have fun, but she'd heard their giggles and vulgar remarks. No wonder she'd always been uncomfortable around Toby. Her blurred vision distorted his face, turning it vicious and ugly.

He removed his hand. "Don't scream and I won't hurt you. I don't want to hurt you."

"How could you do that to a little girl? I was only eight."

"You didn't mind being blindfolded and playing my games."

"You filthy swine. How do you know if I minded or not? You snuck up on me from behind and took me prisoner. You lied and did terrible things. I was a child half your size and I did mind. I hated what you did to me." She was dizzy and wanted to vomit. She started to scream, but Toby slammed his hand over her mouth again. She bit the soft area between his thumb and forefinger, spitting out the taste of dirt and grime. "Let me go, Tobias Gallager! Let me go."

Instead, he dragged her to the ground and threw himself on top of her, his heavy body grinding against her. Small rocks and twigs on the ground dug into her back. His weight crushed the air out of her lungs. He held her down, gripping the sides of her head with his monstrous hands, and forced his mouth on hers again. She wiggled and squirmed, kicked and dug her fingernails into his arms and neck, but she couldn't free herself. Her lips hurt, crushed and bruised beneath his mouth. She didn't have enough breath to scream again, and her cries for help were weak, but a fierce need to fight overcame her fear. No way was this vile swine going to overpower her or violate her any further. Sure no one could hear her groans and loud guttural cries she wasn't going down without leaving some lasting marks on Toby. She fought with every ounce of strength, scratching, biting, and pulling hair. He would have a hard time explaining the bloody scratches on his upper body when the sheriff questioned him. This was one time when Toby wouldn't get by with his lies, fooling the sheriff into believing him.

The right moment allowed her to bite his lower lip until she tasted his blood.

Toby groaned but didn't retreat.

"You'll pay for that," Toby shouted when she released his lip.

"And you'll pay for this!" She spit his blood in his eyes.

While one hand still gripped her head like a vice, his other hand grabbed her breast. She squeezed her eyes shut and dug her teeth into his shoulder. *Lord, I know you hear me. Please, please make him stop. Save me from this horrible man.*

Clawing at the ground Kristina's hand covered a loose rock. It was small enough to fit into the palm of her hand, but it had a jagged edge. Without hesitating and with unexpected strength, she smashed it twice against the side Toby's head. Blood spurted against her face. He grunted and went limp on top of her, keeping her pinned to the ground, and in the next breath he stirred, lifting his head, fury in his eyes.

Please, God I need your help.

A dog barked. The bark grew louder and closer. In spite of Toby's weight on her, Kristina expelled a sigh of relief. It was Brownie. His growls and snarls became vicious, and suddenly he tore into Toby's shoulder, biting as he jerked his head back and forth. Brownie tugged and pulled until Toby fell to one side screaming. Still snarling, the dog dug his teeth into Toby's upper arm. Kristina rolled away from the steel trap of Toby's body and crawled away. She stumbled to her feet just as Toby broke free from Brownie's grip. But it was only long enough for him to reach a crouched position before Brownie bit into Toby's haunches several times, tearing holes in the seat of Toby's britches. Toby wailed and cussed. Kristina backed away, thinking Toby would grab her, but to her surprise he began to run away, Brownie right on his heels. The dog seized one ankle, dragging Toby down, but Toby quickly regained his footing and continued to run.

Still shaking, Kristina watched until the two disappeared around the bend in the creek several yards ahead. Worried about Brownie, she wondered if he would return to her. She'd never seen her old pet attack anyone, nor did she think he had the temperament to do so. And at almost thirteen years of age she was amazed he had the strength and energy to come to her rescue the way he did. It had to be a miracle, a special God-given burst of power. She'd asked God for help and he'd sent Brownie. She thanked him over and over.

At last, up ahead, Brownie re-appeared, his trot slower that usual, but he bore the posture of a victorious conqueror. She dropped to her knees to greet him with hugs and tears, and let her faithful friend lick her bruised face. As she stood and gave Brownie a pat on the back, she hoped Toby was still running. "Let's go home."

With Brownie at her side, they cut across the cotton field, the brittle stems scratching and poking her legs. But she didn't care. All she wanted to do was get to the safety of her home and to her parents, to tell them what had happened.

SINCE KRISTINA HAD SENT word that she wouldn't be meeting him, Pilan' set out on a walk, his camera around his neck. There were areas of town and new buildings being constructed that he hadn't paid much attention to, and it was a good afternoon to see those things. He had plenty of time. and he didn't want to spend the rest of the afternoon alone in his room where the air was stuffy and there was nothing to do.

As he walked, he couldn't rid himself of the disquiet that lingered in his mind. He shouldn't have listened to Toby, knowing the troublemaker he was, yet he'd been caught off guard, and he'd taken Kristina's neighbor's word as truth. He should have known better. However, he'd been on the lookout for Toby the last few days, his camera ready to catch him in some unseemly deed. Pictures didn't lie.

He meandered through some streets he hadn't explored, and photographed the newer buildings, the hospital, a six-story hotel, and a big confectionery. As the electric streetcar approached, he snapped a picture and vowed to take a ride on it one day soon. He wondered if Oklahoma City would ever be a place where thousands more families would make their homes, if it would become a major industrial center of economic wealth. Even though it seemed to be thriving already and it was still growing, it was difficult to imagine it as anything quite like Paris, and it was doubtful he could enjoy living here the rest of his life.

As he pondered these things, his path led him to the edge of town where businesses and homes dwindled into open land. Trees and underbrush thickened. He thought about turning back, but upon second thought, he decided he might find some interesting animals or birds to photograph.

Now that he was away from the center of town, he savored the sounds of nature. Crows argued and bossed the blackbirds, smaller birds sang and chattered. A breeze rustled through the brush and trees as Pilan' made his own path. Somewhere in the distance a dog barked. He took his camera from the case.

As he stepped into a small clearing he saw a lone building about a hundred yards away. Curious, he moved closer. The tumbledown hovel appeared to be an old settler's shack. Rotted boards that were once sturdy walls leaned out of kilter. The roof, sparse patches of thin wood and rusty sheets of tin, covered what appeared to be one small room. Purple and white wild flowers dotted the property around the shack, and added picturesque charm to the otherwise drab scene. When Pilan' was nearer he snapped a picture, then another.

The window opening in front had no glass and he approached carefully. Even though the place looked abandoned, he supposed some poor person could live there, but it wasn't likely. Wondering what the past might have left behind, he peeked through the window, his camera ready to capture the interior images. Without hesitating he snapped, wound the film, and snapped again.

"What do you think you're doing? Go away!"

"Toby?" What was he doing in there? Surely this wasn't where he lived.

It had only been a couple of hours since Toby had given him the message from Kristina. A stream of sunshine broke through a hole in the roof, casting light into the gray interior. Toby was crouched in one corner, his head bleeding, his shirt torn at the shoulder and covered in blood. Pilan' had no love for this man, but he also saw an injured person in pain who needed a doctor's help. "May I help you or send for the doctor?"

"No! Go away!" Toby jumped up and lunged toward the door, clearly ready to attack. Pilan' snapped another picture and quickly backed away from the shanty. His camera ready, he waited for the door to fly open.

It didn't.

THE MOMENT KRISTINA STEPPED through the back door she found her mother and grandmother in the kitchen. Mama rushed to her, carefully touching Kristina's face.

"What happened to you?" Mama Leoma's eyes filled with concern as she looked Kristina over. "Your clothes are a mess and your mouth is all red and bruised. What have you done?"

Unable to believe her mother's implication, Kristina's anger flared. This wasn't her fault. "What do you mean, what have I done? The only thing I did was try to defend myself against Toby Gallagher! Brownie saved me from being hurt worse by that savage."

At once, her father strode into the kitchen. He examined her face, gingerly lifting her chin. His touch was gentle, but she winced when his voice bellowed for all to hear. "What do you mean by being hurt? I want to know exactly what he did to you."

Embarrassed and shy about telling her father things that weren't usually discussed, she struggled with her words as she explained everything. Her voice shaking and tears falling she left nothing out. "If Brownie hadn't come along when he did, I don't think Toby would have stopped."

"I'll be paying a visit to his father and talking to the sheriff. I don't know what action they will take, but I assure you Toby will pay for doing this to you, and he won't be working on my farm anymore. I've treated that boy like a son, and this is what he does? He'll be sorry he laid a hand on you. He's no longer welcome on our property. If he shows his face here he'll wish he'd never been born."

Her father's anger was justified, and she was relieved and glad he would never again hire Toby to help around the farm. Her only worry now was to watch out for Toby as long as he was still on the prowl. She wasn't sure if now was the right time to tell her parents what Toby had done to her years earlier, and after thinking it over, she decided she'd wait. She'd take it one step at a time.

Papa turned to Mama, his face resolute, stern. "I'm going right now and have a talk with the Gallagers. There's no sense putting it off. Those boys have just run wild too long, it's time someone stop them."

Mama patted Papa's shoulder and gave a squeeze. "Be careful, dear."

By the time Mama finished her sentence Papa was out the door. Would he come home satisfied that Mr. Gallager would discipline Toby? She rather doubted it. She'd heard other people in town complain that the boys in that family were unruly and mischievous, and were getting into bigger and more trouble every year. What Toby did went far beyond mischief. He needed to be punished by the law. But would the sheriff do anything about it? Kristina sank into a kitchen chair, shuddering to think that most likely nothing at all would be done.

Chapter 13

THE MORNING WAS OVERCAST and sticky, and every bone and muscle in Kristina's body ached as if she been beaten. No matter how she turned in bed she groaned or winced. She felt worse now than when she'd gone to bed, and she didn't want to get up and dress.

Yesterday afternoon in the privacy of Kristina's room, her mother had helped her undress like she had when Kristina was young. Mama had gently cleansed every injury, paying careful attention to the spots where rocks had pierced the fabric of her blouse and broken the skin on her back. Mama had said none of the injuries appeared serious, but she wanted to take her into town this morning to see Doctor Rhodes. Kristina agreed. He could tell them the best salve to use to keep infection away, and it might be to her advantage to let the doctor see what had happened and put it in her record.

The more that people in the community knew about Toby Gallager and his vicious ways, the better the chance to stop him, even if it meant locking him up.

Contemplating what the day would bring, Kristina pulled her body up and sat on the edge of the bed. Taking her time she rose, walked into the bathroom with painful steps, and looked in the mirror over the sink. She cringed at her reflection. Before removing her nightgown, she slid the latch to lock the door, and ran the deep tub full of water.

Getting into the tub was painful, and the warm water burned the open wounds. She tried to wash but the washcloth was rough on her sore lips and bruises. The attack played over and over in her mind. She could feel Toby's fingers digging into her skin, smell his body odor, and taste his blood. She hoped with all her might that Toby was suffering from her bites and smashing the rock against his head, as well as the deeper bites Brownie had inflicted on him. It seemed sinful to have such hateful feelings, but she couldn't help it.

What Toby had done to her ten years ago was bad enough, and now he'd made it a thousand times worse. This would haunt her for the rest of her life, she was sure of it. Even if her faith gave her the strength to forgive him someday, she'd never be able to forget the attack.

She sighed, wondering how she would handle the future. She had no intention of hiding away at home in fear, wasting what little precious time she had left before leaving on the train to Boston. Then she thought about Dyer and his pain. A barrage of added worry and doubt crashed down on her.

What had happened to her perfect world, her perfect plans? Perhaps she'd been immature and foolish all these years to idealize her life into one neat, little package. Looking back on her childhood, and the trials and hardships her family had been through at different times, she wondered what made her think she would escape life's troubles. No one was exempt from some adversity in life, not even her.

Back in her room she slipped into a soft, loose-fitting cotton blouse and skirt. She brushed her hair, securing it behind each ear with hair combs. When she went into the kitchen to help with breakfast, Mama was stirring the gravy and turned to greet her with a light kiss on the cheek.

"How do you feel, sweetheart?" Her mother examined her face, grimacing and shaking her head. "Your mouth looks tender. Do you think you can eat breakfast?"

"I think so." Kristina poured a cup of coffee, added milk to cool it, and stirred in a spoonful of sugar. She peeked in the oven and inhaled a deep sniff. "The biscuits smell heavenly this morning."

"Good. I'm glad you have an appetite. They'll be done in about five minutes."

The table was already set. Grandmother appeared a stern look on her face. "You let me take care of helping your mother, my dear girl."

"Thank you. But I want to help." To keep her mind off her attack, she spooned homemade blackberry jam into a small serving bowl and placed it near Papa's plate. She put the salt, pepper, and butter on the table.

When Mama called the family to the table, the stormy look on Papa's face was a sure sign that he was upset. "I don't know what has become of that Gallager family. They've become—" Papa looked around the table at each of the children and appeared to reconsider his words. "They've become slovenly, to put it kindly. The entire property, including the house, is a rundown mess, and the yard is scattered with trash, which I could smell long before I got there; it was worse than a pigpen. And the old man—Paw Gallagher is all I've ever heard him called—was staggering drunk. When I asked if Toby was there he nearly ran me off."

Mama's eyes grew wide and curious. "I wonder why. They seemed like decent, friendly folks when they moved in. Remember how helpful they were? They loaned you the stove and the boys brought a pile of fire wood."

"I remember very well. They even brought a loaf of fresh-baked bread and a pot of beef stew for our dinner. It was downright tasty. I don't know about the woman's cooking, but the family sure has turned sour."

Kristina smiled. "I remember when Mrs. Gallager cleaned up the stinky mess Dyer made here in this kitchen. That was awful. But she just laughed and took over the job like nothing bothered her."

Clearly feeling well, Dyer groaned and plugged his ears. "Please don't tell that story again."

Papa laughed. "I won't son. The breakfast table isn't the time or place for that. You can unplug your ears and eat your meal."

Now that the younger children were settled with plates of food, Mama sat down to eat. "I don't recall ever seeing them at church. Maybe they go to one of the new churches in town."

"It's not likely," Papa said. "They don't look or act like a family of believers, and they're sure not sociable these days."

Mama looked puzzled. "As I recall they didn't show up for the housewarming when your house was rebuilt."

"No, they didn't." Papa wiped his biscuit around his plate several times, sopping up the gravy then put it in his mouth, but his thoughtful expression was a sure sign he had more to say. "I don't know what can be done about Toby. His father and mother claimed they haven't seen him for two days."

Edward Lee leaned forward, nudging Papa's free hand, late as usual with his questions. "They didn't help you after the tornado blew your house down, Papa?" Edward Lee waited for an answer, his legs dangling several inches above the floor, swinging back and forth causing his body to bounce.

The anger on her father's face softened. He looked around the table and answered in a gentle tone. "No, son, they didn't. But you know what?"

All eyes were on Papa now. Eddie answered. "What?"

"The church family did a wonderful job rebuilding and furnishing this house. I was real lucky getting blessed by so much kindness and brotherly love." Papa stopped and looked at Mama, his smile filled with affection. "Your mother was the best blessing of all."

"Why, thank you, dear. I've been equally blessed." Mama reached over and squeezed Papa's hand. "Now, we need to get done with breakfast so I can take Kristina to the doctor."

Mama's comment brought a flurry of questions from Kristina's younger brothers, but Mama just smiled. "Your sister had an accident. We're going to have the doctor check her over and get some medicine for the injuries."

"How'd you have an accident, Kristina?" It was Edward Lee again, always full of curiosity. He didn't just want to know why, he wanted all the details: where, how, when.

Before Kristina could come up with an answer Mama interrupted. "Never you mind, Eddy. All that matters is that your sister is going to be fine."

That ended the questions. Breakfast was finished. Children were excused and running in every direction. Kristina rose and helped clear the table, and Mama and Grandmother did the dishes in record time. While Mama changed Gracie May and got her ready to go, Papa hooked up the horse and buggy and brought it to the front door.

The ride into town was uncomfortable, each bump in the road causing the pain to intensify. Kristina had no idea how much she hurt until the buggy rolled across the washboard area. The continuous jostling almost brought her to tears, but she clenched her jaw and bore the pain.

Some of Doctor Rhodes's questions as he examined Kristina were embarrassing, but he assured her everything was strictly confidential. She answered honestly. Several times she flinched when he touched her, and she let out a jagged sigh when he finished. It was the first time she'd ever been examined, and her stomach churned.

"Well, young lady, this has been quite a painful summer for you. You're lucky once again that none of the wounds is serious, and you don't need any stitches. Nor do you have any broken bones. But you're going to be very sore for several days, so take it easy. Clean the open wounds daily with warm water and soap." He looked at Mama. "Leoma, those puncture wounds on her back can be cleaned the same way." He handed Mama a jar of medicine. "Put this salve and clean bandages on them each morning for three or four days. They should heal pretty quickly."

"Thank you, Doctor," Mama said as she shook Doctor Rhodes' hand.

He patted Kristina's shoulder, and led her and Mama to the front door. "You ladies take care. Come back if you have any questions."

Kristina nodded and offered a painful smile.

The morning was still young, and she welcomed the fresh air when she stepped out the door. Dreading the ride home, she paused on the walkway in front of the doctor's office. Across the street was the hotel and restaurant where Pilan' worked, and she wondered if he was on duty this morning. She considered asking Mama Leoma if they could go over for a cup of coffee. Sure she was an unsightly mess, however, she realized she didn't want to be seen in public with her bruised and scraped face and arms, and especially not by Pilan'. And Mama would probably want to get back home before Gracie May fussed to be nursed. It was best she get into the buggy and go home.

Unable to sleep a moment longer Pilan' tossed from one side to the other staring into the pale morning light in his fifth floor hotel room. Throughout the night he'd thought about Toby Gallager's message yesterday. The more he thought about the events that followed, the more it bothered him. Something didn't add up. It wasn't that Kristina didn't feel well and needed to stay home that he found disturbing, not at all. It was something in the tone of Toby's voice, his boastfulness, and later finding him covered in blood and hiding in that shack. It was hard to trust a word that came out of the brute's mouth.

True, Toby had been a friend and neighbor of the Soderlunds for many years, so it wasn't completely unlikely that Kristina might have asked him to deliver the message as a favor. But he found it hard to believe she would depend on such an unsavory troublemaker for the task.

Pilan' had never been so frustrated with himself. He should have followed his instincts yesterday, and gone to the creek. A persistent foreboding in his gut told him he should have gone to check on Kristina, but he hardly knew her, and she wasn't his responsibility. Maybe he was over reacting and worrying over nothing. Besides that, he'd decided long ago that getting involved with a woman would only hinder his travel plans, and if he was going to explore the country and accomplish his goals, he'd best stop fretting over a young woman he'd only met a short time ago.

Rising from the bed in one swift move, he walked over to the window and lifted the shade, allowing the pale morning light to filter into the room. Instead of going down the hallway to the plumbed bathroom, he splashed cold water from the ceramic wash basin on his face and hair and dried. Ready for a cup of coffee, he bound down the stairs. Perhaps it was time to give Potts his notice and move on.

Between serving the breakfast customers, and listening to all the reasons Potts insisted he couldn't do without Pilan', he finished a second mug of coffee. He probably should have waited until the end of the day to tell Potts he was ready to leave. Potts knew when he hired Pilan' it was temporary, maybe a month or less. He'd already been there three weeks. To satisfy Potts, he agreed to work another week, two if necessary. That would give his boss time to hire a new waiter. It would be hard to leave old Potts; he was a good man. Pilan' got along well him and the other workers, but he was itching to travel on to new destinations. There were new vistas awaiting him, and he was eager to see them all.

Shouldering a large tray, Pilan' crossed the dining room, delivering breakfast to two tables near the window overlooking the sidewalk. He placed the plate of biscuits and gravy, the last item on the tray, in front of a rotund, cigar-smoking gentleman.

"May I get you anything else?" He waited while the man tucked the white damask napkin into the neck of his starched, pressed, white shirt, struggling to get the napkin between the collar and the rolls of fat that formed multiple chins.

Without answering the customer shoveled a large bite of food into his mouth and grunted, his head moving from side to side. What was it about biscuits and gravy that made people in this town stuff themselves on the gooey mess? He'd tried them once and agreed, Potts did indeed make tasty biscuits and gravy, but Pilan' had nothing to compare them with, so he couldn't honestly say they were the best, and they weren't something he cared to eat again. Perhaps it was an acquired taste. It certainly wasn't like the small, healthy breakfasts of a soft-cooked egg and lightly-buttered crumpets, or fruit and cream-filled crepes that he was accustomed to. The memories made him crave his mother's and grandmother's fine French cuisine.

Movement across the street caught his attention. Glancing through the large window of the restaurant, he saw two women come out the door of Doctor Rhodes's office. He immediately recognized Kristina and her mother.

Without thinking twice he headed for the door. "Hey, Jake, I'll be right back. I'm going to step outside for one minute."

Jake, serving a table nearby, acknowledged with a smile and a nod.

Pilan' hurried through the double glass doors and waved to get Kristina's attention. Dashing across the street in front of the oncoming streetcar, he stopped short when he saw the abrasions and bruises on Kristina's face and arms. "What happened to you?"

Kristina turned her face away, one hand hiding her mouth. He stepped closer, but he hesitated to touch her, lest he might hurt her further. When she didn't answer, he lightly touched her forearm where there were no marks. This was far worse than her injuries caused by her buggy accident, and he wondered if she'd been beaten. Concerned, he waited. At last she looked at him and shook her head.

He turned to the older woman. "Forgive my bad manners, Mrs. Soderlund. Good morning." He held out his hand. "It's a pleasure to see you again."

Kristina's mother seemed to scrutinize him for several seconds before accepting his hand. "Good morning."

Pilan' took her hand and lifted it to his lips, brushing the back of it with a polite kiss. "I haven't known your daughter long, but I'm quite fond of her. I'm sorry for what ever has happened to her."

Turning his gaze back to Kristina's face, he smiled hoping she would share how she had obtained the injuries. Her lips were black and blue and her skin was pale, as if she'd been sick. A fresh bandage covered her right cheekbone. But what startled him most was the anger in her eyes. He wondered if it was directed at him for not showing up yesterday. His mind went back to Toby and the shack. Suddenly he realized why he hadn't slept; he'd been right to suspect Toby.

"Did Toby do this to you?" He focused on her eyes, knowing they would tell the truth even before she answered.

She nodded, her eyes suddenly glazed. "He lied to you and he came in your place. And—"

"He's going to pay for this." Pilan''s hands curled into tight fists at his side. He was rarely angry, and his reaction shocked him, but right now he was ready to explode. "I shouldn't have listened to him. I'm sorry. If I had come in spite of his lies, I might have been able to prevent this from happening to you."

His voice shook, and the anger burned like molten lava crawling up in his throat. He took a deep breath sorry for Kristina's pain and the anguish she must be feeling. "I'm so sorry I wasn't there to stop him."

The first hint of a smile touched Kristina's lips, though he could tell by her sudden frown, the smile was painful. "You don't have to be sorry, Pilan'. It wasn't your fault. She perked up a little more, amusement replacing the anger in her eyes. My dog, Brownie, came to my rescue.

I'm pretty sure Toby is in much worse condition than I am. The bully actually ran away like a coward."

"He didn't go far."

"How do you know?"

"I went out for a walk with my camera later in the afternoon, and I found Toby hiding in an old shack. I took two pictures of him before he realized what I was doing. He was raging mad, but I think he was too weak to do anything. I came back into town and told the sheriff what I'd seen, and I told him where to find Toby."

Kristina's swollen eyes widened and glazed over.

Mrs. Soderlund had stood back cradling her infant, listening until now. "Are you the young man everyone is disrespectfully calling the half-breed?"

"I am, although I'd never heard that term used with such disapproval until I came to America. It's true that I'm from two different races. None-the-less, I'm honest, and I don't like being scorned and blamed for things I didn't do."

Pilan' realized he'd been away from his job for several minutes. He needed to return to work, but he had a sudden thought. He looked at Kristina. "I must go back to work, but I have an idea that might help put Toby behind bars. Would you mind if I took some pictures of your injuries with my camera? Along with the ones I've already taken, perhaps they'd convince the sheriff of Toby's crimes."

Mrs. Soderlund's eyebrows squeezed together, her eyes curious. "You own a camera that makes photographs?"

"A snapshot camera, yes. Of course the pictures have to be sent away for processing, and that takes some time."

Kristina's face brightened. "I'm willing. Can we do that, Mama?"

"It would only take a few minutes, if you don't mind coming to the restaurant kitchen. I keep the camera with me during the day, in case a good picture opportunity arises. I can't think of a better way to put it to use today."

Both women nodded in unison. Mrs. Soderlund stepped forward. "I suppose it would be good if we had photographs to give to the doctor and the sheriff for the records."

He led the way across the street, making sure the women crossed safely, and held open the door of the restaurant. Crossing the dining room, he took them into the kitchen.

Kristina was arranging large slices of ham on a serving platter for dinner when Dyer cried out from the yard. His anguished scream was unlike anything she had ever heard. It was a howl of sorrow mixed with anger and grief. She dropped the platter on the table with a hard clunk, and her mother stopped mashing the potatoes. They both ran out the back door. Kristina's heart pounded as she flew down the porch steps, expecting to see Dyer doubled over in pain from another headache. Instead, he staggered toward them, Brownie in his arms.

"He's dead, Mama. Someone killed him." Tears and sweat blotched Dyer's face.

"Oh, sweetheart." Mama wrapped her arms around Dyer's shoulders. "He was getting old; he probably just died."

Kristina buried her face into her pet's fur, her anguished cries freely gushing.

Dyer wailed. "No, Mama, his neck is broken. I found him under Kristina's window."

Papa ran from the barn and lifted Brownie from Dyer's arms. It was the first time Kristina had seen her father cry uncontrollably. His tears dripped off his chin. His voice choked with fury, he wailed. "What evil person would do such a thing?"

Kristina froze, chills coursing through her body, and she began to shake. "Toby! Toby did this!"

Mama cleared her throat and wiped the tears from her face with her apron. She turned to father. "Welby, dear, while we were in town this morning we talked with that handsome young man Kristina introduced us to at church. He's a very nice fellow, and he has one of those photo cameras. I let him take some pictures of Kristina's injuries. I think—"

"You talked to that stranger after I told Kristina to stay away from him? You weren't thinking, Leoma. How could you allow a man you know nothing about to take pictures of our daughter?" Kristina had never heard her father talk to Mama that way, and she jumped directly in front of him, hands on her hips her nose nearly touching his.

"He's no stranger, Papa! He's my friend, and he's a good person. He also found where Toby hid out after he did this to me." She threw up a hand and pointed to her face. "Before Toby knew what happened, Pilan' took pictures of him. He was covered with blood from the wounds from Brownie. We should send for him and have him take a picture of Brownie today, just the way Dyer found him."

"I'll not have that half—"

"Don't call him a half-breed! He's an honest and decent man—and I like him."

Her father stepped back, shock in his eyes, his mouth gaping open. She'd never spoken to him like that, and her own harsh tone surprised her. But she couldn't stand by and allow her own father to degrade someone he didn't even know, someone she cared about.

Until this moment, she hadn't realized just how much she cared about Pilan'.

Mama stepped to Papa's side and laid a hand on his shoulder. When she spoke, her voice was quiet but firm. "I agree, Welby. Those pictures might help stop that boy from hurting someone else."

"I don't see how a picture can do any good."

Still nose-to-nose with Papa Kristina shouted. "My word and the pictures of my injuries prove everything. A picture of Brownie would show what a deranged, evil, no-good—"

Unable to go on Kristina began so sob.

Mama spoke up again. "Doctor Rhodes knows Toby did this to our daughter. It's in her file now. The pictures will be added proof."

Kristina stepped aside. Her father threw up his hands as if surrendering. After a long pause, he agreed, although, reluctantly. He plunged his hands into the pockets of his overalls and paced in a small circle. "All right. If you think it's a good idea I'll go along with it." Papa was calmer now, new moisture filling his eyes as he cradled Brownie against his chest.

Chapter 14

"SHE'S HERE! AUNTIE IS here," Kristina said jumping up from her chair. She laughed, amazed to see her grandmother run out the front door like a young girl to greet Aunt Myrtle. She'd never seen Grandmother Fisk move that fast. It had been a long time since the two sisters had seen each other, so she understood the excitement they must feel. The rest of the family right behind her, Kristina rushed out the door on her grandmother's heels.

Great-aunt Myrtle, her petite body perched in all its grandeur upon the driver seat, was a sight to behold. Her wide-brimmed hat with piles of black netting, streaming ribbons, and big pink flowers, sat a bit helter-skelter, failing to keep her graying hair in order. Unruly strands fell around her ears and neck, and wisps of hair brushed her forehead. With the spryness and bounce of a twenty-year-old, she stepped down from the vehicle.

Grandmother and Aunt Myrtle greeted each other with a long hug. "Why I declare, Myrtle," Grandmother said, "this is some motorcar you have here. Aren't you afraid you'll kill yourself driving this all over the country?"

"Lordy sakes no, Lillian." Auntie brushed a hand through the air as if shooing away a fly. "This fine automobile is a whole bunch safer than a horse and buggy."

"Oh, I can't imagine that." Head shaking, hands fluttering in the air as if frightened out of her skin, Grandmother stepped aside, and let the rest of the family greet her sister while she chattered on. "Kristina says you gave her a ride in this thing, and now she thinks you're going to teach her to drive it. Please tell me that isn't so."

"I did promise her that very thing. I must keep my word, unless she's changed her mind, of course." Aunt Myrtle minced no words. "You still want to drive my motorcar, do you not, Kristina?"

"Not without my permission," Papa said above all the ruckus.

"Oh, Welby, don't be a spoilsport. Your daughter is eighteen. She's old enough to drive this little motorcar." Auntie whacked the front fender with authority. "I'll even teach you to drive it if you're not too scared."

Papa's chin jutted forward and his chest puffed out. "If you can drive that thing I sure can."

Mama Leoma whistled with two fingers between her teeth. Every one spun around, looking as surprised as Kristina. "Nobody is going anywhere until after we've had our dinner," Mama shouted. She nudged Papa toward the automobile. "You get Myrtle's bags and carry them indoors then wash up."

At last, Kristina had a chance to greet Aunt Myrtle. When she approached, Auntie clasped her hands on Kristina's shoulders, a frown darkened her face. "My goodness child, what in heaven's name happened to you?"

Kristina touched her face, the large scrape not quite healed, mouth still tender. The bruises had turned to a greenish color. Before she could explain Dyer spoke up. "Toby Gallager attacked her, but she and Brownie got the best of him."

Auntie's mouth dropped open, her eyes wide. "Did you do something about this, Welby? Surely that boy didn't get away with this without being punished. Get me your shotgun, and tell me where he lives! I'll take care of him once and for all."

"You're not going to shoot anyone, Myrtle. I've talked to the sheriff and Toby's parents, although I'm not sure it did much good. They claimed they hadn't seen him for days. But we're not done with him." Papa picked up Auntie's tapestry bags and hauled them into the house.

"It'll be all right, Auntie," Kristina said.

"Something like this is never all right. A man should never be allowed to manhandle a woman." Auntie pulled her close and hugged her then whispered. "He didn't . . . you know?"

Kristina understood Auntie's half-question and shook her head. "He didn't have a chance. Brownie came to my rescue. He tore into Toby's shoulder like it was raw steak, and he didn't let up till the bully ran away."

"Good for Brownie." Auntie gazed around the yard. "Where is he, by the way?"

Before Kristina choked out the words in jagged syllables, tears began to fall. "He's dead. Dyer found him the next morning beneath my bedroom window, with his neck broken. I'm sure Toby did it."

THE NEXT DAY WAS perfect for driving lessons. The sky was cloudless, the wind calm, the air warm. Since Kristina had been promised first, Auntie rushed her out the door and into the motorcar as soon as breakfast dishes were done. "Get right on up there in the driver's seat," Auntie Myrtle said.

Kristina was still sad about losing Brownie, but the excitement of driving Aunt Myrtle's car lifted her spirits. Although a bit erratic, it took her no time at all to follow Aunt Myrtle's instructions. The steering wheel was warm in her grip as she turned around in a big, haphazard circle and zigzagged down the lane.

"There's no need to over steer, dearest. You'll get the feel of it."

Auntie was right. It wasn't that difficult, and by the time they turned onto the road into town, she was driving without a single jerk. Her steering was straight and steady. The morning sunshine was bright, the sky clear and blue. Feeling free as the birds, she loved the wind on her face, the exhilaration of speed. "Can I go faster?"

Aunt Myrtle smiled and shook her head. "This is fast enough for now."

She sped along at fifteen miles-per-hour, enjoying the chugging noises of the powerful motor. By the time she steered the vehicle into town, Kristina suddenly realized she didn't know how to stop the motorcar. What if a horse and buggy crossed in front of her or a person stepped out in her path? Her insides quaked. Gripping the steering wheel tightly, her knuckles turned white.

Aunt Myrtle seemed to know exactly what was going through her mind. She was quick with her instructions and pointed up ahead. "Now, just like I showed you earlier, ease to a stop in front of that hotel."

Kristina steered the automobile up to the curb and parked in front of the hotel and restaurant where Pilan' worked. After several deep breaths, she relaxed against the back of the seat. Until now, she hadn't realized how tense she'd been the entire time. It took her several seconds to unwind and collect her wits. She'd just driven a motorcar all the way from home into town in just a few minutes. It was amazing.

"Well, well, mademoiselle. What have we here?" Pilan' stepped through the restaurant entrance and appeared on the sidewalk, a broad smile on his face that could steal any heart.

"Auntie is teaching me to drive her motorcar. Isn't it grand?"

In three long strides Pilan' reached the driver side of the automobile and bowed. "It is indeed. May I assist you ladies down and treat you to a cup of coffee, or perhaps iced tea?"

"You may, young man," Auntie said.

Kristina accepted Pilan''s hand, appreciating his good manners. When her feet were firmly on the ground, one of his hands remained on her waist, the slightest bit of pressure heightening her awareness of his closeness. Her hand remained in his grip a few moments longer than necessary, not that she minded. After he assisted Auntie down, Kristina introduced them. He lifted Aunt Myrtle's gloved hand and kissed it. "It's a pleasure to meet you, ma'am."

Pilan' held open the entry door and welcomed them to the restaurant. He seated them at a table near the window and took their orders. In a flash, he returned with two cups of coffee and placed them on the table. Though the restaurant wasn't busy, Kristina understood Pilan' had work to do. He excused himself, promising to return in a few minutes.

Aunt Myrtle's eyes followed Pilan' across the room until he disappeared into the kitchen. "So, I assume this is the handsome, young man I've heard so much about. I hoped I might get a glimpse of him today."

Kristina prayed her face wasn't as flushed as it felt. She didn't understand why she would blush; she wasn't embarrassed. In fact she was quite proud to consider Pilan' her friend. "Is that why you instructed me where to park? You knew he worked here?"

Aunt Myrtle's grin was a solid admission she'd been found out. No doubt Mama had told her about their earlier visit to the restaurant. Auntie lifted her cup and took a dainty sip of coffee. Sensing her great-aunt had some advice, Kristina was silent, wondering if she wanted to hear it. After all, Auntie was much older, goodness, at least sixty or more. What could she possibly understand about young folks today? Her great-aunt had become an important part of the family, and she was, without a doubt, her favorite relative, yet Kristina braced herself for whatever Auntie was working up to.

"Tell me more about that young man," Aunt Myrtle finally said.

Kristina swallowed. *That's it? No warnings, no archaic words of wisdom?* Here was her chance to disclose her feelings, and to tell the good things she knew about Pilan' to someone who was interested and would listen. "To begin with, he's been unfairly judged by the people in this town because of his looks. If people would get to know him they'd see what an amazing man he is. He's well educated and comes from a wealthy family. But that's beside the point."

"If he's wealthy why is he waiting tables in a hotel restaurant?"

Kristina thought about that. "I don't know. But, I do know he's honest and good. And he's talented. He plays the violin and takes photographs with one of those new snapshot cameras. Most of all, he's a gentleman."

"Those are all good things." Auntie looked suitably impressed. She glanced around and took another drink of coffee. "Does he love God?"

"I'm quite sure he does." Kristina hadn't discussed that point with him, but he'd come to church, and his character certainly indicated that he lived his life according to godly standards.

"You care about him, don't you?" Auntie reached across the table and covered Kristina's hand with her own.

"I do. We haven't had a chance to get very well acquainted, but I'd like to know him better. I hate that my time before going to Boston is getting so short." She dreaded the thought of leaving, not only because of Dyer, but also because of Pilan'. It seemed Dyer was doing much better since Doctor Rhodes had given him the tincture, but she still worried about him. And Pilan'—she was so confused. How could she go away when they'd just met? They had so much in common. Of course, he talked about his travels as if he could pack up and leave any day, so maybe she didn't matter all that much to him. Still, she'd like more time to find out.

Auntie's eyes never left Kristina's face.

Kristina folded her hands in her lap, unsure what more she could say to enlighten her wise, old Auntie, but she went on. "He told me Oklahoma City is just a temporary stopping place during his travels across the country. I don't know if he feels the same as I, or if he'll just up and leave one day. I wish I knew what to expect."

"Well, dearest, there's only one way to find out. I know your father would wring my neck if he heard me tell you this, but I sense something special brewing between you two. Let that fellow know you're interested. Tell him. Don't just go away and live to regret it because you didn't find out how he feels."

Auntie winked and smiled her demeanor surprisingly feisty, as she tucked a strand of escaped hair behind her ear and adjusted her lace-trimmed hat.

This wasn't at all what Kristina expected from a woman of Aunt Myrtle's advanced years. She turned her head away for a moment, an attempt to hide her surprise smirk. Turning back, she sipped her coffee, composing her thoughts before answering. "I don't know, Auntie. I'll have to think about that."

"Well, my dear girl, I wouldn't waste too much time thinking about it."

Pilan' returned to the dining room, delivering a sandwich and mug of coffee to a gentleman at a nearby table. Her heart hammered. *Oh please, Auntie, don't say another word about this until he returns to the kitchen.* His back to her as he served the man, Kristina gazed at his long, lean body. His posture was flawless, as if he'd been to finishing school for young men. Was there such a thing? She didn't think so. He was definitely far more sophisticated than she would ever be, and it seemed unlikely he would be interested in a common farm girl like her. Yet, as she recalled the afternoons when he played his violin and she sang, they had seemed to be on equal ground, in perfect spiritual harmony. How could she ignore the deep connection they'd made with their music? It would be impossible to forget.

When Pilan' had finished serving the gentleman he came to their table. "Would you ladies like more coffee?"

"No, thank you," Auntie said a sparkle in her eyes.

Kristina shook her head and dabbed her lips with a napkin. "No, thank you."

Pilan' looked expectant, smiling. "Then, may I ask a favor?"

Kristina couldn't imagine what he might ask of her, but it couldn't possibly be bad. She was willing to grant what ever it was he requested. "Yes, of course."

"I've never seen such a fine automobile. I understand the Cadillac was named for a French explorer named Cadillac who found his way to Detroit. I would love to take some photographs. May I?"

It was fine with Kristina, but she looked at Aunt Myrtle for approval.

"Oh, yes. You certainly may." Auntie was all aflutter, wearing her best smile. "You're absolutely right about Mr. Cadillac, young man. It would be a privilege to be photographed with my motorcar."

Kristina chuckled to herself. Pilan' hadn't said anything about taking a picture of her great-aunt—only the motorcar—but Auntie, putting on quite the captivating deportment, was ready to have her picture taken. Moments later, camera in hand, Pilan' assisted Auntie from her chair, and led them outdoors.

After snapping a picture of the automobile, he requested another photograph which included Kristina and her aunt, and he helped them into the vehicle. Auntie, of course, was primping and putting on her most alluring pose, her smile almost giddy. It was fascinating to see the way Pilan' handled the camera with such ease and professionalism. He took several pictures from different angles including one from Kristina's side, and another from Auntie's side, each time smiling and clearly pleased, exclaiming his praises. "Wonderful. Ah, yes, beautiful. Magnificent! I think it's wonderful to see a lady driving."

Back at the driver's side, Pilan' leaned close to Kristina and placed a hand on the back of the seat. "I have another request."

"You'd like a ride?" She wasn't so sure about driving with him in the back seat.

"Not today, thank you. I must get back to work." He pulled a gold pocket-watch from his trousers pocket and looked at it. "But, I would like to invite you out for an evening. Would you allow me to pick you up at your home one day soon? We could dine out and perhaps take a stroll around town? I don't have a fine automobile like this, but my carriage is quite comfortable."

Without giving it a second's thought she answered, moderating her voice to cover the exuberance that wanted to escape. Doing her best to sound lady-like rather than an anxious teen-aged girl, she answered. "Yes. I would enjoy that."

"Will tomorrow evening be suitable? About five o'clock? It's my night off."

"Five o'clock tomorrow would be fine."

"Very well then, I look forward to spending time with you." Pilan''s smile was one of victory, satisfaction, as if he'd deliberated long and hard over asking her out and he'd gotten the answer he wanted.

She was still catching her breath as Pilan' strode back inside, pausing in the doorway long enough to deliver a broad smile and a wave.

It was wonderful the way things worked out. She didn't have to say anything to Pilan' about her interest in him as Auntie had suggested. And she didn't wonder any more about his intentions. They were clear. Giddier than she'd ever been, she could hardly wait to get home. She had to plan what she would wear for her first official evening out with a gentleman.

And Auntie Myrtle grinned all the way home.

Chapter 15

"I wish I had a new dress for tomorrow night." Kristina took one last look at her reflection in the mirror and sighed. "But I suppose a new dress won't do a thing to hide my ugly scrapes and bruises."

"Now, now, sweetheart." Her mother gave her a quick hug and looked into her eyes. "That young man isn't concerned with a few minor marks on your skin, any more than you are of his. I'm sure you'll have a lovely evening with him no matter what you wear."

"That's right." Glenda looked through Kristina's dresses. She held up a blue one with a square neckline and long sleeves.

Kristina shook her head. "It's too warm for that heavy fabric and those sleeves. I'd roast."

"I have an idea." Glenda touched a finger to her lips as she looked Kristina over, as if measuring her for size. Her Boston accent tumbled out with her enthusiasm, her r's sounding more like ah's. "Just last week I bought a new dress at Minnie's Lady's Wear, and I haven't worn it yet. I bet it would fit you. It is pale green with a scooped neckline, trimmed with white lace, and it has short sleeves. I just know it would look lovely with your dark hair and eyes."

She couldn't believe Glenda would loan her a brand new dress before she had worn it. If it came from Minnie's, the dress had to be beautiful. Minnie had excellent taste in buying, and carried only the finest and prettiest clothing.

"Are you sure you want me to wear it? I might ruin it."

"Oh, I wouldn't worry one little bit about that. Why don't I go home and fetch it so you can try it on?"

"What do you think, Mama?"

"I think it's very generous of Glenda. It's entirely up to you two."

Kristina looked at Glenda. "All right, if you're sure about loaning it to me."

It wasn't an hour later when Glenda returned with the dress wrapped in a large white table cloth. She carefully unfolded the cloth to reveal the prettiest silk dress Kristina had ever seen. "It's beautiful."

"Try it on." Glenda seemed as excited about Kristina's date as she herself.

Kristina slipped the dress over her head, and let the sheer fabric slide over her under garments and into place. Mama buttoned the back and stood aside with Glenda. Kristina watched their admiring glances in the mirror. Her own reflection left her nearly breathless with awe. The fit was exquisite, the style flattering, emphasizing her shapeliness more than any dress she owned, yet it was still modest.

"You look beautiful," Mama said admiration in her eyes.

"It's perfect." Glenda's jubilation gushed out.

Grandmother and Auntie Myrtle appeared in the doorway and spoke in unison, their voices raised. "Oh, my."

"It's for my date with Pilan'." Kristina turned full circle and addressed the older women. "What do you think?"

Great-aunt Myrtle stepped into the room. "When that young man sees you tomorrow evening you'll steal his heart for sure."

Tomorrow. It was so soon. Suddenly, the things Toby had done came to mind and overshadowed her joy. Her feelings for Pilan' were strong, but she hadn't considered what would happen if the relationship became serious. She was damaged, not good enough for a fine gentleman like Pilan'. What if—

"Kristina. Hello." Mama dragged out the word and waved her hand in front of Kristina's face. "Where are you?"

She blinked, gathered her wits about her, and returned her gaze to her reflection in the mirror. What had she been thinking, going on in her mind about all the what-ifs, and worrying over the past. One date with Pilan' didn't mean she was committing to a long-term relationship. She still had an education to complete, a major goal to fulfill. Her past was irrelevant right now, but the recent assault by Toby was still fresh on her mind, and her emotions were raw.

She supposed she was unlike most of the girls her age. Of those she knew several of them were already married, some already expecting a baby. Even Doris had been courted by two fellows, and she'd probably be married within a year, now that she was seeing Harland.

"I'm here. I was just lost in my thoughts about tomorrow night."

"Well, don't worry, everything will be fine." Mama gave her a reassuring hug while Glenda, Grandmother, and Auntie stood nearby, all smiles, heads bobbing in agreement. "Just remember your etiquette and be your sweet self."

Friday morning the sun woke her early. In no hurry to get out of bed, she covered her head for a moment, hoping to grab one more minute of sleep. Tossing thoughts back and forth all night between Toby and her date with Pilan', she hadn't slept well. A list of must-dos presented itself repeatedly: wash hair, manicure fingernails, clip toenails, and borrow a necklace from Mama or Glenda. What else? Should she wear her hair pinned up in curls, or let it hang down over her shoulders? Would her good church shoes look all right with Glenda's dress?

The smell of coffee interrupted her wandering mind as she came wider awake. Excited about the evening with Pilan', she threw back the sheet and sat up. Feeling as if she could dance on air, she rose from the bed and hurried to the closet. She peeked in and reached for the dress Glenda had loaned her, making sure it wasn't just a dream. Posing in front of the cheval mirror, she held the dress against her, hoping Pilan' would like it. With one hand, she pulled up her hair then let it down to flow over her shoulders. She'd definitely wear it down.

A tap on the door sent her scurrying to the closet to hang up the dress before throwing on her robe.

"It's just me." Mama stuck her head into the room. She was holding an envelope. "Dyer found this stuck on the back door when he went out to gather eggs."

Puzzled, Kristina took the stained and wrinkled envelope, and her mother left the room. It looked as if it had gone through a battle and traveled the world. She couldn't imagine what it contained or who had left it—then she saw her name printed in poor lettering.

Only one person called her Krissy.

She wanted to wad the envelope into a ball and throw it in the trash. Toby was more ignorant than a dead warthog. Why would he write anything to her after what he'd done? Reluctantly, she pulled the single piece of scrap paper from the unsealed envelope. The uneven lines were printed in pencil, the spelling poor.

> *Deer Krissy,*
>
> *I'm sory if I hert you. I don't meen to hert you. I like you and I know you like me. You will all ways be my girl. I won't never hert you again I promise. I'm watching over you every day.*
>
> *Toby.*

Unbelievable. She'd thought for sure after he'd been attacked by Brownie she was rid of him for good. Shaking and frustrated, she rushed into the kitchen and thrust the letter into her mother's hands. "You won't believe this, Mama. I don't know what to think."

Her mother read the note and handed it back to Kristina. "Well, this is proof of Toby's guilt in his own writing. I think you should show it to Doctor Rhodes then give it to the sheriff."

"But do you think I should still go with Pilan' this evening? There's no telling what Toby might do. I think he's plum crazy."

Clearly, he was still up to his malicious mischief. He could be watching her without anyone knowing. After all, he'd managed to put that note on their door without being seen or heard. And for sure he hadn't given up his claim on her. She shuddered, more frightened than ever.

After Papa said the blessing over breakfast, Kristina handed the note to him and asked him to read it. She agreed with Mama about showing it to the doctor and sheriff, but she also wanted Papa's opinion and advice.

"I think the boy is dangerous." Her father tucked the note into his pocket. "I'm going to go into town to have a talk with the sheriff after I finish the morning chores. He needs to see this."

"Please don't give it to that deputy that came out here. Deputy Hank thinks Toby never does anything wrong. That man is stupid."

Dyer laughed, mocking the deputy's snort and funny face.

Mama snickered.

Kristina wondered if her father still thought Pilan' was dangerous and guilty of crimes he didn't commit. She could hardly eat, and pushed her scrambled eggs in circles on her plate. "Don't you see, Papa, it had to be Toby looking into bedroom windows and blaming it on Pilan'. And if he could kill Brownie, who knows what other terrible things he'll do?"

"Maybe now the sheriff will do something about finding Toby and punishing him," Mama said.

After buttering another biscuit her father spoke again. "I'm still concerned about you going out alone with a stranger. He may be perfectly fine, but we don't know him very well."

"I know him well enough to believe I'll be safe with him. He wants to see Toby caught and punished as much as I do." She put down her fork and pushed the plate away. "Please don't say I can't go out with him tonight. Please, Papa."

Mama shot a warning glare at Papa, one eyebrow raised. Grandmother looked as if she were going to put in her two cents, but Grandfather stopped her with his own glare and shake of his head.

No one stopped Aunt Myrtle from making her opinion clear. "That young man is an outstanding fellow. I, for one, believe there's no finer gentleman in town."

Dyer slipped in his opinion, too. "I like Pilan'."

Papa put up both hands. "All right. I can see I'm out numbered. So I won't forbid you to go out with him. But he better respect you and our family rules."

Kristina jumped up from her chair and wrapped her arms around her father's shoulders. She kissed him on top of his head. "Thank you, Papa."

Friday evening when the sun hung low above the horizon, and an evening breeze cooled the air, Pilan' stood at the Soderlund's front door, admiring the fresh coat of white paint on the porch railing and window trim. The spotless, clean windows shimmered, reflecting the golden sunset. A bench and two inviting white rocking chairs with blue cushions looked comfortable, and he imagined sitting side-by-side on the porch with Kristina and watching the sun set. He rather liked the idea even though it was different from anything he'd ever imagined doing. It was a homey, settled, older-person kind of thing, extremely different from his love for travel, adventure, and unusual challenges. His mind was certainly playing strange games since he'd met Kristina, and he didn't know what to think of it.

After he'd worked the morning shift for Potts, Pilan' had spent the remainder of the day thinking about this evening, wondering if he was doing the right thing, taking a lady out to dinner, especially one so young. It went against all his plans, and his father had warned him against getting involved with a woman in America. He clenched his fists and released them, tried to shake out his nerves. No matter what his conscience told him, his heart told him he had to spend more time with Kristina. Something was special about her, something he wanted to be part of. It didn't mean he was ready to jump in to marriage.

Pilan' straightened his shoulders, took a deep breath, and knocked on the door. When it opened, he was greeted by Mr. Soderlund. Kristina's father wore a scowl, but offered his hand and invited him in. Like the heftily-built man himself, his handshake was strong, no doubt from years of heavy farm work. The welcome was stiff, as if the man had been threatened some serious pain from a cast-iron skillet if he weren't polite.

Pilan' thanked him and stepped inside. He glanced around, not seeing Kristina anywhere. The house was small, simple, but there were scattered touches of elegance, indications of cultured female influence. Most likely his grandmother would scorn such modest living conditions, but his mother had taught him not to judge a person by the house he or she grew up in.

Though he knew little about the Soderlund's background, the home showed pride of ownership. Well maintained, it was orderly and clean. In spite of being raised in a palatial home, Pilan' found this space to be warm and inviting. And delicious aromas wafted out from the kitchen. Too bad he hadn't been invited to have dinner with this family instead of taking Kristina out.

By the time Kristina entered the front room, he was being scrutinized by three younger siblings, two grandparents, Kristina's great-aunt, and Mrs. Soderlund who was cuddling the baby. Mr. Soderlund still scowled. The older man, obviously Kristina's grandfather, studied him seriously. The women looked him over thoroughly, visually examining his clothing, hair, and who knew what else. The grandparents looked friendly enough, and they seemed to be cultured and wealthy.

He was glad to see Kristina when she entered the room. She was stunning. His jaw dropped before he gained control of his reaction. He quickly shut his mouth. Exquisite in a light green dress, she was more womanly than he'd noticed before. A tasteful pearl necklace circled her slender throat, and her shimmering, wavy hair rippled down over her shoulders. Hoping she didn't notice his shaky hands, he gave her the bouquet of pink roses he'd purchased at the new florist shop.

He considered bowing, but thought it might be too arrogant or formal. "You look beautiful."

"Thank you." A radiant smile, and a hint of face powder, camouflaged the fading injuries on her skin. He could hardly see them.

In all his adventures and exploring, he'd never seen a more beautiful sight.

WHEN KRISTINA ENTERED THE living room, she paused for a moment to still her racing heart. At first glance she thought a handsome prince had magically appeared in her plain, little farm house, and for the briefest time, she felt embarrassed by her meager surroundings. From what little she knew about Pilan"s background, her home was a mere shanty compared to the mansion he'd grown up in. She quickly scolded herself for thinking such petty thoughts. He'd probably shown an interest in her, not for where she lived, but for the person she was. Apparently he saw qualities in her that he admired. Exciting new sensations billowed up inside her unlike anything she recognized, causing her to shudder inside. This was the first time a man had called on her for a dinner engagement. Indescribable feelings of newness, adventure, and discovery bubbled from deep within.

She accepted the roses and smelled one, inhaling deeply. "Thank you. They're beautiful."

"Not nearly as beautiful as you. You look stunning."

She giggled. "We do make a stunning couple with our scrapes and bruises, don't we?"

Mama took the roses from Kristina's hands. "I'll put those in water for you."

"Thank you, Mama."

She smiled and said goodbye, barely noticing the curious stares of the children, and the grins of the adult women. As Kristina took Pilan"s arm and walked outdoors, she vaguely heard her father's reminder to be home before too late, and her mother wishing her a good evening. If only Glenda could have been there. When the door closed behind them she took a deep breath, relieved to be over that hurdle, happy to be alone at last with Pilan'.

Chapter 16

When Pilan' took her hand and assisted her into his carriage, his touch was warm, gentle, yet strong. Kristina turned to watch him climb up on his side of the carriage. She marveled at his slim, yet masculine physique. His black trousers emphasized his long legs, and the immaculately pressed white shirt fit him like an expensive tailored shirt, highlighting his well-toned chest and muscled arms. His thick, raven-black hair looked freshly cut, but covered the back of his neck. She tried to ignore the strange quivering in her stomach. How could any man be that perfect? If he had a flaw of any kind it wasn't visible. Probably beneath his fine clothes was a hidden flaw—a giant hairy mole or something. Perhaps there were inner faults that lay hidden beneath the surface—not that she was looking for faults, but she'd always been warned not to put much store in good-looks. Yet, it was awfully difficult not to.

They rode in silence for a time. With the unpredictable summer weather, one never knew when a storm would ruin a special day, but God had blessed them with a pleasant evening. A glance across the landscape revealed nothing but cloudless, deep-blue sky, and the air was still, just warm enough to keep a chill away.

Pilan' steered the carriage down the lane to the main road, keeping the horse at a slow pace. He held the reins lightly, his back straight, as if he'd spent a lifetime driving royalty around the countryside. He had a regal air about him that she hadn't noticed in men in Oklahoma City. Yet, he appeared relaxed, without an ounce of arrogance. Kristina wondered what he was thinking. Her own thoughts rambled, all the while mixed with giddy, new, emotional feelings that had her riding on air.

Suddenly, without warning she remembered Toby's note. Fear crept into her mind. He could be lurking behind the bushes somewhere along the way just waiting to do something terrible, like hurting Pilan', or attempting to snatch her away. If Toby had a weapon he could be dangerous.

Movement in the tall grass beside the road up ahead caused her to stiffen. Her heart dropped. She began to shake.

"Whoa." Pilan' pulled back on the reins, drawing the horse to a stop. He reached over and touched her hand.

Her skin grew clammy and she lowered her eyes, as if she were to look ahead her worries about Toby would be confirmed. Eyes closed tight she leaned against Pilan' for protection. He laughed. "It's nothing to be frightened of," he said. "Look up the road. Hurry or you'll miss them."

Trusting Pilan', she opened her eyes and looked. Embarrassed by her foolishness and swallowing her fear, she straightened and resumed her lady-like position. A few feet ahead a mother raccoon waddled across the road, followed by four babies.

"Oh, how cute." She'd seen raccoons before, but never a little family like that. She cooed and giggled. "It's too bad you don't have your camera."

"Yes, it is." When the raccoons had scampered across the road and into the safety of low-growing brush, Pilan' urged the horse back into a slow walk.

"I've never seen that kind of wildlife in Paris."

"But it must be beautiful there." Kristina had heard very little about France in school; it sounded pretty. She couldn't imagine traveling thousands of miles to such a place.

Pilan' smiled, as if seeing home in his mind. "Paris is a beautiful city, but you have many beautiful places in this country, too. I think God created a grand world for us to enjoy."

What a wonderful thing for Pilan' to say. She nodded, wondering if he planned to travel around the entire world. It seemed impossible. Even thinking about going to Boston was almost beyond her imagination. People who crossed the country in covered wagons and on horseback before the trains came along, had to be brave and hardy souls. Leoma and her husband, Papa and her real mother, and thousands of others right here in Oklahoma City had come halfway across the country and settled here. It still amazed her. It was going to be hard enough spending days on a slow, noisy train just to get to Massachusetts. It didn't sound like much fun, no matter what her grandfather said. Would crossing the Atlantic on a ship be any better? It sounded more interesting, for sure. She rather liked that idea, but then she'd never been on any kind of ship or boat.

Soon she and Pilan' approached Doris Langley's house. Mrs. Langley was in the yard picking roses. Doris stood nearby. *Won't they be surprised when they see us?* She hadn't had a chance to tell Doris about her dinner date. She turned to Pilan' and pointed to her friend. "That's my best friend, Doris, and her mother Anna Jo."

"I recognize your friend—the red-headed woman on the other bicycle." Pilan' shot Doris and her mother a broad smile and nodded.

Doris's jaw dropped to her chest. Mrs. Langley stared, her brows nearly becoming part of the red hair on her head. The pleasure of seeing their expressions tickled Kristina. She could just hear Doris next time they spoke. She lifted her chin, smiled, and gave a brief wave. Doris clamped her mouth shut and waved back, smiling as if she approved of Kristina's escort. Pilan' drove on at the same pace, but Kristina's heart raced far ahead. Riding into the heart of town with a very handsome young man was intoxicating, and Kristina felt very grown up.

For a moment she wondered what people would say if they saw her with the man they called the half-breed. She had no intentions of cowering or hiding her pride in being courted by such a fine man. When people got to know him better, they'd be sorry they ever looked down their snooty noses at him, or suspected him of being anything less than a perfect gentleman.

She was sure now that Toby had been blaming Pilan' for the bad things he'd done, and if she was right, he would be found out. With the help of Pilan''s pictures, he'd be caught and punished. But right now many people were still suspicious of Pilan'.

"You're awfully quiet." Pilan'"s comment pulled Kristina back into the present. "Are you all right?"

"Yes. Just letting my mind wander." She flashed Pilan' a happy smile, and vowed there would be no more thoughts of Toby to ruin the evening. She had to stop worrying. Her time with Pilan' was too special to allow anyone or anything to douse her joy.

At the intersection of Main and Broadway, Pilan' turned onto Broadway and pulled the carriage to the curb. She waited until he stepped down and came to her side of the carriage, allowing him to help her down. He held her hand long after her feet were on the sidewalk. With her hand in the crook of his arm, she entered the large establishment directly in front of them. It was a tall, attractive building with dark green awnings over the double doors and large windows.

Eating in cafes wasn't something her family did. Other than the cup of coffee she'd had at Potts', she'd never eaten any place other than home. Shaky and feeling out of place, she grasped Pilan'"s arm tighter, then feeling silly, she loosened her grip. She didn't want him to know she was nervous. Several of the tables in the dining room were occupied, and as she glanced around she didn't see any familiar faces. There were so many new people in town it was easy to feel lost in the crowd, like a stranger. *Is this how I'll feel in Boston?* She supposed it might be, and she realized she would have to get accustomed to changes and new experiences.

A dapper gentleman dressed in black slacks and a white long-sleeve shirt, guided them to a table against a wall near the back of the room, away from other customers. She sat down as gracefully as possible on the chair the waiter pulled out for her and folded her hands in her lap. *Remember your etiquette.* Etiquette at home around the kitchen table with rowdy younger siblings was surely not the same as here in this fine restaurant. But Pilan', being a cultured gentleman, immediately put her at ease with his reassuring smiles and relaxed behavior.

When Pilan' opened his menu she did the same, studying the variety of meals offered. Since she was hungry it made ordering simple. The pot roast sounded irresistible, and it turned out to be every bit as tasty as it smelled.

KRISTINA WAS EASY TO talk with. Pilan' had never enjoyed the pleasure of another woman's company as he did hers, and in a short time, it seemed as if she'd been his friend for years. They both frequented the library and appreciated books. Her love of music rivaled his own passion for it, and he'd already been blessed by her singing more than once. He wasn't sure if she liked to dance, but he hoped so.

"Do you have special plans for how you will use your musical talent?" He imagined Kristina directing the church choir, or teaching choir classes at high school.

When Kristina answered, he sensed some hesitance or sadness in her voice. "Yes. I think I've mentioned I'll leave soon for Boston to attend the school of music for two years. I'll live with my grandparents during that time."

"That's wonderful. I'm sure you'll do very well." Of that he had no doubt.

He'd told Kristina about his travels, but suddenly, he hated the idea of being so far away from her. Education was important, and he didn't want to deter her, but if she went east and he went west he may never see her again. Urgency grew within him unlike anything he'd experienced before. He fought between wanting to spend more time with her to explore his growing feelings, and sticking to his travel plans.

"I know you have to go away to school, but I wish you didn't. I'd like to get to know you better."

"I feel the same way, but soon you'll be off exploring the country."

Was that regret he heard in Kristina's voice?

There was a long silence. Why had they come together now when the timing was all wrong? He didn't want to fall in love, yet his heart beat with the possibility.

He changed the subject, asking questions about Kristina's family, and he told her about his family and his childhood. It was the first time he'd enjoyed such a full, interesting conversation with a woman. So many of the women at home were only interested in marrying into wealth and buying expensive clothes and jewelry. Their conversations were shallow. He found talking with Kristina stimulating, colorful. Her family history was quite fascinating. When Kristina talked about her brother's illness, Pilan''s heart was touched by her concern for Dyer. It showed her maturity and compassion.

Eventually the conversation returned to their goals and dreams for the future. He wanted to know more about Kristina's long-term plans.

"After college I plan to return here and open a music studio to teach voice and piano."

"You play the piano?"

She nodded modestly. "Are you going to spend your entire life exploring the world?"

He laughed. "No. Next year when I return to Paris I plan to open a dance studio."

"A dance studio?" He smiled at the shock and surprise that filled Kristina's eyes.

"Yes. For several years I've planned to open one. From the time I was two or three years old—as far back as I can remember—my grandmother lifted me into her arms and waltzed me around her ballroom. I grew up loving to dance, and I took lessons during all my school years."

"Your grandmother has a ballroom in her house?"

"Yes. It was there I realized my passion for dancing." He paused. "I love music, too, but it's dancing I want to teach." He paused, a thought forming in his mind. "Can you imagine what you and I could do by combining the talents and gifts God has given us? What a perfect combination—music and dance."

"Oh, yes." Kristina's voice was filled with enthusiasm and genuine interest. "I don't know much about dancing, but we certainly do make excellent music together."

"We do, don't we?" He held her gaze, his heart bursting with amazement.

He took a bite of his pork roast and chewed, wondering if they might have a future together. All odds were against them, the chances nearly impossible, yet his mind overflowed with ideas and possibilities, and for a moment he thought he'd been airborne. It was that same feeling as the first time he'd met Kristina by the stream, when he'd played his violin and she sang.

He finished his meal. Most of Kristina's dinner was gone, and she was no longer eating. "Would you like coffee and dessert?"

"No thank you." Her smile indicated she was quite satisfied.

He didn't want to take her home yet, so when he'd paid the bill he made another suggestion. "The evening is early. Shall we take a stroll around town?"

"I'd like that."

Taking their time, Kristina's hand tucked in the crook of his bent arm, they walked up Main Street, stopping now and then to look in store windows. He made an effort to show an interest when she admired the latest fashions in the window of a clothing shop, and he noticed she did the same when he stopped in front of a hardware store.

A few blocks up Main Street they boarded the electric streetcar, and rode it back to Broadway where his carriage was parked. The sun had set and dusk spread its golden glow over the town. As Kristina stepped down from the streetcar Pilan' offered her his hand. He liked the feel of her soft hand in his own, and continued to hold it as they walked to the carriage.

As they crossed the street, movement by his horse and carriage caught his eye. Evening shadows almost hid the person from view. A warning in his gut stopped him. Putting Kristina behind him, he held her back. "Someone is snooping around my carriage."

Kristina grabbed his arm and tightened her grip.

Suspecting who the culprit was, he called out. "Toby?"

No answer.

Pilan' approached cautiously, keeping Kristina behind him, moving to the other side of the carriage. Sure enough, Toby lurked in the shadows, his large form clear now. Pilan' stopped several feet away. He had no intention of getting into another scuffle with the man. Kristina braced herself against Pilan"s back and shoulders, her fingers gripping his upper arms.

"Good evening, Toby." Pilan' kept his voice casual, calm, hoping to dissuade the troublemaker from causing a scene. "What brings you here?"

Pilan' stepped up on the sidewalk, gaining a clear view of the man. Toby glared, meanness distorting his features. Even from several feet away in the dim light, everything about him appeared wicked and filled with wrath. Pilan' sent up a silent prayer asking God to intervene. He was apprehensive, but he didn't want Toby to think he had the upper hand.

Pilan''s greatest concern was for Kristina. Toby had already hurt her enough, and he would do whatever it took to protect her. But fighting wasn't the solution. He'd been taught that gentlemen don't fight, and he didn't want to dirty his hands on someone like Toby. The man didn't seem very smart, but surely he was wise enough to avoid a confrontation in the midst of so many people in the center of town. Several men walked by on both sides of the street, and sitting at tables just inside the windows of the restaurant were three couples.

Toby stepped closer. "I told you, half-breed, Kristina's my girl. She's—"

"I'm nobody's girl, Toby. I don't even like you. I don't want anything to do with you. If you don't leave right now I'm going to get the sheriff." Kristina could clearly speak for herself. Pilan' liked that.

Toby laughed. "You ain't going nowhere without me, Krissy."

Pilan' turned and put an arm around Kristina's waist, holding her tightly against his side. He could feel her shaking, and he was sure it was anger more than fear. Pilan' warned Toby, "You better leave like she said."

Just then, a burly, middle-aged man who could probably wrestle a bear and win stepped up to Toby. With one massive hand, the man grabbed Toby by the back of the neck. "You causing trouble here boy?"

Toby shook his head.

"Looks to me like you're bothering these fine folks. Move on now, and mind your own business."

Toby started to walk then stopped. "I ain't done with you, half-breed!"

"You'll wish you never messed with me," Pilan' said calmly. There was no point telling Toby about the pictures he was going to turn over to the sheriff when he had them developed. "You'd best stay away from Kristina and me."

The bear fighter nudged Toby then gave him another push, almost making him stumble. The man's deep voice rumbled. "Keep going, young man. Get on out of here!"

It wasn't until Toby was almost out of sight that Pilan' breathed a sigh of relief. He thanked the man, then checked the wheels on his carriage and looked over his horse and the hitch, half expecting to find something Toby had tampered with. When he found everything to be all right, he helped Kristina into her seat and drove toward her home.

Holding the reins with one hand, Pilan' reached for Kristina's hand. He didn't want the unfortunate incident with Toby to ruin the evening, and he was glad when she willingly intertwined her fingers into his. They rode in silence, sharing an occasional glance and a smile. But he couldn't help being on the lookout for trouble along the way.

LIGHT FROM HER HOUSE came in to view. The evening was coming to a close much too soon. Fearing she might not see Pilan' again before she left for Boston, Kristina dreaded saying goodnight to him. When he pulled back on the reins and brought the carriage to a stop halfway up the lane, her pulse quickened. *He must have read my mind. Why else would he stop?*

Pilan' shifted in his seat to face her. She turned, looking in to his eyes. "I must see you again before you go away to school," he said. "Is that possible?"

"I'll make it possible. I was thinking the same thing."

Pilan''s face inched closer. Her pulse pounded in her throat. Her eyes drifted closed and she took a deep breath. His lips gently touched her waiting mouth. They were warm, soft. The kiss was short, but dreamy and sweet, perfect; she knew it wouldn't be the last.

Chapter 17

THE CHURCH WAS FULLER than usual today. Kristina glanced around her. Almost every pew was full. News had spread, thanks to her mother, that there would be a special music presentation during this morning's service. Perhaps that's why so many people were here.

Kristina wondered what people would say after she and Pilan' did their song together. He hadn't come in yet, but she was sure when he walked to the front row and sat down next to her, all heads would turn and murmurs would drift through the sanctuary. She shifted in her seat, trying not to appear anxious, even though her belly was full of jitters.

She thought about the little church where her parents had gotten married, where she'd sung her first solo at the age of five. She'd been comfortable there. It was small and familiar, but when it became over crowded a bigger church had been built. This one was quite grand, with a tall steeple and bell tower, and the basement doubled as a social hall, and in emergencies, a shelter from tornados. It even had a kitchen. All of her closest friends from the old church still attended here. The building was warmer in the winter and cooler in the summer, but the long wooden pews were still hard and uncomfortable.

Where is he? She glanced over her shoulder again, hoping to see Pilan' come through the door or down the aisle.

During the last week, she and Pilan' had practiced in the music room at home during every available minute. They'd tried a few songs with Mama playing the piano, but in the end, they had decided she would sing with Pilan''s violin accompaniment. They would perform *Amazing Grace*, the way they'd done it the first time they'd sung and played together down by the creek. There it had been a natural joining of their souls, spontaneous and unpracticed, but over the past few days, they'd worked on the music until the timing and every note was flawless.

Surely, people would change their minds about Pilan' when they heard him play. Nothing in this town compared to his talent, and added to his obvious faith and good character, how could they not admire and trust him. If any of the folks in the congregation were among those who called him half-breed, or spread rumors and doubt about him, Kristina hoped they'd repent and God would change their hearts.

The organist began to play. Reverend Gilroy entered the platform from a side door up front and stepped up to the pulpit. He was still young and fit, and had a touch of premature gray at his temples. Across the aisle, Mattie Gilroy and their two children sat on the front pew, very much the proper family. Mattie nodded, smiled, and gave Kristina a little finger wave, signs of reassurance. She'd heard them practice, and helped spread the word about their special number. Before the minister spoke, Kristina caught a glimpse of someone coming up the side aisle on her left and she turned. Looking regal, his violin in hand, Pilan' slipped into the pew next to her.

"I apologize for being late," Pilan' whispered.

"Where were you?" She didn't mean to sound like a nagging housewife, but she was beginning to imagine something terrible had happened to him, and though whispered, her words came out sharper than she'd intended.

"I'll explain after the service." He smiled and patted her hand before taking it into his and holding it snugly between them. She didn't resist.

The congregation stood for the opening prayer. Unsure about holding hands in church, Kristina slid her hand from Pilan''s gentle grip and stood. Her legs wobbled and she asked God to steady her nerves. After Reverend Gilroy's prayer a song was announced, and she turned to the page in the hymnal, sharing the songbook with Pilan'. The familiar song lifted her spirits but words in the third verse tugged at her heart and threatened tears. *"Are you anxious - what shall be tomorrow? Tell it to Jesus alone."* Until now, she hadn't realized how anxious she was about standing up front with Pilan' to sing, about going to Boston, and about saying goodbye to him. She was more anxious about the next two years than she'd realized. There had been sleepless nights and anxiety over the incidents with Toby Gallager as well. She shifted on her feet. *Tell it to Jesus.* She did.

During the last verse she listened to Pilan' sing, pleased to hear a fine tenor voice, strong and melodious, that blended in perfect harmony with hers. Her thoughts shifted from her worries and marveled at his talent. She wanted to sing with him forever.

Feet scraped against the hardwood floor and pews creaked as everyone was seated. Kristina settled modestly close to Pilan'. She sat quietly, putting her thoughts and concerns about the future behind her. She was grateful for his friendship, and for the time she had with him, though it wasn't nearly long enough. Still in awe of his voice, she wondered what it would be like to sing a duet with him, perhaps with Mama accompanying them on the piano. Mama would certainly like that.

As Kristina waited for the minister to announce the special number she and Pilan' had prepared, something tender and beautiful grew inside her. A strong connection to this wonderful man she'd only known a few weeks blossomed within her, and she didn't want it to come to an end. They had too much to learn about each other, too much to share. Her thoughts straying, she imagined romantic dinners with him, waltzing with him, and traveling to Paris with him.

Oh, my. She had to clear her mind. *Get a grip, woman.* In moments she and Pilan' would stand on the platform in front of everyone and present their music. She hoped and prayed the emotional depth and richness of the song would touch the hearts of everyone in the congregation.

Finally, it was time. Reverend Gilroy introduced them and invited them to the platform. Legs still shaky she stood. Pilan' paused and gestured for her to go ahead of him. She moved forward, walking slowly, as gracefully as she could, slightly lifting the hem or her skirt as she proceeded up the steps. At the center of the platform, she waited for Pilan' to step up beside her. Glancing sideways she gave him a timorous smile. He nodded and winked.

Confidence radiated in his broad smile. Her heart flip-flopped. She smiled back at him, a full smile this time. For a moment, the flash of white teeth in Pilan''s handsome, dark-skinned face, almost made her forget why she was standing next to him. She calmed herself with a deep breath. He lifted his violin to the smooth plane of his strong jaw, and tucked the polished instrument beneath his chin. As she waited for his introduction, a sea of faces looked up at them, some with smiles, some solemn.

Papa, Mama, and all her siblings were lined up on the second pew, all dressed in their Sunday best. Gracie May was snuggled in Mama's arms sound asleep. Her grandparents occupied the last two spaces on the same pew. She spotted Doris and her family, as well as Doctor and Mrs. Rhodes. Doris smiled. Kristina's gaze moved to the back and she saw Jake, Pilan''s friend, from the restaurant. It was the first time she'd seen him in church. Movement at the entrance drew her attention to the double doors.

Toby!

Certainly he wouldn't come into the church to make trouble. Was it possible he thought about changing his ways, and maybe giving his life to Jesus? She was sorry to admit her doubt. Whatever the reason, she couldn't think about that right now.

You handle Toby, Lord.

Jitters rolled over her body, her stomach churned. She clenched and unclenched her hands. It wasn't the first time she'd sung in front of the congregation, but that little nervous twinge in her stomach always came back, and seeing Toby made it worse. She glanced at her parents again. Their smiles helped settle her nerves. She turned her thoughts to the song she was about to sing, and sent up a quick, silent prayer, asking God to make this moment a blessing to those who listened. Even Toby. A hushed murmur rippled across the sanctuary then quieted.

The moment Pilan' drew the bow across the strings, absolute silence fell upon the congregation. Reverence flooded her soul. A long, deep breath filled her lungs with air. On cue, she began to sing. Nothing but the sound of her voice and the strains of heavenly violin music surrounded her. The presence of God filled her, directed her voice.

PILAN' PLAYED THE FAMILIAR song with great devotion as Kristina sang the words. Just as the first time they'd joined their music down near the creek, the music seemed to float on wings of air, filling the sanctuary with prayerful song. The crowd of about two hundred people, Pilan' estimated, blurred as he focused on each note, striving for perfection. His heart was full, soaking in the magnificence of each word Kristina sang. Her enunciation was perfect, clear, her angelic voice purer than any he'd ever heard. But mostly he marveled at the passion she put into every measure, every note. Most certainly, her talent was a gift from God. When the song ended he paused, basking in awe. The congregation was silent, as if spellbound, then, something he'd never heard in a church occurred.

A resounding applause filled the sanctuary.

He acknowledged the audience with a warm smile and a slight bow.

As he assisted Kristina down the steps with light support on her elbow, and took his seat on the front pew next to her, he was satisfied he'd done well. Of course, he deserved only half the credit and applause. Or, perhaps, all the applause was for Kristina. Still, he hoped the congregation's response was a true indication of how the people would receive him from now on.

He'd been to one other service at this church, and he felt he was still considered an outsider, the half-breed. There were a few who had shaken his hand and exchanged small talk, but he didn't feel like part of the group. He supposed feeling like a member of the church family would take time, time he didn't have. He reached for Kristina's hand and gave it a squeeze, continuing to hold it. It felt right in his grip, and he wished he could hold it forever.

He bent his head toward her and whispered. "You were magnificent."

"Thank you. So were you." Her airy whisper came with a smile.

Pilan' knew he should be paying attention to the message, but the reverend's sermon failed to capture his attention. All he could think about was the amazing woman next to him; the only woman who warmed his heart and touched his soul.

His plans had been well laid out, and he wondered if he was crazy falling for a woman when he knew she didn't fit into the scheme of things. An emotional struggle such as this was the last thing he'd expected when he set out for the journey of a lifetime. Though he knew Kristina was due to leave for Boston in a few days, it didn't eliminate the turmoil he was battling.

And then, there was the problem of his horse.

BEFORE SHE EXITED THE door of the church, Kristina sensed something bad had happened to Pilan' earlier, and she wondered if it had anything to do with Toby Gallager and his reason for stepping into the church. The moment she and Pilan' had finished their song, Toby had slipped out the door as quietly as he'd come in. So far as she knew, he'd never stepped foot inside any church until this morning. Why today? Why during the special music? How did he even know she was singing? Coincidence? Unlikely. She shuddered.

Even though Pilan' had played his violin with perfection, and he'd smiled down at her now and then during the sermon, he seemed distracted. The moment Reverend Gilroy had closed the service with prayer, people crowded around them, making it impossible to question Pilan' here. She shook another hand, received a hug, accepted compliments, but she didn't sing for the praises or recognition. Those accolades weren't important, although, she had to admit, very humbly, she appreciated them. But what she really wanted, was to escape the crowd so she could be alone with Pilan'.

Jake made his way up the aisle through the throng of people and slapped Pilan' on the back. They shook hands then he smiled at Kristina. "You two were amazing. That was beautiful."

"Thank you," she and Pilan' said in unison. It seemed everything they did was unified.

Mama Leoma stepped up beside Kristina and put her free arm around her shoulders, baby Gracie still cradled in the crook of Mama's other arm. She smiled at Pilan'. "We'd love to have you come home with us for Sunday dinner. I have a big beef roast in the oven. There's more than enough."

"Thank you. I'd be happy to come for dinner." Pilan' returned Mama's smile. "My horse went down this morning, so I'll need to ride along with your family if there's room."

"That would be fine if you don't mind a child on your lap. One of us can bring you back into town later."

Kristina jumped at the opportunity to volunteer. "Oh, I'd be happy to bring you back into town when you're ready."

"Then it's settled." Mama looked pleased. Pilan' looked even more pleased.

As Mama walked away Kristina turned to Pilan'. "What happened to your horse?"

"He was sickly and getting old. When I bought him I thought he had another year or two in him, but I guess I was wrong. The veterinarian checked him out before I came to church, and he was pretty sure the old horse just died during the night."

"How awful. Are you sure someone didn't poison him?" Her mind automatically went to Toby, and she wondered if he'd done another hateful deed. She hoped not.

Pilan' shook his head, doubt on his face. "It didn't appear so."

Still troubled, she made her way to the door and stepped out on to the porch. The noon sun was bright and she squinted for a moment, allowing her eyes to adjust. Then she spotted Toby and Dyer nearby, talking with each other. Dyer looked relaxed, not in any danger, but she couldn't imagine why Toby was talking to her brother in what appeared to be a friendly manner. The church yard was full of adults visiting, boys and girls playing tag, and a few young people gathered in a small group. It was typical for a summer Sunday after church, before everyone went home to Sunday dinners and afternoon chores or naps. But the scene with Toby wasn't typical; it downright puzzled Kristina. Not about to interfere in the conversation between Dyer and Toby, she'd wait until she got home to ask Dyer about it.

It didn't take Mama very long to have Sunday dinner ready. Kristina helped set the table and dipped the mashed potatoes and gravy into serving bowls, all the time aware of Pilan' in the next room talking to the other men. The younger children were in the back yard playing, but the moment Mama stuck her head out the door and called them, they rushed inside filling the kitchen with pandemonium.

When the family was crowded around the table and Papa had blessed the food, everyone eagerly settled into filling their plates. Pilan' was well-mannered, as he'd been on their dinner date, and seemed comfortable with the family. Dining around his family table had to be more formal and elegant than her family squeezed around the plank table in the kitchen, but he seemed at ease. He didn't hesitate to ask for butter and jam for his hot rolls, or to refill his glass with iced tea. She liked the way he interacted with adults and children alike.

Kristina waited for everyone to begin eating, and the chatter to die down so she could ask Dyer about his conversation with Toby, but before she could ask, he spoke up. He must have known what was on her mind.

"I suppose ya'll saw Toby at the church today," Dyer said. "Seems he's agonizing over his violent ways. I've been talking to him lately about repenting and giving his life to Jesus, but he's plumb scared." Dyer paused and popped a hefty sized bite of meat into his mouth and chewed.

Papa stopped eating. "Is he serious?"

Dyer nodded. "I reckon. As nervous and shy as he was talking about it, I'd say he's doing some serious thinking."

"Do you think he'll really change his mean ways?" Hard as it would be to forgive Toby, Kristina hoped he would change. But she couldn't help being skeptical, knowing the way he'd been acting recently.

She remembered when Toby was a little boy with a kind heart, and she wondered what caused him to turn bad. She believed God could change the meanest human, if the person was ready and willing to let him. Hard as it was to imagine, maybe it wasn't too late for Toby, if he was sincere.

Pilan' spoke quietly. "I do think he should pay for the things he's done. What if he thinks he can get out of his punishment by going to church and saying he wants to turn his life around then continues the way he is?"

Everyone was quiet for a moment. Kristina agreed and wondered if Pilan' was right. It sounded like the kind of trickery Toby was capable of.

"Didn't act like that's what he was doing," Dyer said.

Pilan' spoke again. "I sent off my photographs to be processed, and they're evidence of some of his crimes."

Thinking about what Toby had done to her made Kristina tremble. Her appetite was gone. She wanted to tell everyone what had happened when she was eight, but this wasn't the proper time or place. Such things weren't discussed openly, and after keeping it inside all these years she wasn't sure she wanted to tell anyone else. Sometimes she still wondered if what happened back then was just the kind of games or exploring all children did. A game like Toby had said. There were times when she felt guilty, angry, and defiled. Mostly, she just wanted to forget it. But Toby's recent brutal attack wasn't a childish game. She'd never forget it.

"He'll pay for what he's done," Papa said to Pilan, "and I hope your pictures help. All those years I had him working here on our property I thought he was a nice boy. I wish I had known what he was doing."

Mama turned to Pilan'. "When you get those pictures we should turn them all over to the law and let them handle him. But we need to pray that the young man is sincere about changing." The voice of wisdom always came from Mama. "Maybe the spirit of God is working on his miserable soul."

Dyer spoke up, sounding more like a seasoned preacher than a boy of thirteen. "I agree; he'll have to admit his guilt and accept his punishment. But, we can't deny him the opportunity to be saved. Jesus didn't die for the sins of only good people. He died to redeem everyone who believes in him. That includes low-down rascals like Toby."

"Well said, son," Papa said. "You keep talking to him until he comes around. Be careful, though, to use sound judgment."

"I will."

Though the conversation made Kristina uncomfortable and she'd lost her appetite, she was proud of her brother. He'd make a wonderful preacher in a few years.

Mama offered the meat platter to Pilan', and asked if anyone wanted more potatoes and gravy. "Maybe if he comes to the Lord he'll have some influence on the rest of his family. It won't hurt us to keep them all in our prayers."

Chapter 18

The open suitcase on the foot of her bed was still empty, a glaring reminder that Kristina's days at home were short in number. It shouldn't be so hard to fill it with the clothes she'd set aside to take to Boston. Everything was washed and pressed, and two new dresses hung in the closet ready to be packed. But the nearer her departure came, the more hesitant she was. Her heart was torn, her insides in turmoil day and night.

Even though Dyer hadn't had another headache since Doctor Rhodes had given him the medication, she still worried about him. It had been only a couple of weeks since he'd begun taking it, and the doctor had said there was no guarantee that the tincture would work. What if he got worse while she was away? Unable to stand the thought, she paced across the bedroom and swiped a fresh tear from her cheek.

And what about Pilan'? She wasn't ready to say goodbye to him. Life without him would be dull, unhappy. She couldn't imagine not hearing him play his violin, or singing along with him. There would be no joy in singing down at the creek or in church.

Her grandmother was ready to begin her journey home, and she reminded Kristina frequently how thrilled she was to have her go home with them. She'd asked Kristina at least three times today if she was packed and ready to leave. Her grandmother's prodding made packing all the more difficult, but she had to get it done. Her university tuition was paid, her train ticket purchased. It would break her grandparents' hearts and disappoint her parents if she tried to back out of going. She couldn't do that.

Discouraged and confused, she plopped down on the edge of her bed and gazed out the window, wishing for an easy solution to her dilemma. From her vantage point Kristina watched the sky darken, gray clouds building in the south adding to her gloomy mood. She lifted her long, heavy hair off her neck for some relief from the heat. What she wouldn't give right now to stick her bare feet in the cool water of the creek. But she wasn't in the mood, and going down there this afternoon was out of the question with all her packing to finish. She stared at the empty suitcase. There was no point ignoring it any longer. It was time to stop fretting and pack her clothes.

Thinking ahead to what she'd need in the fall and winter, she neatly folded a sweater and put it into the bottom of the suitcase. With the first piece of clothing packed, she didn't know whether to feel relief or dread. She should be excited but she wasn't. Heavy-hearted she blew out a puff of air, folded a winter skirt, and placed it next to the sweater.

Someone knocked on the front door. Assuming it was one of Dyer's friends coming to visit or play some game the older boys enjoyed, she didn't leave her room. Someone else could answer the door.

The muffled, male voices coming from the living room were more mature than any of her brothers or their friends. Curious, she stuck her head out of her bedroom door, listening and peering down the hallway. Unable to see anyone, or hear the conversation well enough to determine who was there, she stepped back into her bedroom. Another skirt half folded in her hands, she paused when Mama stuck her head through the doorway.

"You have a visitor, sweetheart," her mother said.

"Just a moment." Not expecting a caller, she quickly brushed her hair back from her face, and checked her reflection in the mirror. "Who is it, Mama?"

"Pilan'." Her mother smiled and left the room.

Pilan' hadn't mentioned on Sunday afternoon that he'd pay her a visit today, but her heart raced in anticipation of seeing him. She wished she'd put on a nicer dress this morning. The one she had on was plain, simple, an old, everyday dress. He might think she looked uncomely, but there was no time to change. She didn't want to keep him waiting.

Heart fluttering, she walked toward her grandfather's voice; he mentioned the train trip to Boston. When she entered the living room her grandfather had Pilan''s attention, but Pilan' immediately turned toward her. He appeared serious, anguished. Goodness. Was her grandfather upsetting him?

Pilan''s usual cheerfulness had been replaced with a frown. Even her smile when she greeted him didn't seem to change his grim expression. He politely, but quickly, excused himself from the conversation with Grandfather Fisk and spoke to her. "I have only a few minutes, but I must talk with you. May we speak in private?"

"Yes, of course."

She held out a hand and he took it. His touch was so exhilarating she could hardly keep her feet on the floor, yet the look on his face almost stopped her on the spot. Maybe he'd received news of some tragedy in his family. Why else would he look so miserable? She led him into the library where they could talk alone, and she sat down on the settee, patting the spot next to her. He hesitated then sat down. Concerned, she waited for Pilan' to speak. The room became hot and suffocating.

After a long silence, he turned to her and looked into her eyes. What she saw on his face was agony. "I came to say goodbye, Kristina."

She released a long sigh and chuckled. After all, they had two more days. "But I'm not leaving today."

Leaning forward, forearms on his knees, Pilan' spoke to the rug beneath their feet. "Yes, I know. I mean, I've come to say I must tell you goodbye. I won't be seeing you again."

Stunned by the sudden change in Pilan''s attitude, she fought back tears. Granted, this had been a possibility all along, but she'd hoped and prayed something would change, that some miracle would occur to prevent this moment from happening. Why couldn't they stay in touch, write, wait for each other? Her throat dry and itchy as Mama's wool knitting yarn, she couldn't speak. The brims of her eyes burned. It seemed she'd known Pilan' forever, and her feelings for him had grown strong. She looked away, trying to compose herself.

Pilan' straightened and squeezed her hand. "Kristina, please look at me." She turned and found him facing her, his handsome face shadowed in sorrow. "This is difficult for me as well," he said, "but we both knew this time would come."

"I know, but—"

"I've thought long and hard about this. It's important for you to get your education, and I don't want to interfere with that. I won't be hanging around Oklahoma much longer. You knew my plans."

"But—"

"We have no choice." Looking away for a moment, Pilan' turned back, his voice raspy. "You can't turn your back on what your grandparents have done for you. Soon we'll be thousands of miles apart, and I'm sure some college boy will catch your eye. You'll forget all about me."

She swallowed hard, the dam of tears released, refusing to believe she'd ever meet another man as wonderful and perfect for her as Pilan'. "No, I won't ever forget you."

"Nor will I forget you, but this is best."

How could this be best when it hurt so much? Falling in love with him had been the last thing Kristina expected or wanted, but she had. She loved him. Maybe the feelings weren't mutual, although she found that hard to believe after the way he'd kissed her. She'd seen it in his eyes, his smiles.

Rising, she walked halfway across the room and turned, arms crossed. "Can I write to you?"

"Once I begin to travel west I won't be in one place long enough to receive mail. I don't know where I'll be from week-to-week."

"You could write to me at my grandparents' house. I'll give you their address if you want it." Almost whining like a child, Kristina was grasping for a way to hold on to Pilan'. She'd never wanted anything more.

After a long hesitation Pilan' answered. "I'm not much of a writer, but I suppose I can try. I just can't make any promises to you about the future, Kristina. It's better if we say goodbye now and part." He stood, pulled out his watch, and studied it for a long time. He came to her, and placing his hands on her shoulders, he kissed her cheek. "I have to leave. I'm sorry."

Without another word, in long strides Pilan' rushed out of the house. Fresh tears cascaded down Kristina's face as she followed him to the front door. She didn't care who saw her sob as she watched the man she loved ride away.

THE TRAIN RUMBLED INTO the station, huffing and puffing steam, brakes screeching. Kristina hugged and kissed Mama and Papa, and her brothers and sisters, her emotions in a jumble. Now she stood between Grandmother and Grandfather Fisk, ready to board. Grandmother carried a picnic basket Mama had filled with sandwiches, a few apples, and a dozen oatmeal-raisin cookies she'd baked early that morning. Tickets in hand, her grandfather smiled down at her.

"Well, off we go, my dear. Are you ready?" Grandfather smiled again, his blue eyes filled with adventure, his silver-gray hair shimmering in the mid-morning sunshine. He motioned with one hand toward the train. "This is our—"

"Wait! Wait!" Doris ran toward her, red hair flying, her hands in the air. She grabbed Kristina into a big hug. "I had to come say good-bye."

Tears sprang to Kristina's eyes, and she wiped a finger across her cheeks to keep them from running down to her chin. How would she stand not seeing her dearest friend for nearly a whole year, especially after losing Pilan'?

"All aboard!"

Grandfather nudged her.

"I'm glad you came, Doris. Thank you." Grandfather was moving toward the train car, and there was no time to chat. She hugged Doris hard and stepped back. "I'll write to you; I promise."

"You better." Doris thrust a small package into Kristina's hands. "Here's a little gift to make sure you do."

"Thank you. And you better write back, you hear?" She kissed Doris on the cheek. "I'll see you next summer."

Heart still heavy and pining for Pilan', and already missing her family and friends, she caught up with her grandparents and stepped up and into the passenger car. She quickly stashed her straw bag on the floor in front of her, and scooted next to the window. Her grandparents took the seats directly across the aisle. Gazing out the window, she saw her family and Doris on the wooden platform waving up at her. She waved back. Her stomach churned, tears dribbled down her face, and this time she didn't bother to wipe them away.

Through glazed eyes Kristina scanned the platform. Pilan was there! In the background, standing in the shadow of the roof overhang, he stood alone, his hands buried in his pants pockets. Hoping he'd see her, she pressed a hand, fingers splayed, against the window. The train jerked and hissed, and began to grind forward. Still waiting she watched him. At last, he lifted a hand into the air and waved.

Tears trickled down her cheeks. Kristina wanted to believe this was not goodbye to Pilan' forever. No matter what he'd said, she was sure somehow she would see Pilan' Rousseau again.

She settled into her seat, sad but hopeful. It felt as if she were being torn away from the man she loved, her family, everyone and everything that was familiar.

The train wasn't two minutes out of Oklahoma City, when Kristina's grandmother stepped across the aisle and sat down in the seat next to her. "You look sad, dear. Are you all right?"

A burning knot in her throat, Kristina nodded and gazed out the window.

"Is it Pilan'?"

Another nod.

Grandmother's voice softened. "Sweetheart, this isn't a time to look back on what might have been. You must look forward to new, exciting things. You have a bright future ahead of you. With your talent and beauty you'll attract many young men. When the time is right you'll fall in love again."

Kristina turned to her grandmother, seeing through glassy eyes. She spoke slowly, deliberately. "I don't think so."

Chapter 19

PILAN' SAT AT THE small table eating another poorly prepared supper, his mood foul. He'd been back on the road for five weeks, and he hadn't had a good meal since he left Potts' restaurant. He found his travels less interesting than they'd been in the beginning—before Oklahoma City and Kristina. His passion for climbing one more mountain or exploring a new city wasn't what it used to be.

No matter how hard he tried, he couldn't stop thinking about Kristina for more than a few minutes at a time. At the least expected moments he'd hear her sweet voice singing *Amazing Grace*, or see her radiant smile beaming up at him. There were nights when she appeared in his dreams, standing in the shade of the big tree down by the stream where he'd first heard her sing. He'd see her silky, dark hair fluttering in the breeze, and he longed to hold her.

What have I done?

He'd fallen in love, that's what he'd done. There was no denying it. What a fool he'd been, getting involved with a woman when he knew it would only lead to heartache. He clenched his teeth together, hoping in time he'd get over her.

He thought about the promise he'd made Kristina after saying goodbye to her, and wished he hadn't agreed to write her. Well, he didn't actually promise he would write her a letter; he'd said he would try. But for the last several days it hounded him. He'd thought about writing to her, but he hadn't sat down with pen and paper and attempted to write a single word. There was no excuse, other than his reluctance to write to anyone. He'd written only three short missives to his parents since he'd left home nearly six months ago.

You promised you'd try.

I know, I know.

It was late in the evening, however, and he was too tired to do anything except finish eating and crawl into the lumpy bed in the tiny hotel room. Tomorrow he'd board the train for New Mexico, not a long distance, but he'd have plenty of time to write while he traveled south. His mind was made up. He'd tear a page out of his journal and write Kristina a letter. Perhaps he'd write one to his mother and father as well.

"More coffee, good-looking?" The flirty, red-haired waitress who had to be older than his mother, held the pot ready to pour, her smile a little too risqué. She winked.

"No. No thank you ma'am." He didn't bother to smile, didn't want to encourage the woman's brazen behavior. Some of the men she waited on at nearby tables seemed to like her shameless flirting, but Pilan' found it unappealing and embarrassing. He'd been brought up in a home with genteel ladies, and he'd been warned repeatedly to steer clear of women like the red-head with heavy rouge on her cheeks, bright red lips, and too much cleavage spilling out over the low-cut neckline of her dress. "They're trouble, son," his father had warned, quoting verses from Proverbs.

As the waitress walked away, her hips swaying, seemingly un-phased by his lack of interest, he took another bite of steak and chewed, thinking the cook could take a few cooking lessons from Potts. The meat was tough and over done, but he was in no mood to complain, and too hungry to leave the meat uneaten.

His mind went back to Kristina as he chewed the rubbery steak, and he thought about what to write. He could tell her about his climb up Pike's Peak, but there wasn't much else to write about at this point. Should he tell her he missed her? No. Even though it was true, that would only stir up feelings in her that would be better left alone. Never mind the feelings he struggled with. *Get over them.*

He grunted. That wasn't happening, was it? Lately he'd been battling with sinful thoughts of her. He wondered how it would be to sleep with her, make love to her, and hold her in his arms all night.

Is this what a spiritual battle was like? What was it his father had once told him? "To have victory over a spiritual battle you must use spiritual weapons, such as prayer and studying God's Word. You must depend on the Holy Spirit," his father had said.

How long had it been since he'd read his Bible? He'd used it when he attended Kristina's church, and that was the last time he'd opened it. *God in Heaven, forgive me. Help me do better.* Maybe with God's help and time, the lustful thoughts and his longing to see her would stop.

Red strutted over to his table and dropped the dinner check on the tattered oilcloth table cover. "Anything else I can get for you, sweetie pie?" She winked.

Jolted from his thoughts, Pilan' wiped his mouth with the flimsy paper napkin and shook his head. "No thank you. That will be all."

He picked up the scribbled ticket. Glad it was the last meal he'd eat in the rundown establishment, he paid the bill. After poorly prepared suppers like this one, he craved the marvelous cooking of the French chef at home, or a tasty dessert baked by his mother. Father had often scolded his mother about all the time she spent in the kitchen learning new recipes, when they had a perfectly capable chef to make the finest of everything from breakfast to dinner and desserts. But mother had taken a keen interest in baking fancy French tarts and other delectable pastries. Over the years she'd perfected many good recipes. Ah, if only everyone could have a small taste of the fine foods he'd enjoyed growing up. He had yet to eat a tastier *patisserie* than those his mother made. The memory almost made his mouth water.

He wondered; does Kristina know how to cook?

Kristina. Would everything remind him of her forever?

Early the next morning, Pilan' boarded the train, his new Appaloosa secured in a special boxcar for the ride. He settled into his seat, his camera ready for interesting sites.

The train chugged and rocked through the uninhabited landscape, the click-clack, click-clack hypnotizing. His mind was almost as blank as the view outside his window. The land was dry, brown, the vegetation sparse and small. It didn't appear he'd need his snapshot camera.

He took out a piece of paper and pen, using a book for support. He put the pen to the paper then lifted it for the third or forth time, rolling it back and forth between his thumb and finger. Except for the salutation, the white sheet he'd torn from his journal was blank.

Dear Kristina,

Words escaped him. Where should he begin?

SIX WEEKS HAD PASSED since Kristina's arrival in Boston. A whirlwind of activities left little time for her to miss her family or to think much about Pilan', yet he was never far from her mind, and he intruded into her thoughts daily.

Mind wandering, she closed the textbook and gazed out the second-floor window of Mama Leoma's childhood bedroom, into the beautifully maintained back yard. What a privilege and joy it was being where Mama Leoma had grown up. It was easy to see why her mother was elegant and gracious, and appreciated fine things. She'd been brought up surrounded with all kinds of finery: Chintz curtains that matched the bedspread, fancy, comfortable, velvet and satin furniture, porcelain knick-knacks, and more. It was a blessing to be there enjoying the same beautiful home, and it made her feel closer to Mama.

Shortly after arriving in Boston, Kristina had registered for school, chosen classes, and purchased books and necessities. Prior to beginning classes her grandparents had spent every spare moment taking her on sightseeing excursions, each one filled with interesting historical facts. When Grandfather was too busy working on weekdays to go along, Grandmother Lillian escorted her. Those outings always included shopping in the finer department stores and lunch out. Already Kristina's closet was filled with new clothes and shoes. New hats lined one shelf, and a variety of gloves shared a bureau drawer with new winter scarves. But the best part of her outings was seeing the sights. There was so much to do it seemed she could spend the rest of her life just seeing the city. No wonder Pilan' loved traveling.

One of the first places she had wanted to see was the Paul Revere House. She'd read about him and his *midnight ride,* and seeing where he'd lived made the story more real. It sure was a tiny house, though. It would almost fit in her grandfather's gardening shed. Reverence and awe had filled her when she sat in one of the box pews in the Old North Church and tried to imagine a Sunday service there. Grandfather seemed to take great pride in educating her about Bunker Hill, and the first major battle of the American Revolution. Her head swam with so many facts and dates it was impossible to remember it all.

Being here with her grandparents was a constant learning experience beyond the school room. Gazing at the Charles River one afternoon, she suddenly understood Pilan''s passion for adventure. The world was full of interesting places and things to experience outside Oklahoma City, and for a frivolous moment, she wished she could join him on his excursions. What a marvelous experience that would be.

Where was Pilan' today? She'd hoped for a letter from him by now, but none had arrived. She stood and stretched, putting her studies aside, wondering if she'd ever see him again. Her heart still ached when she thought about him. Drawn together by music, their meetings down by the creek were still vivid in her mind. She longed for more times like that. The place would always hold precious memories for her, in spite of the bad things that had happened there with Toby. After meeting Pilan' there and singing along with his violin music, the place was even more special in her heart. If she never saw him again, that day was one she would never forget.

Never had she believed she'd want to be courted by a man. Not that long ago she'd declared there was no room in her life for romance and marriage, but Pilan' had changed her mind. Someday she would like to be a wife and mother, perhaps even sooner than she'd imagined, but she couldn't imagine it with anyone other than Pilan'.

She sighed and sat back down at the desk—the same desk her stepmother had used to do her school work. Daydreaming and pining for a man she couldn't be with would get her nowhere. If Pilan' had no intention of writing to her or ever seeing her again, then clearly being with him wasn't meant to be. She picked up the letter from her parents that had arrived yesterday and read it again, grabbing on to the bits and pieces about Pilan'.

> *Our Dearest Kristina,*
>
> *We were thrilled to receive your letter. We are happy to know you are settled in with Grandmother and Grandfather Fisk, and we're glad you're comfortable there. By now you must be studying hard and getting along fine in school. What a marvelous thing to know our dear girl is in college and on her way to a successful future in music. We are very proud of you.*
>
> *All of the children are doing well and I know they miss you. Praise God, Dyer hasn't had another headache and spends every evening with his nose either in his Bible or in his school books. Like you, he is determined to make high grades and he studies hard. We hope the other children will follow in the footsteps of their older sister and brother.*
>
> *We have a new member of the family. Last week Dyer brought home a young puppy, a mongrel Papa says, but he's a cute little thing. He's friendly and playful and good with all the children. Dyer named him Dusty. Don't ask me why.*

Kristina smiled, recalling the day Brownie came bounding around the corner of the house when she was five. She'd called him Brownie simply because he was brown. Maybe the new dog was covered with dust and dirt when Dyer found him and the name fit. She went back to reading the letter.

> *Not long after you left Pilan' came to visit and brought the photographs he'd taken. They were quite good, especially the ones of you and Auntie Myrtle in her motorcar. Of course those of your injuries and poor Brownie were heartbreaking to look at. We took those pictures to the sheriff and had quite a talk with him about Toby. But you'll never believe what is happening with Toby since you left.*
>
> *Remember the day he came to church and talked to Dyer? Well, your brother has been ministering to him, and the last two weeks Toby has been in church. He hasn't gone forward during alter call, but he did visit the sheriff and confess to his bad deeds. Isn't it amazing what the good Lord can do in a person's life? We pray Toby will repent and ask God to forgive him one of these days. Nothing is impossible with our loving God.*
>
> *Pilan' is a fine fellow and we know you were quite fond of him. Have you had a letter from him? I suppose it was best for him to bid you farewell, even though it broke your heart, but you two had such different plans and were headed in different directions. He is gone now, who knows where. Time will heal your heartache, and perhaps you'll meet another fine young man at school who*

> *has the same interest in music as you do. But more important, you must focus on your school work and enjoy your time in Boston.*
>
> *We love you and miss you and count the months and days until you come home for summer vacation. Until then, we pray for you daily and trust the Lord to watch over you and keep you safe. We anxiously look forward to your next letter. Please write it soon.*
>
> *Our love and prayers,*
>
> *Mama and Papa*

Kristina refolded the letter and slipped it back into the envelope, cherishing every word. She found her mother's comments about Pilan' interesting, and wondered if Mama had suggested grandmother talk to her on the train. Perhaps her parents and grandmother were right, but she doubted there would ever be another man as fine as Pilan', and right now she wasn't interested in a relationship with anyone. It was Pilan' or nobody.

It wasn't surprising to hear how Dyer was working on Toby. Her brother was out to save the world and she admired him for his determination, but sooner or later he'd realize that was impossible. Even after seeing Toby at the church, she was sure her brother's efforts were in vain, no matter what Mama had written. The angry feelings Kristina had toward Toby wouldn't go away easily, but she knew it was important to forgive him, whether he changed or not. That was a big step for her, a feat too large at this time. It wasn't in her heart to forgive him for the pain he'd inflicted upon her. It would take time and God's help.

A few minutes later, when Grandmother called her downstairs for dinner, she was still hashing over the news about Toby, and she wondered if he'd come to his senses about her. Glad she was out of his reach she hoped so. She'd never had an inkling of romantic interest in Toby, and no matter how well he cleaned up his life, she could never think of him as a beau. He'd always be the obnoxious, bad, neighbor kid.

Maybe by the time she returned home for the summer he'd be courting another woman, but she couldn't imagine who would want the likes of him. She was just glad to be far away from him. Unlike her burning desire to see Pilan' again, she didn't care if she ever saw Tobias Gallager again.

She jumped up. She'd almost forgotten her grandparents expected guests this evening, and she ran to the closet. Grandmother had asked that she change into something pretty for dinner. Grabbing a pink blouse with an embroidered collar and gray, wool skirt from the closet, she changed in record time. She ran a few quick brush strokes through her hair and dashed down the stairs.

At the bottom of the steps Kristina was greeted by Seymour, the fat, gray, Persian cat. His green eyes gazed up at her as he rubbed around her ankles, then he raised both front paws to her knees, begging her to pick him up.

"All right, Seymour," she said, bending to lift the heavy bundle of fur into her arms. She nuzzled her nose into his soft fur, and scratched behind his ears. "Now I'll have to wash up again before dinner."

Following the sound of voices, she entered the living room, Seymour still in her arms. She lowered him to the floor, hoping none of the fine hair floated into dining room.

"I see Seymour found you. He's never been so fond of anyone else as he is of you. It must be the songs you sing to him." Grandmother smiled as she greeted Kristina with a brief kiss on one cheek.

"He's a good audience." She brushed her hands over her clothes, ridding them of Seymour's hair.

"There she is." Her grandfather ambled over to her and took her hand, leading her across the spacious room to where his guests were seated.

The two men stood, one a sophisticated man with thinning black hair, the other a young man, probably not much older than she. Well-dressed in navy-blue slacks, a white shirt, and a navy sweater vest, the young man was almost handsome. The woman, dressed fit for a night at the opera, smiled.

"I'd like to introduce my granddaughter, Miss Kristina Soderlund," Grandfather said, his hand affectionately resting on her shoulder. "Kristina this is Mr. and Mrs. Morgan, and their son Bentley."

Kristina accepted handshakes all around. "It's nice to meet you."

She wondered if Bentley was the reason her grandmother had suggested she dress in something nice for dinner. No doubt it was. Was Grandmother playing matchmaker, hoping to see a romance blossom?

Bentley's brown, straight hair was cut short, parted on one side, and combed back. In his pale skin his small, light-brown eyes almost seemed dull. And that was some nose he had. She tried not to stare. It was too large for his long, thin face, and very straight, yet somehow his smile made all his features come together halfway nicely.

"My granddaughter is quite the sport," Grandfather boasted. "Can you believe she has learned to drive a motorcar?"

"Is that right?" Mr. Morgan said. "Automobiles are becoming quite the thing, I hear. I'm sure it won't be long before every man owns an automobile, but personally, I don't think women should drive them."

Kristina remembered the thrill of driving her great-aunt's motorcar, and she bristled at Mr. Morgan's opinion. She dreamed of owning one herself someday. If she sounded slightly indignant when she spoke, she didn't mean to. "I believe every woman should own her own automobile. I am quite capable of driving, and I must say I did a fine job of —."

Grandmother jumped up and clapped her hands, diverting everyone's attention. "Well now, shall we all go to the dining room?"

When Kristina returned from washing her hands, she found the only vacant seat was beside Bentley, pre-arranged, she was sure. His manners were almost too impeccable, his appetite modest, if the small portions on his plate were any indication. No wonder he was so thin. He ate like a girl. During the conversation he said very little, and he only spoke to her when he offered a serving dish of food. The two older men talked endlessly about Bentley's career in finance at the bank where both men worked, and she wondered if Bentley was afraid to speak for himself. It seemed his father and her grandfather were trying to impress her, but she didn't find that kind of boasting about one's accomplishments and money impressive. No doubt, his father was proud of him, and that was a good thing, but having both older men speak of nothing else, obviously trying to sell Bentley's attributes to her, grew tiresome in no time.

Still upset about having her sentence about driving cut off, she dabbed her mouth with the linen napkin and turned to Bentley. "Tell me, Bentley, what do you think about women driving automobiles?"

Bentley hesitated, stammered. "I . . . I umm . . . I don't know."

She'd try a different question, another subject. Anything to get him to talk. "What do you do for entertainment?"

"Not much."

His mother groaned and rolled her eyes. "Bentley enjoys the opera, don't you, darling?"

"Yes." His quiet response wasn't convincing.

"He works long hours, and has little time for such frivolous activities," Mr. Morgan said. "If he's going to be successful in the business world, he must keep his nose in the books and work hard."

"But a man needs time for cultural experiences. Life is more than work, work, work." Mrs. Morgan's voice was sharp.

Bentley chewed his food, his eyes fixed on his dinner plate.

So much for conversation with Bentley. It was clear his parents weren't in agreement about their son's social life, but they certainly were in control. It appeared Bentley was indeed afraid to speak for himself. Perhaps the idea of matchmaking was simply wishful thinking on the part of her grandmother and Mrs. Morgan. Clearly, they were going to be disappointed when their scheme flopped. Kristina proceeded to ignore the lot of them, and continued eating her beef Wellington.

When not a crumb of Boston cream pie was left on anyone's plate, and the last coffee cup was empty, everyone retired to the living room. Kristina was happy and relieved to leave the table and the tension-filled conversation among the older adults. She folded her napkin neatly, tucked it beneath the edge of her plate, and rose saying nothing.

"I think it would be lovely, Kristina, if you would grace our guests with a piano solo? Would you mind dear?" It wasn't an unusual request from her grandmother, and she'd half expected it. It was routine after almost every dinner, whether there were guests or not.

"I'd be happy to." She'd rather play the piano than endure the mundane company of Bentley, or listen to his mother and father debate their son's life.

She sat down on the tapestry-padded piano bench and looked through her music. Having no idea what the Morgans enjoyed, she chose one of her favorites, a joyful piece by Johann Strauss. She began playing *Waltzes from Fledermaus*, hoping the lively tune would lighten the mood in the room. As her fingers flew across the keys, however, she noticed at a glance that Bentley and his father appeared totally bored. Well that was just fine. She was totally bored with them, too. In fact, she'd never been so bored in her life.

She finished the song and graciously accepted the compliments from Mrs. Morgan and her grandparents and closed the keyboard cover. She'd done her part to entertain the guests, but she couldn't help but wish for the company of Pilan' Rousseau. At least he would have appreciated her music, and no doubt, it would have set his feet to dancing. *Where are you now, Pilan'? Oh how I wish you were here. I pray the Lord is keeping you safe.*

Two days later when Kristina arrived home after school, her mind on studying for a big test, she found a letter addressed to her waiting on the foyer table. She didn't recognize the hand writing, and there was no return address. The postmark was smudged and difficult to read, but after thorough examination she was sure it said something like Albuquerque, New Mexico. She'd never heard of the city, and the strange name was impossible to pronounce. The only person it could have been from was Pilan'. Test and study forgotten her heartbeat quickened. She could hardly wait to read what he'd written.

"I see you found your mail," Grandmother said, her curious smile uncontrolled. "Do you know someone in New Mexico?"

"No. I think it might be from Pilan'." She didn't want to waste time chatting with her grandmother, or petting Seymour who circled her feet.

"Oh, I see." Her grandmother frowned, clearly disappointed. Probably because it wasn't a note from Bentley.

"If you'll excuse me, I'm going up to my room to read it?"

"All right, dear."

Shoes off and feet drawn up in the large chair by the window, she opened the letter and unfolded the one page missive. It had no date.

Dear Kristina,

I hope this finds you well and doing fine in school. I'm sure you're doing excellent. By now your parents must have written you about the pictures I gave them. I hope they did some good. I saved the enclosed photo especially for you.

She slipped the photo from the envelope and smiled, remembering the day Pilan' had snapped the picture of her and Auntie Myrtle sitting in the front seat of her great-aunt's motorcar. She put the picture aside and continued to read the letter.

There isn't much to tell you at this time. My climb up Pike's Peak was quite an experience. The air up there was thin, and made it hard to breath because of the high altitude. One more thing checked off my list of things to do.

As I write this, I'm traveling by train into the territory of New Mexico, where I hope to learn more about the Pueblo Indians. After a few days there I'll travel across Arizona and into California.

I think of you fondly and wish you well. I will try to write to you again. I'm sorry this is so short, but as I told you, I'm no good at writing.

Enjoy Boston and school.

Sincerely

Pilan'

She read one line again. *I think of you fondly.* Oh, if only he knew how fondly she still thought of him. Desperately wishing she could write to him, she folded the letter, put it back into the envelope, and tucked it away in a drawer with her stationery and other writing materials. She leaned the photograph against the mirror on her dressing table, wishing the photo were of Pilan'.

Seeing her journal on the bedside table, an idea struck her. Even though she couldn't mail Pilan' a letter she could write one. From now on, every day when she prayed for him, she'd write something to him, and if she received another letter in the future, she would answer it in her journal. That way, if by some miracle she ever saw him again, and she had the opportunity, she could share the letters with him. Maybe it was a childish waste of time, but she didn't think so. She put the date at the top of the page and began to write.

When she finished writing she prepared to go downstairs for dinner. The aroma of Miss Bell's excellent cooking drifted up to her room. Her stomach growled.

Still feeling the joy of Pilan''s letter, she hurried down the stairs, the photograph he'd sent in hand.

"What have we here?" Her grandfather nodded toward the picture she held.

"I received this photograph with a letter from Pilan' Rousseau today. He took it with his camera the day Great-aunt Myrtle taught me to drive her motorcar."

She handed the picture to Grandfather. After looking at it he chuckled and handed it to her grandmother. He wrapped an arm around Kristina's shoulders and squeezed. "That sister-in-law of mine is quite a woman, owning and driving an automobile. And so are you, my dear."

"Both you and my sister are a lot braver than I am," Grandmother said. "Myrtle always was more adventurous than I. And she never did let me learn to drive that contraption while we were there."

"It's probably a good thing," Grandfather said. He laughed.

Grandmother swatted his arm and frowned.

Kristina accepted the picture from her grandmother. "So, Grandfather, you seem to approve of women driving automobiles. Am I right?"

"I think its fine as long as they're careful."

"Don't you think men should be careful too?"

"Yes, of course." Her grandfather chuckled. "What did the young man who took the picture think about you driving that vehicle?"

She smiled. "He thought it was fine and dandy."

"He's a good sport."

Conversation at the supper table was light, animated. Grandfather was in a great mood. He talked about purchasing a motorcar of his own. When supper was finished and Miss Bell began to clear the table, Kristina excused herself and went to her room to study. But her mind was on Pilan'; he was a good sport, indeed.

Chapter 20

Time passed swiftly like the seasons. Thanksgiving and Christmas had come and gone. All the festivities of turkey and ham dinners, music performances, and the church cantata were pleasant memories. Kristina had missed being home for Christmas, but it was a lovely time at her grandparents' home, with a large, beautifully decorated tree, a Christmas Eve service at church, and a delicious Christmas dinner. They had generously showered her with brightly wrapped gifts, but it didn't take away her longing for home and family.

When classes began after the break and she was busy in school again, her homesickness lessened. Her time spent in long hours of study, vocal and piano practice helped the time go by more quickly.

One evening, shortly after New Year's Eve when she was sitting in the living room with her grandparents, the telephone rang. Grandmother rushed into the kitchen where the phone hung on the wall and answered it. Her cheerful voice carried into the living room. "Why, yes, dear. Yes, she's here. Just a moment." Grandmother called out, "Kristina, this call is for you."

Thinking it must be her father or mother calling from a borrowed telephone, she ran to answer, excited to hear their voices.

"Hello."

The voice on the other end sounded far away, strange. "This is Bentley."

The conversation was short, awkward. Bentley's voice shook as he invited her to have lunch with him. Feeling sorry for his stammering effort, she almost accepted his invitation. Instead, she graciously turned him down, using the excuse that she was extremely busy with her studies and didn't have a moment free. It was partially true. And why lead the poor fellow on? It was best to say no now, rather than let him think she was willing to be courted by him.

The winter in Boston that year was mild, according to Grandfather, but there was enough snow to transform the city into a winter wonderland, which she enjoyed. Spring arrived early, displaying a glorious profusion of flowers and blossoming trees unlike anything she'd seen at home. Many of the flowers she couldn't name but tulips, which she recognized, dotted nearly every garden in a variety of bright colors. She liked the yellow ones best. Magnolia trees presented their spring wardrobe of pink and white blossoms, and she thought about Pilan' and his camera. Although the colors wouldn't show in the photos, vibrant pictures appeared around every corner. She imagined him taking hundreds of photographs.

It seemed like forever since Pilan''s letter had arrived, so when she received another one postmarked Los Angeles, California, she almost jumped up and down with joy.

Dated April 14, 1906 the letter was short. It told about his ride up Bunker Hill on something called a funicular; it was some kind of little train-car on a track that carried people to the top of a hill. She was fascinated to learn that California also had a Bunker Hill, but it didn't appear to have any historical significance like the one in Boston. It did, however, sounded interesting, and she wished he'd sent a picture.

Kristina could almost detect the excitement in Pilan''s words about his adventure along the coastline from Los Angeles to San Diego and back. His description of the Pacific Ocean made her want to go there. How she wished she could see and hear and smell what he was experiencing.

The last paragraph was brief, clipped.

> *Leaving Los Angeles April 15, train to San Francisco. Don't know when I'll write.*
>
> *Pilan'*

This time, there were no personal undertones, or any indication that he thought of her fondly or missed her. But at least he'd taken the time to write again. Glad for that much, she clung to his words and tucked the letter safely away to save with the first one.

She sat back and thought about Pilan' and his adventurous spirit. How nice it must be to have no set schedule, to go wherever and whenever one pleased. She couldn't imagine how that might feel. Her days were governed by the clock, exams, hours of music practice, and set meal times. Would it always be that way? She hoped not.

PILAN' ENJOYED THE EARLY morning hours when it was cool and few people were on the streets. Sitting in a small café in downtown San Francisco, he downed another cup of strong, black coffee and finished his breakfast. He glanced at a calendar hanging on the wall near the cash register. April 18, 1906. He hadn't paid much attention to dates lately. It didn't seem possible he'd been traveling six months already. He paid his bill and left the café, meandering back toward the hotel. It was several blocks away and he was in no hurry.

He stopped to look in a store window. Unlike anything he'd ever felt, a hard jolt shook the ground beneath him. Startled, he looked around. Suddenly, there was a deafening rumble, and violent shaking almost knocked him off his feet. Glass, bricks, and parts of the building showered down around him, striking his shoulders and head. He dodged what he could as he dashed toward the street. The shaking earth threw him sideways. He grabbed a lamp post, clinging to it. Just ahead of him, the asphalt road and sidewalk lifted into a mound four or five feet high. He couldn't believe his eyes. How was that possible? Terrified, he hung on to the post for several seconds after the shaking stopped.

In shock from experiencing his first earthquake he began to walk, making his way around fallen debris, ignoring his cuts, scrapes, and pain. He almost stumbled over the limp body of a man who had been crushed by the falling façade of a large department store. Tossing aside some of the bricks and wood, Pilan' knelt and placed his fingers on the man's neck. The poor fellow was dead.

People filled the streets, disheveled and dazed. Some women were scantily dressed in nightgowns, some men in pajamas. A gray-haired lady in a housecoat wandered about aimlessly, carrying two howling cats, one under each arm, and another woman with blood on her hands and face, stood in the middle of the street. It was a nightmarish scene he wished he could escape.

Before long, injured people crying for help were everywhere he looked, some gasping for a last breath, others frantically looking for loved ones.

The ground shook again.

"Aftershock," someone yelled. The shaking didn't last long this time, but Pilan''s heart still trembled.

When buildings everywhere erupted into flames he ran, following other people away from the fires. The city became an inferno.

By the time he returned to the hotel where he'd been staying, there was nothing left. He stood in the street staring at the rubble and smoldering ash. It was senseless to think about ever seeing his belongings again. The violin his father had bought him at the age of eight was gone, along with the camera, his journal, and dozens of photographs. All gone. If only he'd been in the room when the earthquake began, perhaps he could have grabbed his most important belongings and fled to the street for safety. But it was too late. Another aftershock hit, but he was too stunned to react.

For three days he walked the streets helping to search for survivors, thankful he'd escaped serious injury. Unlike many, he had on good clothes and ample money in his pocket to survive. When he was able to check on his horse it was too late; it was dead. Pilan was among thousands of homeless refugees escaping the fires, huddling at night in the plaza or wherever they could find a safe place to rest. Outside help came, but food lines were long and water was scarce. He watched as thousands of people fought for space to escape on the Oakland ferry. He'd thought about joining them, but he wanted to stay in the city and help whomever he could.

Late on the third day he made his way up a hill beyond the city. Houses were badly damaged. Some were thrown half off their foundations and leaning at odd angles, others were completely destroyed, but they hadn't burned. Up ahead he spotted what appeared to be a small child hunched over on the sidewalk. Pilan' approached cautiously, not wanting to frighten the child.

A little boy no more than three or four years old, his tear-streaked face smeared with blood and dirt, sat gazing at the sidewalk. Wearing filthy pajamas, his tiny, bare feet were caked in dirt and blood. Pilan' knelt down in front of the child and took his hand. "Where are your parents, son?"

"I don't know." Tears welled up in the child's eyes. The boy seemed lost and in shock. He pointed in one direction, then turned and pointed in another. He shrugged and shook his head, tears on his cheeks forming a river through the dried blood and dirt.

"Do you know where your house is?"

A shake of his head was the child's only response.

"What's your name?"

"Peter." That was a good start.

"Do you have a last name, Peter?" Maybe the boy's parents were searching for him, and Pilan' could locate them.

After a moment Peter answered. "Johnson."

"Well, Peter Johnson, why don't you come with me?"

"Why?"

"We'll see if we can find your mommy and daddy."

Without answering, Peter let Pilan' pick him up and carry him. The boy was almost limp, probably from lack of food and water. After finding food for the child Pilan' would try to find someone who could doctor Peter's feet, and perhaps he could find some stockings or shoes to protect his little feet, but with the whole town in ruin, he couldn't imagine where. Once the child was fed, Pilan' would search for the parents.

A day passed and no one knew to whom Peter belonged. His parents couldn't be found. Pilan' learned from Peter that he'd crawled from the rubble of his house. "It fell down," the boy said.

Peter didn't know if his parents were still in the house or not, and he didn't know how many days he'd been on the street. At first he'd called and called, but they hadn't answered.

It seemed unbelievable that no one had helped the child. Hadn't anyone seen him wandering outside all alone? Pilan' prayed for help, and he hoped that in time the child's parents would be found, but in the meantime, he'd take care of the boy himself. He'd care for him and protect him as long as it took to find a guardian.

But none was found.

He carried Peter everywhere, sometimes putting him on his shoulders, sometimes bracing the boy astride one hip. He stood in long food lines and made sure the boy got food and water, but the rations were small. At night he covered the small, frail body with his arms, and did his best to protect the little guy. Neither slept much.

On the fifth day Pilan' still had no luck in locating Peter's parents, not even a relative, and according to Peter, he had no brothers or sisters. The boy was alone, a four-year-old orphan.

After asking several people what he should do with Peter and getting no reasonable answer, Pilan' sought yet another policeman. The uniformed young man was covered with ash, his eyes red, either from smoke or crying. Pilan' couldn't tell which. He looked exhausted, and as shaken and confused as the rest of the citizens.

"I found this little boy wandering around alone and we can't find his mother or father. Can you tell me what I should do with him?"

Tired and bedraggled, the red-eyed officer shook his head. "I don't know anything right now."

Unable to obtain helpful information, Pilan' was ready to give up, but one thing was certain; he wasn't going to abandon the boy.

Carrying Peter on his shoulders, he walked toward the bay. "How would you like to take a ferry ride, young man?"

"Why?" Pilan' laughed. Why was it that all little children asked why?

"Because if we take the ferry over to Oakland, maybe we can buy some clothes for both of us, and I bet we can find a place to eat a good hot meal and someplace warm to sleep tonight. Would you like that?"

This time Peter didn't ask why. "Yes."

Being at the front of the line, Pilan' was first to board the next ferry. He found a spot against the railing near the front of the boat. He held Peter close to him as other passengers squeezed around them. The boat was crowded, but apparently more orderly than it had been the first few days when people were panicked and fighting for a place on board. As they moved across the bay, even though the water was choppy, the damp breeze was a relief from the smoldering city, and for the first time since the earthquake, Pilan' took a deep breath and relaxed a little.

It was a welcome sight when rays of sunshine broke through the fog. He thought about Kristina then, and wondered if she'd heard about the disastrous earthquake. If he could find writing materials he'd send her a short note.

He'd written to her from Los Angeles telling her he was going to San Francisco, so most likely she'd assume he was still there. After the way he'd said goodbye to her, she might not care where he was, or if she ever heard from him again. Still, if Kristina had heard about the earthquake, and he was sure she must have, she was the type who would worry if she thought he'd been hurt or in danger. The least he could do was put her mind at ease. Thinking about what to write, he realized he still cared for her more than he wanted to admit.

As the ferry approached the landing on the Oakland shore, Pilan' was surprised to see huge crowds of people milling about and more long lines. When the craft came to a full stop, he carried Peter ashore and was immediately directed where to go for help.

"Take the lad to the church three blocks up that way," said a stout woman in a long, wool coat and bonnet. She pointed straight ahead. "You'll find medical help there. Looks like that handsome face of yours could use a bit of nursing, too."

"Thank you." He'd thought very little about his own injuries. He only knew a spot on his head hurt, and his shoulders were sore. He must look frightful after days without bathing or shaving.

He followed a line of people as instructed. As he walked toward the church it was clear Oakland had suffered a great deal of damage from the quake, too, but they'd been spared the fires. In spite of their losses, it seemed the town had been quick to organize relief workers for the thousands of homeless people who flooded in from San Francisco.

In a few short minutes he found himself and Peter in a large church which had been turned in to a makeshift hospital. He showed a worker Peter's feet, and was led to an examination table. When the child's feet were cleaned and bandaged, Pilan' offered to pay for the service, but his money was refused and his own injuries were doctored free of charge as well.

"Will you need food and shelter?" The young woman, no more than sixteen or seventeen, had helped administer care to both Peter and him. Her voice was filled with compassion, gentleness.

"Yes, thank you."

By evening they had been given free clothing, shoes for Peter, two hot meals, and a place to sleep. *You are good Lord. Thank you for your loving servants who are ministering to the needs of all these people who have come out of desperation. Thank you for the provisions you've given us today, and for a warm place to sleep tonight.*

Until Peter was sound asleep Pilan' stayed beside him, watching the little boy, praying a family member would be found.

Pilan' woke at sunrise, thankful for a decent night's sleep. With the care and assistance they'd received in Oakland, there was no reason to return to San Francisco. There was nothing but ashes left of his belongings, and he doubted it would pay to check back with the people with whom he'd left Peter's name. The folks here in Oakland could accomplish the same results in the search for Peter's parents.

Three more days passed with Peter in his care, and Pilan was growing fond of the boy. "What do you say, Peter, shall we check out this department store and see what they have?"

"I guess so." Still quiet and clearly full of despair, Peter rarely said much.

"I bet they have toys." Although it was badly damaged, the department store was operating and full of grappling shoppers.

Pilan bought Peter five new pairs of pants, several shirts, a stack of underwear, and other necessary items of clothing, all at very high jacked-up prices, but he didn't mind. He'd made arrangements for Peter to stay in a special home for lost children, and he wasn't going to leave the child without plenty of good clothing and a warm jacket. Pilan"s personal selection of clothing consisted of a few necessities and a small suitcase to carry them in. He didn't want a lot to haul around. The small toy department didn't have much to choose from, but Peter found a metal, toy fire truck he liked. Pilan' gladly paid the exorbitant price, happy to see Peter smile for the first time.

Later in the evening, using a makeshift dinner table in the church and borrowed writing materials, he penned a quick note to his parents and a longer one to Kristina. He wrote about the earthquake and what he'd experienced, assuring them he was all right, and he told about finding Peter and caring for him. He dropped the letters at the post office, which promised delivery, and then he bought a train ticket to Portland, Oregon.

Leaving Peter behind was difficult and it tugged at Pilan"s heart, but it was impossible to keep the child. He was surprised by how much pleasure he'd experienced from caring for the little boy; it made him optimistic about being a father someday. Did Kristina want children, he wondered?

The shelter where Peter would stay assured Pilan' they would make every effort to find the little boy's parents or next of kin. He would be in good hands, thanks to the benevolent residents and churches in Oakland.

He hugged Peter goodbye and was ready to leave, when he stopped abruptly and turned back to the woman in charge of the shelter. "May I leave my name and an address where you can contact me later? I would like to know if you find Peter's family."

"Yes, Mr. Rousseau. I'd be happy to notify you."

He jotted down his name and the address for Potts's restaurant. It was the only address he knew, and it might be awhile before he got back there, but something was drawing him back. He'd explore the Oregon coast then return to Oklahoma City.

Kristina sat down at the supper table, the atmosphere somber. A month had passed since she'd received Pilan"s letter from Los Angeles saying he was going to San Francisco. Since news about the catastrophic earthquake she'd done little else than worry. She didn't know if he'd left San Francisco before the earthquake, but according to the date of his letter, she feared he was there when the quake occurred. She prayed he wasn't. According to the newspaper accounts thousands of people had lost their lives or were refugees on the streets. It was practically all the newspapers had reported for weeks. *Oh, Lord please let Pilan' be safe.*

She couldn't bear the thought of him dying. Even if he never came back to Oklahoma or wrote her another letter, Pilan' couldn't die. He was a wonderful young man, talented, and full of adventure. He had so much to give the world. People like him weren't supposed to die young.

Heavy hearted and worried, she'd hardly eaten since the first news about the earthquake. Her plate still three-quarters full, she took a small bite of green peas and pushed it aside.

Grandfather spoke up his voice firm, reassuring. "Even if your friend was in San Francisco, he could very well be alive, Kristina. Let's not believe the worst without knowing."

She nodded, trying to agree with her grandfather, but her heart didn't agree with her head. With no way to communicate with Pilan', and no way to know where he was, it was impossible to shake the terrible feelings.

She'd never heard of anything so devastating, or seen pictures like those in the daily newspapers her grandfather received. How could anyone have survived such a tragedy? And how could those who weren't killed survive the aftermath: the fires, lack of shelter, lack of food and water?

Kristina couldn't imagine what it must be like to feel the earth shake so hard it would knock down big buildings, or throw a person off his feet. It was terrifying. She was glad they didn't have earthquakes in Boston or Oklahoma City. Of course the tornados in Oklahoma were terrible, too, and she'd seen utter devastation left in the wake of more than one in her short life. Still, to think about the earth shaking and cracking made her shudder. It was hard to picture a large city being totally destroyed.

"We'll pray your friend is safe, and believe that you'll hear from him before long," Grandmother said, reaching across the table and patting

Kristina's hand. "God is merciful. The Bible says he who trusts in the Lord is kept safe."

She wanted to believe Pilan' was safe, wanted to trust that God had protected him if he'd been in the earthquake. "Yes, but what about all those who died? Good people who believe in the Lord die sometimes. Why does one person deserve to live or die any more than another?"

"There are some things we can't understand, dear," Grandfather said. "Only our creator knows when it's time for someone to pass away."

"I know." Her grandparents were right. Hard as it was to understand, she would pray for Pilan' and expect to hear from him.

Dinner finished, her grandmother rose and gave Kristina a hug. "Please let us know if you receive any news of his whereabouts."

Grandmother no longer seemed against her friendship with Pilan', and Bentley's name hadn't been mentioned since his telephone call. On more than one occasion, however, her grandmother encouraged her to develop new friendships with some of the fine male students at school. Kristina had simply smiled and gone about her studies.

Later that evening, in the privacy and comfort of her room, Kristina snuggled into the big chair. Unable to study, her mind wandered. She secretly wished she and Pilan' were traveling around the world together. What a wonderful experience it must be to see far away places with such rich histories. Now that she'd been in Boston a few months, it no longer seemed distant or unique. She was glad for the opportunity to go to college there and see the interesting sites, but she realized the world was a much bigger place, and there was so much more to see. She closed her eyes and sighed. Maybe someday she'd be able travel to new and exciting places.

Again, her mind drifted back to San Francisco and Pilan'. It was torture not knowing where he was. If only she'd stayed in Oklahoma City and begged him to stay a few more days, perhaps he wouldn't have been in San Francisco yet. She felt as if part of her life had been ripped from her, her heart torn in two. Was this even slightly how it felt to lose a husband? Mama Leoma must have been torn apart worse than this when her first husband, Jeremy, had died. She'd give anything now to be home to talk with her mother, to feel the comfort of her arms.

Chapter 21

KRISTINA STOOD CENTER STAGE waiting for her cue. She didn't feel like singing—didn't want to sing, but the mandatory solo was part of her final grade for vocal class. Long, slow weeks had passed, and still there was no news from Pilan'. Even though she would rather be in San Francisco searching for him, she wanted to do well tonight. She had a promise to keep.

Glancing over the audience, she spotted her grandparents in the third row and smiled. She had given them her word to keep her grades up and to do her very best. They'd made all this possible for her, and they expected her to keep her end of the bargain. She didn't want to disappoint them.

The orchestra began to play. She steadied her breathing and filled her lungs. As soon as she sang the first note, she focused on the music and words, her intonation precise, her soprano voice hitting the high notes with perfection. The music filled the innermost recesses of her heart, and yet, she didn't feel the same passion as when she sang with Pilan''s violin accompaniment. If only he could be here now, accompanying her, sharing this moment.

Her last note barely out, the audience rose to its feet and gave a roaring applause. She curtsied. The standing ovation continued. Surprised, she curtsied again and left the stage.

All that remained before the end of the school year was a final piano recital.

IT WAS A SUNNY Saturday morning in May. The aroma of ham and eggs mingled with coffee and lingered in the air. Miss Bell had cleared the breakfast table, and Grandmother was in the garden planting flowers. Grandfather sat in a big leather chair in his office reading the newspaper, his usual Saturday ritual. Kristina pushed clothing back and forth in the closet, deciding what to pack for her trip home and what to leave for the next school year and winter.

The first year of college behind her, she was anxious to pack her suitcases. She looked forward to the train trip back to Oklahoma City. All her brothers and sister must be a head taller, she thought, and Mama's letters had said that a hint of beard was beginning to appear on Dyer's face. She couldn't imagine. Her mind going top speed, she scolded herself for all her daydreaming. Only two days remained to practice for her final recital.

Kristina had prayed for Pilan' like Grandmother had said weeks ago, and as best she could, she turned him and her worries over to God. There were still times when she caught herself fretting about his survival and his whereabouts, but when that happened, she quickly stopped herself and thanked God that he was in control.

Her mind shifted, and she thought about how Mama Leoma had traded in her life-long dream to open a bookshop for marriage and a family. Had it been worth it, Kristina wondered, for Mama to shove her passion aside? Pilan' had a passion for adventure and a plan to open a dance studio. It appeared he had no intention of giving them up. Kristina had a passion for music and a plan to open a music studio. After pondering her situation further Kristina reinforced her determination not to follow in her mother's footsteps. With or without love or marriage, Kristina would soon be the proud proprietor of a music studio.

Suddenly, as if God had put the thoughts into her mind, she realized she was wrong to belittle Mama's decision to trade her bookshop for marriage and a family. She was glad Mama Leoma had sacrificed her dreams in order to marry Papa and have children. After all, if she hadn't wet-nursed Dyer he would have died. Kristina wouldn't have her brother today, and that was a heart-wrenching thought. Mama had helped turn Papa's life around, and he was a wonderful father. She'd instilled the love of books and music in Kristina, and encouraged her to attend college. New love and appreciation for Mama welled up in her heart, and she could hardly wait to get home.

The story of how God whispered to Mama Leoma came to mind. She'd loved hearing Mama tell the tale over the years, of how when she wanted to give up and die, God's whispers nudged her to obey, to nurse Dyer, and how God promised to give her strength and faith to carry on when she was in the depths of grief over the loss of her husband and baby daughter. Kristina took a deep breath and wiped an unexpected tear from her cheek, overwhelmed with realization of what an amazing woman Mama was.

Oh, Lord, never let me criticize Mama again for her decision to give up her dream. I realize now she was obedient to you, and you put her in our lives for so many good reasons. Teach me to respect her more, and to become more like her. Thank you for blessing me with a wonderful mother.

At last, Kristina boarded the train. Making the trip alone as an independent woman, she was pleased with her accomplishments and excellent grades. She'd miss her grandparents, but she'd see them again when she returned for her final year of school. Counting the days, then hours, until she'd see her father, mother, brothers, and sisters, her heart filled with warmth.

There was so much catching up to do. Ten months had gone by, and she imagined little Gracie May with a mouth full of teeth and toddling around the house. What a bundle of fun she must be. She thought of each of her siblings with tenderness, anxious to see how they'd grown and changed. And with fondest affection she thought of Dyer. What a fine young man he was becoming. Now *there* was a fellow with unwavering passion and a heart for God. Her mother's recent letters had made no mention of his health, except that he was doing well, so Kristina assumed he no longer had the terrible headaches. Anxious to wrap her arms around him, she breathed a prayer of thanks for God's care of her brother while she was away.

She fell into the train's rhythmic rocking motion and click-clack on the tracks. It was almost musical. Kristina tapped the toe of one boot, and moved her head back and forth. Several times the train's movement lulled her into a dreamy, semi-sleep and thoughts of home.

And Pilan'.

She'd been home a week, and Kristina couldn't get enough of being in her mother's kitchen, and watching the younger children play. She'd hardly put Gracie May down since she'd walked through the door. Kristina loved holding the toddler, playing little hand games with her, and singing to her. She couldn't remember being so enthralled with the other children when they were small, and she wondered why she now enjoyed this closeness with her youngest sibling so intensely. Perhaps it was because she'd been away so long, or maybe, because she was more mature. Both perhaps. She nuzzled her younger sister closer and breathed in the sweet baby smell.

"If you keep carrying that baby around all day she'll forget how to walk," Mama said, smiling, turning the fried potatoes.

Baking ham and cornbread in the oven smelled wonderful. "It's just so good to be home and to be with everyone. I missed you all so much." Kristina spotted a booklet on the counter top. It didn't look like a cookbook; it was more like a small catalog. She picked it up. "What's this?"

Her mother turned and smiled. "That's a catalog of publishers and books. Glenda and I have decided to open a bookshop together when Gracie May starts school."

"That's wonderful, Mama. You'll finally have the bookshop you've always dreamed of."

"It will be a few years before it happens, but your father has agreed to it, and we're working out the details."

A knock at the front door interrupted the conversation.

"Gracie May and I will go see who's here, won't we Gracie?" She bounced the baby up and down on her hip as she danced out of the kitchen and through the living room, half expecting to see Doris or Glenda at the door.

It was Toby. Surprised to see him on the other side of the screen door, she froze.

"Hello, Kristina."

"Hello." He didn't call her Krissy. Something other than the clean, fresh haircut and the new, well-fitting clothing was different as well.

He had a peaceable look that she hadn't seen since childhood, and even though she'd heard all about his church-going, she was uncomfortable.

"I heard ya came home for the summer?"

"Yes." She hesitated, lost for words. "Are you here to see Dyer?"

"No. I'd like to talk to ya for a minute. I got some things I need to tell ya."

What could he possibly have to say to her? If he was going to ask her to be his girl, he could forget it. She thought he'd be over that by now. Tempted to say she didn't want to talk to him, she almost closed the door. But his kind demeanor stopped her from turning him away.

"Have a seat on the porch and I'll be right out." She took Gracie into the kitchen and put her down to play on the floor.

"I'll be on the front porch, Mama. It seems Toby needs to talk to me. I can't imagine why."

"Be kind to him, sweetheart, he's a different young man these days. I know he did some bad things, but Dyer has helped him turn his life around."

If only Mama knew all the bad things Toby had done.

"You mentioned that in your letters. I still don't know why he needs to talk to me."

"Toby needs the acceptance and kindness of Christian friends. He's repented and he has taken his punishment like a man. Now we must do our part to show him Christ-like love."

She understood and agreed with her mother, but if he started sweet-talking her about courting her she'd chase him off in a hurry. "Well, I won't be long."

Kristina found Toby waiting on the top porch step, hands folded between his knees, his head lowered, apparently in deep thought. She stepped outside and sat down beside him saying nothing.

He didn't speak.

The smell of soap and cologne instead of alcohol was a pleasant change in him.

"What do you need to tell me?" She wanted to send him on his way as quickly as possible.

Toby raised his head and peered into her eyes, his face serious, somehow older looking. "I came to apologize for the bad things I done to you. The good Lord's been working on me to do things right. Sheriff Higgins worked me over right good, too. Done some jail time and other stuff he made me do." He paused and looked at the ground.

"What kind of things did he make you do?"

Toby dug his curled fingers into his knees. "Had to go around and tell the folks I wronged what I done and apologize, but you was still in Boston. Made me dig weeds, paint buildings, stuff like that."

"I see." She waited, wondering what else Toby had to say.

"The sheriff talked real good to me, like a real paw, and he treated me like a regular person. My own paw ain't nothing but a mean old drunk, and he don't care none about me. I don't want to be bad anymore. I'm trying real hard to change."

"I'm sure your father cares about you. Maybe he just doesn't know how to show it. I heard you were going to church and trying to change your life."

"Yeah. Anyhow, I'm real sorry for hurting you, and for all the mean things I done. I'm terrible sorry about your dog, too. I was so awful mad when he jumped me, I lost my mind. I know now it's a good thing he attacked me, or I would've hurt you worse. You suppose you can ever forgive me?"

Toby's voice cracked. Tears welled up in his eyes and he turned away. His shoulders shook and he sobbed. Deeply moved by his apology, Kristina reached out with one hand and touched a quaking shoulder. Clearly, God was working on his heart. She knew she had to forgive him.

Her words came surprisingly easy. "I forgive you, Toby."

He turned back to her, his eyes red and glazed, his body close but not touching her. "Thank you. I can't tell you how worried I was that you'd never forgive me. I been praying every day that ya would."

"I can see you're sincere, and I appreciate your apology." She paused, not wanting to sound all preachy, but she went on. "The Bible says I should forgive others when they sin against me so God will forgive my sins."

"I'm pretty sure you ain't never sinned in your life."

She smiled. "We're all sinners, Toby. We must be thankful God is a loving and forgiving God."

"That's what Dyer told me." Toby straightened and smiled. "I have something else to tell ya."

"All right." Uh oh, here it comes; he's going to ask if he can court me. She held her breath.

"You was always special, like my sweetheart. But I was plain stupid to treat you the way I done. I was wrong, and like I said, I'm sorry. Anyhow, I been courting Etta Ziegler since Christmas, and I treat her real good. We're planning on getting married."

"Etta Nadine Ziegler?" Shocked, Kristina let out a long breath.

"Yup." Toby's face brightened.

That was a surprise. Etta was a year behind Kristina in school and quite a pretty girl. Toby must have drastically changed his ways in the last ten months to catch the eye of a nice girl like Etta.

"She wants to get married in October." Love beaming from his eyes, Toby's smile grew. It was amazing to see the transformation in him.

"Congratulations."

"Thanks. What ever happened to that half-bre—I mean that fellow that had his eyes on you?"

Kristina's throat choked up. She hadn't talked about Pilan' much since she arrived home. It hurt too much. "I think he died in the San Francisco earthquake."

"Why would you think that?" Toby's voice rose and he seemed genuinely shocked and interested.

"He wrote to me at my grandparents' house. The last letter was from Los Angeles, California, and he said he was going to San Francisco that week—just a couple of days before the earthquake happened. I haven't heard from him since."

"Aw gee, Kristina, that's awful. I heard that you two said your final goodbyes before you went off to Boston, but it sounds like you still like him." Dusty came over to them, and Toby reached out and scratched the dog behind the ears.

"We did, but I never wanted to part ways with him, and I hoped I'd see him again."

"Sounds to me like you fell in love with him."

It seemed strange talking to Toby about love and relationships after all the bad things that had happened, but he was so different now, and forgiveness seemed to change things. Tears surfaced and threatened to fall. "I did; I still love him. He was a wonderful, talented man."

"Yeah. I was mighty jealous of him."

"He was very proud of his French and Indian heritage. Did you know that?"

Toby stood shaking his head. "I could tell he was a good man. Well, I gotta go. I'm sorry for ya. I hope you'll get over him and find another man someday."

Now she shook her head. "I don't think so."

Chapter 22

Potts shook Pilan''s hand then grabbed him into a bear hug. "Good to have you back, my friend. Your job is waiting if you want it."

"Sure. Thank you, Potts. It's good to be back. I never thought I'd miss this place, but I have to tell you, I sure missed your good cooking. I haven't had a decent steak since I left here."

"You get yourself settled in upstairs, and come on back down. I'll throw a big, juicy steak on the stove. You going out to see that pretty little Kristina right away? I hear she's home from that fancy college out east."

"I—"

"Hey there, buddy!" Jake burst into the kitchen and grabbed Pilan''s hand in a hearty handshake. "Man, I'm glad to see you."

"Likewise, Jake. You been staying out of trouble?"

"Why sure. Between working here for cranky old Potts and courting my new gal, I don't have time for carousing."

"So you have yourself a woman, huh?" Pilan' figured half the women in town would be chasing after Jake. He was a fine looking man, and a good, upstanding one, too. Any woman would be lucky to snag him.

"He's got him a pretty one." Potts lifted the lid off a big pot and stirred the contents. It smelled like beans.

Pilan' grinned, feeling at home again. "Is that right? Tell me about her, Jake."

"Her name's Nessy. A few months ago she moved into town with her family. Came from some little town in Ohio."

"She's a beauty," Potts put in, still stirring his pot of steaming food. "I was just asking Pilan' if he's going out to see that sweet little Soderlund gal when you barged in." Potts replaced the lid on the giant kettle, and rested a hot, heavy hand on Pilan"s shoulder, curiosity in his eyes.

Jake eyed him. "Well are you?"

"I'm planning to, as soon as I get settled in my room and get some decent food in my stomach."

Jake fingered his chin between his thumb and forefinger, a troubled frown on his face. "I caught a glimpse of her and Toby talking on the library steps the other day. I thought they looked awfully friendly. If you wait too long, Toby or some other fellow is going to snatch her up."

"I hope not. I was a fool to tell her goodbye, thinking my travels were more important than she was. But why would she be talking with Toby after what he did?"

"I hear he's changed his ways. Paid his dues and took his punishment like a real man. Now he's got a steady job and he's going to church."

"I hope I'm not too late, if she'll still have me, that is. After all, I did say what seemed to be a final goodbye."

"Well, I wouldn't waste time then." Jake grinned and winked.

Potts handed Jake a plate of food. "Better take this out to old Frank while it's hot or he'll be yelling. You can gab later."

Potts turned to Pilan'. "We want to know all about your adventures, where you went, what you saw. And if you want to start working tomorrow morning, I'd be mighty happy to have your help."

"Tomorrow would be fine. We can catch up on everything then."

Pilan' told Potts he'd be back down in half an hour for his steak dinner, and went up to the second-floor room he'd rented. He didn't have much to unpack. He'd been lucky to find a good violin and a leather-bound journal in Portland, but he still hadn't replaced his camera. He could use a few more clothes, too, now that he was done traveling. If Kristina would have him he'd settle down in Oklahoma City.

There was a lot to do: establish a new account at the bank, write to his parents, and look for a permanent residence. But first thing after getting some good food in his stomach, he'd ride out to the Soderlunds to see Kristina. He hoped she would still talk to him, and that Toby wasn't there to run him off.

A short time later Pilan' returned wearing fresh clothes, and pulled up a chair. He dug in to the steaming, rare steak. Thick and tender, it was done just right. Potts sure knew how to feed a man. Fried potatoes were piled extra high, and the serving of beans almost ran over the edge of the plate. He'd eaten about half the food when a young man, surprise on his face, pulled up a chair next to him and sat down.

He had to look twice, then again, before he realized it was Toby. For a moment Pilan' wanted to throw him out on the street, but he knew Potts wouldn't appreciate losing a customer.

"You mind if I join you?" Toby's tone was polite, his appearance and attitude transformed like Jake had said.

Pilan' acknowledged with a quick nod. "I suppose not. How'd you know I was here?"

"I didn't. Matter of fact, I thought you were long gone. I stop in here now and then for supper after work. I figured I should come over and talk to ya."

He wasn't sure he wanted to hear what Toby had to say, but he answered. "I'm listening."

Jake appeared. "You want to order, Toby?"

Jake's tone held no love for Toby, and he was quick to take the order and leave.

"All right, go ahead, talk." Pilan' disliked having his first good meal disrupted, especially by Toby. "I heard you've been seen with Kristina. Are you here to rub it in my face?"

Heat burned in Pilan's gut. He couldn't imagine a fine woman like Kristina falling for a no-good coot like Toby, no matter how much he cleaned himself up. Not willing to let his food get cold, he continued to eat, wondering what kind of dim-witted story Toby would come up with.

"No. I just thought I'd apologize to you. Things are different with me now."

"Is that right?" Pilan' wasn't convinced.

"I already went out to apologize to Kristina for all the bad things I done to her. I'm sorry for the way I treated you, too."

Somewhat dumbfounded and extremely skeptical, it took Pilan' a few seconds to speak. "All right. And you're not courting Kristina?"

"Ah shucks, no. Like I told Kristina, I got me another girl and we're planning to get married."

"What about the other day when Jake saw you with her on the library steps?"

"We just crossed paths. I was returning Etta's book when Kristina came out. I'm telling ya straight up. And Kristina thinks you're dead; she's grieving like a widow woman. If I was you I'd high tail it out to her place and put her mind to ease."

Puzzled, Pilan' wiped his mouth and almost stuttered. "Why would she think I'm dead?"

"Said she never got no letters from ya since you were in Los Angeles. She thinks ya died in San Francisco when they had that big earthquake. Boy that was something awful, wasn't it?"

"You have no idea; I was there. I wrote Kristina a letter and told I was all right."

"I guess she didn't get the letter."

"Thanks for telling me all this, Toby. Now if you'll excuse me I have to go. Enjoy your dinner. I'll pay Potts for it."

"Thanks. Good luck."

Pilan rushed to the kitchen and paid Potts for both meals.

"Where you running off to? We haven't had a chance to talk." Potts served up a plate for another customer and handed it to Jake.

"You and I can talk all day tomorrow while I work. Right now, I'm riding out to the Soderlund place."

Chapter 23

"You look exhausted, dear," her mother said. "This isn't like you. Are you sure you're all right?"

"I didn't sleep much last night."

Kristina rose from the supper table and helped clear the dishes. Lack of sleep and recurring nightmares had left her fatigued. She'd been having disturbing dreams about Pilan' being crushed by falling bricks and glass, savagely destroying his handsome face. In one dream he staggered through piles of debris and ash, his body emaciated, eyes sunken. Awakened several times last night, she had finally refused to go back to sleep.

"You've been dragging and looking down all day. Bad dreams again?"

"Yes. But these were awful; they were horrible nightmares." Unable to hold back the tears, she began to sob. The dreams and nightmares had begun soon after news of the earthquake, but they'd never been as ugly and disturbing as those last night.

Her mother wrapped her arms around her and held her. Kristina cried for several moments, then pulled back and wiped her face with the apron she wore.

Birdie came in the kitchen and looked up at Kristina. "Don't cry sissy."

Mama knelt and spoke quietly to Birdie. "Your sister isn't feeling well, but she'll be fine in no time. You run along and entertain Gracie, please."

Birdie trotted out of the room and Mama turned to Kristina. "Why don't you go lie down and rest. I'll finish doing the dishes."

"Thank you. But I think I'll walk down to the creek. I'd like to be alone for a while." She removed her apron and hung it on the hook in the pantry.

TEN YEARS HAD GONE by since the first time Kristina had taken refuge beside the creek in the shady overhang of the big oak tree. She stood there, arms crossed, watching the rippling water, listening to the soothing rhythm. The water was low, gliding lazily over the rocks and sand. Dozens of tadpoles darted about in a small pool near the shore. As children, she and Dyer had scooped them up in jars. She smiled at the memory.

She'd spent a lot of her youth here: singing, reading, dreaming. So much had happened in this spot, some of the best times, and some of the worst. It was familiar, comfortable, yet different now. She started to hum a tune, but her voice went silent. She couldn't sing.

Birds still sang and chattered in the branches above her. The grass was still soft and cool, the water cold and refreshing. Nature still whispered her music, but something was missing.

She sat down, her back against the old tree, her knees drawn up, and she closed her eyes.

THE SODERLUND PROPERTY LOOKED the same. The early-evening sunlight painted a welcome portrait of the house, with its white paint, wide porch, and the same comfortable looking chairs. Greeted by Dusty, Pilan' gave the dog a quick pat, then bound up the front porch steps and knocked. His heart pounded. If what Toby had told him was true, he hoped Kristina would be as happy to see him as he would be to see her. He prayed that would be so. It seemed as if hours dragged by before someone came to the door.

"Pilan'? Oh, Lord in heaven! You're alive?" Mrs. Soderlund threw her cupped hands to her mouth, her eyes wide and filled with shock.

"Yes ma'am. I'm alive. I've come to see Kristina."

It took Kristina's mother several seconds to respond. "Won't she be shocked out of her wits to see you? She believes you died in that big earthquake."

He didn't want to spend time explaining. "Is she here? May I see her?"

"You'll find her down at the creek."

"Thank you. If you don't mind I'll leave my horse and buggy in the yard."

"Yes, of course, dear. That's fine."

Pilan' hurried to his buggy and fetched his violin, leaving the case behind. Instrument in hand he set out across the yard. Mr. Soderlund came out of the barn and stopped abruptly, staring as if he'd seen a ghost.

"Hello, Mr. Soderlund." Pilan' waved his violin in the air and kept walking at a brisk pace.

"But—"

"We'll talk later."

His steps swift and long, he made his way to the path. The sky was deep-blue with scattered pink and purple clouds, the air warm and sultry. His hair clung to his neck. But all he cared about was Kristina. Her special get-away in view, he hastened his stride. As he came closer he could see her beneath the tree, her head resting on her knees. He slowed, taking in the sight of her lithe figure, and the long dark hair that cascaded over her shoulders. He stopped a moment and caught his breath, sending up a small prayer, asking God to take control, to bless him with Kristina's welcome. He had a lot of explaining to do, and he prayed she would accept him back into her life.

He lifted the violin to his chin, and touched the bow to the strings. Softly, slowly, he began to play.

Soft music caught Kristina's attention. Faint at first, it sounded like violin music. But that was impossible. The only violinist she knew was Pilan', and he was gone. The music came closer, more distinct, the song familiar. *Sweetheart Be Mine*. She'd sung that song for Pilan' last year. Was she dreaming again? Puzzled, she lifted her head and listened.

The music seemed to come from home. She jumped up and looked across the cotton field. There on the path, sunset highlighting his ebony hair, she saw Pilan'. How could that be? In her miserable state of mind she must be hearing and seeing things. Certain this was another dream she closed her eyes for a few seconds. When she opened them he was still there. A chill coursed through her body leaving goose bumps on her arms. Too stunned to believe her eyes, she couldn't move.

Pilan' lowered the bow from the violin and walked toward her. She gasped for breath. He was alive.

A thousand questions running through her mind, she walked slowly at first, taking in the sight of him then she ran to him, her heart exploding in her chest.

KRISTINA STOOD BEFORE HIM, the initial shock on her face replaced by surprise, her eyes wide and searching his face. She was more beautiful than before, more mature, elegant. Her dark eyes held a thousand questions. Pilan' reached for her hand drawing her near. Without hesitation, she came into his embrace and he held her, neither of them speaking.

Pilan' pulled back and looked into her face. Tears streaked her rosy cheeks. She spoke between quiet sobs. "I can't believe you're here—alive, I'm so glad you're all right. How did you know where to find me?"

"Your mother told me you were here."

He hugged her again. What a fool he'd been to go away thinking he could forget this woman. He wanted to see her smile morning, noon, and night, hear her voice every day, and hold her forever.

Kristina's hand in his, they walked to the shade of the tree. Without speaking they sat down on a blanket he recognized from the flower patch, where he'd photographed her the summer before. The sun dropped below the horizon, its deep, amber glow washing over Kristina's face and hair. She looked like a goddess from some museum, yet she was warm, soft, and supple.

He didn't wait for questions, and he was sure Kristina had many. "I understand you didn't receive my letter from San Francisco. I can't imagine why."

"Then you did write? I thought you were... that you died." Kristina's words were choppy.

"A few days after the earthquake I wrote you a letter from a town across the bay. They assured me the mail would get delivered."

"I didn't receive it." Her voice was soft, her tone questioning. "But why did you come back? I thought when you said goodbye you didn't want to see me again."

"I was crazy to think I could go away and forget you. I couldn't get you off my mind. And you had plans of your own. As I recall, you weren't going to let man, money, or love get in the way of your dreams?"

Kristina groaned. "You're right. But you became part of the dream for my future. I didn't expect a man to come along and change my heart the way you did."

"Looks like we both have the same problem." He reached out and stroked the back of one finger down her cheek where the tears had dried.

"What problem is that?" Kristina frowned.

"Love."

Kristina's answer was in her dreamy eyes. Her nod was slow, sure.

He leaned closer, looking into her lovely brown eyes, his lips itching to taste the sweetness of her kiss. It had been so long since their first kiss. Would it be as special now? Kristina leaned toward him, meeting him half way. Her lips were soft, warm, tantalizing. The kiss was even more remarkable than the first one. When their lips parted he sat back, afraid if he didn't leave, he wouldn't be able to stop touching her.

"It's getting dark." He stood. There was so much to tell her, and he wanted to spend more time with her, but he didn't want to worry her parents by keeping her here too late. He reached for her hand and assisted her up.

"I don't want to go home," Kristina said.

Her admission thrilled him. "I don't want to go back to the hotel. Would you like to take a ride? My horse and buggy are at your house."

"I'd like that. I'll let my parents know we're leaving."

Chapter 24

A month passed as if it were only a day. Kristina picked up the letter her grandmother had forwarded from Boston. Tattered and worn, Pilan''s letter postmarked April 24 from Oakland, California, had finally arrived—almost four months after he'd written it. Unable to visualize what he'd gone through, she read it again, her heart overflowing with compassion for Pilan' and the little boy Peter. The letter was further confirmation of Pilan''s integrity and kindness. She glanced at the clock on her dressing table and gasped at the time. Pilan' would arrive soon. She slid the letter back into the envelope and put it into a drawer.

The blue, silk dress she'd bought the day before slipped over her body, and she buttoned the pearl buttons down the front. The shirtwaist style was the prettiest thing she'd found yesterday in Minnie's dress shop, and it was the perfect dress for her date with Pilan' that evening. The strand of pearls and pearl earrings Great-aunt Myrtle had given her on her last visit were just the right accessories She didn't know what Pilan' had planned, probably another fancy dinner at one of the new restaurants in town; he'd suggested she dress up for a special evening.

As long as they were together she was happy. Sometimes they simply sat beside the creek and talked or sang, and other times they enjoyed a picnic in the park. On several occasions Pilan' had come to her house for dinner, and afterward they'd played board games with her younger siblings. If they sat in the parlor to talk it was never without interruptions from clamoring children, but Pilan' didn't seem to mind.

A flash of lightning lit up the room, and thunder rattled the window. *Oh, Lord, please stop all that banging around up there. Can't you send the storm in a different direction this time?* It was probably wrong to talk to God like that, but surely he must understand how important her date was with Pilan'.

Turning away from the window, she examined her reflection in the oval cheval mirror that stood in the corner of her bedroom, pleased with her new look. A faint hint of rouge brightened her cheeks with a rosy glow, and her lips shimmered with the new pink lip color Minnie had suggested. A light dusting of face powder was applied last. The makeup was just enough to enhance her looks, and she hoped it was in good taste and Pilan' would approve.

There were a lot of firsts in her life these days besides the cosmetics. For the first time ever, she was going to be in a wedding. She'd be standing up for Doris when she and Harland got married the following spring. She was being courted by a man; that was a big first. And for the first time, she realized she could have a loving relationship without giving up her plans for the music studio. Pilan' wouldn't allow her to give up her dream. Lately she'd begun to understand Doris's desire for romance and marriage, although, Kristina still wasn't keen on having babies for a long, long time.

She lifted the stopper from the elaborate bottle of Violette de Madame Perfume, one of many extravagant gifts Pilan' had given her. She'd heard the French perfume by Guerlain was very expensive. After breathing in a long whiff of the opened bottle, she dabbed a tiny amount behind each ear. She never tired of the sweet jasmine and woodsy fragrance.

The sound of a horse's hooves sent her dashing to the window. Coming up the path was a shiny, new carriage being pulled by a magnificent, black horse. Her heart raced at the sight of Pilan' at the reins.

Kristina took one last glance in the mirror, making sure her hair was perfect. By the time she went to the door Pilan' was coming up the porch steps, a large bouquet of colorful flowers in one hand. He was extremely dashing in a dark-gray three-piece suit. His smile spread when she pushed open the screen door and invited him in. A gust of wind nearly ripped the door off the hinges, and another bolt of lightning, much closer this time, crackled, sending a chill down her spine. Pilan' hurried through the door.

He kissed her and gave her a careful hug. "I don't want to mess up your hair; it's lovely. You look especially beautiful this evening."

Pilan''s compliments were never spared on her. "Thank you. You look quite dashing yourself," she said. "I see you have a new carriage and horse."

"Yes, finally. I couldn't borrow or rent them forever."

Dyer rushed in from the yard. "I'll put your horse and carriage in the barn. I don't think you're going anyplace for a while."

"But we—"

Ignoring her, in a mad dash Dyer led the horse to the barn and disappeared inside just as the rain began to pelt the house.

Her shoulders dropped and she groaned. "I don't believe this is happening."

Pilan' had experienced several storms, but never anything like this one. He gazed out the living room window. Hard rain turned to hail. He'd never seen such large chunks of ice drop from the sky. Everything in its wake would be damaged, and he was grateful that Dyer had taken his horse and carriage to shelter right away.

He turned to Kristina, one hand on the small of her back. "I'm sorry our plans are being dashed by this weather, but Dyer is right. Unless this blows over right away we'll have to stay here."

He could see the disappointment in her eyes. She took the flowers and thanked him, talking over her shoulder as he followed her to the kitchen. She sounded hopeful when she answered. "Maybe it'll stop soon."

"Perhaps."

But the wind blew harder and roared, thunder boomed louder, and hail pounded on the roof like drums.

He peered out the kitchen window while Kristina filled a vase with water for the flowers. Outside the trees and plants bowed low. After a few minutes the hail turned to heavy rain again, and the sky became an eerie green. He'd never seen anything like it.

In another room Birdie and Gracie's cries turned to wails. Mr. Soderlund rushed into the kitchen, Birdie under one arm like a sack of potatoes. "Everybody get to the cellar! Now!"

Pilan' had no idea where the cellar was. Why would they all go into a cellar? Was it some kind of shelter from the weather? Was the storm going to get worse? In Paris it might be foggy and rainy for days at a time, but that was no reason to rush into a storage cellar.

Kristina stuffed the flowers in the vase and left them on the counter. She grabbed his hand, leading him out to the service porch. On the way through she grabbed two long overcoats off a hook and gave one to him. Following Kristina's lead, Pilan put on the coat, grateful that his new suit wouldn't be ruined. He put his arm around Kristina's shoulder as they raced the few steps outside to the cellar door. Mr. Soderlund was already there holding the wooden door up.

Mrs. Soderlund, with Gracie May in her arms, was already half way down the steps, the younger children right behind her. By the time Pilan' and Kristina reached the bottom of the steps there was very little room to move in the small space. Dusty bound down the steps ahead of Mr. Soderlund, his wet fur smelly, his whimpers and barks shrill.

This wasn't exactly the romantic evening Pilan' had planned.

Dyer settled Dusty on the floor, and Mrs. Soderlund calmed the fussing little girls while her husband lit a lantern. At the top of the room a small glassed-in opening served as a window, and it offered little light except when lightning flashed.

When everyone calmed down Dyer spoke up. "Mama, you should tell the story about the first time you and Papa ended up in your storm cellar before you were married."

"No, not that story again," Frankie whined.

Pilan' had heard the story a few weeks earlier when he and Kristina sat down by the creek exchanging tales from the past.

"I think we can forego that story tonight," Mrs. Soderlund said. "I'm sure it's not as romantic as what Pilan' had planned for this evening."

In the pale, golden glow of the lantern, he could see a puzzled look on Kristina's face. "What do you mean, Mama?"

"Nothing, dear. Nothing." Mrs. Soderlund's voice smacked of a little fib. Pilan' held his smile in check. "I just imagine he had something much nicer than this in mind."

Mrs. Soderlund was certainly right. Everything was awry. He'd arranged a candlelight dinner, with silver, crystal, roses, and white linens on the table. There was to be music playing on the new phonograph he'd purchased, and he'd asked Potts to move some tables to create an area for them to dance a waltz or two. He and Potts had it all set. Jake had even agreed to wear a tuxedo while serving them.

Instead, Pilan' was stuck in a hole in the ground with Kristina's father, mother, five younger children, and a smelly, wet dog. By the time this storm ended it would be too late to go into town. And who knew what conditions he'd find along the way. He couldn't risk taking Kristina into town tonight. Potts and Jake would were probably worried by now, but it couldn't be helped.

"Pilan'?" Kristina's voice burned with curiosity. "What is Mama talking about?"

Should he tell her or wait for a more appropriate time? There was so little privacy and space, and with all the commotion around him he could hardly think straight. Drawing Kristina against his chest, he rested his chin on the top of her head. He closed his eyes hoping to calm his inner brouhaha. It felt as if the storm was raging within him, not outdoors. After a moment he lifted his head and peered into her eyes.

"It's nothing, really. Just a private candlelight dinner I had planned." He looked into her dreamy, questioning eyes, winking once. How did he get so lucky, falling in love with such an amazing young woman?

"Some special evening this turned out to be," Kristina said her voice sullen.

He filled his lungs with a deep breath of stuffy, musty air and smiled, wishing things had been different tonight, but one thing was certain, nothing could diminish his love for Kristina. He whispered in her ear. "The evening isn't over, my love."

The pounding rain slowed. The wind ceased to roar and howl. Mr. Soderlund moved halfway up the cellar steps, his ear directed toward the door. "The storm is over."

Kristina's father pushed the door open, and Pilan' followed the family out of the cellar. The sky was clear with a few stars beginning to sparkle, the air warm and damp. The moon, almost full, was just creeping up over the horizon.

Pilan' needed to stretch his legs, walk a little. "May I help you check out the property, Mr. Soderlund?"

"Sure. You come too, Dyer," Mr. Soderlund said.

The yard was littered with branches and leaves, but the out buildings and livestock had been spared any damage. Pilan was happy to find his horse and carriage in the barn, dry and unharmed.

"We're lucky it blew over us this time," Mr. Soderlund said. "I've already had one farm destroyed by a tornado; I sure don't want to lose another one."

"So tornados are as bad as earthquakes?" Pilan' couldn't imagine that.

"Well, I've never experienced an earthquake, but at least we can go to the storm cellar and protect ourselves from tornados. I don't suppose there's anyplace to hide from one of those earthquakes."

"You're absolutely right." If Pilan' had a choice, however, he'd take the occasional fog and rain in Paris.

A short time later, alone with Kristina on the front porch, Pilan' took her hand and looked down at her. "I'm sorry the evening was ruined. Sometimes the best plans go bad, thanks to Mother Nature."

"True." Long-faced, clearly, Kristina was still unhappy.

He removed his suit-jacket and hung it on one of the porch chairs. "I had a special dinner arranged for us, phonograph music and all. I even arranged to have a dance floor so we could waltz."

"Waltz?" Kristina's raised brows surprised him. Had she never waltzed?

"Yes. Like this." Taking her into his arms in the proper position, he began to dance. Her smile faint at first spread, her long face gone. She followed his lead as if she'd been waltzing all her life. "Very nice, my dear."

"Thank you, my love."

Kristina's words were musical, endearing. Ending the dance he pulled her to him, his arms around her, his hands splayed against her back. Holding her slender body against him, he smiled to himself. He wanted to hold her everyday, hear her laughter and singing forever, and dance her around a room whenever he pleased.

He pulled back, leading her by the hand to the bench. He wiped a hand across it, making sure it was dry before they sat down. After a few seconds, he got up and knelt before her. He cleared his throat, contemplating how to begin. Everything he'd mentally rehearsed escaped his mind. "You know I love you, Kristina."

"And I love you."

"You mean everything in life to me. You're my first love, and you will be the last. I know we'll be apart while you finish school in Boston, but I can't wait until next year to ask. Will you be my wife?"

Eyes wide, Kristina beamed with happiness. Her voice was cheerful. "Yes. I'd love to be your wife."

He was glad she didn't hesitate or say no. Pilan' dug deep in his pants pocket and took out the small, white box. He opened it and removed the ring. "Will you accept this ring and wear it as a symbol of our betrothal?"

"Oh, yes. Of course I will." Kristina smiled down at him, her eyes warm, filled with delight. He took her hand and slipped the ring on her finger then kissed the soft, delicate skin on the back of her hand.

Standing, he drew her up from the bench and into his embrace. He kissed her, relishing the sweetness of her mouth.

BREATHLESS, KRISTINA GAZED AT the magnificent ring. Even in the dim light that shone from indoors through the windows, she could see it was set in gold, the round center stone flanked on each side with rubies and diamonds. Never had she seen a more amazing ring. Being loved by a wonderful, handsome man and having this stunning engagement ring, she had to be the luckiest woman alive. Her attitude about marriage had certainly changed. A marriage proposal from Pilan' was the last thing she had expected this soon, yet she knew deep down she'd hoped for it. The months without him had felt empty and lonely. Now she'd never have to feel that void again.

"This ring is beautiful. I'll treasure it forever." More-so, she would treasure Pilan' forever.

"I hoped you would approve of the Tiffany setting." Pilan' lifted her hand, examining the ring. "It looks lovely on you."

He kissed her hand then took her into his arms again. His embrace was warm, comfortable, a safe haven.

"I can hardly wait to show my parents and Doris, and tell them the news of our betrothal." And won't Auntie Myrtle be pleased? She could hardly wait to see the look on her great-aunt's face.

The screen door opened and her mother stepped out onto the porch. "Would you two like to come in for supper? You must be starved by now."

Kristina pulled away from Pilan' and hurried to her mother, presenting her left hand. "Look, Mama. Pilan' asked me to marry him. Isn't this the most stunning ring ever?"

"Oh, yes. Is that a real Tiffany?"

"Yes," Kristina said, nearly bursting with giddiness.

An unexpected change instantly masked her mother's face with concern. "What about school and your plans to have a music studio? Sweetheart, I hate to see you give up your dreams. And your grandfather—"

"Don't worry, Mama. I'm going to finish at the university. Pilan' and I have a lot to talk about and prepare for, but I'll be on the train for Boston next Tuesday as planned."

Chapter 25

"You look so pretty," Kristina said as she hugged her friend. Doris was radiant in her snowy-white wedding dress of organdy over satin. Fashioned by Mrs. Langley, the headpiece was a halo of satin and pearls and had a long stream of fine net attached that flowed down the back like a waterfall. "Are you ready to walk down the aisle and become Mrs. Gunther?"

"I'm ready." Doris turned to her, placing a hand on Kristina's cheek. "Oh, Kristina, thank you for helping me and for standing up for me. I couldn't have done it without you."

"You're welcome. I'm glad I could be here to share your big day. She hugged Doris again. "Let's go. It's time to go get you married."

Moments later Kristina stood next to her best friend as Reverend Gilroy talked about the marriage vows. Her mind rushed ahead to next summer, and she wondered if she would be ready to stand at this altar and pledge her life to Pilan'. Concern flashed through her mind, and she was uncertain if she'd done the right thing accepting his proposal. It was so soon and there was so much to consider, like establishing her business. Like she'd told Auntie, her plans didn't include marriage and babies, at least not for a long time. Now she was engaged. She loved Pilan', she had no doubts about that, and she wanted to be with him, but everything was happening so fast.

The minister paused. Kristina turned her thoughts back to the ceremony. It was time to sing her solo. She was pleased that Anna Jo had asked if she would sing one song accompanied by Pilan''s violin. She joined him off to the side of the platform.

The words of *Thee Only I Love* rang true to her heart as she sang. Filled with undeniable love, her fears and doubts melted away. She'd never love another man as much as she loved Pilan'. She couldn't imagine spending her life with anyone else. Gazing up at him she smiled, the lyrics directed at him.

When the song ended sniffles and sobs rose from the congregation of guests. The minister declared Doris and Harland husband and wife, and sent them out with a short prayer.

Kristina was first to congratulate her friend. "I hope you two will be very happy."

"Thank you," Doris said. "Just think, next summer you'll be doing this."

Before Kristina could respond, guests crowded around to greet the newlyweds.

Pilan' pulled Kristina aside. "Well my sweet, are you ready to set a date for our wedding?"

Taken by surprise and not yet prepared to answer, she laughed, her giddy response resembling a Shakespearean performance. "Mr. Rousseau, it is thee only I love, but I cannot yet set a wedding date."

Brows raised, love in his eyes Pilan' placed one hand on his heart. "I shan't wait forever mademoiselle, or I shall surely die."

Kristina chuckled and slipped her arm through his bent elbow continuing the drama. "But if you die my love, I shall be an old maid forever. I could not bear it."

"Oh brother!" Dyer burst onto the scene. "What theatrics you two."

They all laughed.

SUNDAY AFTERNOON PILAN' STEERED the carriage up to the front steps of Kristina's house, and pulled back on the reins until they came to a stop. Remaining in the seat he took Kristina's hand. "You've been quiet all the way home from church. Is something wrong?"

Kristina shrugged and looked away.

"Are you having second thoughts about our marriage? Is that why you haven't set a date?"

Turning to face him, Kristina's eyes were glazed, tears pooling. "No. Yesterday after Doris and Harland's wedding a man and woman I hardly know said some terrible things to me and Mama."

"What did they say?" He'd never seen Kristina this upset. What could anyone say to a special young woman like her to bring tears to her eyes? Concerned, he moved closer and put an arm around her shoulders.

She opened her mouth then shut it.

"Tell me, darling. I'm going to be your husband. You can tell me anything."

"It's just—"

He smiled and with one forefinger lifted her chin. "Must I find these people and beat them up for upsetting you?"

"No, silly." Kristina grinned then grew solemn again. "Yesterday when I was leaving the wedding with my parents, Mr. and Mrs. Walsh made a nasty remark about me *running around* with a half-breed. It happened right in front of the church, and they made sure I heard it. I guess the Langley's invited them to the wedding, but they even said they had stopped attending our church because of me."

"That was rude and cruel. I'm sorry you had to experience such hatefulness." Pilan' had a hard time understanding why people were prejudiced and mean. Beneath his calm façade he wanted to lash out at the couple for hurting Kristina, but he knew it was wrong to seek revenge, even verbally. It would make him no better than Mr. and Mrs. Walsh. "You must realize that as long as we're together, you might hear such remarks from time to time."

"I suppose. But they made it sound as if I'm bad, like some harlot. I was so upset I wanted to scream at them, and tell them how stupid and unchristian they were. I can't believe there are still people in this town who judge others by the color of their skin. Everyone knows what a good man you are."

"No matter where you go, sweetheart, there will always be prejudice. There will be good and bad. Forgive them, just as you forgave Toby, and if you see them again speak kindly to them."

"How can I do that when they are against you? At least Toby apologized to us both."

"The world is full of ignorance. You must learn not to let such remarks bother you. I am where God wants me, and I refuse to allow people like the Walshes upset me."

Still solemn Kristina nodded. "You're right."

Comfortable and wanting more time alone with Kristina, he didn't want to go inside yet, even though the aroma of Sunday dinner wafted toward him through open doors and windows.

He spoke with hopefulness. "You'll still be my wife then?"

"Yes, of course." Appearing more at ease Kristina gazed at him, her eyes soft her lovely face aglow. "I was going to tell you something at dinner, but since you brought it up I'll tell you now. I've decided on a wedding date. Is June twenty-ninth next summer agreeable with you?"

He expelled a quiet sigh of relief. Taking Kristina's hand he kissed it. "It sounds perfect." He paused, pondering. Perhaps now would be a good time to tell her his news. "I have a surprise for you as well."

Her face suddenly eager with curiosity, Kristina's smile danced in her eyes. "What? Please tell me now."

"All right. I've purchased a large parcel of property on the other end of town near the park. While you're in Boston, I'll be having our home built. I'll want your opinion and help in the planning, of course."

"Oh, that's grand, Pilan'."

"What would you think of having a music room for your studio and a ballroom for my dance lessons right in our home?"

"It's a nice idea, but do you think people will come to our house, rather than a studio in town?"

"I believe they would. The location is convenient, and it's a lovely setting for a large, inviting home. I thought perhaps after dinner I could take you there."

"I'd like that. I wish we had more time to plan before my departure. There's so much we need to discuss."

He was happy to hear some enthusiasm return to his future bride's voice. "Once you're in Boston I'll have many questions. I'm sure we'll keep the mail service very busy."

Kristina leaned in and planted a light kiss on his mouth. "I'll write to you every day."

He chuckled, remembering what a poor letter writer he was. "Perhaps I will install a telephone in my temporary house, that is, if your grandparents have one in their home. Being in Boston, most surely they do."

"They do. Oh, Pilan', wouldn't that be wonderful if we could talk to each other while I'm away?"

"I'll have to see what I can arrange."

It was a pleasant summer afternoon for a ride, no storm clouds to ruin the day. Pilan' was anxious to show Kristina the property he'd purchased. As he neared the plot of land he smiled to himself, listening to her enthusiastic chatter about what type of house she'd like.

"And we should have a least three bedrooms, an indoor bathroom, of course, and if possible, I'd like a small library."

"I have a much larger home in mind," he told her. "If we're going to have a ballroom and a large music room, I believe that calls for a grand two-story estate with several bedrooms, perhaps a Greek Revival or Georgian style. And we will have a large library as well as a parlor. Would that meet with your approval?"

"I haven't a clue what either of those styles is. But I'm sure what you decide will be wonderful. But—"

"Money is no concern, my dear. Perhaps I can find some pictures for you to look at. That way you can decide what you like. You'll have the finest home in the city and I'll spare no cost to make sure it is well furnished."

"Really?"

"Indeed. Nothing but the finest for my bride. You'll have electric lights and a telephone as well."

"How exciting. I do hope you will allow me to help choose the furnishings."

"Most certainly. Left to my untrained eye for color, I fear I'd do a poor job of that. When you return home in the spring we'll have a good time shopping for everything."

"How will I keep such a large home clean, and have time for my piano and voice students?"

He smiled down at his lovely bride to be, amazed by her simplicity. "You will have a maid, and I think we'll want a cook as well."

Brows lifted and eyes wide, Kristina's mouth dropped. "Oh. How wonderful."

Pilan' slowed and guided the horse to a shady spot beneath a clump of big trees. "Here we are. What do you think?" He spread his arms and scanned the property looking from left to right.

Kristina gazed outward. "It's a beautiful spot. How much of it is yours?"

"Ours my love. Let me assist you down and I'll show you." He leaped to the ground and ran to the other side of the carriage. His hands on her waist, he gently set Kristina on her feet. Turning, he swept a hand from east to west, pointing to a small stand of trees in the distance and another in the opposite direction. Straight ahead was bare land, behind them the city.

"All of that?"

"Yes. And over by that line of trees," he pointed north, "there is a wide stream. When I learned it ran through the property I knew this was the place for our home."

"How wonderful. Thank you. But how will you tend to so much land if you don't plant crops and hire farm hands to work for you?"

Pilan' laughed. "Dear, sweet Kristina, there will be no crops, no pigs, or chickens—unless you insist on having them."

"No thank you. I have no desire for farm animals."

"I must say I'm happy to hear that. Once the house is built I'll hire a crew of men to landscape the property with plants and trees. There will be shrubbery, grass, and flowers, and a gardener or two to maintain it. Remember my darling, we will be teaching students to sing, play the piano, and dance. We will be busy following our passions, fulfilling our dreams."

Folding the last garment and placing it in her suitcase, Kristina was glad she'd left a closet-full of clothing at her grandparents' home. It made packing much easier. If her grandmother had her way, however, it would require a dozen suitcases to return home at the end of the school year. One extra piece of luggage she was counting on for sure, though, was for the wedding dress she hoped to purchase in Boston.

Thinking about Pilan"s words Sunday afternoon, she closed the suitcase and paused, once again admiring her engagement ring. It was still hard to believe she was betrothed to such an amazing gentleman. As long as she lived she would love him and admire him. She had no doubt he was the man God had chosen as her mate, but it was still surprising the way God had brought them together and allowed them to fall in love so soon. However, with Pilan', her dream of opening a music studio was now closer to becoming a reality and even more exciting.

Mama came into the room, eyes red. "It looks like you're ready to go."

"Oh, Mama, have you been crying again?" Kristina pulled her mother into a hug. "I'll be back in nine-and-a-half months. It is I who should be crying since I'm going away. I don't know how I'll stand being away from Pilan' and my loving family for so long."

"I know, dear, but I'll miss you so much. I just can't believe you're all grown up, traveling halfway across the country alone, and engaged to be married."

"Goodness, Mama. What will you do when Pilan' and I go to Paris for our honeymoon?" Granted they would be gone only three months, but Paris, France was over three-thousand miles across the Atlantic Ocean. Kristina had a hard time fathoming that. For some reason the ocean made it seem so much farther away.

"I'll pray for your safe return, and look forward to visiting you in that magnificent mansion Pilan' is going to build."

"Good." She hugged her mother long and hard. "Now, we better call Papa and let him know I'm ready to leave. Pilan' will be waiting at the train station."

Chapter 26

KRISTINA'S FINAL YEAR AT Boston University School of Music went by faster than a staccato music measure. She tucked her degree safely inside one of her six suitcases. Ready to board the train, she could hardly wait to be back in Oklahoma City and in Pilan''s arms. Being apart for the past five months was entirely too long, even with weekly telephone calls.

Pilan' had come to Boston two weeks before Christmas and had stayed an entire month. During that time they'd spent many hours discussing their new home which was well under way, and they had shopped for a few furnishings that were immediately shipped home. He had purchased a new camera and had numerous pictures to show her, but it was difficult to tell what the house would look like from the photos of construction. By the time she arrived home the house would be finished.

Luggage was being put into the baggage car, and people began boarding. Her grandfather pulled an envelope from his jacket pocket. "Before you go, we have something for you."

Kristina accepted the envelope and opened it, finding a card and a check inside for three-thousand dollars. "Oh, you needn't give me anything. After all you've done for me this is far too much."

Her grandmother took her into her arms. "No it isn't, dear. We are so proud of you, and it's been our joy having you here. That's our way of congratulating you on the fine job you've done, and of letting you know we love you. We thought perhaps you could use it to buy a piano for your studio. The rest you can spend on your house."

"I don't know what to say. Thank you." Kristina wiped a tear from her cheek.

The train hissed and blew steam, reminding her it was about time to board. Her grandmother gave her one last hug. Kristina hugged her back, new tears threatening to surface. Grandfather kissed her cheek as he assisted her up the steps of the passenger car. "Thank you again, Grandfather, for everything. I love you."

Seated, she lifted the window and looked out, spotting her grandparents on the platform. Her grandmother wiped her eyes as Grandfather stood smiling. Kristina waved and shouted. "Thank you. I love you both."

Waving back they called out. "We'll see you next month when we come for your wedding."

THE DELICATE FRENCH SATIN slid down her body, the cool silkiness pure bliss. Kristina smiled at her reflection in the cheval mirror, admiring the lace overlay and the fancy beadwork at the scooped neckline. Doris, reaching over her round, growing tummy, worked at fastening the tiny satin buttons down the back.

Dreamy eyed, Doris looked up. "This is the most beautiful wedding dress I've ever seen. Wait until Pilan' sees you in it," she crooned.

"Do you think he'll like it?"

"Are you daft? He'll love it, especially with you wearing it. You look ravishing." Doris was still as dramatic as always.

"Thank you. Can you believe I'm actually getting married?"

"Sure. All that talk about not wanting marriage and a family was just nonsense. I knew when you started seeing Pilan' it was all over for you."

"Remember how frightened I was when you said he was watching me from the library steps?" Kristina often joked with Pilan' about that day, but he understood her fear after she explained to him what had happened when she was eight.

Doris laughed. "You rode like a demon was chasing you."

"In a way one was." She turned to Doris. "This may be a strange time to tell you something I've never shared with you, but I suppose now the time is right."

"Really? What? I didn't think we ever kept secrets from one another."

"Only this one, because I didn't know what to do. When I was eight years old I was playing in the barn and three boys grabbed me from behind and blindfolded me. They . . . well, one of them hurt me."

Eyes wide Doris whispered. "You mean?"

No explanation was needed. Kristina nodded.

"No!" Eyes instantly glazed, Doris threw her arms around Kristina. "You poor thing. Why haven't you ever told me?"

"I never told anyone until recently. I owed it to Pilan' to tell him. I didn't even know who did it until the incident with Toby the summer before I went away to college."

"It was Toby?"

"Yes. I don't know who the other two boys were, Toby didn't tell me, but they were mainly bystanders."

"Oh, Kristina. I'm sorry that happened to you. No wonder you were afraid at first. I bet that was the reason you were so against marriage, too."

"Perhaps, but time and prayer has a way of healing old wounds. Toby has turned his life around and he apologized to me last summer. He accepted his punishment and asked my forgiveness, so I forgave him."

Doris wiped her eyes with a handkerchief. "That had to be one of most difficult things you've ever done."

"Surprisingly, it wasn't as hard as I expected."

"Let's not talk about this anymore. Goodness, it's your wedding day. We should be talking about happy things."

"You're right."

Eyebrows knit Doris sniffed the air. "Do you smell smoke?"

Kristina lifted her face and inhaled. "I do. I wonder where it's coming from."

"I don't know." Doris swished away the air with one hand. "I'm sure it's nothing to worry about. Here, let me fasten your pearls and help with your hat." Pearls fastened, Doris lifted the lace-covered, wide-brimmed hat from the box and placed it on Kristina's head. "What a pretty thing this is."

Mama Leoma burst into the women's washroom lounge where Kristina had changed into her wedding dress. "Fire! We have to get out right now!"

"The church is on fire?!" *No God, not on my wedding day.*

Mama grabbed her hand and pulled her from the room. "Get out right now, Doris. Come!"

"My flowers! I have to get—"

"Forget them!"

Smoke thickened and fire crackled nearby. Her mother rushed her and Doris down a narrow hallway and out a side door, nearly dragging them to a safe place away from the building. Reverend Gilroy directed everyone away from the burning building.

Watching in terror, Kristina sobbed. She searched the crowd for Pilan', but she didn't see him anywhere. Two water-pumping fire trucks arrived and sprayed streams of water on the building, but the blaze gained control.

"Pilan'!" Kristina screamed over and over, her father and mother holding her back. "Let me go, I have to find him! Pilan'!"

Pilan' ran from the sanctuary, down a hallway toward the back of the church searching for Kristina. "Kristina! Kristina!"

Jake grabbed him from behind by one arm. "We have to get out of here!"

"Not until I find Kristina." Flames hissed and cracked as it consumed one wall and part of the ceiling. A hideous roar and crash came from behind. He tried to pull away from Jake.

"Everyone else is out! She probably escaped through another door." Jake seized him by the shoulders, moving him forward. "Come to your senses, man. We have to get out!"

A flaming piece of ceiling crashed to the floor next to him spewing embers. Smoke burned his throat making it hard to breath. He tried to jerk free again, but Jake's grip was too strong. Jake coughed hard, but he continued to hold on. Feeling weak, his vision blurred, Pilan was barely aware of being dragged out the door until fresh air and water hit him.

"Pilan'!"

The woman's scream sounded familiar.

"Kristina?" His voice was weak, raspy. "Kristina?"

"I'm here. I'm here, Pilan'."

Eyes burning, throat raw, he coughed repeatedly while gazing up at the most welcome sight he'd ever seen. Kristina bent over him, tears in her eyes. He reached up and touched her face. "I was searching for you. Thank God you're alive."

"I thought I'd lost you." Already on her knees beside him, Kristina kissed him. Hot tears formed in his eyes taking away some of the sting. "Where's Jake?"

"Jake's right here," Kristina said. "He's all right."

"Excuse me young lady." Doctor Rhodes knelt beside her. "Let me see how your groom is doing."

Kristina stood and waited nearby where he could still see her. He didn't want to let her out of his sight. Mr. and Mrs. Soderlund, and her grandparents gathered around her. Pilan' heard the worry in her voice. "Will he be okay, Papa?"

"I'm sure he'll be fine," Mr. Soderlund said.

The doctor asked questions and listened to Pilan''s lungs. "Take some deep breaths, son."

He did as the doctor said and coughed several more times. After a few minutes Doctor Rhodes assisted him to his feet. Pilan' grabbed Kristina and pulled her into his arms, holding her close to him. A moment later realization struck him. Their wedding was ruined.

"I expected to carry you across the threshold of our new home as Mrs. Rousseau this afternoon, and we have a train to catch for New York tomorrow. What will we do now?"

KRISTINA JUMPED INTO ACTION. Her face was smudged and she smelled like burning rubbish, but nothing was going to destroy her wedding day. She located Reverend Gilroy. "Can you ride out to our estate in two hours and perform our ceremony?"

"Why, yes. I'd be happy to. There's nothing I can do here."

"Thank you." She turned to her mother. "Mama, do you think you can get the florist shop to make a small bouquet of flowers for me real fast? It's nearby and shouldn't take long."

"I suppose so, dear, but wouldn't you rather delay the ceremony until another day?"

"No. Our train leaves early tomorrow morning, and we have a ship to catch in a week in New York." She turned to her father. "Papa, help Mama spread the news that the guests are invited to our new house for the ceremony at four o'clock. We're going to get married in the ballroom."

"Why didn't I think of that?" Pilan' took her hand. "Marvelous idea my love."

"You look beautiful. No one will care about the little smudges of dirt on your dress." Doris carefully brushed the spots some more. She fussed with Kristina's hat, straightening the ribbons and the soft poufs of net. "Almost everyone is here. They came bearing gifts and baskets of food. The kitchen is overflowing with picnic baskets and baked goods. I don't know how they did it so fast."

"How wonderful. You know how our church folks are. No occasion is ever without a feast." Kristina glanced at the mantle clock across the parlor. "It's time. I'm sure Pilan' will be waiting."

She picked up the elaborate cascading bouquet of white roses and delicate fern, amazed that the florist was able to put something so beautiful together on the spur of the moment.

Entering the ballroom her eyes went straight to her groom. Wearing a fresh suit and white shirt, his face was scrubbed clean and hair combed. Except for a small red spot on his jaw, he looked as if nothing had happened at the church fire. His smile broadened as she walked down the aisle of parted, standing guests and came to him.

The ceremony was short, simple, yet perfect. Oblivious to everyone around her, Kristina became Mrs. Pilan' Rousseau.

Her husband took her into his arms and kissed her like she'd never been kissed before. Hoots, hollers, and applause drowned out her beating heart.

"I love you, Mrs. Rousseau"

"And I love you, my handsome Mr. Rousseau."

W‍HILE WOMEN ARRANGED FOOD on the large dining room table Pilan' had something special to do. Keeping the surprise from Kristina hadn't been easy. He found Jake and spoke in a low voice as he slipped a key into his friend's hand. "Would you go to the carriage house and bring the automobile to the front door?"

Jake grinned. "You bet. It'll probably be the only time I get to drive it."

Kristina walked up, almost too soon. "What are you two up to?"

"Not a thing. Jake was just saying he's going outdoors for a breath of fresh air." Pilan' kissed his bride on the cheek, thinking how lucky he was. "Are you having a good time?"

"Yes, I am. Almost every woman here had to have a tour of the house. Auntie Myrtle and her new husband are quite impressed, and I do believe there are a few envious ladies in town."

"No doubt. But we mustn't ever flaunt our wealth or good fortune. I want our home to have an open door and be welcoming to all visitors."

"I agree. Goodness, I feel extremely fortunate to have all this. Thanks to you I'm going to live far beyond my greatest expectations. I will always thank God for bringing us together and for every gift he provides."

"Speaking of gifts, let's step outdoors."

Kristina cocked her head sideways, curiosity in her eyes. He took her by the hand. Just as they stepped out the wide front door, Jake pulled up in the new automobile, honking the horn.

"Oh, look," Kristina said. "Jake bought himself a fancy motorcar. I love that red upholstery and shiny white paint."

Pilan' laughed. It was just like his wife to admire what someone else had, and to be happy for them. He smiled down at her. "It isn't Jake's automobile, and I'm glad you like the colors. That fine Cadillac is my wedding gift to you."

"Truly?" Eyes wide his bride gasped. "Truly?"

"Yes. Truly, my love."

"I have a small wedding gift for you, as well, but it isn't nearly as grand." Before rushing to look at the motorcar Kristina excused herself. "I'll only be a moment. I'll be right back."

As promised, his bride returned in an instant bearing a small gift, elegantly wrapped. He removed the wrapping paper. "A journal?"

Kristina smiled. "You can read it later. It contains my letters to you. Now, I want to take a good look at my new motorcar."

Chapter 27

1912

"I'm going to get you, Missy." Laughing and clapping her hands, Kristina chased two-year-old Melody Rose through the wide, carpeted hallway. It was a game her daughter played lately when it was bath time, bedtime, or just about any time Kristina wanted her to obey.

Pilan' stepped out of their bedroom suite and jumped in front of Melody, instantly sweeping the toddler up into his arms. He tickled her, kissing her bare tummy. "You have to let mommy dress you my little princess. Be good now, or we'll be late for Uncle Dyer's church service."

"Good catch. Thank you." Kristina laughed and took Melody from Pilan''s arms. She hugged her tiny girl, and kissed her chubby cheeks several times as she walked to the sunny nursery. She adored their daughter. "Now, little miss, we want to look extra pretty today. It's a very special day for Uncle Dyer."

"I pretty."

"Yes, you are the prettiest little girl in the whole world." Melody was a combination of Pilan''s extreme good-looks and Kristina's personality. She had her father's piercing blue eyes and both parents' dark hair. "Now let's put on your new yellow dress and get ready for church."

She and Pilan' normally attended the rebuilt church where they'd planned to get married before the fire, but today was special. They'd driven an extra fifteen miles north to attend Dyer's first church service. Papa and Mama had also come with all the children to support him.

Sitting on the front pew, Kristina caught her brother's attention and winked. Dyer grinned. He appeared comfortable behind the pulpit, and he appeared very grown up and handsome in his new suit and tie. Just twenty years of age, he looked mature and confident. He'd been playing church and ministering to friends since his childhood, dreaming of this day. This was his passion.

It was a small congregation, perhaps thirty people, but there was space to grow. Kristina had no doubt, with her brother as the preacher every pew would be full in no time.

An attractive blonde woman came to the platform and led the congregation in the opening hymn, and Kristina wondered if she was the girl Dyer was interested in. Dying to find out, she could hardly wait until the service ended.

After a familiar hymn, Dyer prayed an eloquent oration that touched Kristina's heart. It was sincere, beseeching God to bless the people in the church, praising the Lord for his goodness and blessings. Before the "amen" Kristina wiped tears from her eyes. Pride for her brother filled her soul.

"And now," Dyer said, "I would like to welcome you all, and I especially want to welcome and introduce my family. They came a great distance to be here today."

Introductions complete, Dyer motioned for Kristina and Pilan' to come to the platform. "I've invited my sister, Kristina, and my brother-in-law, Pilan', to bless us this morning with a special musical number."

Kristina put Melody in her mother's charge and walked to the platform, Pilan' right behind her with his violin. Taking their places, Pilan' lifted his violin to his chin and began to play *Sunshine in the Soul*. Kristina sang the hymn with conviction, the words ringing true to the depths of her soul. She especially liked the second verse and sang out loud and clear. "There's music in my soul today . . ."

Her heart overflowing with joy, at the close of the song, she slipped her hand through Pilan''s bent arm, and returned to her seat.

Absorbed in Dyer's sermon on trusting Jesus, Kristina listened closely, taking in the truth of her brother's message. *How true little brother. You're so right.* She shifted on the wooden pew and sighed. Seven years earlier she was determined to do things her way. She had vowed that nothing would stand in the way of her plans. No man, love, money, or tradition. Yet, a time had come when she realized she had to relinquish her stubborn will and trust God. How happy she was that she'd listened to that still, small whisper to her soul.

Had she stuck to her way and her plans, she wouldn't be married to Pilan' and she wouldn't have their darling daughter. Even though she would have a music studio, it wouldn't be as lovely or successful as what she and Pilan' had built together. God had provided far more than she'd ever dreamed of having.

Pilan''s dreams to travel, and one day open a dance studio where he would teach ballroom dances, were also being fulfilled. Like Kristina, he'd been set on doing things one way, his way, and he'd thought there was no room for change. Yet, he had recognized that God had a better plan for him and he obeyed. His ballroom was magnificent, and he had a steady stream of students, both young and old, coming to him for instructions. The house was constantly filled with music and laughter.

She thought about Mama Leoma, an amazing woman who was willing to give up her dreams of owning a bookshop, in order to take in a stranger's starving newborn son, and wet nurse him to save his life. Then she had married Papa, the baby's widowed father, and had four more babies. Today Mama had the bookshop she'd dreamed of, and the starving infant boy stood behind the pulpit in front of them, a much greater blessing, Kristina was sure, than anything else Mama could imagine. Tears pooled in her eyes again, and she wiped them away with her much-used handkerchief.

Dyer brought his sermon to a close and prayed. Instead of stepping down right away and going to the back of the church to greet his parishioners, as was common, he motioned the pretty blonde to come up and join him on the platform. He took the young lady's hand, his cheeks turning pink. Oh my goodness! Kristina couldn't believe her eyes. What was her brother doing?

"Ladies and gentleman, Father, Mother, I would like to introduce my fiancée. This is Anne Marie Johnson. Anne Marie will also be helping with music every Sunday." He paused, smiled at his fiancée, and blushed some more. "God bless you all. You're dismissed."

Mama jumped up and rushed to Dyer and Anne Marie's side. Pilan' stood and took sleeping Melody Rose into his arms.

Kristina sighed, smiling, and contented beyond measure.

CPSIA information can be obtained at www.ICGtesting.com
Printed in the USA
BVOW04s1528200214

345535BV00001B/1/P